ZERO ALTERNATIVE

Luca Pesaro was born in Italy but has spent most of his adult life in the US or UK. After long years gaining a degree and masters in the pseudo-science that is Economics he got bored, jumped the gun and became a derivatives trader in financial markets. Zero Alternative is his first novel and he is hard at work on his second thriller. He is married to an awesome lady and they have two children who always manage to annoy, surprise and delight beyond any reasonable expectation.

ZERO ALTERNATIVE

Luca Pesaro

THREE HARES PUBLISHING

Published by Three Hares Publishing 2014

First published in Great Britain in 2014
www.threeharespublishing.com

Three Hares Publishing Ltd Reg. No 8531198
Registered address: Suite 201, Berkshire House,
39-51 High Street,
Ascot, Berkshire, SL5 7HY

ISBN-13: 9781910153086

For Francesca, because I couldn't ask or wish for more.
And for my Dad, who didn't have enough time to see it,
but I know he's smiling.

PART ONE – THE DESCENT

***'Money is just like the metric system:
you work more, you earn more
and there's always an extra zero to be added.
It's only a zero, though.'***
Biagio '71

SHORT – Finance: *In finance short selling (also known as shorting, being short or going short) is the practice of selling securities or other financial instruments that are not currently owned, with the intention of subsequently repurchasing them ('covering', 'hedging') at a lower price.*

From Wikipedia

CHAPTER ONE

Monday, October 1st –6.02 A.M.

The trading floor was drowning in blood and fear.

The blood at least was metaphorical, a deep crimson red of computer screens flashing Stock Market quotes ready to spiral into monetary black holes. The fear was real though, and palpable. Droplets of sweat crawled on dealers' faces, defying the air-conditioned chill. Grim nods and ticks multiplied as bankers wandered between the rows of monitors, waiting for the canteen to open and the caffeine to start flowing.

Scott 'Yours' Walker inhaled deeply as the glass doors slid shut, enjoying the sudden but familiar adrenaline rush. The financial markets around the world were about to stagger through a nasty morning, followed by a very bad afternoon. *This was going to be fun.*

The thirty-six-year-old trader hurried to his desk in the cavernous open space chosen by Dorfmann Brothers as the nerve centre of its Investment Banking operation. On the far wall, near the massive windows that overlooked Broadgate in the City of London, a few clocks highlighted various time zones worldwide. Walker ignored them: China and Hong Kong were shut for the Golden Week holiday, so East Asia was meaningless. Tokyo had just closed after a precipitous plunge in its Equity and Bond markets but Japan was crumbling anyway: the country had been imploding for months and the world had stopped caring long ago.

The problem was, again, in Europe.

Walker glanced to his right and saw that his eight monitors were already lit – Steph must have logged him on, just as he had told the junior trader to after seeing the results of the Italian snap election. *Good boy*. Random threats of violence and job loss for lateness always seemed to focus minds. The young Frenchman was nowhere to be seen though: probably helping out another one of the testosterone-fuelled dealers on the Volatility team.

'Yours?'

Walker turned around, almost bumping into Anna Guarzelli, a lifer in the bank's risk-management team. She held a coffee mug in front of her chest like a shield, her hand shaking slightly. 'You're early,' she said.

'If you don't get up on a day like today...' Walker shrugged.

'True. So... what do you think?'

'Welcome to financial hell.'

Guarzelli grimaced. 'Nice, as usual.' Her pupils scanned the floor nearby and she lowered her voice. 'Seriously though, is this as bad as it looks?'

'Yes. Can you imagine Italy defaulting and walking out of the Euro?'

'Not really,' she sighed. 'We had a meeting, a couple of weeks ago... The top guys wanted scenarios for this, and we couldn't quite answer. If a country that size breaks off – we are talking unimaginable losses. Bank failures, maybe even a Depression worldwide. Someone mentioned zombies in the street, and they were only half-joking.'

'*Una merda totale*,' Walker swore in Italian.

Guarzelli winced, her wrinkled eyes somehow incongruous in the glare of the arc-lights and the base buzz of computer fans. She must have been pretty once, but almost twenty years of studying dangers everywhere had taken their toll. She sipped her coffee carefully. 'Do you think the European Central Bank will step in?'

'No, *non oggi*.'

Guarzelli shot him a dark look. Though a full-blooded Italian, unlike Walker, she always refused to talk shop in anything other than English. She probably just wanted to make sure that her back was covered, hidden cameras and all. Then again, Anna *was* risk control – he should stop goading her, really. Reluctantly, Walker put aside his mother's musical language and returned to his father's public-school flattened American English.

'They can't go in guns blazing,' he continued. 'Not because some actor nut has gate-crashed the elections. It's strictly an internal political matter, and those EuroTower goons will sit on their backsides in Frankfurt, waiting.'

'But Rossini was only supposed to get around twenty per cent of the votes, not a near majority. The man has won by threatening to take Italy out of the EU, for God's sake. They have to do something.'

'Like what? Send a couple of armoured battalions to Rome?'

Guarzelli's stencilled eyebrows rose and she finished her drink. 'I can't believe how the pre-election polls got it so completely wrong. The markets will be shocked, and terrified.'

'I know...' Walker tried to hide his glee: the market had been wrong, but he – and DeepShare – had called it right. He wondered where DM was, to hug him, but the little mathematician hadn't arrived yet. He shrugged and continued. 'Look Anna, it's fear and greed, same as it's always been. Things will get a good shakeup and the world will go on. It's just the usual game, no?'

'Sometimes I hate traders.' She glared at him. 'Only because you have the right position to make money today... It's going to turn into a bloodbath. For the floor, for Dorfmann. The entire Street will suffer, badly.'

Walker nodded and edged towards his seat, attempting to get away before he said something too annoying. He didn't want to waste any nervous energy on a Risk Manager – it was going to be a long enough day without starting an early fight. 'Is Jack Morden in yet?'

Guarzelli grunted. 'I got him the reports earlier. He must be...'

The trading floor fizzled and went dark.

A fire-alarm siren exploded in the sudden silence, inevitably followed by the monotonic announcer: 'This is not a drill. Please leave the building from the nearest possible exit...'

Walker looked around in the semi-darkness, ready to break something. 'You've got to be fucking kidding me.'

...

This could cost me millions. It had already cost him almost twelve minutes: quite a lot more than he needed to go out, smoke, and come back in as soon as the first blockage around the Dorfmann entrance cleared up. Walker made it back to his seat and forced himself to calm down – the market opening was still almost half an hour away, plenty of time to get organised. At least Steph was already at his desk, bent over the squawk box, growling at someone, 'Don't care if you are busy... over here NOW!'

Walker smiled grimly. Stephane Buvier was in his mid-twenties, short with dark hair. Very much from Paris. He spoke English with a mild French accent, which only came out in full force when he was nervous or angry, like now. But as he strained to hear the muffled reply from the tiny speaker, he was chewing on his best pen. Something bad was going on.

'Steph. What's up?'

The Frenchman jumped, turned to him and tried a smile. 'Hi Boss, it's... the system guys. They just told me that after the outage we won't be able to log into ORK for a couple of hours.'

Walker froze. *Please, not today*. 'How the fuck am I supposed to trade without the bloody thing?' ORK was the electronic dealing system that allowed every trader to buy and sell shares, Futures and Options directly onto the market. All orders were routed through it, and all executions were instantaneous.

'Can... can't you deal by phone, with the Futures guys on the Street?' asked Steph.

Walker stared at him. 'Do you have the faintest idea of how many billions I'll trade in-and-out today? The markets are going to be all over the place, and voice broking is far too slow to make *real* money.' He sighed and tapped on a mouse, but his rightmost screen remained dark. 'We'll need to be ultra-fast, or this could turn into a disaster. And the rest of the guys will get slaughtered without ORK.' His stomach gave an unpleasant lurch, still simmering with the ocean of vodka he had drunk the night before. Straight 42 Below, as well.

'You're right, Boss...' Steph sat down, looking sheepish. 'Are those IT jokers coming over, at least?'

The Frenchman nodded his chin towards the back of the trading floor. Two engineers were approaching, both wearing worried expressions. In any Investment Bank technology supports acted like the enzymes that kept a body functioning, from changing smashed keyboards to hooking up all the various complex systems. But they also played the part of a punchball when things went wrong. Especially *trading* things. A new good techie was a lot cheaper than a new good trader. Traders knew that. Tech guys did, too.

'What the hell is going on?' Walker kept his voice low. He didn't like abusing support people, unlike a lot of his colleagues who seemed to consider it an amusing non-contact sport. But he was approaching boiling point – the adrenaline had been coursing through his system for the last ten hours, rendering him almost sleepless, and 6.24 a.m. was far too early for a headache.

'It's been a cyber-attack, Yours.'

'And?'

'They took us out – apparently everyone in London is off the grid.'

'Out of what? Just ORK?' Walker seethed. It was a ridiculous scenario. Without direct access, it'd be like trying to box with one hand tied behind his back.

'Yep. We've lost connection to the Frankfurt servers.'

The older of the two techies had spoken, a tall black man in his early thirties. *Ben – or Brett?* At the moment Walker couldn't care less.

'Just hook it to our backup. The bloody thing falls over every three days, anyway.'

'I'm afraid it's not only that. Someone also blew up the main switch near Eurex. I mean, *physically* blew it up, with explosives. Apparently those madmen at Hackernym are claiming credit, the Germans are saying.'

'Bloody anarchists,' Walker swore. Still, he knew that Dorfmann had other electronic highways – no bank would entrust all its communications to a single channel these days. He smiled at the techies, trying to sound reasonable. 'Fine. What about the Algo pipeline?'

'The...' Ben, or Brett, coughed nervously. 'Scott, Yours... we can't access that, I think.'

'Really?' Walker exhaled, and tried not to raise his voice. 'You mean we've spent forty million dollars to buy some rundown shithole near the centre of Frankfurt, stuffed it with atomic clocks and Cray Supercomputers, and now we can't use the damn thing?'

'You know that line is dedicated to High-Frequency Trading. We... we don't have permission.'

Walker swore again, more loudly this time. The High-Frequency group was effectively a bunch of rocket scientists holed up with monster-fast machines that traded the markets by themselves, trying to profit from fluctuations in share prices by executing billions of transactions every day. They were like an army of tiny piranhas swimming below the surface of the market, nibbling away at minimal amounts of money, unheard and unseen. Walker despised them:

somehow they seemed to represent a lot of what had been going wrong in Finance during the last decade – borderline legal contraptions that were mainly used to create a tilted playing field. And dangerous, too, though as usual people were happy to pick up pennies in front of a steamroller.

The only good thing about the damn machines was that they were fast, so fast that the speed of light was a constraint. Because the extra few hundred miles of cable between the Stock Exchange computers and the bank's floor in London caused a lag of 0.004 seconds, the Algos would have stood no chance. They had to be close. They had to be next door to the bloody exchange in Germany.

And they were, which meant they still enjoyed the market access that Walker desperately needed. 'That's just insane. We need to trade, and those guys will have to be shut off, if that's what it takes,' he growled.

'It's not my call...'

'All right then.' Walker glanced around the floor, looking for the overpaid, spineless idiot that was supposed to be his direct boss. He saw him next to an overflowing filing cabinet a dozen yards away, near the back of the floor. Jack Morden was deep in conversation with God, or the next best thing in Dorfmann's building. Standing close to him was the tall, wide frame of Chris 'Beano' Friedman, the chief executive officer of the London Office. *Sweet.*

Walker turned to Ben, or Brett. 'There's the guy with the authority. Go and talk to him.'

'But...' The techie swallowed. 'Jack's talking to Mr Friedman.'

'Good. Even more authority, then.' He could understand their nervousness. Friedman was someone who got things done. The man had been a legendary trader in the late nineties, and now ran a tight ship in Europe, always hands-on, always aware. He was quick, and smart, and hard. And he didn't suffer fools gladly.

The floor-lights flickered off and on again, but at least the computers stayed alive. Walker scoffed, glanced at the techies and pointed over. They stared at each other for a second, then shrank smaller and shuffled towards the managers.

Walker grinned and headed for the trading floor exit, checking if the cigarettes were still in his jacket pocket. There was *one* thing he didn't like about Beano.

Under pressure, the guy could turn into a psycho.

His angry bellows would echo across the floor as he swore and chewed some poor banker's head off. Friedman had been known to throw telephones, chairs and once, memorably, a pink umbrella belonging to one of his daughters had gone through a flat-screen monitor.

And right now the pressure within Dorfmann Brothers was at submarine-depth level. At least Beano would get the IT morons to hook up to Frankfurt – unless he killed them first.

As he approached the glass doors a new crowd of traders, researchers and salespeople started flowing through the entrance. It looked as if a school bell had rung, but instead of screaming children you got a bunch of well-dressed investment bankers. Everyone's phones had beeped with the roll call at precisely eleven the night before, and nobody wanted to be seen coming in late, not on a day like today.

Walker nodded and smiled at a few worried faces, then left the floor in search of his first coffee of the morning.

Months Earlier...

The billion-dollar meeting was in a grubby pub down in Charlton, The Sun In The Sands.

Judging from the outside the place looked as if it had seen better days, probably around the end of the fifties. But from the inside, probably not. The Englishman tried to hide his distaste and approached the bar, nodding to the over-tattooed, flabby barmaid.

'Pint of bitter, love,' he said.

She nodded and started pouring as he looked around. The American sat wedged behind a tiny corner table, studying his glass of beer. A small group of builders downed lagers near the pool table while a twenty-something black man hunched over the bar, tapping away on a smartphone. Slouching against the stained wall, a drunk kid in a hoodie burped loudly. Faded pictures from the blitz hung around the wall. Dreariness oozed from the ceiling.

The Englishman dragged his drink along the counter, sipped it and stepped over, sitting down in front of the American. 'You wanted to see me.'

'Yes.' A pause. 'What we're trying to pull off is still massive, but things are moving along nicely now.'

'How?'

'I've already got four on the Board. I only need another two.'

The Englishman nodded, giving nothing away. When the silence lengthened he just took another sip of his beer. The American stared at his dirty glass, considered it for a second and gave up. 'Now they want proof though, something tangible. It's a big step for them,' he said.

'Blackspring is on the ground, but it might take a while. A few weeks, months maybe.'

'That's not be a problem, as long as you can deliver the machine. You know I trust your vision, but... they'll need some data, soon,' the American sighed.

'I see.'

'Here, have this.' The American opened a small box and pulled out an odd-looking mobile phone. The handset was thicker than normal, and about twice as tall.

'What is it?'

'It's military grade. Sat-phone, untraceable, effectively impossible to intercept.' He glanced around and grimaced. 'At least you won't drag me to these shitholes when we need to talk privately.'

The Englishman took the offering and stood up, his pint still half-full. 'Fine, I'll let you know as soon as I have better samples.' Seconds later he stepped into the sticky, humid air of a warm London summer and hailed his driver from the carpark.

Inside the pub, the American slipped to the toilet to wash his hands. The kid in the hoodie smiled, winked at the barmaid and rushed out, a heavy gym bag slung across his shoulder.

Coffee with DM – 6.26 A.M.

Walker hurried through a security scanner near the middle of Dorfmann's circular entrance hall, glancing at the tropical plants that cascaded from the first-floor balcony. He couldn't see any yellow leaves yet, but winter *was* coming. And if DeepShare had it right, this time the Crisis could be almost terminal. He shivered, concerned about the direction in which things appeared to be travelling. Very little had been learnt from the previous disasters; China was in a mess and Europe no better, but the financial world rumbled on uncaring. He wondered again if it was time to get out of banking, whether the nausea at the bottom of his stomach would disappear then. But if big events were coming, he wanted to have a front-row seat. And maybe, one day, with DM's DeepShare...

A couple of guards grunted at him when the metal detector beeped but Walker ignored them, rushing to the exit. Idiots. He was leaving the building, for God's sake – what would be the point of taking a bomb OUT of a bank?

The problem was that everyone felt itchy. Security had been comprehensively tightened in the last couple of years, up to and beyond airport levels. As the economic downturn deepened, social tensions had escalated and the hostility towards bankers was now reaching dangerous levels. Groups like Hackernym were growing bolder, and BreakWallStreet marches and occupations mushroomed around New York, London and most Eurozone capital cities.

Walker stepped out of the building into the crispy autumn air just as Broadgate Circle was starting to brighten after dawn. He tried to shrug off his unease, and lit the cigarette that was already dangling from his lips, looking around to check which coffee kiosk had the shortest queue.

Sharply-dressed City-dwellers were flowing into the banks and brokerages around the plaza, most with eyes down and no desire to speak, their minds focused on what was about to unfold in the European markets. Walker joined a few Dorfmann analysts and was waiting for his turn at the counter when he noticed a narrow-faced woman staring at him from one of the stone benches that dotted the Circle. He locked eyes with her and took a step in her direction but the smart-suited lady picked up a copy of the Financial Times and stood up, gliding away through the crowds to the far side of the Circle. *Do I know her?*

An older man bumped him from behind and Walker realised the queue had shifted; then he glimpsed a skinny figure in a brown overcoat scurrying to a Dorfmann side entrance and raised his hand in greeting. 'DM, there you are! Let's get a coffee.'

The forty-year-old Swiss-Burmese glanced around, his head turning as he tried to focus back to the real world. Even though Walker saw DM Khaing most days, he was still taken aback by the sheer intensity of the man's eyes, and the gauntness of his features. The mathematician was starting to look like a mad hermit left out to dry on the slopes of Mount Sinai.

Walker slid forward, waving his hand. 'I'm here, you big geek.'

'Scott. Go away, I'm late.' DM's voice had a raspy quality, and was much deeper than anyone would expect from such a slight frame.

'You're always late. Don't worry – I'm sure some of your grunts have already fired up the monster.'

'DeepShare's been running all the time. But I've got a meeting with Fontaine on the beta version...'

Walker chuckled, steering his friend towards the nearest kiosk. There were only a couple of people ahead of them in the queue. 'Fontaine has other things to worry about this morning. Your meeting will get pushed back, we have a derivatives trading pow-wow in fifteen minutes.'

'The Italian election?'

'Of course. What does Deep say, now that the results are in? And didn't you get a text on your office BlackBerry last night?'

DM shrugged. 'The mainframe is still crunching scenarios – we should have something back after the first couple of hours of trading. When the market patterns are clearer I'll get an alert ' – he smiled tiredly – 'and no, I didn't see the text. You know I switch the phones off when I get home. I was working.'

'Yeah, what else?' Walker pointed to the pretty girl behind the counter, waiting for their order. 'What do you want?'

'Earl Grey.'

'That's not a *breakfast* tea.'

DM looked sheepish. 'My sleep patterns are a bit odd.'

Walker grunted and threw away the butt of his cigarette. 'Very odd, like you hardly sleep at all. Or eat, even.' He nodded to the girl preparing the tea. 'A chocolate croissant as well, before this man faints. And a double espresso. Cheers.'

DM's appearance was even more dishevelled than usual, his skin sallow, a shadow of blue-black stubble on his normally clean-shaven cheeks. Walker paid and picked up the hot drinks as his friend bit into a chunk of the warm pastry. They sat on a bench close together, keeping their voices low. You never knew around bankers and brokers.

'Are you all right, mate?'

'I'm thinking.'

'About what? Come on, DeepShare got the election results perfectly. It's the first Class A Event it predicted, and the timing was spot-on.' Walker took a quick drag of his Marlboro, exhaled. 'Four months ago a Rossini victory was unthinkable, but we saw it...'

'It's not just that. Tsun, in Hong Kong... he's gone.'

'Gone – where?'

'No idea. He hasn't showed up at the office since last Wednesday, and no one has seen him.'

Walker shrugged. Tsun was one of DM's head quants in Asia, but he wasn't exactly reliable even at the best of times. 'He's probably holed up somewhere in Macau with a couple of whores, as usual.'

'He's gay.'

'So what? I'm sure they cater for that at the casinos.'

DM glared at him. 'You're just over-excited because you'll make a killing today. Besides, you nudged Deep in the right direction.'

'Still, it worked.'

'Yes. It's great at making money, and now we have proof. But that was never the point.'

Walker sighed. The man was such a perfectionist. 'I know. And we'll put in even more work – whatever you think is necessary. Still, it looks like you're getting close to saving the world, you idiot. Smile, at least.'

'Maybe a *little* closer...' DM grinned at some internal joke and looked up at the clear sky, losing his focus. Within a few seconds he drifted off, his croissant forgotten.

Walker sipped his coffee and waited. He was used to this. The mathematician lived in his own world, a sort of alien universe where fractal patterns, chaos theory and deep internet data-mining flashed in bright primary colours through his synapses. All the time.

The unholy mixture of a genius and a prophet, DM was the architect of a machine that spoke, God-like, about the future. A machine that had haunted his dreams since a broken childhood, when, as a young boy, he had been chased away from his mother and his country. Walker had been helping on the unofficial – and secret – DeepOmega for years, and yet parts of his friend remained submerged, locked into pain-toughened steel safes. The truly brilliant were often obsessive, but DM was going to hurt himself if he didn't slow down.

Walker pulled out another cigarette, lit it and blew a cloud of smoke in DM's face. The mathematician recoiled, coughing, and shot him a wounded glare.

'Couldn't you just nudge me?'

'It's more fun this way. So what's eating you, apart from that idiot Tsun?'

'I'm...' DM fidgeted, his left hand rubbing at an old scar on his right arm, just above the wrist: one of his many Burmese civil-war scars. 'I'm a bit worried, that's all. Odd things have been happening.'

'Is it the police again? How much junk have you been doing?'

'A bit... maybe a bit more than usual.'

'Shit. Are you still buying it from the same old guy?' Walker struggled to keep his tone of voice even. DM was a dopehead – not hard stuff, but he regularly bulldozed his way through mountains of weed. His routine was simple: he would get home from work, roll a massive joint and put on some classical music. Then he would smoke more, and more, until he became *properly* stoned. At that point he would fire up the massive mainframe he kept in his house and work through the evening and night, lost in his own drug-sharpened mathematical universe.

'Yes. It's not the police though. I think... I think someone is following me, watching me.'

'Right.' Walker stared at his friend. 'Like before the summer, when you couldn't get rid of that death smell in your place.' He took a deep breath and stood up, annoyed. DM had been caught up in the millennia-old trap that had entangled many mystics, saints and rock stars before him: being high actually supercharged his brain. But he also suffered the usual side-effects of mild hallucinations, panic attacks, paranoia.

'You're having a psychotic episode, mate.'

'No, I'm not. Not this time. It's real. After my deputy resigned...'

'Jim Zhu? What does he have do with it?' Walker groaned.

'When he left, five months ago, he tried to take the access codes to the mainframe.'

'Yeah. And they revoked his FSA registration because of that.'

'Fucking rightly so.' DM slammed his paper cup on the bench, spilling a few drops of the dark tea inside.

Walker almost recoiled in surprise – his friend practically never swore.

'So he's never going to work in the City again.'

'You'd think so. Well, the idiot somehow resurfaced at Frankel last week,' DM continued. 'Senior role, too. Bastards.'

'Really? They tried to hire you again last year, didn't they?' Frankel Schwartz was the Godfather of investment banks. You couldn't count the numbers of central bankers, ministers and Treasury Secretaries they had produced over the years. Conspiracy theorists all over the world believed they were the master puppeteers behind the scenes. Then again, you could find lunatics screaming that man had never landed on the moon. And Area 51 was full of aliens, or whatever. Walker fumbled with his jacket, looking for another cigarette. He glanced at his watch: seven more minutes before they had to attend the morning meeting. 'How much did Frankel offer you – three million?'

DM shrugged. 'Five, actually. When I said no, the offer went up. As if that would make a difference.'

'Well, they're investment bankers. They think it's just a question of price.'

'They're fucking crooks, that's what they are,' swore DM, his voice starting to rise. 'What they did with sub-prime, and LIBOR, and all those nasty bonds they sold everywhere...'

Walker glanced around, noticing a few people were starting to look at them. 'Calm down, mate. You read too many NoHedge blogs. Besides, they are much bigger than us – most investment banks are, really – and their systems are supposed to be the best. They could have helped with Deep.'

'Maybe, but I trust the coder quants in Bangalore – it would take years to get such a good group together. No, I'm too close to go anywhere else.' He looked up, smiling, his words dripping with sarcasm. 'And it's not always about the cash, you WOP oaf.'

Walker sighed inwardly; this was more like their usual banter. 'Beautiful words. So how do you know you're being watched?'

'I've noticed the same people hanging around a few times. On the Tube, near my grocers. I think they might be renting a flat in the opposite building. I've seen light reflecting off something like a telescope in one of the apartments there.'

'You've got to lay off that bloody stuff you're smoking. For a while at least.'

'I'm serious.'

'Me too.' Walker lit his cigarette, becoming impatient. 'And who would be following you, anyway?'

DM glared at him. 'Aren't you listening? It *must* be from Frankel, someone high up there. They have Zhu and they've known about Deep, at least the Alpha version, for a while.' The mathematician jumped up, his expression stormy. 'They want it real bad, I know.'

'Come on, trying to buy you out is one thing but... This is ridiculous. Frankel Schwartz is a big investment bank, not the bloody Hydra you make it out to be.'

'I wouldn't be so sure.' DM stepped back, his intense eyes burning with rage. 'You know what Kissinger said,' he rasped.

Walker looked at him blankly. 'What?'

'Even a paranoid can have enemies, Yours.'

The mathematician swore again, spun on his heel and rushed to the side entrance that would take him down into Dorfmann's basement. Walker let him go, then he finished his cigarette and stubbed it out. DM was falling to pieces. The man needed to be taken away for a few days, to decompress. He worked through the options for a second, then smiled: Monaco.

They hadn't been to the Cote d'Azur in years, not since the '08 crash. A long weekend, roulette, and stunning girls. He knew a trader at a Swiss bank who would rent them his Dossani yacht, a 36-foot sleek beast moulded in carbon fibre, with all the proper toys. Another week to unwind his trading book and make the bank some serious cash, and they'd head off. They both needed a break, badly.

Walker's BlackBerry beeped and he checked it: two minutes to the meeting. He dodged a pregnant lady wobbling past him and slipped, but as he regained his balance he glimpsed the same well-dressed woman staring at him again from across the plaza. Suddenly uneasy, he pivoted and took a few quick steps in her direction. She dropped her paper, turned and slipped behind a kiosk.

When Walker reached the corner she had vanished into thin air. *What the hell was that?* His phone beeped again and he swore, making his way back to the bank's entrance.

CHAPTER TWO

The Previous Night. Sunday, September 30th - 7.41 P.M.

The ring swayed before his eyes and Walker stepped aside, twisting and dodging a left hook. The glove grazed his padded helmet, but just as he prepared to respond a right fist clattered into his ribs, winding him. The world slowed as he half-fell to the ropes, barely managing to avoid a straight punch that would have broken his nose. Someone shouted and his opponent danced back, a nasty smile on his lips.

Coach Newstead left his corner and hurried to Walker, helping him climb back up. The old pro stared at his eyes, trying to decide whether to stop the sparring.

'Are you okay, Scott?'

Walker shook his head, his vision still blurred. 'Yeah.'

'You sure? We can have a short break.'

'No, I'm fine.' He took a deep breath, ignoring the pain in his lower chest. 'Just another round.'

Newstead nodded, glancing at Teddy, the seventeen-year-old who was battering Walker. 'Left hitting only, tiger.'

'Yes Coach.'

'Box!'

Walker rushed in, feinting and changing guard to a southpaw stance. He swivelled and avoided a left hook, then pushed off his right heel and slipped a lower cross, aiming for the solar plexus. His opponent swatted him aside as he had expected, his right hand darting through for a jab that rattled the youngster.

Teddy shuffled back and stretched his neck, his eyes narrowing. 'Not bad, white guy.' He crouched lower and approached, unleashing a series of left jabs, his fist moving so fast it almost blurred. Walker defended out of instinct, parrying a couple and managing to avoid a third. He tried to slide away from the corner of the ring leaning into the ropes but his foot slipped on a sweat stain and he lost his balance for a split second.

He didn't even see the punch that knocked him out.

...

Walker stepped out of the shower, his body still aching from the punishment. A deserved one, since he'd never learnt to stop when he was overmatched. He had needed to while away the hours and the tension before the Italian election results, but the best kids down at Fisher's Youth club were obviously becoming too quick for him. Sighing, he dried his short dark hair and checked himself in the mirror – no cuts or lumps, just the usual intense grey eyes set under a high forehead. *No worries; at least I'm still a decent-looking bastard.*

He jumped into a pair of jeans and a T-shirt and poured himself a drink in the open kitchen in his loft-style living room. After lighting a cigarette, he walked to the ceiling-height windows and looked out at the Thames, swirling darkly four floors below. To his left, less than a hundred yards away, the bright lights of Tower Bridge painted a maelstrom of red, blue and white into the London night. Beyond them shone the skyline of the City, where new buildings continued to shoot up, defying the gravity of another economic crisis. Astonishing, how Finance could still find ways to expand and pay when entire economies crumbled.

It felt as if... as if the parasite was killing the host, slowly bleeding it dry. Walker's mild soul-sickness threatened to return, and again he wondered what he was waiting for. The entire world seemed strained, ordinary people were suffering. Maybe it was time to think of ways to help repair the damage. Not much he could do alone, but DeepShare might...

He coughed a few times, fighting a sudden wave of nausea. He flicked his cigarette away and watched the tip spiral into the water before going back inside. The 60-inch TV on the wall was on, volume muted. A few Italian politicians argued around a cowlicked host who'd seen better days, filling air-time and waiting for the election exit polls to come in.

Another twenty minutes.

He grabbed a bottle of 42 Below from the fridge, picked up his phone and lowered himself gently onto a leather couch. His body felt like he'd just walked out of a car crash but the adrenaline was already starting to pump again. Flights of fancy about helping to shape a better future were all right, and maybe one day he could afford them, but right now he needed to be sharp, focused. If he and DeepShare were wrong and the Italian election went as expected... the next few weeks would turn into a financial massacre for Walker Ltd.

His trading portfolio would take a battering in the market, bleeding away like an unstitched open vein. He would personally lose Dorfmann a fortune in the run-up to Christmas, and that fat idiot Fontaine would lean on Jack Morden to have him fired if he closed the year down fifteen or twenty million. Spineless Jack wouldn't stand in the way of the head of trading – the idiot didn't really care, not if it could cost him money when the envelopes were handed down on Bonus Day. Then again, maybe it would be better to be pushed, if he couldn't jump.

He exhaled and readjusted his legs on the sofa, trying to get comfortable just as his phone rang with the slightly odd melody that signalled a video-call.

Luigi.

Walker smiled and gestured at the TV, transferring the call onto the big screen. The image split down the middle, Italian politicians still silently jabbering away at each other. Luigi Seu's ruddy face materialized on the left-hand side of the screen, his blue eyes glinting. His short beard was half-grey, the cropped hair receding beyond a widow's peak.

It looked as if he had finally lost some weight.

At least a bit.

Maybe a third of one per cent.

He also looked like he was already half-drunk, sitting in his massive kitchen in Lugano, a large brandy glass at his elbow.

'Yo, bitch. Whassup?' he smiled.

'Hi ugly.' Walker switched to Italian – Luigi's English was perfect but very flat, while his friend's funny Sardinian accent shone through in his mother tongue. 'I'm in pain. Serious pain.'

'Been down sparring? Those kids are too good for you. You should have quit already, like twenty years ago when they rehashed your nose in the Trials. Why the hell did you pick up that barbarous hobby anyway?'

'When you're a skinny orphan at boarding school in Dulwich, it's not a bad idea to know how to defend yourself.'

'Maybe,' Luigi sighed. 'But now?'

Walker shrugged. 'I needed to take my mind off things.'

'Drinking helps.'

'I can tell. When are the ladies due back from America?' Walker was godfather to Luigi's daughter Lia, a feisty three-year-old.

'Next Friday, I hope. I've been eating out for a week and I'm starting to get bored. So, you still think Rossini is going to win the election?'

'Yep. Was I wrong three months ago when I told you the previous government would collapse?'

'No, but you're an idiot now. Rossini's five to one at the bookies, and it's a rip-off. The man and his Three Star Party have no chance to get more than fifteen to seventeen per cent of the votes, I reckon. You should get ten-to-one odds.'

Walker smiled: this was the hook. Luigi was an inveterate gambler, even with his closest friends. Casinos, horses, dogs, anything was good for a wager. 'Are you making me a market?'

Luigi missed a beat. 'Maybe.'

'Why do you always try to take my money?' Walker sniggered. 'Is it because you're only a lowly broker?'

'Yeah. And I want to join the god-like beings, like you. I dream of being a trader, every night.'

'You're just jealous, mate.' Luigi's job as an Over-The-Counter broker consisted in helping dealers shift risk across banks and hedge funds. He earned a small commission on all trades, working as the ultimate middleman. And, though it paid well, he often got bored with it.

'Jealous of all those idiots who take enormous punts with other people's money? Of course I am.'

'Great. I'll take those odds, then.'

'Dream on. Just because of our decade-old friendship, I might offer you seven to one.'

'Eight.'

Luigi grunted, as if suffering a great injustice. 'You're done. The usual?'

'Yes sir, for a grand. Great British Pounds, not your worthless Swiss toilet paper.'

'Good. At least with your cash I'll shrug off this damn austerity drive.'

'You, saving?'

Luigi grimaced and looked at his empty glass. 'It's why I've scaled down to this cheap Grand Marnier junk, instead of the hundred-year reserve. Too many penny-pinching Protestants around Switzerland are having a bad effect on me, apparently.'

'Good man. Problem is, when those other scrooges in Brussels and Frankfurt push too hard for cuts, countries implode. Greece is in ruins, Spain has become a German protectorate, for God's sake. And Italy – there's a riot in

Rome every time Parliament tries to vote a new law. That's why I'm sure Rossini will win the elections. He's the man with a plan.'

'Leaving the Euro? That's insane. The country would go under in weeks, and the rest of the world would get a heart attack.'

'Maybe. But I don't know if there are any good solutions left at all.'

Luigi sighed, looking annoyed. 'And here's the reason you've been so damn bearish on the markets, and short. You're trying to make money as the world slides into a depression. Very nice.'

'Look – traders react to events, they don't cause them. I can't do anything about it, but prepare.' It was true but it could be sickening at times, and that's when working with DM helped.

'React. And make money.'

'That's my job.' Walker sat back on the sofa, sipping his vodka. 'Come on, you know me – I'm getting tired of all this banking bullshit. One last big trade, if I'm right. Then I can go off, do something useful with the rest of my life. And if I'm wrong and the world gets better, I promise I won't complain.'

'Oh yeah.' Luigi grinned like a wolf cornering its prey. 'So why have you been whining in the last few weeks, as you got murdered by the market drifting higher?'

'That was just my bruised ego talking.' Walker faked a shrug and glanced at his watch – 9.59 p.m., just one minute to go. 'Be quiet for a second and let's check out the exit pools.'

Luigi looked away with a snigger, concentrating on an unseen TV to his right. Walker turned up the volume on the split screen where the Italian politicians had quietened down and a digital clock ticked away the last few seconds. Time seemed to slow, but finally a bell rang in the TV studio and blue graphics flashed on the screen.

Rossini-Three Stars – 38%

PD – 20%

GrandItalia – 14%

FI – 9%

Walker blinked, rereading it to be sure.

'Holy shit!' Luigi's voice boomed from the speakers. 'That's unbelievable. The son-of-a-bitch has done it.'

Walker smiled, finishing his vodka in one shot. 'You owe me some cash. You, and all those idiots in the markets.'

Interlude

The satellite phone rang just as late evening turned into night. The Englishman rushed to answer it, hoping the kids hadn't been woken by the loud noise.

'What do you want?' he asked, annoyed.

'Did you hear about the Italian mess...' The American sounded both excited and scared.

'Of course.'

'And does it... did it think...'

'There was a chance for the 1.8 model. I'd guess their 3.1 prototype was surer.'

'Can you deliver some timed-logs, at least? That's the sort of thing we need.'

'Maybe. I'll look into it tomorrow.'

'Hurry up. The window might be closing.'

The Englishman sighed and cut off the call. Had the twat been trying to put pressure on HIM? Ridiculous. And scary how people could get so high up in business without a functioning brain.

Late Night

How long does pain last?

Twenty-five years was longer than the jail-time you'd do for murdering someone. Walker sighed and put out another cigarette before checking his watch. 1.17 a.m. – he had burnt through a full packet of Marlboros while half-listening to the election analysis of the Italian media and political second-liners, the 42 Below bottle was almost empty and his throat felt like a dry patch of tarmac leading into the Gobi desert.

Food – he needed food. He turned the TV off and called his favourite delivery restaurant. They were normally fast, but the guy said one of their ovens was out and it would take a while. Which was fine. He didn't have anything better to do and sleeping was out of the question for the time being, anyway. Stirring the ice in his glass, Walker sipped the last of the vodka and tried to ignore the dull ache in his jaw. Then he gave up and grabbed his calculator, a notepad and a pen, trying to think through his trading book. There had never been any real hope of distracting himself with sparring, or alcohol.

The young amateur boxer he had been had somehow grown up to become a Prop Trader – a polite way of saying he spent his days punting around with the bank's money, using his expertise and Dorfmann's lightning-quick systems to try and predict the stock market's behaviour. He now shadowboxed against the Eurostoxx: an index composed of the fifty largest European companies, the Old Continent's equivalent of the Dow Jones Industrial Average. And like half-decent heavyweights who nonetheless carry a packed punch, volatility traders like him could make enormous profits, or losses. It was pure adrenaline at its best, and soul-crushing almost as often. But at least the bad hits hurt his pride more than his body.

Pride. Did it have a price, too? Walker shrugged, tired, and refused to think about it. He scribbled a few numbers, punched some keys on the calculator and considered another cigarette before deciding it was the one that would make him throw up. He was about to cancel his pizza when he remembered he hadn't yet spoken to Steph, his junior, and grabbed the phone. The line rang for a few seconds before a rough voice picked up on the other side.

'Hallo?'

'Don't tell me you were asleep.'

'Boss. No, my...' Steph's breathing was a little heavy. 'My girlfriend is here, from Paris.'

Walker smiled. 'Good, shove her off and tell her to wait. You'll make it up to her with the ring you can buy after bonus day.'

'Sure, hold on.' Some quick-fire French followed and Walker heard a scraping noise. 'What's up, Yours?'

'What's up? The fucking market is going to crack tomorrow, that's what. I need you to be in by five o'clock, at the latest. Fire up the systems, and launch the new spreadsheet. You'll be trawling brokers from six thirty.'

'Shit. Are we going to be all right?'

'Steph. Concentrate, for fuck's sake. I own a lot of Options, right?' Walker could understand the Frenchman's brain being addled by sex, but after six months on the desk he expected better. Even at 1.33 in the morning. He forced himself to be patient: no point in having a confused guy around in the morning.

'Yes.'

'And what else did I trade last week?'

Steph paused, and Walker could almost hear his brain clicking into gear. 'You sold a ton of Futures, short.'

'About one hundred million. That will turn into over half a billion with the market crashing, because of Option dynamics. Which means?'

'You'll... make a fortune when you buy them back cheaper?'

Walker grinned, enjoying the mild torture. 'That's right. How much, do you reckon?'

'Ehrr... just give me a sec.'

Walker counted to three, then answered his own question without glancing at the calculator. *Too slow, really.* 'Thirteen million, and you should probably add another ten, as Option prices scream up.'

'*Merde.*'

'So yeah, we'll be all right. But to lock in the profits, we'll have to trade like mad.'

'I guess –' Steph almost choked. 'So... how do we do it, exactly?'

'That's where the art comes into it. I don't know, yet – I'll have to see how things break when trading starts. Sleep tight, and don't forget to set your alarm clock. People have been fired, or killed, for less.'

Walker cut the connection and poured another vodka, thinking. Sleep could wait a little longer, he guessed. He hadn't wanted to overburden the young man, but the question Steph had asked was absolutely key. Having set up the perfect book for a crash, the real skill would now lie in knowing *when* to hedge: do it too early in a big drop and you could waste most of the potential profit. But cut the Futures' short-risk too late, and your losses would be catastrophic when the market bounced.

Timing is everything.

Walker shuddered, suddenly cold. Timing.

He was there when his mother died for the second time. *The hospital room is small and cramped, saturated with the smell of disinfectant. Tubes run into her mouth and arms, under the sheets. She is thinner, almost skeletal, and pale. Her eyes are closed – ever since the accident that killed my little sister Sarah. Ever since the fucking double-decker crashed into their car. Almost a month has passed but she's not waking up. I touch her hand, and it's cold. It's hard to think. It's hard to breathe.*

Abruptly one of the monitors beeps twice, then continuously, with a loud, persistent noise.

Dad and a nurse rush into the room and Dad grabs me and leads me out. There are tears in his eyes.

Time stops, sometimes.

Walker stifled a sob and forced himself up. His hands grabbed the notepad, crumpled the sheets of paper into a ball and sent it flying across the room.

Even Later

The little Chinese man screamed when the cigar burnt his nipple. It was a piercing howl, the type that came up from the diaphragm, bursting through lungs and windpipe before crashing out. Not that it would help him, but it was a good scream.

The woman waited for it to finish before the tears and blubbering started again. She puffed out some Havana smoke, and sighed.

'How can you possibly not even have a partial copy?'

The little man's voice shook and he sobbed. 'I… he always asks me to work on different things, I told you.'

'Yes, yes. All unrelated, all unconnected. Or so you think.'

'Please… I really don't know…'

'We'll see.'

The second scream wasn't nearly as good as the first one, she thought.

CHAPTER THREE

Morning Meeting – 6.41 A.M.

Walker crossed the trading floor, barely acknowledging the greetings of colleagues moving about their workstations. The massive hangar-like room was almost full now, phones starting to ring on the hundreds of dealerboards sitting below thousands of brightly lit monitors. A voice echoed around the squawk boxes and speakers – the high nasal pitch of Dorfmann's Chief Strategist lecturing the troops about the talking points of the trading day. Walker tried to block the noise out; the man was a blubbering fool who hadn't got anything right for the last five years. He still didn't get that they were living in a post-Lehman world, with different rules and new Empires rising, ready to fight for the spoils. Walker could hear the words looping in his head, like so many times before: *Look, you guys should tell your clients that today will be a great buying opportunity. The market hasn't been so cheap for a long while, the forward PEs and the dividend yield...'*

Rubbish. It was the usual claptrap, simplistic bullshit fed to post-grads at over-expensive business schools across the world. Investment banks were populated by idiots. And the fact they still had thousands of clients eagerly listening to such drivel only proved that the rest of the financial world was made up of even bigger idiots. Walker exhaled and told his inner cynic to shut up. He was strangely unsettled, and it wasn't the market opening in a few minutes that bothered him; he had been preparing for that through the night. But what DM had said – and the blank face of the well-dressed woman outside watching him – still gnawed at his consciousness as he approached Fontaine's office for the morning meeting.

Frankel Schwartz was run by a bunch of cutthroat bastards, that much was true. Though they had survived the 2008–09 crisis better than most of their peers, the large investment bank had been recently hit with several lawsuits and investigations. Through the years they had gone over the edge too many times, selling toxic rubbish and fudging rules, buying influence and political protection, and now they were starting to pay. Their reputation as the smartest on the Street was taking a beating, a few high-profile clients and hedge funds had cut ties and their underwriting business was suffering. Still, Frankel was a trading behemoth, across all asset classes. Walker wouldn't want to work at such a ruthless place anyway – no matter the money – but their research and systems were second to none, and their connections unparalleled. Its share price may have been suffering, but Frankel continued to be the best franchise on Wall Street. By far. *DM is seriously losing it.* Walker swore and forced himself to focus on the bloody meeting. The day was too big to get distracted.

He entered Olivier Fontaine's office just behind a group of senior traders, a few more already standing in the large glass-bowl room with views over Broadgate. Fontaine himself sat behind his massive desk, a fat man sliding into obesity with thin blond hair that stuck to his skull like dying moss. Walker despised the Belgian. He had climbed high, but only on the backs of broken traders. Ruthlessly taking credit whenever he had a chance, arse-licking the managers he could see were on their way up. The man had no morals, no conscience, and was now supposed to run all the dealers on the damn floor. What a joke.

Fontaine gestured for someone at the back of the office to close the glass door, then started speaking in his monotonous voice. 'First, all the trading systems and ORK are back online.' He glanced about, smug, as if they should all be personally grateful to him. 'Then, as you all know...'

Walker tuned him out and looked around the room, studying the familiar faces. All the Equity and Derivatives Trading areas were represented in force. Next to him a couple of older boys from the Cash desk were nervously exchanging glances with a tight group to Fontaine's left, the Risk Arb people. In theory their books were supposed to be neutral, but when markets tanked most of their spread positions would widen and go haywire, and shakier deals could be pulled in a flash. They were going to take a bloodbath, but if the turbulence proved short-lived they should have a chance to recover. Other desks were represented by their heads, all wearing worried expressions – the only team apparently missing was Automated Trading, DM's group.

Fontaine turned to spineless Jack Morden, who was standing next to the door with Mendes and Setter, two of Dorfmann's most senior Volatility traders, both a few years older than Walker. *We're the linchpin*. The Vol group ran by far the biggest risks on the floor; this was not going to be pretty.

Fontaine sipped from a mug and cleared his throat. 'Jack. Consensus here seems to be that we open down five or six per cent before stabilising.'

Morden nodded, checking with Mendes and Setter. 'That sounds about right.'

'What are the desk positions like down there, and lower?'

Morden looked sick. 'Horrifying. A large client needed a lot of protection and purchased billions of Options from the desk a few days ago – and we haven't covered them yet.'

Walker had to restrain himself. He had told the idiot to buy all those damn things back from a few other investment banks, fast. But Morden had been greedy, and now it would cost a fortune to hedge.

Fontaine grimaced. 'How much?'

'A lot – about ten million a point. If the market doesn't stabilize and Option prices scream up we could be in serious trouble. Down at least a hundred bucks on that alone, maybe more...'

The door opened suddenly and DM rushed in, followed by a couple of his quants. Fontaine shot him a dark look. 'Hello sir, you're just in time. What's DeepAlpha's view?'

'Sorry Olivier, I...' DM trailed off and focused on a printout, his brow furrowed. 'The market view... it's mixed at the moment – I guess it will be clearer once the markets start trading. But Deep's not signalling any major catastrophe ahead. When we simulated a minus-seven-per-cent opening, Alpha actually wanted to use the lower prices to buy back half of its short exposure. It doesn't look at Options, though.'

A few people around the room audibly breathed out.

'Really? That's interesting. What about DeepBeta?'

Walker smiled, feeling like the kid who's hidden the candy. DeepShareBeta was a more powerful version that DM was drip-feeding into Dorfmann's computers. It was really just an incremental improvement to keep the bank happy while they secretly developed the real monster – Omega.

DeepOmega sat under lock and key somewhere in cyberspace, its servers scattered around the world by the secrecy-obsessed DM. The mathematician, using the cover of the Beta version, had been driving Dorfmann's quants everywhere to produce most of the multiple parts of his Frankenstein dream. No-one knew the full picture but him – dozens of different experts worked on slices of the program that only DM could assemble and perfect in his drug-induced nirvana at home. In theory it was illegal to take that sort of stuff out of the bank, but the man was both a paranoid genius and the head of the department. Who was going to notice unless he told them?

Even Walker had no idea where the source code for Omega sat, or how to access it. His friend had one hyper-secure, custom-made tablet that was the only pipeline in and out of the massive software, and the only way to speak to his oracle.

'Beta is the same – if anything even more optimistic. But it crashed before the final run, so it's only a preliminary,' DM said.

Fontaine stood up and glanced at the big clock to his right: 6.47 a.m., thirteen minutes to the opening of the

European Futures. The cash markets and all single stocks would open an hour later, but the Futures would drive the action, as always.

'Fine, get back to your desks and let me know how things are going. No panic, but if the Eurostoxx breaks lower than eight per cent down on the day... I want the heads of desk in my office, pronto. Good luck guys, Dorfmann is counting on you.'

Walker resisted a gag reflex as the glass office emptied quickly, the traders eager to get back to their teams in time for the bell. He was about to leave when he heard Fontaine's voice calling him back.

'Yours, I need you for a minute.'

'Sure.' He turned around and saw the Head of Trading gesturing to a seat. 'What's up?'

'I just wanted to congratulate you. Great call. I know your positions have suffered in the last few weeks, but you were right.'

Walker sat down, suddenly worried. A compliment first – that was never good. 'Thanks. We'll see how it pans out today.'

'Any views?'

'I don't think it's the big one, yet. We might drop seven or eight per cent, but as the Americans come in the market is probably going to bounce. And I suspect Rossini won't say anything major in Italy today; he'll be cautious for a while, get used to Rome first.'

'Okay. I'm a little more worried than that, though.'

'Are you turning more bearish than me? That's a first,' Walker said.

'I've got an entire trading floor to worry about,' Fontaine snapped. 'You heard the guys, if it's down ten per cent, or more, we'll be in deep shit. Hundreds of bucks of losses, more if it cracks. I...'

Walker shifted, uncomfortable. *Here it comes.* Whatever it was.

The Belgian hesitated for a split second, then continued. 'I don't want you to hedge your book, cover your short or sell out any puts. Not without my approval.'

'What?' Walker lurched forward, aghast. 'Are you joking?'

'I'm serious. We need your Options to protect the rest of the guys who are on the wrong side of the market.'

'You mean I'm the only one who called this right, and now I can't trade it? My own damn book?' Walker seethed; this was ridiculous.

'No, but I want you to check with me before you lock in the profits and close positions down.'

'What if we disagree?'

Fontaine's eyebrows arched up. 'We'll see.'

Walker struggled to keep calm: it wouldn't be a great idea to insult the big head of trading. He took a deep breath, still angry.

'This is insane. I can't run around the floor looking for you – not today, when I'll need to be quicker than ever. You know my style, for God's sake. I trade my guts, especially intraday.'

Fontaine just stared at him. Walker ignored the Belgian's look, stood up and continued. 'If I don't hedge in time and the market bounces, I'll give back most of my profits.' He paused, then continued in a lower tone. 'You know that as well as anyone.'

Fontaine jerked out of the leather armchair, his eyes blazing. As a trader on the desk he had made exactly the same mistake on a large position a few years earlier, and the barb had cut him too close. 'You'll do as I tell you. If you lose out because markets come back, I'll take care of you. Trust me, it won't be forgotten.'

Right. Like he hadn't forgotten all those poor bastards screwed to get the damn fishbowl office. 'Fine, I'll let you know.'

Biting his lip to keep from exploding, Walker stormed out of Fontaine's glass hovel and hurried to the fire stairs for a quick cigarette before the Futures opened.

A Phone Call

'Are you ready?'

'Of course I am,' the woman scoffed. 'The background stuff has come through, and I've met the manager. When will the target show up?'

'Sometime. Soon, I imagine.'

'Every extra night will cost you.'

'I know,' the man sighed in his own nasty, annoying way. 'Money is not an issue. Just make sure you do your job right.'

'Have I ever let you guys down?' she said.

'No. And now would not be a good time to start.'

Trading - 6.56 A.M.

The deepest circle of Hell is not hot enough for you, Fontaine.

Walker returned to his desk and sat down with a sigh, grabbing the rightmost keyboard underneath his eight monitors. He started typing away angrily and Steph glanced at him, surprised. 'Boss, is everything all right?'

Walker shrugged and kept working. The pre-open indicator for the Eurostoxx Future was already down almost five per cent, seeming to drop a few ticks every second.

'What are you doing – anything I can help with?'

'Like I told you last night, I'm putting a few limit orders in the market. When it opens, I'll buy back the Futures I sold short last Friday for a five-million profit on the gap. We'll still be short three hundred bucks or so afterwards, anyway.'

Steph nodded, his eyes widening. The reality of trading such large sums was starting to weigh on him, now that it wasn't a theoretical possibility any more. He looked afraid of making mistakes, the sheer size of the money involved terrifying him. But in the last few months he had been adapting, always working his head off to help make prices, speak to brokers or anything else the senior dealers on the desk needed him to do. He was a smart kid, learned fast. It was time to see if he had the fearlessness, the ruthlessness to go for blood when it was swirling in the water.

Traders needed the humility to cut positions and start again when things went wrong, but for Walker the best quality of the great ones was the arrogance to sometimes stand against the Market and say, 'That's enough. This is wrong and I am right, and I will prove it. With cold, hard cash.' He blinked, just realising that Steph had asked him another question.

'What?'

'I said, do you need me now?'

'No, I'm almost done. Ask around the guys and see if someone else wants help. I'll give you a shout later, to trade Options with the OTC brokers.'

Stephane shot off towards the desks at the other end of their row and Walker concentrated on his Bloomberg terminal, ignoring the flashing messages on the instant chats.

Twenty-three seconds to 7.00 a.m.

He took a deep breath, still seething at Fontaine. He would be damned before he let the fat bastard ruin his trading. Cursing in a low voice, he rechecked the orders in ORK, grabbed a mouse and stared at the expanded Future ticker on the screen. Four seconds, three, two...

The numbers flashed by, so fast it was impossible to distinguish them. 2704, 2693, 2684 – the market was dropping like a stone.

'Whoa!' Somebody shouted from across a couple of rows away.

2654.

A blood-red, unpleasant figure. Followed by a sudden, creepy stillness.

The prices had stopped moving, only one displayed on the ticker instead of the usual two – bid and offer – that normally shifted up and down in unison.

The Eurostoxx Futures were suspended limit-down. The circuit breakers had kicked in.

'What the hell is going on? I can't input anything.'

Walker turned and glanced at one of the trainees who had managed to secure a temporary spot on the desk a few weeks before. 'It's a trading halt.'

'What?' The pimply young man looked confused.

'Whenever market moves become too disorderly, the Stock Exchange freezes for a while.'

'Why?'

Walker sighed. He didn't mind explaining things to trainees – he had been one, a long time ago – but this kid could be slow. 'A short break, and a new dealing price. Hopefully at the re-opening markets will behave with a little more logic. Now the forced sellers are out, and people know that at least some buyers are sniffing around. It's only a matter of finding the level where things can stabilize. The second attempt should be much quieter, with the early panickers out of the game. Maybe.'

'I see. So...'

'Just wait.'

Walker turned back and glanced at his orders on the ORK monitor – they had all been filled. He'd just bought one hundred million dollars' worth of cheap Futures in the first second of trading. *Quality.*

The voice of a broker rumbled from the squawk boxes: 'The Eurostoxx and all European Futures markets are suspended for the next fifteen minutes. I repeat, in *fifteen* minutes there will be another opening auction, starting level 2667.' A short pause, interrupted by the sounds of quick fingers tapping away at a keyboard somewhere.

'Globex has also informed us that since the Dow Jones, Nasdaq and S&P Futures have all been offered limit-down for over two hours, the US will not restart trading at all until New York comes in, at nine thirty a.m. local time, fourteen thirty in London.'

Walker realised he had been squeezing his infrared mouse like a vice and released the poor thing. He stood up, searching for tech-support to ask for a new one. From the corner of his eye he noticed that Tony Mendes was approaching his desk, a sly smile on his round face. 'Hi mate – since the market's dead for now, do you fancy a quick coffee and a smoke?'

Walker looked at his monitors: his risk-management system gleamed darkly in the middle of the top row, highlighting his current position and daily profit-and-loss. His book was showing a temporary gain of twenty-seven-point-four million dollars. He shrugged and decided to ignore all those urgent messages for a few more minutes. 'Sure. Let's go.'

...

The little sailing boat swayed on the waves, turning in a lazy circle around the anchor line. The woman looked at Sprague, her accomplice, who was effortlessly dragging a few weights across the quarterdeck.

'I'll take those. Go and get Tsun.'

'Uh uh.'

She liked the fact that Sprague never spoke unless it was absolutely necessary. With a grunt she shifted a heavy lead ball and then another before untangling the plastic cables they would need to tie up the thin Chinese man. Glancing behind her, she thought she could see a distant light on the horizon but the Hong Kong skyscrapers were probably too far away.

Sprague staggered out of the cabin, carrying the unconscious man on his shoulder. 'Where?'

She pointed to the opening where three metal steps led down to the murky waters of the South-China Sea, and helped him lean Tsun against one of the railings. They tied the weights to the man's ankles, checking the knots twice before Sprague pulled out a small, silenced handgun.

The woman slid to the side. 'Just make sure you don't spatter the entire boat. This has been a monstruos waste of time already.'

'Okay.'

The muffled explosion was almost lost in the wind and she smiled as only a few blood drops splashed back onto the deck. Sprague leaned over and kicked the body overboard, where it bobbed up for a second before sinking without a trace.

...

The two traders left the Dorfmann building and went for a quick stroll around Broadgate, enjoying the sunlight. It was one of those rare but pleasant autumn days, the sun shining and the weather mild. Tony borrowed a Marlboro, as ever, and lit it with Walker's lighter. He had been trying to quit smoking for years without any real success but had finally graduated to not buying packs anymore, preferring to pinch cigarettes whenever he could.

'So how much are you up, you jammy bastard?'

'Twenty-five million, maybe more.' Walker shrugged. 'Hard to tell with the Option market still closed, but I guess the models are not going to miss out by much.'

Tony whistled softly. 'Jeez. Not bad, my friend.'

'How are *you* getting on?' He knew that Mendes had closed most of his book in the previous two weeks. The man was not a deep thinker, but his market instincts were often astounding. He had been Walker's supervisor and mentor when he was just a desk junior, and had taught him many of the darker secrets of Volatility trading.

'No disasters, yet. Down a mill, maybe two if it gets worse – nothing to worry about. I'm still going to finish the year well-up; I'll just have to sit on my hands from now till Christmas.'

Walker nodded, silently agreeing. December 31st was the goal-line for traders and salespeople, when budgets were closed and the bonus calculations finalized. If someone had had a good year they tended to lay-off risk in the last quarter to avoid any nasty surprises. Dropping a bundle of money near the year-end was not an ideal strategy to maximize your own payout when the Envelopes were handed out in January.

And traders cared a lot about their bonuses, not only for the cash itself but because – in a world where P&L was calculated every second, and money made or lost sat as the ultimate measure of quality – getting paid astonishing amounts was proof that what they were doing was *right*. Money to a trader was like goals to a striker, Michelin stars to a chef, adrenaline to a base jumper. It was evidence of their professional worthiness, their importance, and their quality. Often, for many, it was the very air they breathed.

Mendes finished his cigarette and turned to Walker, eyebrow cocked. 'So, have you started hedging yet? Twenty-five bucks is a great *year* for anyone, you can't afford to see it vanish.'

'Not really. Apparently I'm not allowed.'

'What? Why?'

Walker fought to keep the anger at bay: a good poker-face was standard requirement for a trader. 'Olivier Fontaine is using my book as protection for the entire floor. I can't sell off my Options and cash in the profit without his approval.'

'That's shite.' Mendes sipped his coffee slowly, considering. 'Un-fucking-believable. I've never heard of anything like this. They must be really worried.'

Walker grimaced. 'I think they have problems in Fixed Income as well – the bond markets are going bananas and the Italian BTPs are tanking. The boys downstairs are going to get caught in the crossfire.'

'Well, there goes my hope of a decent bonus this year, I guess.' Mendes looked around, making sure no one could overhear. 'What are you going to do? Be a good little soldier for Fontaine?'

'Dunno.' Walker lit another cigarette, his brain in overdrive. 'What do you think?'

'It's a hard call. The book is your responsibility, but going against Olivier could land you into all sorts of shit. Especially if you get it wrong.'

'True.' But Walker's instinct told him to go for it. He knew he could get the trade right. 'I don't trust that fat Belgian twat.'

'You shouldn't.' Tony Mendes had been screwed by Fontaine years before, as well.

'Then maybe it's easy.'

Mendes checked his watch, gesturing with his head at the Dorfmann building. 'Time to go. Be careful, my friend.'

'I will.'

CHAPTER FOUR

Running DeepShare

Walker unlocked his computers and fired off a few quick messages on the Bloomberg Instant Chat, replying to the brokers and traders that he always kept online to his terminal. *Time to make or lose some millions, boys and girls.* His personal mobile phone rang and he glanced at the screen – Mosha Micovich was calling, for the third time. He hadn't talked to the big Serb for over six months, but he could guess what this was about. Finally he answered, stepping away from the desk into an empty office nearby.

'Ugly one, long time no speak.'

'Hi Scott, how goes it?'

'I can't complain. Enjoying the fireworks today?'

Mosha grunted, his voice dropping a couple of octaves. 'We are going to get murdered. Fuck Rossini. Fuck my stupid traders.'

'You in trouble?'

'Yeah, lots of it.' The Serb paused, clearing his throat. 'Any chance you might have some Options to sell?'

'What do you think?'

'With a nickname like "Yours", I expect you'd be well placed for a big market drop.'

'Indeed.' Walker smiled, remembering dozens of discussions through the years with the hedge-fund manager. They had been at school together – never particularly close but always ready to argue economics or finance – and somehow they had managed to keep in touch throughout their careers. They were often fighting opposing views, Mosha the optimistic bull, Walker the doom-and-gloom bear trader. Still, if the Serb was prepared to pay well for protection, Walker would rather sell it to him than to some unknown grunt at a rival bank. Besides, Mosha had all sorts of weird connections and you never knew...

'How much do you need?'

Mosha exhaled. 'Twenty-thousand puts, front month or similar. To start with.'

'I'll see what I can do. Call Luigi Seu in half-an-hour.' *Screw you, Fontaine.*

'Will do. Thanks, mate.'

Walker turned off the phone for good and glanced at the time: only three minutes to the Futures reopening. The pre-auction quotes were drifting lower, flickering around 2640 – a little less than seven per cent down on the day for the entire market. He stuck in a few more orders to buy another one-hundred-million-dollars' worth before glancing at Steph, who had just returned to his own desk.

'What?'

The young Frenchman looked a bit nervous. 'A couple of the senior salespeople want to know if you could make prices for their clients. They need to buy puts for protection and everybody knows you have some to sell.'

Walker shook his head. 'I believe we still have a Flow desk for that kind of thing, right?'

'Yes. But the guys...'

'Then tell them to fuck off. Politely.'

Steph bit his pen, nodded and scurried off towards the dozen or so rows of Sales and Structuring, near the floor exit. Walker picked up one of his dealerboard phones, pressed a button and waited while the machine dialled Luigi's number. Seconds later the Italian's voice boomed from the handset, excited. 'Yo, bitch!'

'How did you know it was me?'

'Because I'm the best broker around.'

Walker laughed. 'Sure. Listen, Mosha Micovich will be calling you later. I'll sell him twenty-thousand November puts around the opening print, but then I want you or one of your kids to be on standby for my own orders from nine o'clock onwards. When you hear me or Steph, I expect you guys to drop everything and pick us up.'

'As ever, great Lord. But that level of service...' Luigi paused expectantly.

'You greedy bastard. Fine, double the usual comm for today, one basis point of notional on my side.'

'Really?'

Walker bit his tongue, but it was too late. He went through a quick mental calculation to figure out how much extra money he'd just spent. He had doubled the commission owed to the broker, up to one-hundredth of one per cent. It didn't sound like much, but on a day like this he might easily trade over one hundred thousand Options.

That was close to three billion's worth – three hundred grand of fees on Dorfmann's side alone. And Luigi personally got almost half of that in his paycheck.

'Yeah,' he sighed. *Just forget it, and worry about the big picture.* He could hear the Italian's smile in his voice as he replied, 'That's why I love you.'

'I can imagine. Now go away and let me know when someone out there starts getting desperate.'

...

When the stock market finally reopened, it had returned to some semblance of normality. Walker watched the Eurostoxx drop a few points fast, then bounce a little to start trading in a wide range. He dealt sporadically, struggling to stay calm as his stomach churned.

Liquidity was scarce and the contracts gapped up and down, but the market felt a little saner as some traders and computers started finding their feet, especially the machines that now accounted for the largest slice of the volumes. It wasn't likely to last, though.

A shout echoed from one of the salespeople rows, down into the Southern European – the Club-Med – desks. Walker ignored it and bought another thirty million dollars worth of Futures, mainly to pass the time. Unlike the machines, most humans were still rattled, both on the trading floor as arguments exploded with annoying regularity, and around Option markets, where prices jumped haphazardly, quotes disappearing within seconds of being posted. One of the prices Walker was about to hit flashed away and he swore, slamming his desk.

'Temper, temper. You're too old for that. And by the way, since you're cleaning up, I expect you to buy the drinks tonight.'

Walker turned around and saw Thomas Setter, the ancient forty-seven-year-old DAX trader, standing behind him. 'Jeez man, it's a bit early to worry about beers.'

'It is never too early.' Even after years in London, Thomas' thick German accent had never lost its edge. 'I will book a couple of tables at the Brasserie Rock; tell the desk juniors to come along on your tap.'

'Fine.' He shrugged. 'No managers, though.'

'Of course. By the way, should I call my wife? Just in case...'

'In case of what?'

'I hear the Dancing Snake in Finsbury Square got a few new girls at the weekend. South American and Spanish, proper dirty. I can get a broker to pick up the tap...'

Walker sighed. 'Thomas, fuck off and let me get some work done.' He turned back to his computers and dived into some serious trading.

...

Later, when the nicotine craving started niggling, Walker checked his watch. It felt as if several days had passed but London was still a few minutes short of half past ten. *Time to make the big call.*

Rossini was due to speak in about thirty minutes, around 11 a.m. GMT, to tell the world what his intentions for Italy were, and prices would move in a flash after that. Walker thought he knew what he wanted to do, but this was a decision that could make or break the rest of his career. He studied the screens for a while, making sure that all his positions were correct, then buzzed DM on the internal line.

'Hey, are you busy?'

His friend's voice echoed tinnily from the small loudspeaker. 'Always. Actually, I was about to come over.'

'Good. Fire stairs?'

'Sure, see you in a minute.'

Walker unwrapped a fresh packet of Marlboro Gold and crossed to the back of the trading floor, past hundreds of bankers hunched over their monitors and phones. He pushed open the de-alarmed fire escape, descending a few steps to the empty 'smokers' landing'. Though it was obviously against all regulations, a small outdoor ashtray stood near the glass wall; it was taken away every once in a while when there was some inspection, but always magically reappeared within a few hours.

Walker guessed that Dorfmann preferred ignoring the tiny fire-hazard to seeing its nicotine-addicted traders, salespeople and analysts disappear from the building. Someone had even unplugged a couple of the smoke detectors and replaced them with small security cameras. He lit up his Marlboro and exhaled, trying to relax and let his mind trawl through the various market scenarios.

Seconds later DM appeared through the door, grimacing. 'God, it stinks in here.'

Walker nodded gravely. 'You should try it at three or four in the afternoon.'

'You guys are mad. What's up?'

'Wanna go to the Snake tonight? We deserve a celebration.'

The mathematician looked at him, surprised. 'Sure. I'll meet you there around ten, if you want. Is this really why you buzzed me?'

'No, of course not. It was just Thomas being a fucking idiot at the wrong time that threw me.' Walker shrugged, pulled on his cigarette. 'I'm about to make a huge trade, mate. What does Deep think of the market now?'

'Alpha is very unclear.' DM grinned. 'It still wants to hedge partially and wait.'

'I don't give a shit about Alpha. What about our Omega – anything new out of it yet?'

DM pulled out a mini-tablet from one of his suit's pockets. He smiled like a magician unveiling a trick and unlocked it, handing it over. 'The monster is about to reverse its virtual portfolio and buy – it's certain the market will turn back up.'

Walker glanced through the numbers and graphs on the small screen, tapping away at it as he calculated through the possibilities. When he was finally satisfied he nodded and gave it back, sucking a long drag of his cigarette.

'Good to know I'm not losing my mind.'

'Maybe you are.' DM's voice dripped with sarcasm. 'Trusting a silly machine on its very first real-life test.'

'I trust my guts, mate. DeepShare has just made me feel better about it.'

Balancing Act

Walker returned to the floor, sidestepped a couple of salespeople deep in conversation and almost bumped into 'Beano' Friedman, Dorfmann's European CEO. Friedman's office was two floors below, in the middle of fixed income, but as a former Equity Derivatives trader – an awesome one, really – he often liked to hang around his old stomping ground on busy days, and check how things were going, in person. Walker knew him quite well: had, in fact, been hired on his desk by Friedman, then Head of Derivatives, when he was still a graduate trainee.

'Yours, are trying to kill me?' Friedman's thin cultured voice belied a massive six-foot-four, overweight rugby-player frame.

Walker stepped back, smiling. 'I'll let the bond traders do that. They get violent when they lose money, I hear.'

'Bad day, I'm afraid,' Friedman sighed. 'You should be cleaning up though, right?'

Walker was always surprised by how well Friedman seemed to know the bank's books, down to the details of many individual traders' positions. He probably spent his nights going through risk reports across the board. Friedman had become the chief executive of Europe just after the 2008 crisis struck; the lack of understanding of his predecessors – and the damage it had caused the bank – must have scarred him badly.

'I can't complain, Beano.'

'Taken much profit yet?'

'Nope. It's not an easy shout at the moment.'

'It never is,' chuckled Friedman, patting him on the shoulder before heading towards the office of Dorfmann's

Head of Research. After a couple of steps he turned, his tone more serious. 'You've made the right calls in the past, Yours. Don't start doubting yourself now.'

Walker nodded, smiling, and hurried back to his desk. The Futures were dropping again, trading near the lows of the day. He checked the time: 10.42 a.m., just minutes until Rossini was due in a press conference.

The tension was increasing once more and terrified traders returned to selling heavily, trying to reduce risks. Computers got into the game and pushed the market through the previous low point, gapping it down another twenty ticks.

The Eurostoxx is off almost eight per cent; a few more points and trading will get suspended again.

Taking a deep breath, Walker grabbed his new mouse and started buying large amounts of Futures through ORK. He turned to Steph, who was typing away at one of his keyboard.

'Yo, it's time. Drop that, whatever it is. Call Luigi Seu and start selling some of our puts, the December expiry first. About ten to fifteen K, all the ones we have on the book for that maturity. Tell him to speak to the smaller guys first, I'll need the whales later.'

'Sure boss.' Stephane picked up the phone and got Luigi to work.

Walker looked back at his ORK, then rechecked the risk-management system. To lock in his profits for the day, he would need to sell most of his Options while buying back the thousands of Futures he was still short of. It was a delicate exercise, a no-net tightrope walk that could blow up in his face if his timing was off. He fired off two more purchases, one thousand Futures each. The numbers in his book updated in real-time as the market bounced back a few points, perhaps because of his aggressive buying.

Time to rock and roll. He stood and glanced at Steph, who was deep in a phone conversation but managed to give him a thumbs-up sign; a second later he walked off the desk, heading for Fontaine's office.

As he approached the glass partition, Walker noticed that Jack Morden was in the room with Fontaine; both were standing behind the massive glass table studying a row of monitors. The Belgian saw him coming and nodded.

'Yours, anything going on?' Fontaine asked in a gruff voice.

Walker stared at his two bosses for a second, then answered, 'I'm hedging the book, before the press conference in Rome.'

Morden blanched. 'All... all of it?'

'Yes. Rossini is going to sound reasonable, and the market will bounce. No Italian default for today.'

Fontaine walked around his desk, coming to stand in front of him. 'That's not what our strategists say.'

'Right. Because Mayweather's been calling it so well up to now.'

'I don't care. We agreed...'

Walker interrupted him. 'We agreed to speak. Now I've told you what I'm doing. It's my book, I'll make the decision.'

Fontaine exploded, cursing. He turned to Morden, who was quickly shrinking into the floor, then snapped back, his fat chin wobbling with rage. 'Fine, grab your money and run. But if we get killed today, no matter how much you make... Don't expect to be paid.'

Walker took a couple of steps back and opened the door. 'I don't. All I expect is to be *right,* again.' He slammed the glass panel and returned to his seat.

...

'I'm on location. Should I go for it, later?'

'Probably, but I'll let you know soon.'

'Okay. Any last-minute advice?'

'Just do whatever you have to. He's the key.'

...

Steph was finalizing the December trades when Walker sat down next to him. The Frenchman muted his phone line and looked at him expectantly. 'All done, boss. What now?'

Walker studied his screens for a moment. The Eurostoxx had stabilized once more, but it was still down about seven and a half per cent, hovering near the day's lows.

10.52 a.m.

Walker pointed to his ORK and stood up. 'Start buying Futures, I want to cover all my shorts in the next few minutes. You'll need about three thousand here. Get them in small clips, one-hundred-odd a piece. And don't let the machines sniff us out too early again.'

Steph nodded and came over, taking his mouse and keyboard. Walker checked his work for a split second, then grabbed a handset and reopened the phone line to Luigi's brokerage firm.

'Luigi, is the trade with Mosha done?'

'Of course.'

'Great. Make sure he pays you triple commission – he owes me now. Did you find someone else in real trouble for me?'

'Ah, *Signore*. Of course I did. There are some very sweaty traders out there; a large hedge fund and two banks in particular are panicking, and they are scaring whatever few Option sellers we've got left.'

'Good. Get a couple of your guys to help on the lines – I want to sell to all of them at the same time. I need to see bids on twenty K of November puts, forty K of March...'

Luigi interrupted him. 'Whoa. Forty thousand?'

'What, too big for you? Stop fucking around and call these three whales you've harpooned – you know who will want what, I guess.'

'Okay, okay. I'll ring you back when I have the prices.'

Walker looked up at one of the massive TVs scattered around the floor. Both CNBC and Bloomberg Television were showing live pictures from a studio in Rome, a roomful of journalists waiting for Mario Rossini to start his first press conference as Italian Prime Minister-Elect. He tapped Steph on the shoulder.

'Good job. Leave it now, I need my chair back.'

Steph stood and Walker glanced at his screens, making sure the portfolio was in order. He fired up the Dorfmann Option-pricing model and inputted the details of the trades he had asked Luigi for. The system would run complex mathematical models to compute the correct values according to real-time data.

Jesus.

Option prices were exploding even further. He could feel fear seep through his monitors.

The Futures lurched lower, hovering just a few ticks above the trading-halt level. Walker bought thousands, firing orders away as fast as he could. Finally the suspension kicked in and the Eurostoxx stopped trading as it reached minus eight per cent on the day. A five-minute break would follow, before another reopen.

Walker picked up his phone and shouted down Luigi's line. 'Talk to me, you bastard.'

'I've got them – just a sec.'

He craned his neck and checked the prices on Steph's system to make sure they reflected his own. Not a good time to make a mistake.

'Okay, for the Novembers I can pay you seventy-three Euros each.' Luigi's tone carried an edge of tension: the deal was huge.

'The March is 202, and the June bid is 264. Three different buyers, for your full size. Hold on...' Luigi muted his line for a second. 'March is now up to 205. June is 268. They really want these babies.'

Walker bit his tongue and stared at his screen. Dorfmann's system valued his Options at only 521 Euros each, but things were moving so fast that he could sell them to the market for 546. There was blood in the water.

The extra twenty-five points meant close to a further ten million dollars in profits, if he sold now. *Sweet.* He looked up at the giant TV screen to his right – in Rome, Mario Rossini had entered the conference room and was shaking a few hands, flanked by a couple of his political minions.

'Scott?' Luigi's voice quivered. 'Are you there? I don't know how long I can hold these prices.'

Walker smiled. 'Good job, man. I guess you know what I'm going to say now.'

'Hopefully...'

'You're done, Luigi.' Walker took a deep breath before finishing in a louder tone. 'Yours.'

Interlude 2

The Englishman dialled the number slowly, relishing the fact that New York was still in the middle of the night. The phone rang a few times before a groggy voice finally answered.

'Yeah?'

'It might be time.'

A short break, static on the line. 'Have you spoken to the Australian?' the American asked.

'Yes. Pienaar is ready. But you need proof, and I want it to be rock-solid.'

'So when?'

'Let's see how the markets play out. I'll know for certain in a couple of hours.'

'Okay – just let me know if... when it happens.'

'Fine.' The Englishman closed the call, his mind running through the next few steps. The American had sounded on edge, even scared. He scoffed and put the phone down on his desk. When you played for big stakes, you couldn't worry about collateral damage.

CHAPTER FIVE

End of Day

The trading floor fell silent as most eyes focused on the TVs scattered above the desks. Someone turned the speakerphones to the CNBC audio channel: the simultaneous translation of Mario Rossini's speech was about to start.

Cameras zoomed in and Rossini stood, his dishevelled grey hair almost glowing in the artificial lights. The former actor looked like a mad prophet about to present the new Commandments, his intense gaze staring right through the screens.

Walker swallowed, a metallic taste in his mouth, and prayed that the next Italian Prime Minister wouldn't pull one of the stunts that had made him famous. The politician's fiery rhetoric was legendary; he had won the election by relentlessly attacking the European Union and promising an end to what he called Italy's debt slavery.

Walker looked around the floor, counting the seconds down. Ties had been loosened, shirts semi-untucked. The air stank of sweat, and little crowds of bankers had formed underneath a few massive LCDs that were stuck to the concrete columns around the floor. Olivier Fontaine emerged from his office and waddled nearer the Vol trading desk. His eyes settled on Walker for a second, a look of pure hatred in his narrow eyes.

Walker ignored him, turning as Steph slid into his own chair and whispered, 'It's bad around the floor – one of the risk juniors told me.'

'How bad?' Walker said.

'Three hundred something. If it goes on...'

'Christ.' Walker leaned against the backrest, staring at Rossini, trying to guess what was going through the man's mind. *Did I get it wrong?* He had purchased close to three-quarters of a billion dollars of Eurostoxx Futures, turning his book around in the hope of a strong bounce. If the market continued to tank, he'd give back a lot of his profits and the desk would get absolutely crushed. Fontaine would fall on him like a mountain of rusted nails, unlikely to be satisfied till he had ground Walker's career into fine dust.

Rossini started speaking, the English translation just a split second behind. After thanking his supporters he cracked a joke, then continued, 'As you all know, we believe that the Euro has been a disaster for Italy. It has cost the country millions of jobs, and some of its freedom.'

Walker's heart skipped a beat. The freshly reopened Futures collapsed in a tidal wave of red, gapping down a further four per cent in little more than a heartbeat.

The market had cracked.

Bile rose in his throat, and he almost gagged. A groan spread around the floor, someone shouted and phones exploded in a cacophony of rings. Walker glanced at his profit-and-loss window, struggling not to vomit. He had just lost twenty-two... actually, make it twenty-four million in less than three seconds. And it was only going to get worse. *This could break Dorfmann. And me.*

He could feel Fontaine's stare burning holes into him but somehow forced himself to look up at the TV. Rossini had stopped speaking, was sipping from a glass of water. The politician's burning eyes scrunched up with amusement as he sat back in his chair, exchanging a glance with his minions. He cleared his throat and started again. 'But this is a crucial time for our country. We have decided not to look for destruction, or hate – we must work within the rules. As Prime Minister I will study all issues carefully, without haste. Italy needs time and strong leadership, and our friends in Europe last night assured me that we will have all their support. *We will do everything possible to stay in the Euro.*'

Someone on the floor raised his voice, stunned. 'What? Is he really...?'

Walker slumped in relief, his entire body tingling with adrenaline. Strangely his father's face flashed through his mind and he shuddered, looking back to his screens. The blood-red was gone. All of it.

The Eurostoxx screamed upwards in relief, and the market exploded towards the stratosphere. Within forty seconds it was almost unchanged on the day.

For a while at least, the Crisis appeared over.

Drinks

Walker reached the Brasserie Rock a few minutes before six in the evening. The atmosphere was electric, and the relief that the day had not turned into a complete disaster was firing up the hormones of the survivors. The bar was teeming with bankers and brokers, ties askew, shirts untucked. Quite a few younger ladies were already wearing low-cut blouses, short skirts and high heels. He wondered how many of them kept eveningwear at the office, and how many just came along from home or university trying to catch a wealthy banker-fish.

Using his elbows, Walker made his way through the crowds at the entrance and searched for his colleagues. He noticed a few known faces – after almost fifteen years in the City his acquaintances in Finance were in the hundreds – but he carefully avoided any eye contact. He needed a drink, or five, before he could start any kind of conversation. Someone bumped him from behind and he turned, grabbing the bottle that Tony Mendes thrust at him with a wink.

'Yours...'

Walker leaned forward; the noise in the Rock was just a few decibels short of an airplane landing.

'... we've got a spot outside. It's too loud in here.'

He nodded and followed Mendes back out, into a wide beer garden where dozens of wooden tables creaked under giant buckets of ice-cold lagers. The evening was mild and the open bar was also packed, but at least you didn't have to breathe the sour stink of sweaty bankers. They had almost reached the spot where their colleagues stood around a couple of small wrought-iron tables when Mendes slowed and turned about, his head drifting closer to Walker's.

'That was a gutsy one today – Fontaine could have skinned you alive. When did you decide to go for it?'

'Just after the reopen. I bumped into Beano and he gave me the final nudge, I guess...' Walker stopped short and looked down at his friend. 'Wait, did... did you talk to Friedman after our chat?'

Mendes' eyes crinkled up in amusement. 'Me? Of course not. I would never go over Fontaine's head like that, would I?'

Walker laughed, raised his bottle and touched its neck against his friend's glass. 'I owe you one.'

'I'll remind you on Bonus Day.'

They reached the tables and Walker got a small cheer from the Dorfmann crew. There were about twenty of them, from the Derivatives area; Steph was there, deep in conversation with Liam Gander, another desk assistant who had come up to the floor from the Middle Office cave just a few days earlier. Thomas Setter and a couple of Exotic traders were chatting to Alice Cramer, a saleswoman in her late twenties who looked like she had just walked off the cover of Playboy magazine. One of her colleagues stood silently next to her, very pretty in a short cocktail dress but overshadowed by the stunning Cramer.

Walker put down his beer and grabbed a plastic glass full of ice. Ralph House, one of a trio of Dorfmann Flow traders, grinned at him and picked up a bottle of crystal-clear liquid. 'Yours, I think you are looking for this, right?'

He poured a generous dose of the ice-cold drink into Walker's glass just as he noticed the brand. 'Jewel of Russia. Obviously you had to pick this one, since it's on my credit card...'

'We couldn't find anything more expensive.'

Walker sighed, downed the vodka in one shot and shook his head, dizzy.

House refilled him and turned around to answer someone's question. Walker found a bit of space and lit a cigarette, savouring the hot smoke and waiting for the nicotine and alcohol to dissolve the last few strands of adrenaline coursing through his veins.

He looked around the beer garden and groaned: impossibly, more people seemed to have materialized out of thin air. Even their own group was growing all the time, as a few secretaries and more traders and salespeople joined them at the lower level of Broadgate Circle from the Dorfmann building. He took another drag from his Marlboro and inevitably Mendes arrived, like a truffle hound excited by the smell of tobacco.

'Have you got a spare one?'

'Sure. Your wife will smell it on you, though.'

'I'm allowed one a day, with drinks.'

'This is the fifth cigarette you've pinched from me this afternoon.'

'Well, she's not here is she?'

Steph and Gander joined them, both smoking as well. Gander must have been only a few months out of university, still shy around the senior traders. He nodded to Walker and Mendes, then stammered, 'Sc... Scott, can I ask you a question?'

'Yep.'

'If I'm not too nosy, why do... why do they call you "Yours"?'

Mendes cracked up, his laughter turning into a cough when he inhaled too much smoke. 'I thought everyone knew about that!'

Gander and Steph both shook their heads. Mendes glanced at Walker and grinned. 'It's because this man has never met a financial instrument he doesn't like to sell short. He might be the best bear-trader you'll ever meet, but apparently he's yet to see a level of the market that he doesn't find too expensive...'

Walker's private phone vibrated. He pulled it out of his inside pocket and unlocked it, checking the screen. *Mosha.* He walked a few steps away, towards the outer edge of the garden where he found a quieter spot. Mendes' voice faded away and he answered the call, 'Hi mate.'

'Thanks, Scott. I owe you big time.' The Serb's voice sounded tired, and worried.

'You do. How did you get on in the end?'

'Not good, but it could have been worse. And don't worry, I always repay my debts.'

It probably came with the territory, Walker guessed. 'I know.'

'Listen – I'm in London next week. Let's meet up. And if you need *anything...*'

'I'll think about it.' He grinned.

'Great. I'll buzz you. Ciao.'

Walker shut off his phone and was about to go back to the Dorfmann tables when he heard someone calling out, 'Yours, where are you?'

'Here.' He slid the phone away and raised his hand.

Alice Cramer walked towards him holding two glasses full to the brim of a transparent liquid. Her hips swayed slightly as she glided around a group of semi-drunk brokers, smiling when she saw him. She had long reddish hair and was still wearing her work suit – her skirt a little too short for Dorfmann, really – but she had changed into a semi-transparent top under her jacket, her ample cleavage pushed up by a sheer satin bra. *Fine, I'll admit she IS quite hot.* She passed him a glass and her dark blue eyes sparkled.

'I hear you like the strong stuff.'

Walker nodded and tried a sip; the vodka carried a weird earth-like flavour, a hint of bison grass and something else, impossible to place.

'Me too.' Cramer's voice dropped an octave lower as she leaned closer. 'I'm told this is a special brand.'

'What's the occasion?'

'You are...' Her tone was almost husky as she placed a hand on his arm. 'How does it feel to be the Hero?'

Walker shrugged, reminding himself to be careful. 'There were no heroes today. The floor dropped nearly a hundred bucks, I think.'

'It could have been a lot worse. Especially without a certain trader.' She stood on tiptoes and moved closer, her toned body pushing against his arm and shoulder. 'How much did you make, today?' Her mouth almost brushed his ear as she whispered, her long hair caressing his nose and cheek.

'Sixty-eight.'

'Wow.' She exhaled softly, her breath tickling his earlobe and sending a shiver down his spine. 'I'm impressed.'

'You shouldn't be. It's only a number on a computer monitor.'

'A large number, though.' She stood back a little, her hand still on Walker's arm. 'You live near Tower Bridge, right?'

'Yes.'

'Let me know when you're done here. We'll share a cab back.'

He nodded and watched her moving gracefully back towards the Dorfmann group. After a few steps she turned around and flashed him a smile, then disappeared into a heaving throng of people. Pop music started blaring out from a few waterproof speakers scattered around the outside bar.

Walker lit another cigarette and shook his head with a small grin. *This could turn messy.* He tried to ignore the sparkling in his veins and bit on his tongue. It wasn't the first time that Cramer had come on to him, but the last thing he was looking for was an office romance. Much better to spend some hard cash at the Snake, and avoid problems in the morning.

CHAPTER SIX

Fear

The clicking sound was soft, nearly inaudible.

Normally DM would have missed it but his Wagner playlist had just ran out into silence and his drug-heightened senses tingled, raw and sharp. He strained his hearing and stared at the entrance. Another gentle scraping noise and the doorknob moved a few millimetres. He typed a combination of numbers and letters on his keyboard and the computer screens turned black, plunging his living room into semi-darkness.

DM stood up and crossed to the open foyer, careful not to step on any of the discarded junk that lay on the floor. He reached the door and was preparing to look into the peephole when the panel slammed open, hitting his face and sending him sprawling. The back of his head bounced on a table and he rolled to the floor in blinding pain, his brain shutting down for a few seconds.

When he regained consciousness a man was standing astride his body, a black ski-mask covering most of his face. The intruder was pointing a small handgun at his chest.

'Get up, you stupid fuck.' The thug's voice was curt, with a strong Australian accent.

DM struggled to his feet, tears of pain blurring his vision. He glanced at his computer, realising that in seconds the fail-safe he had turned on was going to burn his hard drives and flash-memory to digital ashes. 'What do you want? I've got some money...'

The intruder slapped him hard, a small ring opening a cut on his cheek. DM staggered back, shocked, and half-sat, half-fell on his sofa. The man stepped closer, shoving the gun in his face.

'You will only talk to answer questions.' He gestured towards the overflowing bookcase where the mathematician kept his expensive sound system and hissed, 'Turn that thing on and play your classical crap. We don't want to be overheard, especially if I have to make you scream.'

DM stood gingerly and crossed the room, almost stumbling onto a discarded takeaway box. His pulse was racing and his heart felt about to explode, overwhelmed. Trembling, he switched on the stereo and as the music restarted he saw the intruder drawing the heavy curtains closed. The Australian gestured for him to come nearer and made him sit at his workstation, lighting a table-lamp.

DM blinked – the stranger's shadow projected on the wall, like a huge reptile about to bite his head off.

'Log on to your computer.'

'I can't...'

The intruder slapped him again, twice. Hard. 'Wrong answer.'

DM could feel himself shaking. A soft, wet feeling spread across his legs and he sobbed, tasting the blood from his split lips.

'I... it won't work. The hardware burnt itself out after you came in, as a security measure.'

The big man stared at him, unblinking. 'Fine.' He pulled up a second chair, just in front of DM's.

'Really?'

'I guess we're just gonna have ourselves a very nice, long conversation.' The Australian sat down, shifted the handgun to his left and grabbed DM's wrist with his right hand.

Then he snapped the mathematician's ring finger, breaking it.

DM screamed, a short sharp howl of pain that was drowned by Wagner's aggression. The intruder shoved the gun barrel down his throat and he stopped, gagging.

'You need to learn to suffer quietly, mate, or we won't get along very well tonight.'

The Dancing Snake

Walker lit a cigarette as he stood with Stephane Buvier in the short queue at the entrance of the Dancing Snake. A few bankers, a bunch of rich kids and a small stag-do. All participants at various degrees of inebriation. He wondered how drunk he looked, then checked his watch. It was well past ten – DM should be on the way, or inside already. Steph nudged him and Walker noticed that the nightclub bouncer was pointing at him. He recognised the massive man from the last time he had been around, an expensive evening only a few nights before, and smiled. The queue parted, letting them through. Grudgingly.

'Have a good time, sir,' the bouncer rumbled, opening a red velvet rope into the Gentlemen's Club.

Walker nodded and hurried through the foyer into a poorly lit, cavernous room. A few dozen men were scattered around the lowered floor, most sitting in small groups at tables and alcoves, others enjoying the views alone. The bass beat thrummed in the semi-darkness and he headed for a gleaming copper bar in the farthest corner, Steph just behind him. He grabbed one of the stools and leaned on an elbow, his head spinning softly.

A gorgeous black girl in her early twenties – wearing a sheer top with nothing underneath – smiled at him. 'Anything to drink, sir?'

'Double vodka on ice, and a glass of still water.' Walker turned to Steph, who nodded. 'And a Gin and Tonic, thanks.' He handed the girl his American Express Black. 'I'll be running a tab.'

As he waited, Walker glanced to the nearest of three stages where a few good-looking women were dancing sinuously to the rhythm of some African music. Suffused lights shone on the central one, a redhead Russian-type doll with enormous breasts who was in the middle of a striptease.

'Been here before, Steph?'

'Only once, after Bonus Day last year. It's a bit expensive for me, we tend to hang around the cheaper places down Shoreditch.' The Frenchman looked around, his eyes widening at the sheer amount of scantily clad beauty on display. 'But this is awesome, much better than Spearmint Rhino.'

There were scores of women scattered around the club, some pole-dancing, others just walking the floor between tables or sitting in the smaller nooks, sharing a drink with clients.

'Best lap-dancing club in London, and not as strict as most.' Walker sipped his vodka, then drained a glass of water and asked for another. Though it was only a Monday and the nightclub seemed quieter than usual, the quality of the girls was still outstanding. You could find anything, from skinny Eastern Europeans to voluptuous African-American types. Any hair and skin colour, eyes of all conceivable shape and tint, and quite a few bodies to die for.

A tall plump girl with dark hair approached them, wearing a skimpy bikini-top underneath a fishnet shirt, her heavy breasts in danger of bursting out. She stopped in front of Stephane and smiled at him coyly. 'Good evening, guys, would you like a private dance?' Her high voice lilted with a strong French accent. Steph swallowed and looked at Walker.

'How much?' Walker asked.

'Fifty pounds for ten minutes, seventy for the two of you.'

'Ehrr.' The Frenchman squirmed, stuck.

Walker shook his head and decided to rescue him. 'What's your name, darling?'

'Chantelle. Please, I feel sooo lonely tonight.'

'Not for me, but maybe my idiot friend here...' He glanced at Steph, who was nodding quickly. *The call of the wild, bloody French people.* Walker sighed and signalled to the bar girl. 'Put it on my tab, love.'

Chantelle gave a little hop, one of her large breasts almost spilling out. She took Steph's hand with a big smile. 'Great. *Allons-y.*'

The Frenchman stood, almost dropping his drink before looking at him. 'Yours, thanks – but I really shouldn't leave you alone...'

Walker gestured at the roomful of women. 'I'll survive, don't worry. See you later.'

The showgirl was studying Steph – must have realised he was not a regular. She pulled him away and started talking in a lower voice. 'By the way, no touching, monsieur. It is strictly...'

Walker lost the rest of the conversation as the music grew louder for a few moments before quietening down again. He finished his vodka and stood up before some other girl could approach him. Quiet nights made for an easy market: worth having a look around. Glancing at the stage again, he noticed that all the dancers had left. A thin man in his fifties entered from a side door, wearing a tuxedo and holding a microphone.

'Gentlemen,' his deep voice boomed, 'in just a few minutes our brand new star, the stunning Falena from Spain, will delight us with a special and exciting dance. It's her first night at the Snake, so give her a good cheer and enjoy the show!' He grinned, climbed down from the platform and left, as a few of the girls returned to their poles and the music picked up again.

Walker checked the entrance, then his watch. DM was over thirty minutes late. It wouldn't be the first time the mathematician had forgotten an appointment, but he loved the Dancing Snake. It was one of the few places where he seemed to forget his uptight, intense nature for a while. Walker exhaled, circled the stage and climbed some steps to the smoking area, a smaller glass-walled room with several easy chairs and sofas that looked onto the main hall.

An overpowering waft of burning tobacco stung his nostrils, and he almost gagged. The smokers' room smelt like a giant ashtray that had been left too long, overflowing with ashes and butt-ends. Walker breathed in through his mouth, and lit a Marlboro. *I should quit, really. This is just nasty.*

Maybe next month. Or the one after.

He signalled to the girl patrolling the area for a drink and slouched in one of the leather armchairs that faced the main stage lower down. Seconds later his vodka had arrived and he took a tentative sip, almost gagging again. His senses felt dulled, and his head swam on a lake of alcohol. He wondered how many drinks he had burnt through, tried to count them and gave up. Too many. He was drunk.

At least he had closed almost all of his positions by the end of the day, so the following morning he could take it easy, nursing the massive headache he could feel stirring at the back of his skull. He lit another cigarette from the still-burning tip of the previous one and flushed away the harshness with a large glass of water.

Maybe he should have taken Alice Cramer up on her offer. Her firm body still lingered like a warm ghost against his shoulder and arm – she had felt ready, and excited. By the money, most likely. Sixty-eight million in a day. Prop traders at Dorfmann generally got paid a slice of their profits, between five and ten per cent depending on their track record and how well the bank had done. His book was now up over sixty bucks for the year, which meant he could expect the largest bonus of his career, something northwards of... At least four million, maybe a lot more if the floor didn't blow up. Holy shit. The big trade had landed.

He had done it.

He could get out after January, if he wanted. This was what he'd been working his arse off for, for the last twenty years. After his father had died, the life insurance had covered Walker's boarding school fees, and little else. He didn't have any relatives in America, or know anybody in Italy. He had been stuck in London: alone, poor. Excitement was only the second reason he had chosen to become a trader. Paying off debts, and then the thrill of finally having money to burn had been the main one. But it hadn't lasted.

Trading still fired up his blood, though the adrenaline hits were fewer and far between, with the kicks coming more from the losses than the wins, these days. Gambler's syndrome. *Get your money, and get out.* And the last few years had broken something within him – he was tired of the greed, of the incessant pressure for profits, day after day, no matter the long-term consequences. He had behaved like a perfect professional to the last, but there had to be a better way. He should be enjoying his big win instead of just feeling burnt out, hollow. And it wasn't just the alcohol speaking. He needed a new reason, something to fight for.

The world felt as if it was driving towards a cliff, oblivious, just rolling along. And maybe DeepShare could really turn out to be what DM dreamed. Walker shrugged – it was certainly worth a try, better than killing himself to make an extra few bucks. He downed the last of his vodka and stood up, deciding to try a final look for the mathematician. If DM hadn't arrived yet, he would grab his credit card and stagger home to throw up and crash. Swaying slightly, he left the smoking room to return to the main floor.

The music had stopped and the main platform was dark. Walker guessed a show was about to start; he searched around but there was no sign of DM, though Steph was due out of his private dance any minute. He wondered if the young Frenchman had abided by the no-touching house rule, or whether the pretty Chantelle had let him take a few liberties. The Snake, maybe because it was a members-only club, was one of the few top quality places in London where the decision was down to the showgirl.

Two spotlights flickered on, lighting up the stage just as a South American beat echoed around the room.

A man's voice boomed, 'Please welcome our beautiful Falena!' and scattered applause rose from the guests. Walker glanced at his watch: five past eleven and DM was nowhere to be seen. The idiot had forgotten, or doped himself to sleep. He was about to leave when the side door opened and a stunning woman made her entrance, gliding to a stop a few feet away.

Walker stared at her for a second, transfixed. Then he grabbed a chair and decided to stay for the show.

CHAPTER SEVEN

Falena

Pienaar stopped the video-recorder and studied his notes, methodically checking off the points he had been asked to investigate. It had only taken a couple of extra broken fingers and some small electric shocks, but the mathematician had co-operated fully in the end. They had delved into the workings of DeepShare, looked at how the enormous program had evolved from a chess-playing software into a market algorithm, to how it now used all sorts of data to try and predict the future.

A lot of what DM had said went right above his head, but the Australian had appreciated the way the machine scoured the web, from social networks to obscure newsflows and blogs. There was something God-like in its view, mixing the obvious with the inscrutably deep. But the mathematician hadn't given away his last secret, yet.

DM moaned, his head still sunk in his skinny chest. He feebly fought the tape that tied his naked body to the chair and gave up. Pienaar reached closer and shook him awake.

'Please...' He coughed, tears in his eyes. 'Please, can I have some water?'

'In a minute. There's something else we need to talk about.'

'Oh God, no more. I've told you everything...'

'No, you haven't. Just one more thing – where is *DeepOmega? How do we access the source code?'*

DM shook his head and sobbed, great shudders wracking his thin body.

...

Falena started dancing, her long dark hair swaying under a tight hat peppered with feathers. The music boomed with a primeval sound, accelerating and slowing almost randomly. Her body was laced in a skintight suit, the snake-patterned garment stretching and rippling as she moved with liquid grace. And, though she was gliding around the entire stage, somehow she seemed to return close to Walker's seat a little too often, her dark almond-shaped eyes fixed on his face, a faint smile on her full wide mouth.

Walker watched her without moving a muscle, mesmerized as she slowly ripped off first the leggings and then the lower part of her top, leaving her in a G-string and bra that showed off a perfect toned body, with the firmness and delicate proportions of an athletic ballerina. Falena was beyond gorgeous, her high cheekbones and straight, slightly long nose giving her the appearance of a Greek goddess of war – or lust.

'Wow, who's that?'

Walker glanced to his right, his eyes immediately returning to the stage. Steph had come up behind him and was staring at the showgirl, his mouth agape.

'No idea, but I'm going to find out soon,' whispered Walker, adrenaline and desire washing away the fumes of the vodka. Falena shone like the ultimate ideal of quite a few girls he had taken out of the Dancing Snake in the past. He was addicted to jet-black hair and full lips, and preferred lithe bodies like hers to the pneumatic breasts and gym-sculpted shoulders sported by most lapdancers. Her oval face and slanted black eyes could have been designed just to fire up his blood. He forced himself to sit back, realised that Steph was still talking: '... DM here yet?'

'No, I don't think he's coming.'

'Ah, all right. What are you going to do? I'm quite beat, and my girlfriend...'

Walker kept his eyes on the dancer as Falena unlaced her bra, slid nearer him and threw it in his lap. Her breasts were larger than you would expect from her slim frame, with wide aureoles, nipples pointing upwards in the lightly chilled air. He leaned forward and placed the snake-printed underwear on the stage, smiling as she gave him a quick nod of thanks.

'I'll stay a while longer, I think.'

Steph grinned. 'Do you mind if I scoot home?'

'Go ahead, I'll see you in the morning.'

The Frenchman nodded and patted him on the shoulder, heading towards the foyer. The music reached a thumping crescendo and Falena reacted to it, her arms and legs shooting out in a final frenzy that was almost martial-art intense in its controlled violence. She threw off her hat-piece, somersaulted and landed on her feet without a hitch, then bent lower and twisted her body into a prone shell just as the last few notes echoed and died.

The Dancing Snake might have been half-empty but the few customers still erupted in loud applause and Walker himself stood, clapping. Falena quivered and lifted her head, looking at him through strands of black, sweaty hair. Her eyes glinted and she gave him a little satisfied smile.

Walker turned around and searched for the manager, George, then saw him at a corner of the copper bar studying a ledger. He approached the man and leant on a stool, rapping his knuckles on the counter.

'I'd like to book a private dance with Falena.' His throat felt dry, creaking from too many cigarettes.

George didn't look up. 'She's at top rate, one hundred pounds for ten minutes, but there's a few people ahead of you.'

'I'll give her five hundred quid for half an hour. And two hundred for you, but I'm not waiting.'

The manager looked up then, smiling as he recognised him.

'Ah, Mr Walker. Of course, I'll see what I can do.' He picked up a pen from behind the bar, scribbled a few lines on his ledger. 'I think we can accommodate you.'

'Thanks.'

'A smoking suite, I believe.'

Walker nodded. 'I'd love the larger one at the back.'

'Certainly. If you'd like to come with me... though it might be a few minutes until Falena gets changed.'

'That's all right. Please have one of the girls bring me some water, a bottle of 42 Below and another one of whatever the lady is partial to.'

The manager signalled to the barmaid. 'I believe it's champagne.'

Walker followed George towards the far side of the stage, his senses tingling. 'Then the '02 Cristal, of course.'

Eros and Thanatos

The private suite was wide, about the size of his own bedroom and lit by a few dim, hidden lamps. Walker sat sprawled in the corner of a fat L-shaped couch, his jacket off, smoking and sipping at a glass of water. His head spun, colours flashing randomly whenever he closed his eyes, and he felt a little nauseous from all the alcohol in his system. He was trying to concentrate on the quiet jazz music in the background when Falena came in.

She looked even more gorgeous than before, if possible. Her face was not made up; her lustrous hair was unbound and cascaded well below her shoulders. Seen up close her skin was unblemished: a darker shade than he had thought as she danced on the stage. She was also a little shorter, maybe five foot eight.

She wore a light blue dressing gown, barely held together by a belt at her waist. As she approached him she let it slip off, coming to stand in front of him in a black strapless satin corset, suspenders and tights. He sat up straighter, finished his drink and studied her face; her eyes glinted mischievously and she twirled around, giving him a wink.

'I hoped it might be you.' The showgirl's voice was husky, the excellent English obviously learnt in the US, with only a tinge of Latin cadence to it. 'Do you like what you see?'

'It's shocking.'

Falena flashed him a smile and glided forward between his legs. She placed her hand on his shoulder and pushed him back, making him slide against the backrest, then she leaned into him and her hair covered his face. Her mouth nuzzled his ear and she whispered, breath hot against his cheek, 'I'm told I should treat you nicely, Mr Scott.'

I bloody hope so. Walker's fingers left the sofa and traced the contours of her hips, lingering on the back of her thighs and slipping upwards. She readjusted herself, planting a knee on the cushion between his legs and drawing closer, breasts pushing against his chest. His palms caressed her firm cheeks and descended again, along the seam of her tights, all the way down to her calves.

Falena bit his earlobe, nuzzling the line of his jaw until she reached his mouth. Her tongue darted forward and she licked his lips, but before he could react she drew back and shook a few strands of hair away from her face, a sly smile on the ruby-red, wide mouth. 'I'm thirsty, did you get me anything?'

Walker pointed to his right. 'It's over there, behind you.'

Falena stood, always moving with an impossible elegance. She gave him her back, went to the glass coffee table and slowly bent lower, allowing him a great view of her perfect buttocks. She glanced behind her with a smile and gave her hips a wiggle, making him chuckle. God, she was good.

As she busied herself with his drink Walker lit another cigarette, her musky scent still lingering in his nose. He closed his eyes and took a deep breath, savouring the smoke mixed with her perfume. Again, lights flashed behind his eyelids and his head spun, though not unpleasantly.

Heartbeats later Falena was standing in front of him once more, his vodka tumbler in one hand and her bottle of Cristal in the other. She handed him the glass, lifted the champagne to her lips and took a long drink, her eyes closed. A few rivulets made their way down her chin and into the hollow of her neck. She rested the bottle on the floor and motioned to him. 'Make me some space.'

Walker put his glass aside and readjusted himself, one foot against the sofa's back and the other on the carpet while she snuggled into his legs, naked shoulder into his chest. He chased the drops of champagne into her corset and she shivered, then slid the cigarette from his lips, gave him a quick kiss and inhaled, purring like a satisfied cat. Walker relaxed, ready to simply enjoy what looked likely to turn into a hell of a night. His fingers ran through her thick hair, caressed her neck and traced the curve of her spine, lingering on the zip that would open her bodice.

'Wait,' she whispered. 'Did you like my show?'

'I loved it. It was worthy of the night butterfly.'

Her eyes lit up and she smiled, putting the cigarette back in his mouth. 'Like a *falena*! How did you know that's what it means?'

'My mother was Italian.'

She drew back a few inches, her hand crawling up and unbuttoning the top half of his shirt. 'I love Italy, I've always wanted to go. What is it like?' Her fingers reached inside his collar, drawing down his pectoral ridge and coming to rest on his nipple, teasing it.

'It's the most beautiful country in the world. And you, are you really Spanish?'

'Mexican. I'm half-Maya, that's where my Bird Dance comes from.'

Walker smiled, his hand brushing her lips and lifting her chin up. 'Please don't tell me your real name is Kukulcan, or Quetzalcoatl.'

Falena stared at him in mock anger, then her head darted forward and she kissed him hard, her mouth opening hungrily. He did not resist and let his lips part, her tongue probing inside him. She tasted of smoke, champagne and cinnamon, and he drank her flavour, unashamed. *Definitely worth the price of admission.* She locked her palm onto the back of his head, drawing him nearer and biting on his tongue, deeper. Then she let him go and kissed his eyes closed, lips sliding to his ear. Her hair tickled his face and he felt a stirring in his groin, the erection almost painful in his jeans.

Walker caressed her shoulders and unlaced the corset, her full tits tumbling out. He almost ripped off the garment; his other hand already cupping her left breast, worrying the hard nipple. She sighed in his ear, trembling slightly, and whispered, 'Layla, my real name is Layla.'

...

Pienaar despised weakness, because it was a lot more fun to break people when they struggled and tried to resist.

'No... I can't give it to you,' the little man had sobbed. 'It's my whole life.'

'Really? We'll see about that.' He walked to the coffee table and shuffled his instruments, checking and repositioning them, making sure that his captive understood what he was preparing. Pain always starts in the mind.

He finally picked up a couple of electrodes and the heavy battery and returned to his seat, dangling the copper wires from his fingers.

'We'll try something new, now,' he grinned.

His free hand snapped forward and he ripped off the thick tape that covered the mathematician's shrivelled penis and his testicles.

DM screamed.

...

Blood thumping in his temples, Walker let his fingers slide from Falena's chest to her hard belly, tracing the contours of the navel and lower, down to the front of her G-string. Her breath accelerated in his ear and she shifted a little, mouth searching for his lips. No holds barred, then, he guessed. She slid her hips close and spread her legs wider as he drew the slim cloth aside. Her shaved vulva glistened, warm and inviting, and he slipped his thumb inside her just as her tongue burst through his mouth.

Her back arched and she drew him deeper against her crotch, swayed for a second, then took her head back to look into his eyes. Her skin was flushed red and she bit her lower lip, trying to suppress a grin. 'You're making me hot.'

'You *are* hot.' It was an astonishing performance, and for a second he wished it were fully real. Then he shrugged, deciding to just let his body have some fun.

Layla trailed her hand along his shirt and lower, lingering on his erection and giving his cock a gentle squeeze through his trousers. Moments later she stood up, squaring her shoulders to let him look at her magnificent breasts, the wide areolas a darker shade of brown. Quick as a cat she bent lower and picked up his packet of Marlboros, lighting one and drawing a breath before passing it over. Then she handed him his glass again and slowly raised the champagne bottle, lifting it level with her eyes.

'I love Cristal. Thank you.'

Walker took a long swig of his vodka, grimacing at the unexpected, metallic flavour of the drink. It tasted odd, just a little too sharp. He breathed in some smoke, again feeling a little nauseous, shrugged and finished the tumbler in one go, the ice clinking against his teeth.

Layla licked the top of the champagne bottle sensuously and took it in her mouth, allowing a few rivulets to dribble once more down her throat. She twisted her head to one side and looked at him askance, with the ghost of a smile.

'Oh, look, you've made me soil myself...' her fingers slowly drew the clear droplets down to her breasts, and she continued, '...now you'll have to clean me.'

Shuffling closer to Walker, she planted her legs again between his knees, placing her palms on the sofa, just wide of his head. Her firm tits were just inches from his eyes, dripping Cristal onto his chest. 'Come on.'

Walker grinned, shifted his back and slid on the cushion, his hands going to her shoulders and quickly lower. His head threatened to explode from the burning heat at the centre of his brain, and light flashed in a million colours behind his eyelids.

His mouth opened to the warm softness of her breasts, his tongue avidly licking the pearls of drink from her hard nipples. His teeth teased her aureoles and then he went lower, along her sternum and almost reaching the navel before moving to the other side of her body, this time with more hunger, delighting in the taste of her skin.

Layla moaned and pressed her breast into his mouth, her fingers worrying the nape of his neck. Walker's hand slid to the sides of her legs, moving up to her thighs and buttocks, working towards the inside. She shifted her feet, opening up for him as his fingers burrowed inside her, caressing her clitoris. She moaned again, but after a few seconds she pushed off the sofa and straightened up, giving him a playful slap on the cheek. 'My mama always told me not to trust good-looking men with grey eyes.'

I bet she did.

Layla lowered herself to her knees, her breasts against his erection, and opened the last few buttons on his shirt. He rested his head on the back of the sofa and closed his eyes. Her mouth slid along his chest, licking and biting, and he decided he was going to implode. His heart thumped painfully and his throat felt raw, gritty. There was a buzz in his ears and parts of his brain grew detached, somehow floating on a dark sea. Still, the fire in his belly and hips was growing hotter as her lips descended to his stomach, fingers tracing his abdominal muscles, caressing one of the yellowish boxing bruises. Was she really...

Her head dropped lower and her mouth closed around the side of his hard cock, nibbling at it through the fabric of his thin jeans. After a few seconds she teased him with a sharp little bite and drew back, that satisfied smile back on her lips and in the glinting dark pupils.

'Now we're even.'

Walker sighed. 'I don't remember scoring any goals, yet.'

'True. But we can't, *here.*' She stood up, glancing around the small private room.

'I could have a word with the manager, if you want.'

Layla nodded and picked up her dressing gown, wrapping it around herself. 'I hope your place is not on the other side of London.'

Walker jumped to his feet and almost fell, the room spinning around him. He steadied himself and smiled, giving her a quick kiss on the lips. 'It's not far, not far at all.'

Dark of the Night

Pienaar swore several times, almost shouting. He was enraged, and in the last few months his anger had proven more difficult to control.

The mathematician had fallen unconscious again, his shallow breath laboured. The Aussie walked to the stereo and turned up the volume of the music before slipping into the kitchen to grab a glass of water. He returned to the tied man and poured it on his head, ripping off the tape that covered his mouth.

DM grunted, bloodshot eyes flickering open. His pupils were dilated and sweat covered his tortured body. He coughed sickly, then threw up some bile and sobbed again.

'Now, now, there's no need for that.' Pienaar grinned and lifted the battery, placing it between his captive's feet. He unwound the wires, connecting them with the electrodes taped to the mathematician's testicles, then looked up into his shuddering face.

'Please... I can't...' Tears glistened on DM's thin cheeks, mixing with the mucus from his broken nose.

'Where is the real DeepShare? How do we access it?'

'No.'

'As you wish.' Pienaar twisted a knob on the battery and DM's body jerked, straining against the ties. His mouth opened in a silent scream, face contorted in a rictus of unimaginable pain. Then his head snapped backwards and bounced, chin coming to rest on the emaciated, bruised chest.

Blood dripped from his nostrils and a fat crimson droplet fell from his ear, splattering the carpet. Pienaar lunged forward, immediately sensing something was wrong. His hand shot up to check DM's pulse.

'Fuck.'

The mathematician's heart had given out under the stress, and pain.

This could turn into a serious inconvenience, but hopefully one of his associates would have better luck. Besides, the little Burmese coward might have let something slip that he had missed – he would need to check the recordings with care. Pienaar grabbed the satellite phone from his coat and dialled a number from memory.

'What?' The Englishman's voice at the other end was rough from sleep.

'He's dead.'

Silence. The line crackled with static, then went quiet. The Aussie could hear some breathing, short, machine-gun like. Bloody amateurs.

'Dead? How... why?'

'Accidents happen in this business.'

Another intake of air. 'Did you get the software, at least?'

Pienaar almost giggled. It sounded like there was more fun on the way. 'No. The thing burnt itself out. Sounded good, though.'

'So you have nothing?'

'Maybe. Don't forget the other target.'

'I never forget anything, you stupid fuck. But this is a nightmare. What are you going to do now?'

Pienaar sighed, pretending to ignore the insult. For now. 'You tell me. Should I plant some of the stuff around the place?'

'Yes.' The Englishman paused for a heartbeat. 'Have it look like a real drug bust-up. And make sure Walker pans out, or...'

'Of course.'

...

The apartment door slammed shut as Walker searched blindly for the light switch, his mouth tangled with Layla's. She was already shrugging out of her overcoat when she stepped away from him and turned around, studying the room. Dropping the heavy jacket on his couch, she walked past one of the thin metal columns that speckled the open space and glided towards the large triple windows, her eyes fixed on the London night outside. The City buildings shone across the river, a skyline dotted with thousands of artificial fireflies.

'It's beautiful here.'

Walker joined her, his arms embracing her slim frame from behind, hands coming to a stop just below her breasts. He inhaled her perfume and nuzzled her neck, keeping his eyes open to avoid the nausea that threatened to overwhelm him. His head ached, a throbbing pain just behind his temples that had been made worse by the short taxi ride, but a weird sort of energy seemed to burn through his muscles.

Layla twisted in his arms, her mouth coming up to meet his, and they kissed hard. His hands went to her back, searching for the zip of the dark velvet dress she had changed into. She unbuttoned his shirt while still kissing him and pulled it off his head, kneeling to caress his bruises. 'How did you get these?' she said.

'Boxing. I guess I'm becoming too slow.'

Layla straightened and stepped away from him, her back against the windowpane. She looked him up and down with a smile. 'It keeps you in good shape though, especially for a banker.'

'How did you...'

She raised her index finger in front of her full lips. 'Shush, it's a trade secret. Do you have any music?'

Walker nodded and went to his stereo, fumbling with the dials. His headache was fading a bit now, as waves of heat came up from his loins into his neck and face. He brushed away a few droplets of sweat from his forehead and managed to switch the radio on just as Layla slid up behind him, her hands coming to rest on his shoulders.

He turned and saw she was already naked, wearing only stockings and a satin suspender. Walker bent and kissed her deeply, her mouth opening to swallow his tongue. Her skin felt cool against him, or maybe he was just burning up.

Layla's hands dropped to his waist and fumbled with his trousers, pulling them off to reveal his hard erection. She caressed his cock, gently, then gave him a little shove and pushed him to the couch.

Unbalanced, Walker fell backwards onto the leather cushions and lay unmoving, his head spinning. The semi-dark room seemed to shift and twist impossibly, and bright spots of colour flashed across his eyes. Then Layla was on top of him, straddling his hips with her legs.

She leaned down and kissed his forehead and eyes, her full breasts just below his mouth. He tried to reach them and suck at her nipples but she forced him back, her mouth licking his nose and moving down to wet his lips. She readjusted herself and slid lower, nuzzling his neck and biting his skin, then lower again to his abdomen.

Walker laid back and closed his eyes as her hands reached his groin, cupping his testicles. He could hear his own breathing become more ragged, like a massive fever had broken through the barriers and was now raging across his body. His legs were leaden, and he could hardly feel his feet and hands.

Layla's tongue flicked around the base of his cock, teasing, then she gave him a soft bite higher along the shaft, working her way towards the tip. He sighed, a deep rumble in his ears. She played with his foreskin and gave him another little nuzzle, then her mouth opened and she swallowed him, just an inch or two at first, then out, before taking him deeper, again, and again. And again.

The heat in Walker's head became a searing fireball, imploding as a sudden wave of ice came from nowhere to grip his brain.

Darkness.

CHAPTER EIGHT

The Morning After

Walker woke up with a splitting headache, nausea engulfing his senses like some dark tide. He climbed up from the couch unsteadily, feet tangling in an old blanket, and rushed to the bathroom. He almost didn't make it, vomit burning at the back of his throat just as he dived for the toilet to throw up, his chest heaving and shaking.

After a minute or so he managed to stand and splashed some cold water on his face. His head shrieked, and when he checked himself in the mirror his eyes were bloodshot and sunken, the skin blotched red. All the bruises on his naked body seemed to be turning a nasty shade of violet.

Water – he needed water. He stumbled out of the toilet and shuffled to the fridge, trying to recall the events of the previous night. He could remember returning home from the Dancing Snake, hard kisses, a warm body and sudden blackness...

Layla. The bitch must have slipped something in his drink. Walker grabbed a bottle of water and gulped it down, eyes scanning the living room. Dozens of his books lay scattered on the floor and a few drawers in the ancient oak desk he kept near the kitchen were open, papers strewn around. His computer had been ransacked, only the monitor and keyboard remaining, while the mainframe and hard drives had disappeared.

Walker finished the water, fighting a second wave of nausea. His brain threatened to explode and he almost threw up again, the room swaying about him. He reached the window and steadied himself, glancing around the open space as if his custom Sony double-tower could magically reappear somewhere else. DM was going to be monumentally pissed off. Walker had kept some bits of DeepOmega on his machine at home, even though it had made his friend uncomfortable. And now they were gone, because of the Mexican whore. If she was even Mexican at all. Probably not.

His mind flashed back to the private suite at the Snake, and the weird aftertaste of the vodka she had prepared for him in there. He could still taste the metallic flavour at the back of his throat, and almost gagged again. Screwed by some sort of date-rape pill, like a fucking idiot. Many nights of hard work were gone but – knowing DM – his friend would be a lot more concerned about the security of their precious Omega version. They needed to talk before he called the police.

Hurrying across the living room, Walker searched for his jacket. He found it near the entrance and picked it up, going through the inside pockets. His own phone had disappeared but the bank's BlackBerry was still there. Small blessings.

He sighed and checked the time before unlocking it. 8.14 a.m. – DM should already have arrived at the office.

He tried the mathematician's mobiles first, but both were switched off. Then he dialled the Automated Trading secretary but she told him that DM hadn't shown up yet. It was odd, but he was probably on his way.

Another stab of pain skewered Walker's brain and he downed a handful of aspirins, suddenly remembering the cash hidden in his bedroom. He rushed to check the underwear drawer, not expecting much. *You clever fucking bitch.* The wardrobe was open, clothes lying on the floor. And his money had disappeared, over ten thousand in Pounds and Euros he kept for emergencies. A bloody expensive night.

Cursing his own stupidity, he headed for the shower and prayed the paracetamol would kick in quickly, before an entire side of his head dropped off.

...

Walker left the elevator and crossed Dorfmann's entrance hall, rushing past the security guards and their metal detectors. DM had not arrived or called yet, and half past nine was too late even for his standards. Walker wondered what to do – he could head to his friend's house, but would risk missing him if the mathematician was making his way to the bank. Or he could wait a while longer, but he was getting seriously spooked after what had happened the previous night.

Stepping into the crisp morning air, he lit a cigarette and almost threw up again. His head still hurt but it was now a milder, deeper ache somewhere at the base of his skull, instead of the blinding flashes of pain he had suffered earlier. He started pacing around the plaza, trying to make up his mind, when a hand burrowed itself in his side, taking his arm and squeezing it hard.

'We need to talk. Keep smiling and walk on.'

Walker turned and gasped: Layla was snuggled against him, almost unrecognisable underneath a broad felt hat and enormous sunglasses.

'You... what the fuck are you doing here?'

'I have a small gun up my sleeve, and I told you to smile. Just keep going and give me a kiss.'

Without waiting for a reply she nudged him towards one of the side roads that would take them to Liverpool Street Station. They ducked into a tiny alley behind an older office building and she twisted, forcing him into a long, lingering kiss as they disappeared from the Circle's view. Walker struggled free and pushed her back, holding onto her arms.

'Are you going to shoot me now?'

She stared at him, her eyes glinting with amusement. 'No. I could prick you with my steak knife, though,' she shrugged. 'A little lie, just to get your attention.'

Walker swore and took a step back, his shoulders brushing the wall. The surprise had passed and now he was just angry. 'What the hell do you want? Are you after more money to return –'

'Listen to me,' she cut him short. 'There's something nasty going on and you're deep into it.'

Walker paused and studied her face: she looked nervous, her eyes dancing around and checking their surroundings. He decided to let her talk for a few seconds. The bitch really was gorgeous.

'Look, I was just hired to do a job,' she hissed.

'What job?'

'You. I had to get inside your flat and take some files, without triggering any alarms that might spoil the data.'

'Jesus. Who are you?' DM had installed a series of smart failsafes in Walker's PC: if someone tampered with the machine they would burn his hard drives. How the hell could she have known that the alarms would only be deactivated by his fingerprints?

Layla waved a hand. 'That's not important. Someone has set the entire thing up, given me your profile and placed me into the Dancing Snake. Very thoroughly organized, real pros.'

Walker shook his head, incredulous. *This is insane. She's after something else, don't believe a word she says.* He found a cigarette and lit it. Layla took it from his hands and gave the Marlboro a long pull before returning it.

Walker thought hard, exhaled and decided to play along with the story, see where it was going. 'Who hired you?'

'Probably one of those private security firms, like they use in Iraq or wherever. No real idea though, that's not the type of question I ask.'

'What do you mean?'

'I'm an independent contractor. Someone gets in touch with my agent, a fee is agreed for the job and I'm given the information on the target. If I can deliver whatever is asked for, I get paid. I don't want to know who or what hires me – it could turn complicated.'

Astonishing. He just didn't have a clue if it might be true. 'So my computer...'

'It's gone. But when I went to drop it off early this morning, the courier guys tried to force me to tag along.'

'Where?'

'Somewhere unpleasant, I'd guess. There was a man, a big Australian with a nasty scar and a couple of thugs. He said I needed to follow him to get my fee. That's not the way it's usually done, so I refused. One of the thugs tried to grab me but I got away. Barely. They took your stuff, though.'

'And you expect me to believe all this?'

'Believe what you will. But I told you, the sting was set up perfectly, someone must have worked on this for months. They knew everything about you. If they suddenly turned weird and tried to take me out...' Layla's voice trailed off.

'What?'

'It must be because something has gone seriously wrong in some other part of the operation. What the hell was on your hard drives anyway?'

Walker's world lurched. *Oh shit. DM.* 'I need to go.' He dropped her arm and turned away.

Layla grabbed his shoulder and pulled him back. She was a lot stronger than he expected, and quick. 'Where are you going?'

'To a friend of mine. He has a lot more stuff than I did on his computers, and he hasn't showed up at the office yet. He might be in danger.'

She nodded slowly. 'That could be true. But I'm coming with you.'

'No, you're not. You're a fucking criminal, and I should take you to the police first.'

Layla stepped sideways, her eyes angry. 'Don't overestimate yourself.'

'Why are you here?'

'There's no time for this. Look, your friend might be in serious trouble, and I'm the only one who can get in touch with these guys. If I get away now, you'll never see me again.'

Walker considered it for a second. He didn't have anything to lose, and she probably knew a lot more than she'd been telling him. 'Okay, let's go.'

…

They jumped into the nearest black cab and Walker gave the driver DM's address – the mathematician lived in a rundown part of Shoreditch, less than ten minutes away. Walker's heart accelerated in his chest, his palms sweaty. He took out his phone and dialled.

Come on, come on...

The answering machine came up and he swore. Taking a deep breath, he checked that the taxi's mute button was on before turning to Layla. 'I'll ask you once more, and if you don't give me a straight answer I'll drop you off, right now. Why are you here?'

'I wasn't paid, and I want my money. To get it, I have to find out what the hell is going on.'

Walker's head spun with possibilities. Was this real? Was he truly sitting in a cab with a hot honey-trap who'd just robbed him? Everything just felt wrong. Very wrong. The London streets flashed by as they travelled against the flow of traffic. City skyscrapers gave way to rundown council houses, depressing husks populated by the unemployed just a few minutes outside the largest financial centre in the world.

Walker wondered whether DM was all right. Maybe they'd drugged him as well... He shook his head, trying to clear his thoughts. Who were *they* – Frankel? Another bank? Perhaps someone had really been following the mathematician, keeping him under surveillance.

The world seemed to shrink around him, and he forced himself to breathe. It felt as if he was falling into one of DM's nightmares; maybe it was true that even a paranoid could have enemies. The woman next to him was proof that something extremely weird was happening. Or she could just be a lunatic playing out her own insane fantasies.

'Is your name really Layla?'

She glanced at him, coming back from whatever thoughts were going through her head, and pulled off her sunglasses before stuffing them in a Gucci backpack. 'Yes, strangely enough. I'm not sure why I told you, last night.'

'I'm honoured.'

She ignored him, her eyes cloudy. 'Not the name I was born with, but the one I chose for myself. I have others, if you prefer.'

Walker sighed, exasperated. It wasn't exactly a reassuring answer: how many names did a sane person need? He checked out of the window and recognised the neighbourhood: another couple of minutes and they'd be at DM's place. He shrugged and tried to change the conversation. 'Why do you need more money? You stole over ten grand from me.'

'They owe me twenty-five.'

'Shit. You're not cheap.'

'You have to pay for quality,' Layla said. 'And I *did* get you.' She looked at him with a small smile to take the sting out of her words. 'Why on earth did you keep so much cash at home, anyway?'

'I don't quite trust banks.' Walker remembered the date perfectly, October 7th, 2008 – less than a month after Lehman Brothers went under. The day the financial world almost imploded.

'Weird, for an investment banker.'

'That's exactly why. I was there, on the trading floor, when the system went to hell. The largest bank in the UK had enough money to last for about eight minutes, and the rest were not in much better shape. I took some cash out then, been keeping it at home ever since. You never know.'

Layla stared at him. 'Are you kidding me? I do the same, but for other reasons...'

'I'm sure.' Walker tapped the cab's glass partition. 'Anywhere here is fine, mate. Thanks.'

...

DM's door was locked, and the curtains at the bay window looking onto his scruffy little garden were drawn. The small detached house, on the corner of a quiet side street, had its usual rundown look that DM never seemed to worry about. Maybe the mathematician was on his way to the office, and he'd laugh – *after taking my head off for being so dumb.* Walker rang the bell, then shivered, fighting to keep his foreboding feelings at bay.

No answer.

He tried again a couple of times and the muffled sound echoed from the inside, without reply. 'What now?'

Layla shrugged, pushed him out of the way and knelt next to the door, rummaging in her black backpack. She pulled out a small set of odd-looking keys and glanced up at Walker.

'Keep an eye on the street,' she muttered before she started messing with the door handle, sticking tiny instruments into and around the keyhole.

Seconds later he heard a sharp click and the door swung back a little. 'Let's go,' she said.

Walker shook his head. He shouldn't have been surprised, really. He followed her inside the dimly lit corridor, just a few steps behind her.

'Fuck.' Layla had already reached the living room when she froze.

Walker stepped into a sticky puddle and looked down at a red splash on the carpet. The blood was already half-congealed.

Please God, no.

He rushed forward and saw DM's naked body lying in the middle of the floor like a discarded rag, bruises and burns on his battered torso. His friend's face was a mess, the nose broken and twisted out of joint, lips grotesquely swollen and blood spatterings everywhere.

Dropping to his knees, Walker took the mathematician's hand and leant down to check for a heartbeat in the tortured chest. There was no point, and he forced himself to swallow a sob, tears burning in his eyes. How could something like this have happened, and why?

He glanced around the room, trying to find something, anything not to look at the broken face that lay unmoving below him. The place had been ransacked, files strewn everywhere. DM's computer was gone, with only a few unhooked cables remaining.

Layla came up behind him and gently laid a hand on his shoulder. 'I'm sorry.'

Walker ignored her, struggling to control his grief and rage. *You wanted to save the world, my friend. If this is the result, maybe the fucking thing is not for saving.*

Decisions

Pienaar entered Walker's apartment and shrugged out of the stolen postman's jacket and cap. He opened his bag, pulling out a syringe full of dark liquid before heading to Walker's bedroom. He spattered a couple of tiny droplets of the dead man's blood on a pair of trousers and a dark shirt, then a few more in the cracks between the wooden floorboards, both in the bedroom and living room. After working Walker's bathroom, he finally got dressed up again and left the flat for the underground carpark.

...

It had felt like hours but must have been only a couple of minutes; Walker forced his hand open and let go of DM's cold, rigid fingers. He stood up just as Layla came back into the living room, pulling off a pair of thin latex gloves.

'There's lots of drugs hidden around the house,' she said, her voice low.

'He liked his hashish.' Walker could see the mathematician's intense expression as he rolled the artistically large joints he could assemble like a Jamaican sculptor. Then he glanced at the DM's battered body and almost gagged.

'No, I mean hard stuff. Coke, pills...'

'That's impossible...' DM hadn't drunk, ever. Nothing that could kill his precious brain cells had been allowed to enter his body. 'I've never seen him do anything worse than marijuana, and we've been friends for a long time. I'd have known if he was on heavier shit.'

'As you say.' Layla shrugged. 'Then someone else must have put them there, maybe make it look like drug crime.'

She looked at him nastily. 'Everyone knows the City is full of addicts.'

'Really.'

Layla stuffed the gloves in her bag and pulled out the felt hat and sunglasses. 'I'm going to get out of here. I wouldn't touch anything if I were you.'

'Why?'

'When the body gets discovered, you'll become a suspect. A major one. I guess you and this poor man –' she pointed at DM's body – 'were working on something... let's say unofficial. Big, secret, and worth a lot of money. Now you two have finished the job, the "something" works and you were last seen staggering out of the Snake, very drunk. Perhaps you decided to pop here, had a fight...'

'That's ridiculous. Besides, I was with you.'

She smiled, explaining things slowly as she would with a small child. 'True, but since your alibi is about to disappear into thin air, I'd think twice about using me as proof of your innocence.'

'Disappear? I thought you wanted your money.'

'It's far too late for that. Someone is already dead, and I'm not going to see a cent. More likely a bullet to the back of my head, if I'm not careful,' she grimaced. 'I told you, these guys are serious pros, and I'm a loose strand. They don't like to leave any traces behind – that's why they tried to take me at the drop-off.'

'What about me?' Walker suddenly remembered the vacuous face of a narrow-faced woman staring at him in Broadgate.

Layla shrugged. 'I don't know – but if I were you I'd be worried. Very worried. I'm sure they didn't want to kill your friend, just steal whatever you guys were working on. Then something went wrong; maybe he even died by accident. But whoever did this is now working off a Plan B, and I suspect you'll be part of it, again. They're going to need a fall guy.'

Walker grabbed a chair and sat down, overwhelmed. *This is insane.* But she could be right. Steph and others knew he'd been drunk and waiting for DM. And the people who had planned this – it must be fucking Frankel Schwartz – they'd try to pin it on him now that they had DM's drivers. He didn't know what to do; this was too far outside his universe. He should just go to the police, but there would be so many questions – he would have to talk about DeepOmega and he didn't have a shred of proof, just two missing computers in a convoluted story. And powerful enemies working against him as he tried to defend himself in front of the law. *You might be truly screwed, Yours.*

'What should I do?' Walker asked, his voice shaken.

'I know what I'll do. Disappear somewhere, and keep my head low for a while. Maybe you should do the same. Besides...' She was obviously thinking aloud, and Walker realised Layla knew a lot more about the murky world he had fallen into that he could ever hope to learn. 'Wait, your computer was alarmed, right? They told me I had to use your fingerprints to turn it on before taking the hard drives, or they would be ruined.'

'Yes, DM did it. He was obsessed by security.'

'Then maybe he had something even better here. This thing you were working on...'

'It's called DeepShare.'

'Fine, this DeepShare. Is there another copy?'

Walker nodded. She was right, they might have got nothing. DM was too careful for a thug to just walk off with his PC and access keys. He took a deep breath, trying to calm down. *Think*. He was reacting like a lost little lamb. And he'd end up like one when the wolves came, if he didn't wake up fast.

'Yes, the real thing is somewhere on the net, in super-secure servers. DM only kept some bits he was working on at home, and it's far too big anyway to run outside the Cloud.'

'Good. Where is it then?'

'I don't have the faintest idea.'

Layla sighed. 'Come on, I'm trying to help you here.'

Walker stood up from the chair and Layla stepped closer, wiping the area he had touched with his hand. She was careful, no doubt. 'I wouldn't trust you anyway, but I really don't know.' *DM's brother*, he thought. They had been close. 'Though there might be someone who does.'

'Good, than I suggest you find this DeepShare fast, since it could be the only thing that gets you out of trouble.' She winked at him and left the living room, heading for the foyer.

Walker followed her, trying to avoid the spatters of blood on the carpet. 'Where are you going?'

'I'm bailing out of this damn country. Do you want a ride?'

Walker stared at her, thinking. Should he listen to the bitch; could he afford not to? 'Maybe you're just trying to deliver me to these guys, to get your money.'

Layla half-smiled at him, gorgeous black eyes glinting with amusement. 'Believe me, if I had wanted to take you to them, you wouldn't have stood a chance.' She opened the door and checked outside. 'Are you coming?'

He couldn't see any other option. But he needed more time to think, to understand. 'I don't have my passport.'

'You won't need it.'

'So you say.' He looked at his hands, speckled with DM's blood. 'No, I'll go and get it. And I want a shower first.'

Layla shrugged, exasperated. 'Whatever. I was only doing it to save your sorry ass.'

'I know.'

'Fine. If you change your mind, I'll be on the eleven-twenty train from St Pancras to Dover. Have a good one, banker boy.' She flashed him a smile and pushed him away. Walker tripped on something, stumbling as she pivoted and ran out of the house. He recovered and went after her, but by the time he emerged onto the street she had already vanished.

. . .

Walker rushed back to his flat, his mind still in turmoil. DM was dead. Someone had murdered him to steal DeepShare. His nausea returned with a vengeance and he staggered to the bathroom, empty stomach heaving up bile while his head pounded harshly. After a couple of minutes he had recovered enough and dried his tears, grabbing the sink. He opened the tap and glanced at his reflection in the mirror; a tiny speck of blood stared back at him, near the top of his forehead.

Walker tried to wipe it off before realising that the small droplet was actually *on* the glass itself. He looked at his hands, but the smudges of DM's blood were dry. Weird, he hadn't even shaved in the morning. He checked around the bathroom and found two more minute red stains on his towel and bathrobe. *What the hell?*

He hurried into his bedroom, blood thumping in his temples. Everything lay as he had left it, including a pile of cleanish clothes on the floor where Layla must have dropped them as she went through his stuff. Walker kneeled down and soon found more droplets of blood on a dark shirt and jeans. What had the bitch said? *Whoever did this must be working off a Plan B, and I suspect you'll be part of it, again. They are going to need a fall guy.* Walker swore loudly.

The buzzer rung and he jumped. The police. Now he was truly screwed. He ran to the intercom system and looked at the tiny screen: the camera showed a postwoman holding some envelopes. He didn't answer, held his breath as she pressed a few more buttons before someone let her in.

He leaned against the doorframe, then slid to the floor. His heart was exploding through his chest, hands shaking with adrenaline and fear. Returning to the bedroom, he packed a few clothes in a small shoulder bag, grabbed his passport and left the flat in a hurry.

Dover

Walker arrived at King's Cross Station a few minutes past eleven, wondering what on earth he was doing. He hurried through the crowds, scanning the platforms, checking random faces. The world felt like a hostile place, and a part of him was waiting for the tap on the shoulder that would mean the end. When he found the right spot the train was already waiting on the tracks, just six mostly empty carriages. He boarded the first one, looking through the seats as he searched for Layla, but she was nowhere to be found. He rushed through the following wagons, glancing left and right, but there was no sign of the woman. Another lie. *Why?*

He retraced his steps, going faster through the train, checking in the toilets as well. Finally a whistle called and the carriage shook, ready to depart. Walker approached the door to disembark and was pushed back as Layla rushed up the stepladder. She had changed into an olive-coloured hunting jacket, with the hood up. As he regained his balance the doors closed and she pulled off the hood, greeting him with a half-scowl.

'You changed your mind. How come?'

Walker exhaled and took a deep breath, relieved. 'I was getting bored.'

She scoffed and found a seat near the exit. 'At least you didn't bring any friends.'

Walker sat across from her, resting his head on the window. 'Is that what you were doing? Waiting to see if I showed up with the police?'

'You can't be too careful these days. But at least you proved you aren't as dumb as you look.'

'Maybe. They might just be waiting for you at the next station.'

She pulled out a tablet computer from her new backpack and turned it on, ignoring him.

'Aren't you worried?'

Layla lifted her eyes away from the screen for a second. 'If you don't want to tell me why you're here, fine. But please don't waste my time.'

...

Dover was almost two hours away and Walker spent most of the trip blindly staring out of the window, remembering the happy times with DM and trying to process the loss. His thoughts twisted in a mess of pain and rage, and a part of him screamed for revenge. Though he was worried about what would happen to him, the images of his friend's tortured body stuck like a dark scar in his brain. He wished he could lay his fists on whoever had done it, but first he needed to prove he had not been involved in his friend's death – that someone else was behind the events. And for that he needed DeepShare.

If anyone had any idea of where DM kept a copy of the access codes, it could only be his one sibling. Walker had met Jiwa-Sai Khaing a couple of times in London, and once on a skiing weekend in Switzerland. JS was DM's older brother and had been a father figure to him as the two boys had escaped Burma, helped by their Swiss relatives, to end up, orphaned, in one of Geneva's most prestigious boarding schools.

JS had later become a senior Swiss-Army officer, a colonel stationed at one of the hidden military bases in the mountains near Zurich. Walker would need to convince him he'd had nothing to do with DM's murder, but the Colonel knew about their friendship. He should listen, hopefully.

Walker forced himself to think one step at a time. Though he had to be careful using his passport, his dual-citizenship meant he always carried an Italian ID that should be good enough to get him past the border into Switzerland. He also had friends in the country, and might be able to get hold of some of his rainy-day money. And once he got access to DeepOmega he'd have a chance to sort this mess out. Maybe.

His mind made up, he concentrated on Layla; she'd been studying something on her tablet for a long time, and he wondered what she was up to. He needed to know more about her, what her reasons and plans were. He glanced around – Dover was still almost an hour away and the train carriage rumbled on almost empty, with no one sitting nearby. 'I want my money back. And my phone.'

'I never took your phone,' she shrugged. 'What the hell would I do with it, anyway? You must have lost it at the Snake. You weren't exactly in good shape over there.'

'Maybe. What about my money?'

She mock-groaned and looked up, a faint smile on her lips. 'Forget about it, we'll need it to pay my fisherman pal, anyway.'

'How much is that going to be?'

'Three grand.'

'You took more than ten. I need the Euros at least – I can't quite use my credit cards, can I?'

'No,' Layla sighed. 'You shouldn't. But you're not going to get very far with a few thousand Euros.'

'Don't worry, I have a plan. What about you?'

'I'll vanish after we reach France.' She readjusted herself on the seat, the light jumper she was wearing on top of tight leggings bulging in all the right places. 'Now be quiet and don't worry about me. I've done it before.' She looked back down at the screen and started typing.

'I'm sure.'

...

Layla's 'friend' knew her as Maria, another one of an impressive collection of names. He met them at a country pub that was so remote even her tablet couldn't find an internet connection. His name was Charlie and he dragged around a weather-beaten face that made him look older than a rock, decorated by a fat moustache and a heavy cap. He sat down at their table with a beer and told them they would have to wait until late afternoon before leaving, as he wanted to land in France well past midnight.

After a couple of hours of stilted conversation Charlie eventually stuck them in the back of his truck and drove to the fishermen's docks in Old Romney, where they boarded his ancient Cuddy boat. He fussed around with a few things and sent them below deck, to a narrow cabin where the old man kept his bunk. After several attempts, he finally managed to start the outboat engine and stuck his head back in as they were looking around the cramped quarters.

'It's going to get a bit rough tonight – Maria, you might want to lie down. The next few hours could become unpleasant.' He nodded and slipped out, busying himself with some fishing nets.

Layla sat down on the tiny bunk-bed with a sigh and shuffled around, trying to get comfortable. 'God, I hate boats.'

'Me too. I get ludicrously seasick.' Walker inched closer to the cot, his back bent to avoid bumping his head on a beam. The Cuddy lurched and he lost his footing, stamping on her shoe.

'Ouch! What are you doing?'

'You'll have to make me some room.'

'What?'

'If you don't want to get splattered in vomit, I'll need to lie down as well. Whatever you slipped me last night is still killing me.'

'Great.' She half-turned and lay back against the cabin wall, freeing about a foot of space just as the Cuddy started gliding along the water, its engine rumbling softly.

Walker slid next to her, his shoulder pressing against her breasts. Layla grunted and pinched him hard before she readjusted her shoulders, slipping one leg onto his thighs, right arm across his chest. She was warm, soft and firm at the same time.

'Don't get any ideas,' she grumbled, her voice low.

'Of course not. Once was more than enough, thank you very much.'

...

Walker must have nodded off for a while before waking with a start as the boat shuddered heavily on the waves; he bounced his head against the low roof of the bed's nook and swore. Layla giggled and shifted against him, trying to find a less uncomfortable position in the near-darkness.

'You were snoring. Not as badly as last night, though.'

'Shut up.' Walker's stomach swayed and he fought to control a backdraft of nausea. His headache had returned with a vengeance.

'Okay.' Layla was quiet for a few seconds before she continued. 'Did DM have a cleaner?'

'I don't think so.'

'Then it might be a couple of days before his body is discovered. That should give you a bit of time.'

Walker considered telling her about the blood drops planted in his flat. The police had probably found them, anyway. In the end he decided not to – she already knew more than enough about him. 'Why are you helping me?' he asked instead.

'I'm almost done helping. From tomorrow morning you are on your own.'

'Still, why? You don't strike me as the good samaritan type.'

Layla took a deep breath, considering. 'Stealing is one thing, murder is different. I guess I just felt sorry for landing you in such deep shit. You're way out of your league, Walker.' She winked at him. 'And you seem like a good guy, for a banker.'

'Thanks.' Was it true, or was she still after something? He shrugged, annoyed. *Whatever*. When they reached France he'd make his own way.

'So what's the plan now?'

'A friend of Charlie's is picking us up near the small beach where we'll land; then we can drive to Reims – it's less than two hundred miles away. I know a quiet place to spend the night, and in the morning you can head to the train station. From there, you'll be able to reach anywhere in Europe quickly, and without needing your passport.'

'That sounds good. Thank you.'

'No problem,' she sighed. 'We all do stupid things at times, and I guess this was my turn.' She nudged him sharply with her elbow. 'Though if I had known how much space you were going to take up, I might have reconsidered.' She grimaced and pushed him away, almost over the edge of the thin mattress.

'Me too.'

...

Sometime later the sea became rougher and the old Cuddy fought and twisted on the waves. Charlie poked his head into the cabin, his croaky voice loud in the small, dark space. 'One hour to go, but it's going to get nasty now.' He was soaked by the heavy rain.

Walker could hear Layla gritting her teeth. 'Great.'

She squeezed him tighter as the boat rocked from side to side, the point dipping under the wind as higher waves rose and crashed around them. He felt like his insides were about to explode out of his ears and mouth, nausea making the tiny cabin turn like a spinning top. Layla groaned, the suffering clear in her voice. 'I'm going to be sick.'

'Don't even think about it.' Walker fought to keep down the pub lunch, his own stomach twisting into a knot.

'I hate boats.'

'You've already said that.'

'Fuck off.' Layla took a deep breath. 'Talk to me, please.' She grabbed his hand, shuddering.

'About what?'

'Anything. Something interesting. I need to take my mind off this...'

The boat lifted in the air and dropped like a roller-coaster, wooden beams groaning under the stress. Layla jerked, sliding almost on top of him. 'Come on, please...' She groaned again. 'What is a DeepShare?'

Here we go. He had to be careful, now. 'It's a computer program. A big, complicated one, and it's none of your business.' He shifted a little, trying not to fall off the bunk. 'What are *you*?'

'Fine, *I'll* talk,' she sighed, her right hand grabbing his shirt and crumpling it as the Cuddy lurched again. 'I'm a honey-trap.'

'That much I figured. Why?'

'Why?' Layla scoffed. 'Sometimes you don't get to choose...' She hesitated, breathing shallowly for a few seconds. Walker waited until she continued. 'I was born in Mexico, near the Chiapas. My family was very poor, worse than you can imagine. It's a bad area, drugs, lawlessness...'

'I've heard of it.' The sea rumbled and roared around them, almost drowning his words.

'You have *no* idea. When I turned twelve, my father gave me a choice. Since I was pretty, I could become a prostitute in a brothel near San Cristobal, the big town. Or he would sell me to the secret police. They needed the money for my little brothers and sisters.' She spoke with a cold, hard edge but Walker could hear a shadow of old pain in her voice.

'Jesus.' Was this just another story?

'At least he gave me a choice. Some of my friends – they weren't so lucky.' She paused for a second, regaining her composure. The Cuddy rocked again, almost throwing Walker off the bed. Layla's hands shook. 'Did I mention I hate boats?'

'You might have. What did you choose, then?'

'The secret police. It sounded better than a brothel. But they trained me to be a kind of prostitute anyway, for information instead of money. For years I was taught to seduce men, and fight. Then they sent me deep undercover in drug barons' country – I lasted eighteen months, which is a lot longer than most. In the end I ran, escaped to the US and set up my own business.' Her voice hardened again. 'I guess the job is the same, but at least I get paid properly.'

'Sometimes.'

Layla kneed him in the crotch, making Walker gasp in pain. 'You were too easy anyway, banker-guy. Certainly not worth twenty-five grand.'

Charlie knocked and opened the small cabin door. 'Get ready, sweethearts. We're almost there.'

France

'What the fuck is going on?'

The phone had rung a few times before but the Englishman had avoided answering while waiting for updates. In the end, suspecting the man was about to explode into inadequacy, he had decided to pick up before the American did something stupid.

'It's all under control.'

'No, it's fucking not. You've killed the mathematician.' The American sounded as if he was about to have a heart attack.

'Mistakes were made. By the people you've chosen, I should add. But we're working on it.'

'What? You've got to be...'

'Don't worry. Just give me a few days, maybe a week.'

'Forget it. It's going to be a murder investigation, now, for God's sake. You need to move much faster.'

The Englishman swallowed, suddenly uncertain. 'I'll see what I can do.'

'You better. If any of this comes out, we're both finished.'

'It won't.'

...

The boat came to a halt less than twenty yards away from the beach, in shallow water. The rain had calmed down and a sliver of moon glinted through the clouds, but the night was still freezing. Walker and Layla waded through the surf and reached the sand shivering, wet to the waist.

Car headlights shone just beyond some low shrubs of vegetation and they made their way to the small battered Peugeot that was waiting for them. Layla got in the front, next to a thin older lady who was sitting behind the wheel. Walker climbed in the back and tried to make himself comfortable. The ice-cold water had shocked his system enough to get rid of the nausea and he felt a little better, but a veil of exhaustion threatened to swamp him and he soon fell asleep as the little car moved along dark, empty country roads.

Sometime later, a heavy backpack landed on his chest, waking him with a jolt.

'Rise and shine, pretty boy. We're in Reims.'

Walker sat up, rubbing his eyes and trying to clear the fog from his mind. 'What time is it?'

'Almost two in the morning.' Shop- and bar-lights flashed by as Layla drove through tiny cobbled streets in an ancient town centre. The old lady had disappeared without a trace. Walker could still smell her sickening perfume and was about to ask what had happened to her when the car shuddered to a halt and Layla got out. He shrugged and joined her under a broken streetlight.

'What now?'

Layla pointed at his clothes, and hers. 'We're still wet. I know a place to spend the night and get some rest.'

'Where?'

'Just by the Cathedral – we're almost there. Come along, it's beautiful.'

She shouldered her bag and rushed ahead, then waited for Walker to catch up. They turned a corner on the uneven stones and stepped into the main square. Walker caught his breath: Reims Cathedral was astonishing, a two-towered gothic masterpiece illuminated by flickering lights that shifted along the facade, reflecting into a thousand colours as they hit the enormous central window. The rest of the square was dark but the spotlights shone on and off the front and sides of the ancient building, where hundreds of statues seemed to twist and move, angels and demons floating on some invisible wind. DM would have loved it.

'I think it's one of the largest churches in the world,' she whispered, awed.

'It's magnificent.'

Layla let him stare at the building for a few moments before turning and walking back a dozen steps or so. She stopped under a broken sign that read 'Hotel du Champagne' and opened a creaky door, telling him to wait.

...

The room was cheap and dirty, but from a corner of their first-floor balcony Walker could see the upper part of one of the cathedral's towers, rising like a prayer into the night sky. He finished his cigarette and flicked it out before noticing a lone figure crossing the empty square, just a few yards away. The man wore a baseball cap and was shuffling along when he looked up, catching the trader's eyes for a second before turning away.

Walker shivered, then he blamed the chilly air and told himself to relax. No point in jumping at shadows. He opened the squeaky French window to reenter their bedroom just as Layla was wriggling out of her top. She stood next to the bed wearing only her underwear and he looked for a second at her body, impressed. *You might be dumb, Yours, but she really is something.*

Layla caught him staring and grinned, her hands going up behind her back. 'No pay, no play, Mr Walker.'

'It's not something I haven't seen before.'

'True.' Layla undid her bra and threw it on the bed, her full breasts hardly moving. 'God, I need a shower. That saltwater has dried me out.' She spun around and slipped out of her flimsy panties, stepping gracefully away to the bathroom.

Ignoring the stirring of an erection Walker inhaled, went to a side table and rummaged in his shoulder bag for a fresh shirt and some underwear. His BlackBerry tumbled out and fell to the floor, the back of it detaching. He swore, picked it up and reassembled the phone, leaving it on the double bed. The hems of his jeans were still damp but he decided to keep them on as the sound of the shower took his mind back to Layla's naked body.

He grabbed another Marlboro and went back to the balcony to get a little more fresh air. His thoughts drifted, spiralling between Layla and what the next few days were going to bring. He wondered whether DM's corpse had been found yet, and what he was going to tell the older Khaing when he met him. His only chance was to convince him that he'd had nothing to do with the murder. He needed help, not someone else contacting the police with his whereabouts. He sighed and took a long pull of his cigarette, glancing down to the corner of the church square. Something sneaked into the shade and he strained his eyes, trying to figure out what the shape was.

One of the cathedral spotlights swerved, pointing downwards and slashing the shadows for an instant and he swore. The light had revealed the same man who'd looked at him earlier, just without the cap. He was half-leaning behind some column, staring at their hotel. Walker dropped the Marlboro and slipped back inside, hurrying to the bathroom. Layla was wearing a bathrobe but hadn't tied it; her hair was dripping and her skin flushed from the hot water. She looked like a wet angel when she smiled at him. 'I'm starting to think you want to get me into bed.'

'There's a guy outside, looking at our room.' Walker struggled to keep his voice even, but he was nervous. He returned to the bedroom and Layla followed him quickly. 'What? Are you sure?'

'I've seen him twice, now. And the second time he was trying to hide.'

'But they can't...' Layla checked around the room and saw his phone lying on the bed. 'Oh God, what the hell is that?'

'It's my Dorfmann BlackBerry. But it's super-secure, and switched off.'

She turned to him, fire in her eyes. 'You *are* a fucking idiot.' She shrugged out of her bathrobe and started getting dressed in a hurry.

'We need to get out of here, now.'

'I'm sorry, I didn't think...'

'Shut up.' Layla was already putting her boots on. 'I'll get down the back and bring the car around.'

'What about me?'

'Go and stand on the balcony, where they can see you. When you hear an engine coming, jump down and run to the corner as fast as you can. And try not to break a leg, or I'll leave you here.' She sighed and put on her overcoat, pointing to the window.

Walker grabbed his cigarettes and headed back out of the french doors. He lit up and inhaled, making sure he didn't glance back into the room. His heart was racing, adrenaline shooting up his veins. He tried to slow his breathing as he had done when he was a kid, just before a fight, and wondered whether he'd been imagining things and Layla was overreacting. It was a Dorfmann phone, and turned off – how the hell could Frankel track it? Or was it someone else? Seconds ticked by, too slowly. Trying not to be obvious, he leaned further out and checked the square but the man he'd noticed was nowhere to be seen.

Where was Layla? She should have brought the car already. Maybe she had driven off, and left him to DM's fate. Why the hell had he trusted her? She'd probably dropped him like a hot pan, and he shouldn't have expected more. He swore, pulled again on his cigarette and fought to stay calm. Then he heard soft footsteps in the night's silence and after a heartbeat a second figure appeared below, a large man striding to the corner near the hotel entrance. *Shit. Now you're seriously fucked, Yours.*

Tyres squealed and a car braked furiously, coming to a stop less than a hundred yards to his right, on a smaller side road leading into the cathedral's square. Walker recognised the battered Peugeot and stepped onto the stone handrail, grabbing it and letting himself drop a couple of yards to the pavement. He heard a shout and fell badly, twisting his ankle and rolling to the ground.

When he got up the large man was clearing the corner, rushing back towards him. Walker turned around – a second thug was running by Layla's car, trying to cut him off while a third had emerged from the shades under the church's main door and was sprinting across the plaza.

Right. Let's see what you got. Walker spun back, his ankle sending a shard of pain up his leg. The big man approached him and he crouched in a boxer's stance, left fist coming up near his face. The thug had a nasty scar running down the side of his mouth and was wearing a tight hat. He took another step forward, glancing beyond Walker.

'Come on, give it up, mate. We don't wanna make a scene,' he said in a thick Australian drawl.

Walker let him get closer and feinted, dropping his shoulder and swaying to the right. His feet shot sideways, keeping his balance and increasing the momentum as he swung from just above the hip to hit the Aussie with a right cross to the chest, aiming for the diaphragm. His fist connected solidly and he followed through on the turn, pushing off his good leg to run back towards Layla's car.

The second thug stopped a few yards away and brought up a small handgun, pointing it at him. 'Enough.'

The third man was approaching from the middle of the square. Walker glanced over – it was their original watcher, once again wearing the baseball cap, but now carrying a long knife.

Walker swore and checked behind him, just as the large Australian was struggling to his feet. *Not there.* He looked back at the gunman and a shadow shifted near Layla's car.

'What do you want?' he asked, his body quivering with adrenaline. Just a couple of seconds...

The man waved his pistol in the air. 'Don't worry and come with us. Everything will be...'

Layla's foot lashed out of the darkness, kicking the gun out of the thug's hand. He turned sharply and Walker was onto him, lower through his defenses, then swinging, his fist crunching bone before he twisted to one side, shuffling and regaining his balance to land two more uppercuts that sent the thug sprawling to the ground.

One down, two to go. And both armed, probably. Breathing hard, Walker checked to his right and saw that Layla was trying to intercept the third man. The big Australian had also recovered and was fumbling with his overcoat. Definitely armed.

'Get into the car!' Layla shouted just as Baseball Cap reached her, his knife flashing as a yellow spotlight from the cathedral fell on them.

Walker rushed to the Peugeot and jumped into the driver's seat, slamming the door shut. He saw Layla dodging the first knife thrust and drove the little car forward, heading for her. She ducked another cut and rolled to her left, bouncing up with a sidekick. Baseball Cap reeled backwards.

Walker leaned over and opened the passenger door just as he reached them. Layla lunged away but the man managed to grab her coat while slashing with his other hand. She grunted in pain and dove into the car just as Walker accelerated onto the larger slabs of stone near the centre of the plaza. He swerved violently and floored the gas pedal. The Peugeot shot off with a screech and slid into a tailspin, glancing the Australian just as he was trying to aim his gun. The big man dropped to the ground and Walker regained control, heading for one of the little alleys that sprang from the cathedral's square.

In a few seconds they were away, wheels skidding on the uneven pavement. Walker took a couple of side roads to make sure they lost the thugs before looking at Layla, who was trying to sit straight and tie her seat-belt.

'Are you all right?'

She swore in Spanish, and fiddled some more until the clasp locked into position. 'No. The son-of-a-bitch cut me.' She opened her coat to check her right arm. 'Turn left here, then left again. We need to get out of Reims. Just follow the yellow signs to the highway.'

Walker nodded, finally remembering to switch on the car's headlights. He was driving too fast, the speedometer reading over ninety as they crossed to a more modern part of town, and he only wished he could go faster. He glanced at Layla, trying to see what was wrong with her.

'Keep your eyes on the road. Don't worry, I'll live.'

'You sure?'

'He just opened up my upper arm.' Her hand came back out of her coat, dribbling with blood. 'It hurts like hell though. *Fuck.*'

Walker flew the car into a roundabout, then switched lanes and drove the Peugeot up a ramp that would take them onto the larger ring road. 'Do you need me to stop?'

'Not now.' Layla gritted her teeth, swearing again. 'Just pop into a service station when you see one, I need something to stop the bleeding.' Her hand returned to her shoulder as she shifted her seat backwards, leaning against the headrest and closing her eyes for a few seconds. 'Slow down a bit, the last thing we need is to get stopped for speeding.'

They drove on in silence for a few more minutes, until they reached the highway and Walker turned south. Layla opened her eyes and looked at him just as he was checking on her.

'Where are we going?' she asked, her voice rough with pain.

'Switzerland. I told you I had a plan.'

'I hope it's a good one.'

'Definitely the best I have.' He reached into his jeans and pulled out a crumpled pack of cigarettes. 'You want one?'

'Oh God, yes.'

Walker lit a Marlboro and placed it between her lips. 'There's a service area in fifteen miles.'

'Good, because I'm bleeding like a stuck pig. I always do, for some reason.'

'You saved my life.'

'Probably.' She sucked on the cigarette and puffed out the smoke, savouring it. 'So did you, actually. We'll just call it even.' She readjusted herself, grimacing. 'And Scott...'

'Yes?'

'The next time you intend to do something so fucking dumb as carrying a *phone*, please ask me first.'

CHAPTER NINE

Lugano

Walker decided to cross the border in Geneva, since the city sat between France and Switzerland and the controls ought to be more relaxed there than anywhere else in the region. *Hopefully.* He drove slowly through town, careful not to break any traffic laws. His foot itched to slam the accelerator forward and get somewhere safer, away from the road. He felt too exposed, checking his mirrors often to see if someone was tailing them, but the town traffic made it impossible to know. Layla was asleep, head resting against the car window, one hand wrapped around her bandaged upper arm.

As he approached the border crossing Walker nudged her and she awoke with a start, eyes still unfocused. 'What? Where are we?'

'Geneva. I need your passport.'

She groaned and rummaged in her backpack, producing a small red booklet. 'It's Spanish, in the name of Paula Carbonero. What about you?'

'I'll use my Italian ID – it might help, I guess. But I'm hoping they'll just wave us through, there's lots of traffic...' He trailed off, uncertain.

'Good thinking.' Layla tried to smile. 'You might not be on Interpol yet.'

Walker grimaced. 'I'll tell you if we get through.'

The small truck in front of them shifted, and they could see a few cars being let through the barrier with barely a glance. Walker's spirits lifted for a second as the white van rumbled through, also without being stopped, and shot forward. He slowed down to a crawl, staring straight ahead as they approached the Gendarmes on both sides of the road. The left one glanced into the car and his signalling disk dropped, stopping in mid-air.

'Fuck,' Walker whispered. From the corner of his eye he saw Layla tense, and wondered if they could just burst through. The other policeman was staring ahead and Walker prepared to floor the pedal, calculating whether there was enough room to swing past the van.

BOOM!

The truck in front screeched as it swerved on the road, sounds of crunching metal exploding through the air. Somehow the driver had lost control and rammed the vehicle ahead, smashing it into the following one. The Gendarmes shot forward, rushing to check the damage. Walker breathed out and skirted the mess, careful to avoid the shattered glass from the headlights of the two cars in front. The border police were screaming at the driver and didn't even turn to look at them as they slid past, into Switzerland.

They drove on, and long minutes later the houses and villas became grander, and then scarcer, until he turned onto the highway that would take them into the south-western part of the country, the Italian-speaking Canton

Ticino. Layla soon fell asleep again, her body twitching as she struggled to find a more comfortable position, but eventually she started snoring lightly, almost sounding at peace.

The night's events and the seven-hour drive had exhausted Walker but he drove on, knowing they needed to get somewhere safe in a hurry. Layla's wound had turned out to be truly nasty, more than an inch deep and five long. He had managed to clean it a little and staunch the flow of blood by bandaging it tightly, but she would need attention soon. It took another tense ninety minutes until eventually he stopped at a service station, just a few miles outside Lugano. He got out of the car, stretched his aching back and wandered past the pumps to use the single payphone. Luigi answered after the second ring, his voice chirpy.

'*Pronto?*'

'Get out of the office and find a place where no one can hear you.'

'What?'

'I'll call you back in a minute.' Walker put the receiver down and went to buy some water before going back to the booth and dialling again.

'Can you speak freely now?'

'Sure. What's going on? And where are you?' Luigi sounded surprised, and a little worried. 'The market is all over the place...'

'I couldn't care less. Listen, I'm near Lugano, and in big trouble. I need your help.'

'Whoa. Anything, man. Just tell me.'

Walker exhaled. 'Can you meet me at your place in twenty minutes?'

'Of course.'

'Don't mention my name, to anyone.'

'Right.'

Walker returned to the car to find Layla awake. Her skin was pasty, deep dark circles under her eyes. 'Hi gorgeous, how are you getting on?'

'Not too bad,' she croaked, taking the water bottle. She greedily drank a few mouthfuls before asking, 'Where are we?'

'Lugano, still in Switzerland. We're going to a friend's house, see if we can sort things out a little.'

'Are you sure? DM's death will be on the news soon. Can you trust this guy?'

'With my life.'

'How about mine?'

Walker smiled and started the Peugeot, heading back onto the highway. 'I can always drop you off here, if you want.'

Layla ignored him and they soon drove into town, along the shorter route by the lake. Lugano was a relatively small city: about fifty thousand people, but growing to double that during the summer. It sat around a pretty lake and was built with typical Swiss neatness around the historic centre. It was a wealthy place, hundreds of well-kept houses dotting the beach promenade and the surrounding low mountains.

Walker turned for Castagneta, the tiny suburb where Luigi lived, just a couple of miles away. They drove up the hills along winding semi-private roads until they reached his friend's place at the bottom of a cul-de-sac surrounded by pine trees.

Luigi's house was a medium-sized villa with magnificent views over the water and the Ticino valley: a two-story wooden chalet on top of a sheer hundred-yard drop to the lake below. Walker stopped the car and looked around; his friend hadn't arrived yet. He got out and lit a cigarette, but after a minute or so a loud engine approached and a green Range Rover turned into the cul-de-sac, braking just in front of them.

Luigi stepped out and embraced Walker, then he glanced at Layla still sitting in the Peugeot and his eyebrows arched up.

'Hi ugly, what's going on? And who's that charming lady?'

'Inside. Is your garage big enough for our car as well?'

'*Si*, of course.' He pressed a button on his remote control and a wide door yawned open. 'Let's get you in and we'll chat.'

...

As Layla went for a quick shower, Walker talked through the events of the previous thirty-six hours with Luigi. When he finished the Italian just nodded silently, stood up and poured himself a large drink. Walker joined him, glancing at the scenery from the massive windows that opened onto Lake Lugano and its valley.

'Sweet Mother of God.' Luigi's voice was shaken. 'What are you going to do now?'

Walker shrugged. 'I'm not sure. I need to speak to DM's brother, but I don't have his number and it's probably unlisted since he's at an army base.'

'Leave that to me – I'll check with the office systems. And I'm going to buy a new phone you can use, in my name.'

'*Grazie.* Then I'll need to take some cash out of...'

'Money sounds good. Can I have some?'

Layla glided into the living room. Her hair hung wetly to her shoulders and she wore a sleeveless white dress; the top of her arm was wrapped in a towel that was already turning pink. She was still too pale and her eyes were sunken and bloodshot but she looked a little more alive.

Luigi glanced at Walker and winked as she headed to the couch, curling up on a pillow.

'I'm out of clothes,' she said. 'This is the last clean stuff I have.'

The Italian finished his drink and headed for the stairs. 'Don't worry, my wife has millions of clothes and she's of a size with you, I'd guess.' He turned and grinned at Layla. 'Though maybe not quite the same shape.'

Layla smiled, then winced, and her hand went up to her shoulder. Walker stubbed out his cigarette and joined her on the sofa. 'Let me have a look at that.'

'It's getting better.'

'I'm sure. Show me.'

He unwrapped the towel and then the gauze Luigi had given her. The cut underneath was still bleeding in places, and the swollen skin was turning a deeper shade of red. 'You have to see a doctor.'

'No, I don't. Just get me some pills and I'll be okay.'

'This is going to need some stitches. Try not to move your arm too much.' Walker stood up, calling out, 'Mate, where are you?'

Luigi came back down with a pair of long boots and some socks. 'Yes? Try these on, Layla, then you can go and raid Susan's wardrobe. I'm sure she won't mind. Or notice, really.'

'Do you know a doctor who can help us?' asked Walker.

Luigi paused, thinking. 'Eh, it's difficult. This is Switzerland, where everything is done properly. There isn't anyone I can trust – any doctor would go to the police for a knife wound. If we were in Sardinia, sure...'

Layla cut him off. 'I'll be fine, I just need some general antibiotic.' She winced. 'And maybe a painkiller or two.'

'That's okay, I have to go back to the office for a while but I can pick something up on the way back. I'll take a cab. Here are the keys to my car...' He paused before continuing, 'I also need to get you a new phone. Any preferences?'

Walker glanced at Layla and she shrugged. 'Just not a smartphone, anything old and simple will do.'

'Done. And feel free to use my laptop while I'm gone.'

Walker sighed, tiredness and the release of tension catching up on him all of a sudden. 'Thank you, man. I owe you big.'

'We'll call it even on the eight grand you won from me on our Italian election bet.'

Walker smiled. 'I thought your word was your bond.'

'I'm not a trader, Yours. Thank God.'

...

Luigi left and Walker brought out the PC from his friend's studio, setting it up on a coffee table near Layla's couch. After a few minutes of typing he checked the message carefully to make sure Mosha would not freak out and contact the police. *'Don't believe a word of what you hear,'* it read. *'Someone is after me, and I might need you to repay that debt soon. It probably won't even be illegal. I'll be in touch in the next few days. Yours.'*

Walker sent the email to the Serb's private account and slid next to Layla, noticing she was shivering.

'Are you cold?'

'A little. I think it's the shock.'

'Wait here.' He went upstairs, searching for a blanket. When he returned she had already taken hold of the laptop and was scanning through some news websites.

'Anything yet?' Walker laid the heavy quilt on her shoulders, carefully folding it around her wounded arm. Layla turned to him and gave him a quick kiss on the lips. 'Thank you. I'm sorry about... everything.'

'Me too.' He glanced at the BBC news-page she had pulled up, and then at the City Life website, but there was no mention of DM or anything else. 'So it's not out yet?'

'Doesn't look like it. But the police wouldn't tell the press for a few hours anyway, not before they have a first idea of what's going on.'

'Good. I'll go and get some money out, then.'

'If you use your passport they'll know where we are. You can't wire it from the UK.'

Walker nodded. 'I know my banking. Home wasn't the only place where I kept some cash hidden, and this is Switzerland. You don't need a passport to use a numbered account, not in the right private banks.'

'That's impressive.' Layla coughed, and then grimaced. 'Maybe I'll offer you a job after all this.'

'I'm too expensive for you.'

'Probably. What about the rest of your plan?'

Walker studied her, considering. She was still shivering, and her bright eyes looked feverish. For the first time since he had met her Layla looked fragile, and a little scared. If it hadn't been for her, he wouldn't be in such a mess. But without her help, he might also be already dead. He shrugged, deciding to go with his instincts.

'I need to meet up with DM's brother, JS. Luigi is going to find his phone number – he's the only one who could possibly know about DeepShare's access codes. I must convince him I had nothing to do with the murder, and if he believes me and he's got something that can help, then...'

'There's a lot of *ifs* in this plan.' Layla leaned back onto the couch, her naked feet pushing against his leg and slipping behind his back.

Walker ignored her and continued, 'I'll work on the software, figure out all the parts I don't know much about. Then I'll see if it can be used to prove I'm innocent and Frankel is behind all this.'

'Is that Frankel Schwartz, the investment bank?' She adjusted herself, trying to get comfortable without hurting her arm further.

'Yes. DM thought they were after him to steal DeepOmega, the secret version we were working on.'

'And how would finding this DeepShare help?'

'I don't know yet – I need to access it first. But you have no idea how powerful Omega is. It was developed for financial markets, but DM has been expanding it for years to do a lot of other stuff. Nothing out there can touch it, especially when it comes to uncovering information and examining patterns of behaviour.'

'And you're positive Frankel, or whoever, didn't take it from DM when they killed him?'

'If they did, what were those thugs doing in Reims last night?'

'Good question.'

Walker stood up, looking around the living room. 'So that's my plan.' He spotted Luigi's car keys and went to pick them up.

Layla had stretched out on the couch, her eyes closed. 'It doesn't sound like much, to be honest,' she whispered.

Walker shrugged. 'I'm going to the bank. If you come up with a better idea, let me know.'

Planning

The Banca Cantonale di Lugano occupied a turn-of-the century building hidden beyond a sharp bend in a peripheral road, on the other side of town. Walker parked Luigi's car a few hundred metres further ahead, in the shade of a massive pine tree. Though he had tried to sound calm to Layla, he was worried about the security cameras that would be spying on him from everywhere around the bank, and inside. The baseball cap he had taken from Luigi's wardrobe felt like scant protection and he shivered in the chilly air, hurrying but trying not to look conspicuous as he tracked back.

The road was almost deserted, and so was the tiny carpark. Small glass doors beckoned from the front of the building, leading him into a foyer of gleaming marble and steel, dominated by a huge staircase rising up the right side. A receptionist waited discreetly behind a small corner desk and smiled at him as he approached, struggling not to stare at the wall-set glass eyes above her coiffured hair.

'*Buongiorno*. Can I help you?' she said.

'I'm...' Walker croaked, cleared his throat. 'I'm a client of Signor Ventura.'

'Ventura? I'm afraid he's away, this week. Will anyone else in Numbered Accounts suit?'

Walker swore under his breath. He didn't want to use his ID, but he needed the money. Desperately. 'Sure,' he answered, trying to sound confident.

The lady picked up a phone and dialled. Walker turned around, looking away from the small cameras only to find himself staring into a bigger one, just above a pair of walnut doors. Trying to avoid them was useless, and he gave up.

A couple of minutes later a heavyset man in a brown suit came down the marble steps, looked at him gravely and offered his hand. 'Welcome, sir. I'm Tom Ghizzoni. Would you follow me to my office?'

Walker nodded and stepped after him, along the half-spiral up to the second floor. His brain spun through scenarios, wondering if they were going to try and detain him as the police arrived. *Just calm down and be normal*. The office door closed behind him with a solid thunk and he sat down, bumping his knee on the desk.

'How may I help you?'

'I have an account – numbered. I need to withdraw some money, but I just realised I forgot my passport and I guess...' Showing up at the bank had been a really bad idea. But he'd be a sitting duck without any cash.

Ghizzoni glanced at his monitor, then back to Walker's face. He waved his hand, and smiled.

'Not a problem, of course. What is the account number?'

'67A2396J.' Walker stared at his feet, fighting to keep still.

'And the password?'

'31Sarah6.' The day and age at which his little sister had died. He wasn't gonna forget that.

Ghizzoni typed something, then frowned and looked back up. 'This is not matching.'

'What?' Walker's heart sank, and he felt sweat breaking out on his forehead.

'I think there's a problem...'

Walker half-stood, ready to bolt. The door was only a few steps away, then it would take about fifteen seconds to get back down to the exit, he guessed. If they didn't seal it shut in the meantime. He thought he heard a siren from somewhere, coming closer.

Ghizzoni banged his mouse, then grinned. 'Ah, there we go. The system was trying to crash.' He flashed Walker a grin. 'So, how much are you going to need today, sir?'

...

When Walker returned to the house Luigi was already back and busy typing something on his computer. Layla sat on the sofa, a steaming mug in her hands, still wrapped up in the old quilt. They both turned to him at once, the Italian asking, 'Did you get the cash?'

'Yes, almost no drama at all. I do love Swiss banks.'

'I found JS's home number, but he's not answering.'

Walker sat down, dropping a heavy rucksack on the floor, and groaned. 'Great. Anything out of London?'

'Not yet.' Layla sipped from her cup. 'I've set a news alert for Dorfmann, so we should know as soon as it hits.'

Walker nodded and opened his backpack, pulling out several thick wads of two-hundred Euro banknotes to place them on the coffee table. Layla's eyes widened and she sat up straighter. 'Jesus, how much have you got in there?'

'Three hundred grand.'

'That should last you a while,' deadpanned Luigi.

'You never know.'

Layla shuffled closer, taking one of the cash piles and weighing it. 'How does it feel to be rich?'

'Rich is something else, and I'm not nearly as wealthy as I was going to get.' Walker breathed out, then went on. 'It doesn't matter, money is only a number on a computer screen, in the end.'

Layla threw the banknotes back on the table. 'Not where I come from,' she said as she lay back down. 'And only a rich man would say that.'

Walker shrugged and lit a cigarette. The woman could be seriously annoying. He inhaled and stared out of the window, silent. Finally Luigi's laptop beeped twice, breaking the tension. '*Vediamo*,' he sighed gratefully.

The Italian came to sit between them as a BBC news website opened on his screen. Down on the left, one of the articles started with a photograph of Dorfmann's building. The caption read: 'Investment banker found murdered at home.' The piece didn't go into much detail, and there was no mention of drugs or anything else, just a brief biography of DM at the end.

'DM's brother will have been notified already.' Layla's tone was sombre. 'They are not allowed to publish before the next-of-kin is informed.'

Walker nodded. 'Let's try to call him again.' He dialled on his new phone but the line rang for a while without answer before cutting off.

Luigi closed the computer, stood up and poured drinks for everyone. 'Still convinced about what you'll do after meeting the Colonel?'

'Yes – you know we can't stay here. If JS doesn't have me arrested, we'll hide somewhere in Italy.'

Layla took her drink from the broker's hands. 'Why Italy?'

'I've spoken about this with Luigi. First of all, it's still a cash-based economy, especially now that the country is in a kind of Depression. You can do just about anything without a credit card, as long as you have money. Also, I'll be able to pass for a local and...'

'And since your first stop will be Sardinia,' Luigi interrupted, 'I can get a lot of stuff sorted out. It's not like the Swiss, with their million rules – they are my people, they understand. My little brother, Paolo, he... Let's say he's got connections. Getting you a trustworthy doctor will be easy, and we might even be able to sort out a new passport for Scott.'

Layla turned to Walker. 'Glad to be involved with the planning.'

'It's just an idea. Besides, I could be in jail in a few hours.'

'No, it's fine. But I'm not coming.'

'What?'

'You heard me. I've got *my own* plan.'

Walker stood and opened a window, letting some fresh evening air into the room. He breathed out some smoke and turned to her. 'I hope this plan doesn't involve your arm dropping off. Do you have some hidden surgeons lying around?'

'No, but I'll sort something out.'

'I'm sure you will.' He exhaled and looked at Luigi, who shrugged and opened his arms, refusing to be drawn into the discussion. 'Look, let's talk about this in the morning, okay?'

'No, let's not...'

Walker's new phone rang and they all stared at it, surprised. He picked the handset up gingerly and answered, 'Hello?'

'Who's this?' The voice on the other side spoke with a strong Swiss-German accent.

'Colonel! It's Scott Walker. I'm so sorry about your brother...'

'Scott,' JS interrupted him. 'I hoped you might call. Do you...' His voice broke for a second, as he tried to stifle a sob. 'Do you know anything more about DM?'

'I do, but I need to see you, to talk.' He waited for a reply, tense.

'I'm flying to London to identify the body tomorrow morning.'

'I'm not in the UK, but in Canton Ticino. What about tonight, where are you?'

JS went silent for a while, absorbing the information. In the end he answered, 'Maybe. Can... can you be in Altdorf around midnight? It's about halfway to Ticino.'

'Absolutely.'

'There's a small bar just outside town called "The Cow", and they're open all night. I'll meet you there.'

'That's great.' Walker sat there, his heart-rate calming down. 'Thank you...'

The line dropped.

Walker looked at Layla and Luigi and half-smiled. 'I'm seeing him later in a place called Altdorf.'

The Italian nodded. 'I've heard of it – it's a lot closer than Zurich.'

'How did he sound?'

'Shattered. He wants to know about DM.'

'Will he turn you in?' Layla sat up on the couch, studying him.

Walker considered the question. He didn't really have a clue. 'It's possible. I don't know him that well, and he's an army guy. But I don't really have a choice, do I?'

'Maybe...'

'No.' Walker tried to sound more confident than he felt. 'If he knows something about Deep – I have to risk it. There's no other way.'

'I should come with you, just in case.' Layla grimaced and stood up, unsteadily.

'It's not...'

She tried to step forward but her legs crumpled and she crashed to the floor, her head barely missing the coffee table. Walker reacted first, kneeling next to the prone body and checking her pulse just as her eyes fluttered open. 'She's burning up, Luigi.'

'I'll check if we have something. Help her to the guest bedroom.'

Walker carried the semi-conscious Layla to bed and slid her under the covers, propping up her head. He was inspecting the wound, which seemed to have reopened, when Luigi arrived with a touch thermometer. The fever was very high and she moaned softly as they redressed the cut on her arm before giving her more antibiotics and leaving her to rest.

Back in the living room, Walker lit another Marlboro and finished his drink, thinking hard. 'This isn't good,' he sighed finally. 'How long is the drive to Altdorf?'

'Less than two hours, I'd guess. I'll come with you.'

'No way, mate. You're risking enough as it is, and someone needs to stay with Layla.'

Luigi sipped his Grand Marnier. 'You're probably right. Take my car, though. I can always say you stole it.

Your piece of junk shouldn't get out of my garage for a while.' He lit a cigarette himself, and coughed.

'I thought you'd quit.'

'I have, but I don't really care right now.' He pointed towards Layla's bedroom. 'Quite something, that lady.'

'Yes. She really is something.' *But what, exactly?*

JS

Luigi's Range Rover devoured the road and Walker reached The Cow almost half an hour early. He left the car in a deserted parking lot near an industrial compound and studied the small bar from the shadows below a broken street-lamp. It looked like a trucker's stop, with three semi-articulated monsters parked near the dingy building. There were no police cars, for the moment at least. A couple of letters on the yellow sign flickered in and out of life and he approached the entrance.

The place was even smaller inside, just a dozen round tables and a low bar nestled along one of the walls. Walker ordered a vodka and tonic to relax and keep awake, and sat down in a corner opposite the exit. The barman was a thin man in his sixties and a pair of burly drivers sat nursing beers on the other side of the room, talking quietly.

Walker sipped at the drink and lay back in his chair, exhausted. His body felt leaden from lack of sleep, and the couple of hours of rest he had snatched at Luigi's before the drive had only seemed to remind him of how battered he felt. He wondered how Layla was doing; she hadn't woken since they had put her to bed, though her temperature had dropped a little by the time he left. She obviously needed a doctor, and soon.

His mind drifted back to DM's tortured body and he almost broke down, exhaustion and sadness threatening to overwhelm him. He had vowed to make whoever had killed DM pay, but he wasn't sure he could get out of it alive him-self. He shook his head trying to clear it and was about to go out for a cigarette when the door opened and JS walked in, scanning the shadowy room.

The Colonel carried a military backpack and was wearing a full uniform, several medals glinting on his chest. He saw Walker and nodded, then asked the barman for a coffee and headed to the table. Walker noticed his eyes were red-rimmed, a hint of stubble on his cheek. He looked very much like his brother, just taller and a lot thicker, but with the same nose and high cheekbones. Walker stood up to offer his hand and JS grabbed it, shaking it firmly.

'Colonel, I'm so sorry.'

'Why are you in Switzerland? What are you doing here?' JS's voice had a cold edge as he sat down.

Walker leaned forward, the speech he had practised suddenly forgotten. 'I had to run. Someone is trying to... frame me. For DM's murder.'

'Frame you? Who?'

'I don't know. Not yet.'

'Did you have anything to do with it, Scott?' The Colonel half-stood, glaring at him. Walker could feel the rage and anger radiating from him.

'No, I swear. Please, JS – he was my best friend.'

JS kept staring at him. He was perfectly still, his hands a few centimetres apart on the table. 'Keep talking.'

Walker exhaled, struggling to calm down and gather his thoughts. The Colonel had looked about to hit him. 'Whoever did it – they took your brother's computer. They were after DeepShare, and that's why they hurt him. I think DM tried to resist; you know how important Omega was to him.'

'Too important, I often thought.' His voice dropped lower, the anger even more apparent. 'Was it an obsession with you, too?'

Walker fumbled with his cigarettes, trying to gain some time. 'Do you mind if we step outside?' He wanted to be nearer the car, where he might be able to get away if things turned sour.

'We're not going anywhere, Scott. Not until you've explained yourself.'

JS was too smart to pull off something like that. Walker slumped back, his cigarettes forgotten. 'I didn't care that much about Omega,' he lied. 'It was DM's dream, not mine. You know he had great plans for it, something much bigger than Dorfmann, or money.'

'Maybe *you* changed your mind.'

Walker sighed. He looked around the bar and noticed that one of the truckers was glancing at them. He lowered his voice. 'Please. I only helped him because I was intrigued. DM must have told you I was sick of trading and banks, that I was even thinking of getting out.'

The Colonel nodded slowly, the tension in his eyes relaxing a little. 'Yes. He spoke a lot about you, when he wasn't going on about that damn machine.'

'We were basically done, JS. That's why he was pushing himself so hard...' Walker's voice caught, and he sipped the vodka and tonic.

'What about the hard drugs the police told me about? Is it a lie as well?'

'Of course. They were planted.'

A pause. 'Really?'

Walker wondered if he could hear relief in the man's voice. He finished his drink and rushed through the story of the last two days – what he thought had happened, and why, trying not to leave anything out. JS listened in silence, never interrupting him, his eyes narrowing again as he heard some of what had been done to DM. When Walker had finished the Colonel shook his head and shuffled to the bar, returning with a tall whiskey glass. He swallowed half of it and shuddered, his hands going up to his face and staying there, for a long time. In the end his hands dropped back to the table, and he exhaled and looked away.

'I didn't believe him,' he whispered.

'What?'

'For the last few weeks DM had been telling me that someone was after him, that he was afraid.'

'Did he say who?' Walker sat forward, relief and tiredness almost overwhelming him.

'He thought it was that investment bank, Frankel Schwartz. I said he was doing too many drugs.'

'That's what I told him, too.' Walker choked, struggled to concentrate.

'He... he's always been a little paranoid, and I...' The Colonel breathed out and wiped his eyes. 'I wasn't there for him.'

'You can't blame yourself. What happened is madness – out of this world. But I'm going to try and make sure that whoever did this will pay. Did DM tell you anything else?'

'I know he trusted you,' he said sadly. 'He always said you were our lost third brother, somehow.'

'Do *you* believe me?'

'I guess... Yes, I do, now.' JS took another sip of his whiskey and continued. 'DM said he would find proof and show me. He was going to use DeepShare against them. Do you have any idea what that means?'

'Maybe. But I can't get into the program.' Walker paused, steeling himself before asking the question that could shape his fate. 'The Omega servers are hidden, and your brother made it too secure. Do you know where the access codes are?'

The Colonel picked up his rucksack and placed it on the table. He unzipped an internal pocket, pulled out a small tablet computer and handed it over.

'DM gave me this a few months ago, for safekeeping. He told me to hide it at the military base – apparently it's the twin of the one he was always carrying around. I know he would have wanted you to have it.'

'Thanks.' Walker took it and turned it on, waiting for the screen to come to life. 'I can't believe he's gone. I miss him.'

A tear ran down JS's cheek. 'The world will miss him. DM was special.'

The tablet pinged, red icons blinking before a few words materialized on the screen. 'Welcome to DeepShare – Omega Version 3.2.'

Walker bit on his tongue and signalled to the barman for another drink. *Now I have a chance.*

...

Walker finished the coffee sitting in front of him and glanced at his watch. It was well past one in the morning and JS had fallen silent, staring at a spot on the far wall.

Walker was loath to disturb him, but he needed to be back in Lugano, planning a way into Italy. He cleared his throat and the Colonel focused back on him, eyes suddenly sharp again.

'So you think Frankel Schwartz is going to come after you?'

'If it's really them, yes. But I'm going to make it hard for anyone to find me.'

'What about the police? If someone's trying to frame you...'

'I have to get a new passport, fast, but I have money and an idea of where to go. It will take a lot of work before I can understand and use Omega properly – I'm nowhere near as good as DM. I'll need time and a quiet place.'

'Italy?'

'Yes.'

'How are you going to get through the border? Interpol must have signalled your name across Europe by now.'

'I don't know yet. I might have to just risk it.'

'Nonsense – from what you told me, you were lucky enough in Geneva...' JS picked up his rucksack and gestured. 'Come with me.'

He paid the bill and looked at the truckers at the table, who had also stood up. They both saluted him and he nodded at them, returning the gesture. '*Danke, Soldaten.*'

'A pleasure, Colonel,' they replied in German.

Walker stared at them for a second, finally realising how close to the abyss he'd been. And not for the last time, he guessed. He followed JS out of the bar with a weary shrug, refusing to feel daunted. A large black Mercedes with military plates was parked near Luigi's Range Rover.

'Do you need anything from your car?' asked JS.

'No. Where are we going?'

'There's a military border pass into Italy less than two hours away.' JS pointed at his uniform. 'I'll take you through; no one is going to stop us if you're with me.'

'Are you sure?'

'Of course. Your friend can pick up his Range Rover tomorrow; I'll drive you to Lake Como and then you can make your way to Milan, or wherever you want to go. What do you think?'

'That's great.' Walker stepped nearer and opened the car door. 'Thank you JS, you've given me a lifeline.'

'Just make sure those bastards get caught. For DM, for all of us.'

...

The Swiss highways lay quiet as the car rolled up and down low mountains, whizzing through the myriad tunnels that dotted the Alps. JS drove silently, lost in his own thoughts, and Walker concentrated on the next step now that he had access to DeepShare. It was past two in the morning when they neared Italy and he decided to call Luigi.

'Yo, is everything all right?' The broker's voice was alert; obviously he hadn't gone to bed yet.

'Yes. The Colonel had the codes, and he's taking me through the border into Como. How's Layla?'

'A bit better. Ah, wait, here she comes.' There was a crackling noise as Luigi passed over the phone.

'Scott, what's up?'

'Slight change of plan. How are you feeling?'

'I'm not dead yet.'

'Can you meet me in Italy tomorrow morning? You'll need to get on a train from Lugano to Milan, and bring my stuff.'

'I'm not sure it's a good idea. I want to...'

Luigi took the call back and put it on speakerphone. 'She looks like a ghost. A sick ghost.'

'I can imagine – Layla, I have no idea what you want to do...'

'Exactly.'

'But fainting your way to Spain, or Mexico, or wherever...'

Luigi came on. 'I've spoken to the doctor – he will be waiting for us in Sassari.'

Layla sighed, audibly. 'Okay, I'll do it,' she groaned. 'But then I go my own way.'

Walker smiled. 'No one will stop you.'

'Nobody would dare to try,' Luigi chuckled.

Minutes later JS parked the car and radioed ahead to let the military guards know he was coming through on urgent business. When the army Mercedes reached the pass they were whisked through without a second glance, a lone soldier saluting them both on the Swiss and Italian side.

Walker breathed a little more easily as they drove down the steep hills and reached Como in less than half an hour. JS parked near the train station, where a few taxis worked the night shift. He got out and hugged Walker, then shook his hand, trying to hold it together.

'What should I tell the police, if they ask me about you?'

Walker thought for a second. 'Say we've spoken, and that you think I might be hiding somewhere in the UK.'

'I will do. Be careful, Scott.'

'You too. I don't know what these guys might be planning next.'

'Don't worry, I live in a top-secret Swiss army base. I'll be fine.'

…

The sick old man closed the phone and lay back, considering. His feet ached abominably with the ghost pain of the recent amputation and he cursed his doctors, though he had ordered them to do anything just to give him some extra time. He told himself pain was only a companion, a recent friend who would keep him sharp until he was no more.

His eyes drifted around the room, ignoring all the monstrous machines that kept him alive and coming to a stop on the original Van Gogh painting hanging in front of the bed. He stared at the amazing self-portrait, the work of a man obviously losing his mind, and he idly wondered what madness would feel like. Then he shrugged and reached for a glass of water, his hand too slow for his impatient brain.

The old man sighed: the recordings were good, but not good enough to bring down the whole house of cards. He needed more, but even if resources were not an issue, time was. Exhausted, he closed his eyes, praying to have just a little longer. A few more weeks, and his penance could start.

Then he could die a happy man.

Milano

Milan's Stazione Centrale was a hulking monster built in Mussolini's time as proof of Italy's greatness. Its Art-Deco style was mixed haphazardly with concrete and chalk to form a monumental building that was a lot cheaper and shakier than it looked. The perfect metaphor for Italy, then and now, Walker decided.

He slipped through the crowds of the morning rush, looking for a display that showed which track he would need to wait by. Layla was travelling on the 7.11 train from Lugano, and he was early. He had found a cheap room to rest in for a few hours after the taxi ride, but his sleep had been wrecked by nightmares and he had soon given up, deciding to stroll through town as he waited for the night to end.

Milan looked a lot worse than the city where he had spent a wonderful year during university. Its wide boulevards and ancient palaces slouched dirty and unkempt. Even the mighty Duomo Cathedral seemed but a shadow of itself, scaffolding semi-abandoned on a botched clean-up of the facade as the government's money had ran out. He half-wondered how much he had contributed to the decay, though it was a ridiculous thought. Most of the damage in Italy was self-inflicted, by its insane political system and the heavy bureaucracy, though Finance and central bankers certainly hadn't helped. Still, it was the sort of thing DeepShare could help with in the future, just as DM had dreamed – maybe even stop the country going down the drain for good when the next crisis hit. If Walker somehow managed to stay alive and out of jail.

Trying to rub the tiredness from his eyes, he found the station coffee shop and ordered a cappuccino and a jam pastry, his stomach rumbling in anticipation. As he waited at the bar he scanned the room, his skin tingling with uneasiness. Though they still attempted to look elegant, a lot of Italians around him were shabbily dressed, in scuffed shoes and worn jackets that in the past would have been thrown away without a thought, especially in Milan. Almost half the customers in the bar were African or Eastern-European, and they seemed in even worse shape than the Italians. A couple immediately approached him, begging for change as he paid for his breakfast. He left them a few coins and finished the steaming cappuccino before checking his watch again – the train was due in five minutes.

Walker slipped out of the bar and hurried to track eleven, his mind in overdrive. Was Layla going to make it, or had she been stopped at the border? Maybe she had fainted again, or decided to leave at some other station... An unpleasant feeling of helplessness coursed through his veins. Though unwell, Layla had proved in the past how resourceful she could be. And now she was carrying over three–hundred thousand bucks of his money. Was she going to steal from him again?

The train rumbled into the station and Walker swore at himself, trying to calm down.

Within a few seconds the doors of the carriages opened and a dozen people came out. One old man had to be helped by a conductor, and a pregnant lady struggled while carrying a young baby girl. The train was only six wagons long, and mostly empty. In less then two minutes all the passengers were gone.

Layla was nowhere to be seen.

I can't fucking believe this. Where the hell is the bitch?

He started walking along the track to check whether she was still inside when a hand tapped him on the shoulder. Walker spun round, ready to throw a punch, but stopped just in time.

'Got you again.' Layla smiled, raising her hands. 'I think I'm too good for you.'

'You probably are,' he groaned. He studied her face – she looked tired, but in better shape than the previous night. At least she wasn't fainting. 'I'm sorry, I was just a little nervous.'

'About what?'

She looked at him and he shrugged. 'Oh God, you thought I was going to run with the money.'

'It crossed my mind.'

'Asshole.' Layla turned on her heel and walked away. 'Where's the train we are supposed to take, before I change my mind and drop you right here?' she hissed.

Walker caught up, pointing towards a nearby track. 'Come on, you *are* a thief.'

'And you are a goddamned banker. I'm not sure what's worse.'

Tirrenia

The second-class cabin on the ferry from Genoa to Sardinia was cramped and rusty, but at least the ship was massive, the sea calm and the evening clear. Walker placed their bags on the floor and glanced at Layla, who was already sprawled on the lower bunk bed. She had been fading during their train journey from Milan, becoming quieter as time passed.

'How are you holding up?' he said.

She grimaced, one hand going up to her shoulder. 'I've been better.'

Walker helped her out of her jumper and started unwinding the tight gauze, noticing it had turned a pallid pink. Layla's entire upper arm was swollen and tender. He touched around the wound and she moaned, then asked him in a low voice, 'Is it bad?'

'I think you'll lose the hand.'

'Go to hell.' She lay back and closed her eyes.

Walker shrugged and rummaged in his rucksack, finding his tablet. When he returned to the bed she was already half-asleep. Which was perfect; he had time to get some work done. He left the cabin, locking the door to go in search of some quick food and a drink, his mind buzzing with plans for the next few days.

...

Walker put down his coffee cup and readjusted his chair, brushing a few crumbs away from the old wooden table. He glanced about but no one seemed to be looking at him.

He turned on the tablet and fired up DeepOmega, digging into the latest financial markets events. After about an hour it became clear that the machine had picked up a scent and was forecasting serious trouble for a large pharmaceutical conglomerate in the US. Exactly the sort of thing he needed to make the hook more appetizing for his old schoolmate. He quickly typed a message to Mosha, explaining what he expected to happen to the company and giving him Deep's target for the share price, before saying he would be in touch again after the events. *I wonder if he's gone to the police already.* Probably not – Mosha's hedge fund was in trouble, and he would be loath to attract attention to himself. This should give the big Serb further room for thought.

After sending the message, Walker returned to their cabin to check on Layla. The room was dark and stuffy and he could hear her murmuring in her sleep. He sat on the bed and swore in a low voice – her fever had not broken and the bedsheets were drenched in sweat. He grabbed some medicines and gave her a sip of water, his hand stroking her hair.

'I'm cold,' she whispered.

'I know.' He lay down next to her and Layla snuggled into him, pressing her body against his warmth. She shivered and her breathing slowed as she drifted back to sleep. He readjusted himself and hugged her closer, then he closed his eyes and tried to switch off, his body exhausted and battered by the lack of sleep and continuous tension of the last seventy-two hours. What felt like minutes later he woke with a start as Layla pushed hard against him, trying to sit up on the bed. He realised she was in the middle of a fever-dream and tried to restrain her, whispering against her hair. She groaned and fought him with unexpected strength, before lying back and speaking in a low voice, her disconnected words almost unintelligible in a sleepy Spanish. 'No puedo... Capitan, no es possible...'

Walker half-rolled her, holding her closer. She tried to turn back, leaning on her wounded arm and moaning in pain. Then she mumbled something, her voice too low for him to understand, until she shuddered and half-shouted, 'Rafa, no!'

She sobbed and her legs jerked, almost throwing him off. '...Rafael, lo siento mi amor.' *I'm sorry, my love.* Tears ran down her cheeks as she wept without waking. Walker dried them with his fingers and kissed the top of her head, not knowing what to do.

Who the hell is Rafa?

Mercifully she soon calmed down and fell into a deeper sleep, almost unmoving. He sighed and lay back, wondering what he was missing and praying the next few hours of the trip would rush by.

...

Walker's watch woke him later, to a sliver of light shining through the cabin porthole. He checked on Layla – she was now resting peacefully, her fever gone, but Porto Torres was less than thirty minutes away. He stroked her hair to wake her and handed her a drink, which she sipped, grimacing. She looked scruffy and beautiful and fragile, younger than her twenty-nine years.

'Where are we?' she croaked.

'Almost there. Do you want me to get you any breakfast?'

Layla shrugged and stood up unsteadily, clasping the top bunk for support. 'No. And you don't need to watch over me all the time. I'm not a child, I can take care of myself.'

'I'm sure you can. But you're hurt, now.'

'It's little more than a scratch. I've dealt with worse.' Layla glared at him.

Walker chuckled and grabbed a couple of thick pills from his bag. The ferry rumbled and swayed and she lost her footing, stumbling. He caught her in his arms, leaning against the door to keep balanced. 'Are you sure? You look like you could do with something in your belly.'

'Do painkillers count as food?'

'Probably not.' He passed her the medicines and she sat back down, drained.

'Okay, maybe a croissant,' she sighed. 'Thanks.'

Walker grinned. 'Don't go anywhere.'

CHAPTER TEN

Sardinia

Luigi Seu had flown to Sardinia the night before and was already waiting in his rented car at Porto Torres when Walker and Layla disembarked. He loaded them in a little Fiat 500 and drove off at speed, heading for the bigger town of Sassari, only about twenty minutes away. Layla sat in the back of the tiny car, half-slumped, her eyes closed. Walker glanced at Luigi, who was accelerating like a madman along the small country lanes, and grimaced. 'Thank God we're off that damn ship. Layla is exhausted, and she needs the doctor.'

'She does look in bits,' the broker said in Italian before smiling at him. 'But even now she's still stunning.'

'You should have seen her at the Dancing Snake.'

'Better not, I might still have nightmares about it,' Luigi said, offering Walker a cigarette. 'I can see why you fell for it.'

'Me too.'

Walker opened the window a touch and lit the Marlboro. The weather was still very warm, and the sun shone bright and harsh on the Mediterranean scrub that infested the island. The roads were almost empty, as the ferry had been. Not a lot of tourists visiting, he guessed.

'How did your brother get on this summer?' Walker knew that Paolo Seu was a skipper; he owned a small yacht for wealthy people to go deep-sea fishing or to explore the myriad caves and stunning little bays of Sardinia's northern coast. Paolo would whisk tourists around tiny islands and coves for a few days, sometimes all the way into French Corsica.

'It was quiet. Too quiet, really. Paolo said that people don't want to spend, or to be seen spending.'

'Even in Porto Cervo? That's a first.'

'Yes. It's been a disaster.'

'Is he going to be okay?' Luigi's younger brother still had a large loan to repay on his boat. And no savings.

'Hopefully. He's had to expand the *side* business, though.'

'Tell him he wants to be careful with that.' Paolo's secondary activity, as Walker had discovered during a particularly *intense* holiday, consisted in importing light drugs from Corsica into Italy. He had been doing it for years – but just as an amateur, and in small quantities, mainly through old friends. 'Harder stuff?'

'No, no. Thank God. Just more of the same, and more often. A guy he knows has connections to the Sicilians.'

'That's no good.'

'Well, they are the ones who'll find you a new passport.'

'Seriously?' Walker glanced at Luigi, who had a grim smile. He finished his cigarette and closed the car window. Layla was snoring lightly in the back. 'That's just what I need now, a Mafia debt.'

'Mmh. We'll see them after dropping Layla off, and you can make your mind up. Hopefully they'll just be happy with cash – but they want to meet you. In person.' Luigi skidded into a couple of turns, speeding the car past a shabby suburb on the outskirts of Sassari. 'Later, though. We're almost at the surgery now.'

They turned off the main road and slowed down through 1960s state-housing blocks that were slowly falling apart, with windows broken and doors ajar. Paint was peeling from the walls and a few children played in a rundown basketball court next to a mountain of garbage.

Walker held his breath, shocked. He hadn't visited Sassari for a few years, remaining on the touristy Costa Smeralda towns where the great hotels and restaurants catered to the in-crowd. But now it dawned on him how the rest of Sardinia had seemingly slid out of the Western world, into a netherland of broken towns and unemployment.

Luigi parked the car outside a dilapidated four-storey building just as Layla stirred. She sat up and stretched, her eyes bright. 'God, I'm tired,' she yawned.

'Just a couple of minutes now.'

'Okay.' She rotated her shoulder, wincing. 'So, how well do you know this doctor, Luigi?'

'He was at school with my dad, and they have been friends for forty years. Besides, he needs the money.'

'Why?'

'Divorce. And a malpractice lawsuit from when he was a surgeon.'

Layla groaned. 'That sounds reassuring...'

...

A few minutes later they met the doctor, an old man with a short white beard. His study was on the fourth floor of a low tower block and it certainly had seen better days, but it still looked almost clean, if sparse, with some medical instruments and a scale waiting by a narrow hospital cot. The surgeon also spoke some English, which was a bonus. After a quick introduction the two men left Layla in his care and returned to the car. Luigi fired up the engine and turned the Fiat around. 'So, are you ready for the Sicilians?' he asked.

Walker thought for a second. He could imagine a thousand other things that he'd rather do. Including a lot of unpleasant ones. 'Not really. Isn't there another way?'

'It's the only one I can think of. Especially since you need the damn passport fast. And they are fast, I'm told. Too much, sometimes.'

'That's fucking awesome,' Walker swore. 'Can we really trust them?'

'It's the Mafia. What do you think?'

'Great.' Walker sighed and stared out of the window, without really seeing the roads rush by. All he could think of was DM's broken face, and the droplets of blood planted in his flat. 'Okay, let's try it. What could possibly go wrong?'

Luigi shrugged back at him. 'My brother thinks they're reasonable.'

'Remind me to have a chat with him, when this shit is over.'

The Italian smiled and drove on, along the state road past Sassari, heading for the gorgeous resort of Alghero, a small medieval walled town on a finger of land surrounded by the sea. 'We are meeting them at the port, docking bay 57.'

Walker nodded and remained silent, wondering what he was getting himself into. Probably nothing as bad as the mess he'd already fallen in. Probably.

…

Bay 57 sat at the farthest end of the tourist harbour. The season was late and most boats and small yachts were covered in tarps, rain-stained and abandoned for a while. Walker and Luigi hurried through the narrow plank-ways, checking behind and around to see if anyone was following them. They soon turned onto a smaller dock, where most bays were empty. The last spot near the harbour was the only one taken, by a sleek four-seater speedboat bobbing in the placid water. Its tall, muscular pilot saw them coming and disembarked from the helm, putting on large sunglasses the same colour as his lifejacket while he waited. Walker shivered, trying to ignore his bad feelings.

'Hi,' Luigi said. 'We are –'

'Is this the guy your brother spoke of?' The pilot cut him off in a strong Sicilian accent.

'Yes.'

He nodded to Walker. 'Get in the boat. We'll take a short trip.'

Luigi moved first but the guy raised his hand, shoving him back. 'Not you, Seu. Just your friend.'

'But...'

'My rules, or you can just get the fuck outta here.'

Walker bit his tongue, swore and stepped forward, taking Luigi's arm. 'It's all right, mate. I'll go alone.' *Shit. What's next?*

The broker hesitated, then nodded. 'Are you sure?'

'Yeah. And do me a favour while I'm gone...' Walker tried to sound more confident than he felt, and almost managed to stop his voice shaking. 'I'll... need a couple of old phones and SIMs. And two laptops – can you take care of it?'

'Of course, but...'

The pilot interrupted him again. 'Sorry, fags – we've gotta be going. Seu, you can wait for your boyfriend at the bus station, later. Now piss off.' He shoved Walker, pushing him towards the boat, then un-moored the small four-seater and jumped on at the helm. Luigi turned around, gave them a worried backwards glance and headed towards the port gates.

'What's your name?' Walker asked as he struggled with the seatbelt.

'My friends call me Salvo. You shouldn't call me. Or talk to me. At all.'

Great. Walker slumped back in his seat, feeling powerless. The boat accelerated quickly, its engine throbbing in a loud bass tone. They approached the open sea and Salvo turned around, digging into a large plastic box at the back.

'Where are we going?'

'Do you know Neptune's Grotto?'

Walker scoured through his memory. He had been there once with Luigi. Neptune's Grotto was tourist heaven, a stunning part-underwater cave a few miles to the west, at the foot of the Capo Caccia cliffs. He remembered an amazing place of eerie sounds and spectral depths, a large cavern dotted with thousands of stalactites and stalagmites. 'Yes, I've seen it before.'

'Good. We're going nowhere near that,' Salvo said. 'Now shut the fuck up and wear this.' He threw Walker a heavy cotton sack dyed a dark shade of brown, covered in yellowish stains.

'How?'

'Just stick it over your fat head, and pull it down to your hips. If I catch you peeping, I'll throw you overboard. After I've shot you.'

Walker swore, but the look of menace on Salvo's thin face convinced him not to try anything stupid. He sighed and slipped the sack over his head, then lower down. It stank of rotten fish and something worse, and he almost gagged.

Time slowed and seemed to stop. Without any reference points he tried to keep track of their turns in the water but soon lost count, struggling not to throw up as the boat rocked up and down, quicker at first, then maintaining what felt like excessive speed. After an eternity the pilot eventually slowed down and Walker sat up straighter, the adrenaline starting to course through his veins. He knew there was a big chance that he would not make it back alive.

The speedboat slowed further, then ground up against some beach, rocking from side to side. Rough hands pulled the sack from Walker's head and he blinked in the harsh light, trying to get his bearings. A new man, taller and heavier, helped him off the stern into shallow water while Salvo splashed around the other side. Walker stumbled onto a small sandy beach, almost choking in the fresh air, then turned and found himself staring into the barrel of a large gun in Salvo's hand.

'Are you going to kill me now?' He stood up straighter, not wanting to give them the satisfaction of seeing his fear.

Salvo and the new thug shrugged. 'Only if the boss says so. Now move.' Salvo pointed with the gun to a narrow opening in the cliff-face and Walker stepped forward, with the two Sicilians just behind. The opening turned into an even smaller passage and he had to twist on one side, his back scraping the rocks as he walked crab-like into the darkness. After slipping past a couple of doglegs he emerged into a wider space, a tall cavern lit by a couple of arc-lights. In the corner, near a pool of translucent water, an older, bearded man waited behind a huge desk. Computers and files were scattered over the dark-wood surface and the man stood, grinning.

'Ah, the mysterious Englishman. Or Italian. We're not quite sure.'

Walker nodded, without replying. He could feel the two thugs a few steps behind him, and the last time he had risked a glance Salvo was still pointing the gun at his back. *How do I get out of this?* He thought of Layla and Luigi, hoping they would be all right.

'You don't talk much, do you?' the bearded man asked.

'Why am I here?'

The man grabbed something from his desk and pointed it at Walker's face. 'Salvo?'

'Yes, Capo.'

Walker grimaced, tensing, but it was only a strange-looking camera, attached to some cable. The flash stung his eyes and he shook his head, trying to clear his vision. Someone shuffled behind him and he felt a hard object press into the back of his neck, just below the base of his skull.

'Don't move a muscle,' Salvo whispered in his ear.

'What... what do you want?'

The Capo tapped a few keys on his computer and glanced back up, smiling. 'You see, we don't like it when strange people come asking for fake documents. You could be anyone, my friend. An undercover idiot from Rome, the DEA... your precious Scotland Yard.'

Walker sighed, fought to keep still. 'I'm not.'

'We'll find out – now.' The Capo stared at his screen, and waited.

Minutes ticked by and Walker shifted his weight from one foot to the other, his legs beginning to cramp. Salvo slid the gun an inch to the right, resting its muzzle behind his ear and pushing his head forward a little. 'I told you not to move,' he whispered roughly. 'My finger could slip.'

Walker tried to ignore the cold steel and concentrated on the desk, staring at some files. He forced himself to think and stay cool – it was the only thing that might keep him alive. His nose itched and he could feel a drop of sweat about to slide into his eye. The gun shifted a quarter of an inch, and Salvo's breathing rumbled in his ear.

The Capo finally nodded, picking up a pair of small reading glasses. He leaned forward, studying something on his monitor. After a while he smiled and straightened, then took the long way around his desk, coming to stand a few steps in front of Walker. 'Interpol has put out a search for you, Mr Scott Walker. You're wanted in London, they say.'

Walker nodded, slowly, making sure not to startle Salvo.

'What did you do?'

'Someone is trying to frame me for murder.'

The Capo's smile widened. 'Of course. We're all innocent here, ain't we, boys?' He gestured to the men behind him and Salvo laughed, the gun dropping away from the back of Walker's neck.

'What else is involved, Scott? Drugs – a woman maybe?'

Walker breathed out, feeling dizzy. 'No. I... the victim was my best friend. I would never have hurt him.'

'Of course. And I think I believe you, a little.' The Capo slipped back around his desk, sat down and shuffled a couple of files. 'So, since you're also a banker, apparently... How much can you afford to pay?'

Into the Mountains

Walker staggered into the bus station and a relieved-looking Luigi rushed to embrace him, steering him towards the small Fiat parked a few yards away.

'Thank God, I was so worried...'

Walker shook his head and lit a cigarette, his hands still unsteady. 'That was... unpleasant,' he croaked.

'What happened?'

'Forget it. And tell your brother to steer clear of those guys. But... they'll get me the passport.'

Luigi let it drop and jumped behind the wheel, starting the engine and almost crashing into an approaching bus. More near misses followed, not helping Walker's mood, but somehow they made it to Sassari and rushed up the old council block to find Layla sitting in the waiting room, chatting in Spanish to the doctor who had apparently spent a few years in Argentina, hence his divorce. Layla looked tired and her face was pale, but her eyes had regained a bit of sparkle. Both she and the doctor stood up when Walker and Luigi entered, and the doctor smiled happily.

'We're done!' he said in English, then handed Layla a brown bag and continued in Italian to Walker. 'I've given her a painkilling shot and a strong antibiotic. Now it's injections for five days, and lots of rest. The infection is ongoing and she needs her strength to fight it off.'

Walker paid and thanked him. He discovered his voice had returned to a steady tone, and asked, 'Anything to keep an eye on?'

'If the wound turns a darker shade of red or she still has a temperature in two days, call me.' The surgeon produced a crumpled business card and left them, returning to his surgery.

Layla studied the pair of them, clearly noticing how edgy they were. 'All good?'

Walker nodded. 'You're cleared. I just had an interesting couple of hours, that's all. You ready to go?'

'I guess. So what did you do that was so interesting? And did you get everything?'

'Yes. But I'll tell you in the car – we still have a long trip, and I'd be happier if you were still under the effect of the painkillers.'

'Me too, especially if you plan on driving like most Italians.'

...

After saying good-bye to Luigi, Walker took the rented little Fiat from the outskirts of Sassari onto the ring road around town, and south to the mountainous heart of Sardinia. Traffic thinned out and soon they were alone on cracked tarmac. Layla glanced behind as he was driving, checking out the large cardboard box in the back of the car.

'What's that?' she asked.

'A small printer/scanner, a netbook for you and my new laptop, a top-of-the-range Sony monster.'

'For DeepShare?'

'Yes. While you get better, I'll use it to see if there's anything we can do to sort this mess out.'

'And then?'

'In a few days you should be able to go, I guess,' Walker glanced at her. 'You're a free woman with a plan, remember?'

'What about you?'

He didn't have the faintest idea. He exhaled, struggling to sound a lot more in control than he felt. 'It depends on what DeepOmega finds. There's a guy I'm trying to bring in to help, but it's going to take a while, I think. He's an old acquaintance, and if I can convince him... let's just say he could bring along some serious firepower.'

'Firepower, like guns?'

'Money. He controls mountains of it.'

'Oh, God. Another banker?'

Walker grinned. 'Worse. Hedge-fund manager, a particularly greedy one.'

'Nice.' Layla sipped some water and stared out of the window. The terrain was changing from coastal shrub to low rolling hills, a few cloud-topped mountains barely visible on the horizon. 'Where are we going?'

'Sadali.'

'What's that?'

'A place I've always wanted to visit. My great-grandmother came from there, and my mom used to tell me stories about how isolated and old-fashioned it's always been. Very pretty, apparently.' And a world away from banks and killers, he hoped.

'Will anyone know you?' Layla sounded unconvinced, and he tried to soothe her.

'No, of course not. It's almost abandoned now, just old people and a couple of bed-and-breakfast hotels.' Walker pointed at the rough hills they were driving through. 'This entire part of Sardinia has become a ghost region in the last thirty years. Younger people have moved on to the big cities, or to the rest of Italy, to find jobs.'

'It sounds lovely,' she deadpanned.

'It is. We'll find somewhere romantic.' He glanced at her and winked. 'Maybe a well-hidden Agriturismo, one of those small family-run hotels that infest this poor island.'

She groaned, refusing to look at him. 'Is this Sadali far?'

'Maybe three hours.'

'Okay.' She leaned back, lowering her seat a few inches. 'God, I'm tired. Can you wake me when we get there, please? I want to check the place out first.' She closed her eyes, then reopened them for a second. 'Won't we need documents for the room?'

Walker shrugged. 'Probably. But a few hundred euros should do it – I'm sure we're not the first couple they see, wanting to keep a little secret.'

'Couple?'

'Just try and look fond of me. You've managed it before.'

'I'll see what I can do.'

Interlude 4

'This is a fucking disaster.' The American's voice sounded angry, and scared.

The Englishman fought to keep calm, though he was boiling inside. 'Listen, I told you it was better to wait. The plan we had in place...'

'There was no time for it – not since the Australian goon killed the mathematician. What are you going to do now?'

'Wait. They'll surface again.' The Englishman sighed. 'Security cameras, money laundering – we have entire investment bank compliance teams looking for them. And Blackspring. Walker will make a mistake, or be seen, and then we'll get him.'

'What about the UK police?'

'They are clueless, as ever. And even if they grab him first... It'll be easy enough to cut a deal – and take DeepShare from him.'

'Maybe. Do you still trust Blackspring?'

'We don't really have a choice any more,' the Englishman said.

The American was silent for a second before conceding, 'No, I guess not.'

'Don't worry. He can't hide forever.'

The Englishman cut the connection and returned to his computer, studying the security company files. He was reasonably certain of where Walker could have gone from Reims, but although Switzerland was a small country, it was proving difficult to locate him. He stood and paced the office for a few seconds, uncertain. Then he sighed, deciding to make a few confidential, dangerous phone calls. The American was proving to be an idiot, but he did have a point – time was running short.

Sadali

The *Agriturismo* was a small barn that someone had converted into self-catering apartments a generation earlier, before deciding to forget about it. An old lady with wispy hair greeted them at what passed for the reception: a cubbyhole she entered from a side door leading to some sort of kitchen swimming in the smell of cabbage and old goats. The place looked near crumbling, but it sat alone near the top of a high hill, reachable only by a dirt track that ran for a few miles from the dilapidated centre of Sadali into the low mountains of the Gennargentu. It was perfect for them.

Walker smiled at the ancient woman, Miss Sanna, struggling to understand what she was saying in a thick Sardinian accent, her vowels clumping together until they all resembled the U's of an upset canine.

'That's great,' he said, interrupting her before she realised he had no idea what she was talking about. 'And we'll need it for a week, maybe a little longer.'

The old lady nodded eagerly and her eyes glinted. Walker wondered when she had last seen out-of-season clients.

'Certainly. And I can give you the best apartment – for just an extra ten Euros a day. No breakfast, but there is a small kitchen in the flat.'

'Wonderful.' Walker pulled out a wad of money and counted out five hundred Euros, almost twice the quoted rate for a week. 'I'm afraid I've lost my ID, though. Can I bring it over when I get the new one?'

Miss Sanna's eyes widened and she glanced at Layla, a slow smile forming on her lips. 'But of course, Mr...'

'Anconetani, Romeo Anconetani.'

'Signor *Romeo*.' The smile widened. 'And the young lady's name?'

Walker handed her the cash, which immediately disappeared into an old chest by the door. 'Juliette,' he answered.

'Naturally.'

Walker ignored her tone. 'And – is there a phone line in the flat?'

'I'm afraid it's broken. But I can call my nephew...'

He glanced at Layla, who shrugged. 'No, that's fine. We just got married and...'

The old lady nodded. 'Don't worry, you are not the first –' she broke off, coughing – 'newlyweds who stay with us. I understand.' She shuffled around the low counter and grabbed a key. 'You can park in front of the room, if you want. Follow me.'

They left the side building and walked around the ivy-shrouded stone walls to a large oak door that wouldn't have looked out of place in a medieval castle. The flat was on the second floor, reached by a musty staircase that creaked and groaned. There was a small bedroom dwarfed by a four-poster bed, a larger living room with a corner kitchen, and a cracked table next to four mismatched chairs.

Miss Sanna drew the curtains and opened the window to let some evening air in; Walker noticed a couple of wide damp stains on the walls and ceiling, paint peeling around the edges. The place was a dump but the view from the window was magnificent, down into the mist-shrouded valleys and hills that rolled towards the distant Mediterranean Sea.

Layla looked around the bedroom and sat on the bed with a sigh, turning to the old lady. '*E' bellissima, grazie*,' she said in pitch-perfect Italian before lying back. Walker stared at her, impressed, and glanced at Miss Sanna.

'Great, we'll take it.'

Her eyes lit up. 'Wonderful! And if you need anything...'

'Do you stay here at night?'

'No, I go back into town at seven. But you can head to the Bar Sport in Sadali in case of emergencies – my nephew owns it. Also, the mini-supermarket there is open on Tuesdays and Fridays. And tomorrow they'll have the fresher stuff, from the big city.' The old lady glanced around the room almost jealously before heading out. 'Have a good time, lovebirds.'

Walker locked the door behind her and returned to the bed. Layla had sat back up and was trying to shrug out of her jumper without moving her wounded arm too much. He went to help her and checked the bandage – the gauze was dry, showing only a few small pink stains.

'How are you feeling?'

'It hurts. But I guess that's just the anaesthetic wearing off.'

'I'm sure. Let me go and get our bags, it's time for another injection anyway. Are you hungry?'

'Not really, but thanks.' She yawned, laying back on the wool blanket. 'I'm just exhausted right now.'

'Get into bed. I'll move the car and bring in the luggage.'

When Walker returned Layla was already in her underwear, propped up against a pillow, her long naked legs crossed on top of an old quilt. She smiled at him as he carried their equipment into the bedroom, almost dropping one of the computer boxes.

'I don't have any PJs.'

Walker grunted. 'You can borrow one of my shirts.' He stared at her for a second. 'Are you trying to distract me?'

'Is it working?'

'Yes.' He unzipped his rucksack and threw her a brand new T-shirt he had picked up with Luigi while they waited for the laptops to be ready.

'Thanks. Do you snore?' She sat up straighter and unhooked her bra. 'Ah yes, of course you do.'

Walker tried to keep his eyes on her face. 'Only when people drug me unconscious.' He gave up and turned around, rummaging through the bags for the medicines. 'Don't worry, I'll sleep on the sofa.'

'That dirty old thing? Nonsense.' Layla smiled. 'You can look now, I'm decent again.'

Walker found some disposable syringes and filled two, one with antibiotics and the other with painkillers. He joined her on the bed and shuffled closer as she presented her healthy arm. She looked at him dubiously. 'Can you give injections?'

'I did a paramedic course during my Italian army service.'

She whistled. 'More hidden talents, Mr Scott.'

'It was compulsory, at the time.' He drove the needle into her shoulder, not carefully.

'Ouch!'

'And it was over fifteen years ago.'

'You could have told me earlier.'

'I guess.' Walker smiled, preparing the second needle. 'I didn't know you spoke Italian.'

'Just a few words... Ah!' Layla pulled back her arm and glowered at him. 'That hurt even more.'

'Sorry. You have a great accent.'

'I'm good with languages, apparently. And Italian and Spanish are quite close. I can understand most of it, though the Sardinians are very hard to get.'

Walker drew the curtains closed – the sun had just set and darkness was closing in. 'Don't worry, most Italians struggle with their accent too.' He turned around and saw that she had snuggled under the covers and was shivering. 'You okay?'

'Don't sleep on the sofa. I can defend myself if I need to.'

'I'll keep that in mind.' He switched off the light and headed to the living room, leaving the door slightly ajar. 'I'll set up the computers; you try and get some rest.'

'Okay, boss. Ciao.'

'Goodnight.'

...

Walker straightened his back and checked his watch; it was 2.47 a.m. and he had been slaving away for over five hours without a break. Layla had fallen asleep fast and had barely moved since, knocked out by the painkillers and heavy antibiotics. His stomach rumbled and he downed a glass of water, then took a sip from the large bottle of vodka he had bought in Sassari, trying to clear his mind of the myriad useless details that DeepShare was throwing at him with annoying regularity.

DM's tablet had given him complete access to the Omega server, and his new laptop was working like a dream but the software was complex and Walker was unfamiliar with lots of areas. And he knew very little of the search algorithms that had been his friend's real area of expertise. But at least there was already a Frankel file running: DM had been trying to trace them, to see if they were indeed the ones watching him.

In its Cyberspace haven, DeepOmega had been digging for weeks on a thorough search for the investment bank's footprints, producing an enormous amount of results. Too much, really – the data was just overwhelming, and Walker couldn't make sense of most of it. He knew he should rerun the algos through the preliminaries, to get Deep to filter them again and make the output usable. But he had no idea how to do it. The markets were obviously jittery about Frankel – its stock had dropped over ten per cent in a week. Still, there were no particular rumors online, aside from the usual...

Walker glanced around, a blaring noise breaking his concentration. He hurried to the window, checking outside from the edge of the curtain. The valley was deep in darkness, lit only by a sliver of moonshine. Suddenly a light flashed brightly from the direction of the dirt road that curved back to town, before disappearing again around a bend.

Walker caught his breath and he strained his eyes. A second light popped up just behind the first one, followed by a loud roar. A truck? *No – motorbikes.*

He turned and almost jumped out of his skin as Layla appeared from the bedroom, hair dishevelled from sleep. She immediately went to the computer and closed the laptop, plunging the room into darkness.

'Car?'

'Bikes. Two, I think.'

'Shit.' She checked around the room. 'Why didn't you get a weapon in Sassari?'

Walker searched the tiny kitchen and rummaged in the drawers, finding a couple of old steak knives. 'This is Italy, not the US. You can't just show up somewhere and buy a gun.'

He returned to the window and glanced outside. The motorbikes were getting closer, rounding the last turn in the road. The engine noise rose to a searing pitch just as Layla came over to take the blades. A shadow flashed past their window, darker than the night sky. They both recoiled, then realised it was only a bird scared by the clatter.

'Where's our car?'

Walker pointed down, just below their room. The old Fiat appeared from the gloom as the first bike turned into the dirt area in front of the converted barn, its headlight beam dancing around. He put up his hand, whispering, 'Wait.'

'Why?'

'They're making too much noise.'

The second bike approached the parking lot just as the first went into a spin, its back wheel sliding through the dirt and raising a cloud of dust. 'I think it might be just a couple of kids fooling around.'

Layla didn't reply. She slipped next to him and checked outside. The driver of the first bike stopped and jumped off with a shout, just as the second went for a wheelie near the reception. His carburetor popped loudly, sounding like a machine gun.

The riders wore no helmets and as the closest turned towards their window Walker glimpsed his pimply, late-adolescent face.

Thank you, God.

Layla sighed, dropped the knives to the floor and turned on the living room light while he swore, opening the curtains. A couple of seconds later one of the kids shouted something. Walker saw him rush back to his bike, pointing at their apartment. His friend swung around and within a few moments both of them had disappeared back towards Sadali.

Walker closed the heavy curtains and looked across the room, just as Layla was picking up his bottle.

'Vodka?' she asked, her voice shaken.

'Please.'

He brought her a glass and they shared a drink. Her eyes were swollen from sleep and her cheeks flushed. Walker exhaled and reopened his laptop, logging off DeepShare. 'That was unpleasant,' he grimaced.

'Very. Are you sure about this place?' Layla leant back on the table and he noticed that goosebumps pimpled her long legs.

'Nobody knows we're here. Look – it was only a couple of teenagers, and they're probably wetting their pants as we speak...' Walker tried to smile and lit a cigarette. 'We'll be fine, and I need some quiet time to work anyway.'

'Okay, I'll believe you,' she shrugged. 'But no more of these shenanigans while I sleep, please.'

'I promise.'

She glanced at his computer. 'Did you find anything?'

'Not yet.' He finished his drink, enjoying the burning sensation as the tension receded. His heartbeat still felt too fast and his head spun a little from the adrenaline. 'It's not going to be easy.'

Layla stepped nearer, looking into his eyes. 'Anything I can do to help?' She was very close, and her pupils seemed to sparkle.

Walker opened his arms just as her mouth came up and they kissed hard, their tongues entwining and probing. Her arms rose to his neck and she let her body slide into him, pressing into his chest. Being careful of her wound, he caressed her back down to the waist, then bit gently on her tongue. His left hand slid under her T-shirt, along the ribs and up her warm skin to cup her breast. She pushed against him, her legs straddling his knee and holding on for a second or two. Then she slipped away.

Her hands went up, she took a step back and looked at him, her eyes cloudy. 'I'm sorry, I can't,' she said.

Walker stared at her, surprised. 'What?'

'I'm... this is not right.'

'Why?'

Layla hesitated, her chin dropping as she glanced at the floor, then at the window. 'I'm not... ready for this, Scott.'

Walker swore silently, biting on his cheeks. Why not? It had felt right, very right. It had felt like the best thing in a long time. He swallowed, looking away from her, searching for the cigarette he had dropped.

'Fine.' He picked the Marlboro up, took a long drag and extinguished it. 'I guess there's other stuff to take care of.'

'It's not that... I'm sorry.'

'Don't worry about it.' Walker exhaled, realising his tone had been sharper than he had intended. 'Really.'

'Thank you.' Layla nodded and headed back towards the bedroom. 'It's very late, you should get some sleep as well.'

'Yeah.'

She disappeared into the darkness and Walker switched the living-room light off, then lit another cigarette. A minute later he shrugged and went into the bedroom to pick up a pillow and a discarded blanket.

'What are you doing?'

'I'll sleep on the sofa.'

Layla sat up on the bed, a darker shadow in the blackness. Walker could smell the faint traces of her cinnamon perfume. 'You don't have to.'

'I think it's better this way.'

She sighed. 'I guess you're right.'

'I *know* I am.'

PART TWO – EXPLORING THE DEEPNESS

'History is full of people and institutions that grew to positions of supremacy only to come crashing down. *Very often hubris – a sense of invincibility fed by uncontested power – was their undoing. Sometimes, however, the rise and the fall was due more from the unwarranted expectations of those around them.* ***A case in point is that over the last few years, the central banks of the largest advanced economies have assumed an almost-dominant policymaking stand.'***

Ludwig Van Boren, formerly one of the most important investment managers in the world

CHAPTER ELEVEN

Plan B

Walker spent the entire day diving into DeepShare's research on Frankel. He'd run the machine overnight, trying to trace the bank's trading activities in the markets for the past few months. A lot of the stuff was impossible to locate, dealt in Dark Pools or over-the-counter with only confidential paper trails, but Omega had still managed to find some gold nuggets in the Exchange data.

A serious flag had appeared, and he sniggered as he tried to piece together its meaning. He had no idea how DM had managed to sneak his software's probes so deeply in the market's archives, but the frenzied aspect of some transactions was unmistakeable. Frankel Schwartz was in big trouble – you didn't deal in such sizes, and with apparent randomness and counter-logic, unless something was going wrong in your books. Unless you had a serious hole below the waterline and were desperately trying to keep your ship afloat, patching leaks up here and there. It wasn't what he had hoped for, but maybe...

Satisfied, he leaned back in his chair and turned to Layla, who was typing something on her netbook. She glanced up without stopping. 'You've been working hard today.'

'I'm in the middle of something complicated.'

'Good complicated?' She closed the computer and walked over to him. Some colour had returned to her cheeks and the wound was starting to heal, without signs of infection. 'What are you trying to do, exactly?'

Walker sipped his coffee and grabbed one of the last few pastries on the table – earlier, Miss Sanna had brought over a ludicrous number of croissants and Seadas, typical Sardinian honey pastries, and had also left them an old kettle along with some Nescafé and milk. Layla had appreciated and devoured several sweets in a flash, hardly pausing for breath.

'I'm not sure, really. DM had unleashed DeepOmega onto Frankel, and most of the results are interesting, but flimsy.'

'Why?'

'The software sees an uncertainty node in the company, and serious vulnerability. The problem is that Omega can't tie Frankel to our events yet – its probability tree folds in the right direction, but...'

'It's not something that would stand up in court.' Layla grabbed his pastry and finished it.

'Once a thief...' Walker glared at her and lit a cigarette. 'That's the point. I don't think the police could use any of it. It's not how Omega works – it just gives potentials, and turning points. I need something harder... names, connections for it to work on. And I don't have any. Which means I'm also scheming to put in place a secondary option, a Plan B, if you wanna call it that.'

'Plan B?'

'Yes. But it's complicated, and very hard to pull off. I'd rather just nail Frankel with DM's death and be done with it.'

Layla glanced at her laptop, then looked back up at him. 'Names, connections. That's exactly what I'm trying to get for you.'

'Are you?'

She caressed the back of his head, letting her hand linger for a second. Then she moved back towards the sofa and half-smiled. 'I've been in touch with my fixer, and a few other people I know. Maybe someone can figure out who the big Australian is.'

'That would help...'

Walker's mobile phone rang, and they both turned to look at it. He picked up the handset, checking the screen. 'It's Luigi.' He turned on the speakerphone.

'Pronto?'

'Hi mate, my brother tells me your new passport is ready.'

'Great. How do I pick it up?'

'One of their people is going to meet you tomorrow around two p.m., at the Santu Antine Nuraghe near Torralba. Salvo, apparently. Do you know him?'

'Sort of.' *Wonderful. Such a lovely guy.*

'You must go alone.'

Walker groaned. 'Why am I not surprised?'

'One day you'll have to tell me the full story,' Luigi said. 'And by the way, how's the lady? Do you need to see the doctor again?'

'She's okay, I think.' Walker glanced at Layla, who shook her head. 'She'll be fine.'

'Cool. *In bocca al lupo*, Yours.'

'*Grazie*. And tell your brother to fuck off.'

...

Plan B. Could it really work? Walker returned to his laptop and put the finishing touches on a new message for Mosha, this time about Deep's take on the next European Central Bank meeting. The market expected interest rates to remain unchanged but Omega saw a very high probability of a rate cut, against all odds. The Serb had replied a couple of hours earlier, quite impressed by the software's success in forecasting the mess at the pharmaceutical company, and now wanted to know how it had come up with the information.

As Walker had expected, the hedge-fund manager seemed a lot more interested in making money than in reporting him to the police, so he had started explaining DM's creature and its almost magical capabilities. And if the ECB event went right, the big fish should swallow hook, line and sinker. He reread the email and attached some background data from Deep, finally firing the message off.

'What's a Nuraghe?'

Walker glanced up, stood and joined Layla at the window, checking the darkening sky. A few clouds were gathering near the higher mountains, though the weather forecast still predicted a balmy few days.

'It's an ancient ruin, some type of cemetery built by the pre-historical Sardinians. There are some astonishing complexes around the island, from four thousand years ago.

Santu Antine is one of the most famous, a great tourist spot – and busy.'

'Sounds like a good place for a drop. Anyhow...' She turned away, heading for the bedroom. 'Those pastries were gorgeous, but I'm starving now. Can we go into town and buy some food?'

'Sure. We'll check out the supermarket, and apparently there's a good local restaurant for dinner, according to Miss Sanna.'

Layla looked at him askance. 'A restaurant? Can we do something like that?'

Walker drew the curtains completely open, pointing to the shrub-infested valley below. 'We'll be fine. You have no idea how isolated this place is. There's fewer than ten thousand people living in an area over five thousand square miles. Most of them tend sheep, and mind their own business. It's safe, believe me.'

'All right, if you say so.' Layla smiled uncertainly. 'I want to try one of those dresses that Luigi lent me, anyway.'

'Don't overdo it, or we'll stop what little traffic there is.'

Layla's smile widened. 'You can be charming, when you want.'

'Obviously not charming enough.'

'Keep trying, you never know.' She winked at him and closed the bedroom door behind her.

Walker sighed and poured himself the last of the vodka, then went back to the window and stared at the sunset for a while.

A Sardinian Bar

The Su Stori restaurant was small, a few tables tucked away in what looked like somebody's living room just behind the bar. It was a bar in the Italian sense of the word, a multi-function place where you could get a cappuccino in the morning, an espresso or digestive in the afternoon and a few drinks in the evening. Layla hadn't quite stopped traffic in the small town square –because there was hardly anyone about – but she made an impression on the old men who sat around sipping on white wine. She looked stunning in a tight blue dress that stopped well short of her knees, her lustrous hair hanging loosely to her shoulders. Conversations had tapered off as they walked in and shared a drink before the owner/waiter, a thin middle-aged guy, rescued them and pointed to a corner table in the back.

'Tonight we have Culurgioni or Malloreddus for pasta, and Porceddu as main. Starters are the traditional cured meats and cheeses,' he said in Italian.

Layla glanced at Walker, mystified, but he just nodded to the waiter and replied, 'That's fine, we'll try both the pastas. And a bottle of Capichera wine, as well.'

'Certainly.'

The guy left and Layla stared at him, whispering, 'What the hell was that?'

'Our food.'

'Yeah, I got that much. But I've never heard of any of it.'

Walker smiled and went to the table, pulling her chair back. He sat down, nodding at the waiter who had already returned with their wine and some water. 'The Malloreddus are pasta shells, with a sausage sauce. I'm not sure about Culurgioni but the meat dish is a suckling pig cooked for hours in a hole underground. It's delicious.'

'Mmmh. We do something similar in the Chiapas and it's wonderful.' Layla sipped her wine and continued, 'I hope they're not too slow, I'm starving.'

'I could see that – you must have bought half the supermarket earlier.'

'I can't live on pastries like this morning.'

'You certainly gave it a go.'

Layla stuck out her tongue at him. 'I'm in convalescence, and the doctor said I need my strength.'

'That's okay, I don't mind plump women.'

'Dream on.'

Minutes later the waiter brought them several plates of starters, piled high with salami, ham cuts, pickled vegetables and cheeses. The warm homemade bread and cool white Capichera vanished before Layla sat back, taking a break. She lifted the glass to her lips and looked at Walker, eyes sparkling. 'God, this feels good. When was the last time we had a proper meal?'

'At Luigi's?'

'Pasta with tinned tuna? I can tell you grew up in England, not Italy. Actually, why do you sound American sometimes?'

'My father was from Boston, and I studied at an international school in the US for a couple of years. As for the food taste, don't blame the Brits – I guess I've just eaten too many sandwiches while staring at computers in the last ten years...'

Walker smelt burning tobacco and glanced at the waiter. The man nodded and wordlessly brought him a small ashtray – Italy's anti-smoking regulations seemed to have fallen by the wayside in Sardinia, like much else. He lit a cigarette and offered one to Layla, who shook her head.

'I only smoke when I'm stressed, or drunk.'

Walker eyed the empty bottle of Capichera, and signalled for another one. 'Won't be long, then.'

Layla ignored the jibe, set her plate aside and leaned forward, face resting on her palms. 'So, apart from poor eating habits, what else does a derivatives trader do?'

'Why do you want to know?'

'I'm just curious. Most of your dossier was gibberish to me.'

Walker finished his last slice of ham and took a sip of water, thinking. What had he been doing for the past few years, really? It was a great question.

'It depends. Some traders make prices for clients and other banks that want to cover risks – like a weird type of financial insurance. Others dream up complex products for retail or pension funds to invest in, and hedge them. In my role, I used the bank's money to – essentially – bet on the stock market's behaviour.'

'Why?'

'To generate profits. If I get it right.'

'So you have to make money from money.'

'Yes.'

'And are you good at it? It all seems so... random. How do you decide what to do?'

Walker lit another cigarette and waited for the thin owner to clear their starters before answering. 'You breathe financial information all the time, news, reports, anything. And you watch the market all day. It's inevitable to build your own opinions, or best-guesses. Then you must trust your instincts, believe in yourself.'

'What happens if you're wrong?'

'That's when skill and experience count. Discipline is the most important asset for a trader – anyone can be right at one time, but you have to be quick to cut your losses, or to know when to let your profits run. If you can do that, forget your emotions and treat it like a sophisticated game of chess, or poker...'

'And can you?'

'Yeah, I'm quite good at it.'

Layla raised her eyes to the ceiling and shook her head. 'Of course. How do you know?'

'I did make money. A lot more than I lost.'

'Which is how everything is measured, I guess?' Her voice carried an edge of sarcasm.

'In an investment bank, yes.' Walker shrugged. 'It's ruthless, but at least there's a baseline. Every day you know how well you've done, irrespective of people's opinions of you. Money is the proof.'

'Is that why you went into the job? Money?'

Walker finished his cigarette, and poured more wine for both of them. 'This is starting to resemble an interrogation.'

Layla sipped at her drink and smiled, her full lips glistening. She brushed a loose strand of hair away from her cheek and pouted invitingly. 'I just want to know what makes you tick. You don't seem like a typical banker.'

'That sounds like a compliment. Maybe.'

'It is. You guys cost me a lot of money in the crisis.'

'We cost the world a lot of money. But then again, the world sort of deserved it.'

Layla looked at him strangely. 'What do you mean?'

'Greedy bankers got most of the blame – still get it, really. But everyone was greedy – people bought houses that they couldn't afford, spent more than they could possibly repay. The world runs on credit – and it got too much of it. Everyone wanted to get rich fast, and an empire of debt was built. That was the real problem. Governments ignored it, either because they didn't understand or because they only cared about the next election. Like a bunch of lemmings, we all jumped off the same cliff.'

The main dishes arrived, and the Culurgioni turned out to be delicious pasta dumplings filled with potato and cheese. Layla dived into them, then stopped chewing for a second. 'What about the banks' role? Or are they just a bunch of poor innocent scapegoats?'

'Banks did go mad, and lent too much. It was a type of Ponzi scheme, where you just danced when the music was on.'

'Couldn't they see it coming? All the smart people and their computers?'

Walker laughed, then almost choked on some bread. 'A bank's time horizon is so short it couldn't see its own navel. Look, the single most important cause of the crisis was stupidity. Everyone got greedy, but the real problem was that a lot of the stuff that exploded was very complex, and nobody had any understanding of the big picture. Most senior bankers were as shocked as everyone else – their firms had become so big and the deals so specialised it was impossible to keep them under control.'

'Seriously?' Layla sounded unconvinced.

'Yes. We are all focused on our little turf, and every area is so monumentally complicated that no one could hope to understand the entire business. Bankers made mistakes out of ignorance and simply assumed things would continue as they always had. But the world changed, and they blew up. Because of their own stupidity they let it get out of control, and nobody reined them in. Besides, it's easy to look away when you rake in millions.'

Walker put his glass down and took a few bites of the closest pasta, then leaned forward and picked up a Culurgione from the plate nearer Layla.

She glared at him. 'Those are mine. You can have the madare… whatever they're called.'

'Malloreddus.' He smiled at her. 'So that's a brief history of the crisis. Easy crime, everyone is guilty.'

'Some more than others, I still think.'

'Probably.' Which was why the world needed DeepShare more than it knew.

Layla finished the last dumpling and sat back with a satisfied sigh. 'So you're innocent, and I'm stuffed.'

'We still have the suckling pig.'

'What? Are you joking?'

'Italians never joke about food.'

'I can't.'

'Don't make me look bad.' Walker stood up, grabbing his cigarettes. 'Let's go out for some fresh air. You just need a little break.'

'I need another stomach.'

…

They headed outside and stood in silence for a while, sipping on their wine and smoking. The tiny central square of

Sadali was empty, with only a middle-aged man crossing the cobbled pavement towards a bar on the other side, near some pine trees. A few cars were parked in front of stone houses that looked as if they were hundreds of years old, and a single street-lamp tried to pierce the evening gloom.

The temperature was dropping and Walker took off his leather jacket, putting it around Layla's shoulders. She nodded gratefully and flicked away her cigarette, snuggling closer to Walker as they both leaned against the building's sidewall.

'Sardinia is colder than I expected.'

'Yes, especially here in the mountains. They even get decent snow in winter.'

'I hate the cold.'

'You are Mexican.' Walker paused and glanced at her. 'I think. Are you really?'

Layla looked hurt. 'Yes. I wasn't lying. All I told you about my life was true.'

'Well, it wasn't that much. What did you do after you left the secret police, and why did you?'

'I was being used, and I couldn't take it anymore. I ran to the States, crossing the border near El Paso.' Layla sighed, her eyes lost in thought. 'I didn't speak much English, but I made it to LA. It took me a while to get the pieces back together.'

Her voice went cold, distant. 'The smugglers raped me in the truck.'

'I'm sorry.'

'I found one, years later. He won't be doing it again.'

Walker shivered and lit another cigarette. 'What did you do in California?'

'A few odd jobs with the other illegals, there's a large community there. Then a friend got me into a rich man's place as housekeeper and cook. The rich man was in the middle of a divorce, and he – he liked me.'

'Did you... like him back?'

'Not really, he was a selfish bastard. And he was trying to screw his ex-wife. But he was stupid, started leaving all sorts of documents around the house. Maybe he wanted to impress me with his wealth.' Layla looked at Walker with a wolfish grin. 'I went to the wife's lawyer and organised my first sting. They gave me ten grand for the bank's papers.'

'How did that feel?'

'Good. And dirty.'

The restaurant door opened and the owner poked his head out, looking for them. '*Il Porceddu e' pronto*,' he grumbled, before popping back inside.

Layla shrugged out of Walker's jacket and returned it. 'I was sick of myself for a while, but it gave me a chance to start again. The lawyer was impressed, and she found me a couple more jobs like that. During one of those I met my current fixer – he's a real pro, and stuff became more complicated.'

'Like me?'

Layla stepped towards the entrance, then she looked at Walker and grinned. 'No, never *that* complicated.'

Olive Tree

'They were hiding in Lugano.'

'How do you know?' The Australian's palms tingled with anticipation. He was still mad at Walker's escape in Reims, and he couldn't wait to get even.

'Banker's connections. He has a lot of money to play with, though.'

'It doesn't matter. Where were they holed up?'

'A friend of his, we think. When can you get there?' The Englishman sounded worried for the first time, and in a hurry.

'Tomorrow morning. Don't worry, I'll make sure the trail doesn't go cold, now.'

...

They finished dinner in a rush, neither having the appetite to make a dent in the suckling pig, and drove back to the Agriturismo. Walker whizzed through the empty mountain roads in silence, with Layla apparently lost in her thoughts. When they reached the hotel parking lot he prepared to carry their shopping up to the room but Layla stopped him.

'Are you going back to work now?' she asked.

'Yep. There's a few things I want to try out.'

She looked at the clear sky, then around the converted barn. 'Let's go for a walk. I'm not ready to get closed up in that dump, yet.'

'Okay, sure.'

Layla found a little track that wound down the steeper part of the hill and they followed it for a few minutes through some dense shrub, emerging into a meadow in the shadow of a giant olive tree. Walker stopped to admire it in the quarter-moon while Layla bent under the low-hanging branches, wiping the ground and leaning back against its trunk.

'Sit with me, Scott,' she whispered. 'Please, it's lovely here.'

Walker joined her and lit a cigarette, the small lighter flame making the shadows twist.

'You never answered my question,' she said.

'Which one?'

'Why you do your job. Is it the money?'

'I was about to quit, actually. After my big trade... I'd have gone, I think.'

'Where?'

Walker thought for a second. 'Travelling, maybe, for a while. I'd had enough of modern finance, and some of its effects were really starting to grate on what's left of my conscience. DM had a dream, and I thought I could help him with it when Deep was ready. Give something back, you know?'

Layla nodded, her eyes sparkling in moonlight. Walker sucked on his cigarette, struggling not to lean over and kiss her. *Forget it. Not now.* And probably not ever. He sipped from a glass of water and continued, 'The money was key at the beginning, of course, but it's always been about the adrenaline, as well. When you make mountains of cash... it's a rush, a massive one. Your mind feels sharper, you're almost more alive.'

'And when you lose?'

'It's the same, especially if you lose big. Even if it hurts.' He paused for a couple of seconds, thinking. 'And being a trader is good because nobody tells you what to do.'

'Come on.'

'Obviously there are things you *have* to take on.' Walker shrugged. 'But in general you can trade your own book as you see fit, within your risk limits. You don't have to be polite, or scurry after people. And the worth of your job is there, measured every second. The politics is mainly higher up in management.'

Layla was quiet for a moment. 'A shrink would say that you seem to have a problem with authority.'

'Maybe. I don't like grey lines. It's too easy to get screwed over, and I've learnt not to trust the world. Too much randomness, too much pain.'

Layla turned away and her tone cut him. 'Is that why you pay for women?'

'My dad loved his family very much. So much that it killed him.'

'I'm sorry.'

'It was a long time ago. When my mother and sister died in an accident... it broke him.' Walker's voice dropped a couple of octaves, becoming rougher. 'He lasted less than a year, afterwards. A doctor said it was a tiny hole in his aorta, but I always thought he just died of a broken heart. I'm not going to go the same way.'

Layla turned back and took his hand, her tone softer. 'Still, caring for someone, or something other than yourself... I can't see how that's bad.'

Walker didn't reply. He sucked a last lungful of smoke and put the stub out with his foot, before standing up and stepping away. 'DM cared, and look at what it got him.'

'That's ridiculous. He was killed because of a machine to make money, not because he found a cure for cancer.' Layla's voice thrummed with an edge of anger.

'No. DeepShare was a lot more than that, especially to him.'

'Why?'

'It uses financial markets, but Omega was supposed to become an instrument to predict the future, extrapolating trends in politics, technology, social moods. It had the potential to become a scientific way of... minimizing wars, revolutions, poverty. A guide, to illuminate the path of leaders – that was DM's dream for his machine.'

Layla stood as well, gliding nearer. 'That's just a dream. An impossible one.'

'You'd be surprised.' Walker glanced at his watch. 'Are we going back?'

'Not quite.' She pulled at his arm and brought him back underneath the tree. 'Surprised at what?' She rummaged in her bag and pulled out the small bottle of rum she had bought earlier. 'I'm not drunk enough to believe you, yet.'

'Yes, you are.'

She gave him the finger, but with a narrow smile. 'We might get killed tonight. Or tomorrow. I need a break.'

'And I need some sleep.' *And some help from God*, he thought.

'Yeah, right. You're drinking all the time, anyway.'

Walker grimaced. 'I guess it comes with the job. As long as I can function.'

'You're not doing too bad.' Layla stepped forward and grabbed his shirt, pulling him against her. She kissed him hard on the lips before stepping back. 'Please, indulge me. I don't want to die without knowing why.'

Walker watched her slide back, straightened his shirt and gave up. 'Look, all the big banks and hedge funds have systems like DeepOmega. They're just less advanced, and no one could count on a genius like DM, who was probably ten or twenty years ahead of his time.'

'Really? He sounds... special.'

'I wish you could have met him.' Walker paused again, choosing his words. 'The markets have become too big, too fast and complicated for humans. Most of the trading is already done by smart machines, using speed, arbitraging correlations, trying to predict future fluctuations and events. A lot of what humans do, these days, is simply to supervise the algos, making sure nothing stupid happens. And even then it's too hard for us – some of this stuff takes place in picoseconds, and the amount of information these softwares can process is too big to even fathom.'

'And what's so different about *your* machine?'

'Deep is the next evolutionary step. It doesn't just look at the next few hours or days, but can go further, predict all sort of happenings.'

'Like what?'

Walker lit another cigarette and lay back against the tree trunk. 'The day I met you... I made close to seventy million dollars, profiting on an event Omega had forecast almost four months ago. It pointed to the week, and the exact result of the Italian elections, before anyone even expected the previous government to fall.'

He closed his eyes, reliving the events in his mind, trying to steer clear of the images of DM's dead body. 'And that was just me, an average trader with an average book. Can you imagine how much money Dorfmann could have made if all the bank's resources had been geared up like my portfolio? We're talking billions, on just one instance. Besides, Deep is starting to predict a much more turbulent twelve to eighteen months to come.'

'That's scary.'

'You have no idea. Look, according to DeepOmega we are nearing another massive crisis – there's little we can do to stop it. And the machine is right, I can feel it in my bones.'

Layla grunted and snuggled closer. 'But I thought things were better.'

'They look better, in some countries. Morphine can do the same with a patient, though she's still very ill. What has been done in the last few years – they mainly kicked the can further along, storing problems for the future. And when those finally blow, it'll be like nothing you've ever seen before.'

'So if DeepShare is right...?'

'Any bank or hedge fund with a tool like Omega could make an absolute killing, tens of billions of dollars – it would quickly become the wealthiest, most influential financial institution in the world. And the people running it would get rich, and powerful, beyond belief. You could even use it to manipulate events, determine outcomes.'

'Which is what DM dreamed of.'

'Yes. And he certainly wasn't gonna let Omega anywhere near a banker's hands. For him it wasn't about the markets, or the money. They were just signals, to help people make the right choice.' He sighed, took a sip of the rum that Layla offered. 'Deep started decades ago as a chess-playing software. These days the chess computers are too good for humans, but they are great teaching and analyzing tools. That's what Omega was supposed to become. For governments, or the UN, or something.'

'Is it there yet?'

'I don't know, probably not,' he said. 'It's certainly great at making money, though.'

'But not at catching bad guys.'

'Not really, no.' He downed more rum and went silent, staring into the distance. *Or not yet.* DM had died too early, and Walker was becoming afraid that he could never fulfill the machine's potential – maybe he just wasn't good enough. 'There might be another way, though, and that's what I've been also working on.'

'Your famous Plan B?'

'Exactly. Even if DeepOmega can't tie Frankel to DM's murder, perhaps I can still hurt them.'

'How?'

'The only way a bank can be properly mauled. By going after its money.'

Layla glanced at him. 'You said there was a vulnerability in their stock.'

'Yes. Maybe a bad book somewhere, or... It could be anything, but Deep thinks we could cause a lot of trouble for them. The problem is that Frankel Schwartz is massive – I would need perfect timing and a serious amount of firepower to really go after them.'

'Firepower? You've said that before.'

'Yes. But my big fish hasn't surfaced yet. And I don't know if he ever will.'

'Are you talking about that hedge-fund guy? What's his name?'

'Mosha.' Walker finished his cigarette and stood up. 'But don't hold your breath. Lots of pieces still need to fall in the right places.'

'It's about time you got lucky.'

Walker shrugged. 'I guess. And as we always say on the floor, I'd rather be lucky than good, anyway.'

CHAPTER TWELVE

Caught

'The car is here.'

'Good. Any sign of them?'

'No. Only the broker, and he's just turned the lights off.'

The Englishman thought for a second. Pienaar sounded eager to move, but too many mistakes had been made already. 'Fine. Follow him around for a day or two, they might still be in Switzerland.'

'What if they are not?'

'Then the broker will know where they've gone.'

'I can tell you now. Italy.'

'Maybe.' The Englishman sighed. Pienaar was becoming too dangerous, but he had no other choice. 'Just keep your eyes on him, and wait for my instructions.'

'Will do.'

'No initiatives.'

The Australian grunted. 'As you say, Chief.'

Santu Antine

Walker woke groggily and struggled up on the couch, only the smell of coffee enticing his eyes open. Layla was still wearing just his T-shirt, her long legs naked and her hair messy from sleep. He noticed she had a new – and smaller – bandage wrapped around her upper arm, the white gauze spotless.

'This sofa is shit. My back feels like an elephant trampled me.'

Layla grinned and handed him a mug of coffee as he looked for his cigarettes, found them on the floor and lit one.

'Good morning to you,' she said. 'I think we're almost there, the stitches are nice and clean, and look...' She lifted her arm and swung it about, reaching behind her back. 'I can even undo my bra now.'

He sighed, grimacing at the bitterness of his coffee. 'Don't, please.'

'Boring.'

'What time is it?'

'Almost ten.' Layla sat next to him and opened her laptop. 'Aren't you supposed to go and get your new passport today?'

'Yes,' he answered, staring at her legs for a second. She studied his face and he realised he needed a shave. *I hope I don't look as crap as I feel.*

Layla smiled. 'You smell like death. Did you stay up late?'

'Five, I think.'

'Any results?'

'Nothing new, really. I'm still running a few deep searches – maybe they'll throw something up later. But it's not looking too good, I'm afraid.'

'Pity.' She slipped sideways and looked down, starting to type something on her computer. 'Now leave me alone.'

Walker shrugged and shuffled to the bathroom for a shower, trying to get back to a more human form. After half an hour he emerged, feeling a lot better in a fresh shirt and jeans. Suddenly his laptop beeped and he swore – the ECB decision that DeepShare had predicted was about to be announced. He ran to his computer and fired it up, just catching the newsfeed from Frankfurt. He turned the volume higher and prayed.

'The European Central Bank has decided to lower rates by a quarter of a point...' droned the commentator.

'Yes!' Walker swung his fist, skipping.

Layla glanced up at him, surprised. 'You look happy.'

'Deep was right, again. Mosha will definitely be ready to listen now.'

'Why?'

'I've just given him proof that I can make him oceans of money.'

'Delightful. Is that really the only thing you guys ever think about?'

Walker grinned. 'No. Sex is important, too.'

Layla closed her computer and stood up, studying him. 'At least you look better.' She checked the time and asked, 'Is it far, this place you have to go to?'

'Maybe three hours. I should be back around six or seven, I guess.' Walker searched for his phone, found it and started typing a number.

'Who are you calling?'

'The firepower, I hope.' He signalled for her to be quiet, then waited nervously as the line rang without answer for a few seconds.

'Hello?'

Walker paused a beat, savouring the moment. 'Mosha, it's Scott.'

'That was impressive, Yours.' An intake of breath. 'I want to see this DeepShare thing.'

'I'm sure you do. I'm about to send you the logs from the mini-crash last week – they will blow your pants off – but after that we need to talk, in person.'

'I have to say, I'm curious about what the hell happened in London. When do you want to meet up?'

'Soon. Are you in Rome?'

'No, I'm in Sarajevo till tomorrow. Then I have to go to Siena for a couple of days.'

Walker thought for a second. 'Siena is good. Can you see me there?'

'Yeah, sure. Don't know what time, yet.'

'Just send me a text, day after tomorrow. On this number. I should be in town by late afternoon.'

'Fine. You're not gonna bring the police down on me, are you?' Mosha sounded nervous, Walker realised.

'Would I?'

'I've heard of worse.'

'Fuck off. I'll see you on Thursday.'

'Done.'

Walker closed the phone and looked at Layla. Did his plan even make sense, he wondered, or was he just running around as the axe prepared to fall? 'Have you ever been to Tuscany?'

'Are we moving again?'

'Just for a day or two.'

Layla looked unimpressed. 'Nope, never been. Is it as overrated as this island?'

'Funny.' Walker sat down next to her and breathed out, trying to convince himself. Leaving Sardinia was dangerous, but they could take a ferry and he didn't really have another choice. 'Listen – this is something I *have* to do. Omega is stuck on Frankel, and it doesn't look like it will produce anything useful soon. Those guys... they might be catching up to us. Mosha is my only option. If I can get him to help, maybe...'

Layla sighed, still unconvinced. 'More maybes. And why would this guy want to help you, anyway?'

'He's an old acquaintance.' Walker shrugged. 'But that's not the reason I trust him. He's in trouble and he needs me, I think. And Deep.'

'For what?'

'Mosha's business is a tad more complicated than your average hedge-fund manager. And he owes me big... honour debts must be repaid in his world.'

'Honour debts? Have you lost your mind?'

Walker glanced at his watch, wondering the same. 'Look, I've got to go but – I'll tell you the story when I'm back, I promise.'

'*Fine.*' Layla glared at him. 'And yes, I'll come to Siena, if you want...' She hesitated, thinking. 'What about the tickets to fly to Tuscany?'

'No planes, we're taking another boat.'

'Now you tell me!'

'I'm smart like that.' He grinned. 'I'll text you when I get the passport, then you can book them. But we need to know my new name first, don't you think?'

...

It's darkest before dawn, they say.

Layla wasn't so sure – it seemed black enough all the time, at the moment. And what the hell was dawn, anyway? Did it mean a fresh start, unencumbered by past mistakes?

Maybe it was just the hope of light, a faint guide out of blindness and uncertainty. Maybe it was love.

She didn't want to tell him anything. It was such a big risk – that goddamned machine could expose her, and too soon. Because she liked Walker. A lot. Too much, possibly. She really didn't want to chance it – not now, when she was almost ready to...

But he was stuck, and he needed the extra information she had. She shivered, though the room was warm. Sometimes you have to take a chance, follow your heart, someone had said.

And that was the problem, because there is no dawn when the darkness lies within your soul.

...

The Nuraghe looked like a fifteen-foot-tall termite nest, built in white limestone covered with moss. Walker rambled through the outer passageways, along twisting paths marked out in chalk, into the smaller outbuildings. The roofs were mostly gone but the walls were higher than his head and he kept wandering through crowds of tourists, looking for a familiar face. Frustrated, after thirty minutes he was ready to give up his search and go back to wait by the entrance when someone slapped his arm, hard.

Walker spun, bracing his legs and dropping his shoulder, preparing to throw a punch. He finished turning, already coiled, and found himself looking at Salvo's thin face. The Sicilian stepped back, hand sneaking into his rain parka.

'Easy, fag. You know how I am when I get nervous.'

Walker stared at him, wanting to break his neck. 'Do you have it?'

Salvo checked around, pointing to one of the smallest outbuildings. The slim mound was covered by a makeshift thatched roof, a low door hanging by its hinges from one side of the entrance. 'Let's see the cash first, moron.'

Walker tapped his jacket pocket and they slipped inside the smaller side-nuraghe. Salvo nodded and squared his back to the panel, keeping the door shut against curious tourists. Walker pulled out an envelope and handed it over.

'It's thirty grand, like you asked. Count it if you want.'

Salvo sniggered. 'That's okay – we know where your friends live. If there's something missing...'

'There isn't.'

The Sicilian grunted and rummaged in his pocket, pulling out a purple booklet and flicking it to the floor. 'There's a driver's licence in there as well, in the same name. The Capo liked you, for some reason.'

Walker glanced down at the Italian passport, without moving. 'Thanks.'

'Whatever.' Salvo half-turned, pushing the door open. Then he stopped and glanced back with a nasty grin. 'You know, I think you did kill the guy in London.'

Walker shrugged, looking straight into the man's eyes. 'Why?'

'Because you're a cold one. Like me. You don't flinch.' Salvo winked at him and stepped out, slamming the panel so hard one of the hinges broke off.

Eating Mexican

Walker returned to the Agriturismo just after nightfall, his new Italian passport in the inside pocket of his leather jacket. The forgery was great – the document had even been treated to look battered, with a few exotic tourist stamps in the middle pages. And Salvo thought he was a cold one: impressive, if slightly tainted praise. He smiled and took the stairs in a rush, eager to show the passport to Layla and find out what she had been doing for the last few hours. As he turned onto the landing he saw something stuck on their apartment door: it was a manila envelope, the words 'Welcome back' scribbled on the front in pencil.

Walker frowned and pulled it off the panel. Inside he found a grainy picture showing the face and large upper torso of a man, with a name typed underneath: 'Francois Pienaar'. His blood froze as he recognised the man's scarred features – it was the Australian thug who had tried to grab him in Reims. The same man who had apparently organised the sting, and who might have been DM's killer. They had been found.

He shouted Layla's name, fumbling with the keys and bursting through the door. His heart pounded as he scanned the room, dread rising from some deep place inside him. The apartment was in semi-darkness, a few small candles flickering on the window sill. A dim lamp illuminated the old table in the middle of the room, made up with plates and cutlery, a magnum of red wine sitting among flower petals. *What the hell?*

'Layla!' he shouted again, scanning the shadows.

'I'm fine – just give me a couple of minutes,' came the laughing reply from her bedroom. 'And don't eat anything.'

Walker swore, his heartbeat all over the place. He stumbled through the room and dropped his jacket on the sofa, still shaking. Just what he had needed after Salvo. But this... He picked up the photograph he had dropped and searched the living room. Layla had moved his PC to the low coffee table and he rushed to turn it on, studying the picture of Pienaar as he waited, fidgeting. In less than a minute he had scanned and downloaded it into DeepShare, suspending all the other processes he was running to unleash the machine on a massive search for the thug. His brain went into overdrive, considering what else he could do.

Nothing. Just let Omega work its magic.

And maybe he could finally grasp a lead on the bastards who had killed DM. He stared at the screen for a while, willing the software to work faster. As if it would help. Then he exhaled and sat back, almost resigned to a long wait.

Soft music started up and he turned on the sofa to see the bedroom door opening. Layla stepped through, with more candles flickering behind her. Her hair was made up in a side chignon, a longer fringe caressing the side of her face. She wore a black satin dress, strapless and figure-hugging. It fell to her ankles, split by a side-slit almost to her hip. When she moved he could glimpse a finger of tanned skin just above her stockings.

Walker stared at her and swallowed, uncertain.

She smiled coyly and twirled around, allowing him a glimpse of her naked shoulders and back. The stitches on her arm were still visible, but fading. 'Well, what do you think?'

'I... I'm not sure I *can* think.'

'The dress feels a little loose. Luigi's wife might be...'

'You look like an angel. A fallen one, maybe, but still an angel.' He stood up, unsteady.

'Nice line,' she chuckled, her eyes sparkling.

Walker forced himself to look away, back to his computer. 'That photograph. Pienaar...?'

'Shush. Not now, please.' Layla flicked back her hair, walked around the table and took his hand, leaning forward to give him a long, lingering kiss. Walker responded and his mouth opened greedily, letting her tongue probe deeper while her hands came up to his neck. She held him tightly, her strength again surprising, until Walker stepped back and searched her face, struggling to keep his composure.

'I thought you weren't ready for... for this,' he said.

'This what?' She glanced at the pots and the table. 'I just wanted to cook something for you, to celebrate. I'm very proud of myself.'

'Layla...'

She bit her lip, blushing. 'I know,' she whispered, pulling closer to peck his cheek. 'But this feels right, now. If you still want me.'

Walker embraced her, bit her earlobe and inhaled her light perfume, the faint scent of cinnamon tingling his nose. Her body was firm and soft against his chest and he nuzzled her lip.

'Yes, of course I do.'

He kissed her again, hard, blood thumping in his head as his hands glided along her shoulders and back, then lower, caressing her buttocks. She pushed against him and he fell on the sofa, dragging her on top of him.

After a few seconds Layla shoved him back and sat up, readjusting her skirt as her leg slid out of the slit. She grinned. 'Not yet, banker-boy. I've cooked for hours, and you're not about to eat it cold. Besides, I promise to answer all your questions. Food first, then you can enjoy the dessert.'

'I have a sweet tooth.'

'Well, you can have it as many times as you want. But later.' She stood up, opening the mini-fridge. 'Drink?'

Walker straightened up, his senses tingling. *Pienaar. And Layla.* She bent down to grab a couple of glasses and he stared at her shape in the low light, forcing himself not to grab at her again. 'Yes, please. A large one.'

'Neat vodka, as usual?'

'I like the roughness.'

'Sometimes I do, too.'

Walker exhaled, looked for some matches and lit a cigarette. 'I guess that's good to know.'

...

'Francois Pienaar. How did you find him?' Walker swallowed another spoonful of the spicy chicken-and-fruit stew and then bit into a tamale, savouring the dried-shrimp saltiness. God, he was starving.

Layla sipped her red wine and played around with the food on her plate before answering. 'My fixer, Anton, had heard of a big scarred Australian, ex-foreign legion. He didn't know the name, but a few of his contacts gave him bits and pieces. Then I got lucky; someone saw that picture in an old Cape Town newspaper and recognised him. Zimbabwean descent, orphaned young. Active mainly in Africa, apparently. And a nasty piece of work, they say.'

'I'm sure. Who does he work for?'

'I don't know. He disappeared a couple of years ago, after being convicted in Lesotho for murdering a minister, and he must be using some other identity.'

'It doesn't matter. I've already set Deep on him.'

She grinned, but her eyes remained serious. 'That's why I was waiting in the bedroom. I knew you'd want to do it straight away. Do you think it will come up with anything?'

'Maybe. If there's anything useful to find.'

Walker picked up a different tamale, sniffed it. 'This is wonderful, by the way. You're a great cook.'

Layla smiled thinly. 'I learnt it at home, before... before I had to leave.'

'But you're not eating much.'

'I picked at it while I was making it. Couldn't resist.' She sipped at the wine again. 'What about this Mosha, what's the story there?'

'The billions he runs in his hedge fund – it's mainly Camorra money.'

'Isn't that like the Mafia?'

'Sort of. Mafia is Sicilian, Camorra is originally from Naples – they're rivals, often. A lot of their profits have been recycled through the banking system, and he is their main investment guy. Most of the money is now clean – has been for a long time – and the business is legit, but obviously a lot of people high up in Italy know about its origins.'

'And no one does anything?'

'Too many interests, too many bribes. The State is partly corrupt, always has been. Don't tell me Mexico is any different.'

'No, of course not.'

'Well, Mosha's been having a bad time, lately. His recent returns are negative, very negative. But I've given him some tips since we got DeepShare back, and they've worked out like a dream. Now I'll show him the stuff on Frankel – if I can convince him...'

Layla nodded, leaning closer. 'You said you've known him for a long time?'

'We went to school together, in the States. Before university, at a place called a United World College. We were never friends, but we somehow kept in touch – the City can be a small place. And he's a bright guy, but he's always been too greedy for my liking.'

'Too greedy? That's rich, coming from an Investment Banker.'

Walker winked at her. 'I don't take morality lessons from a thief.'

'We've had this conversation before.' She stuck out her tongue. 'Is he Italian, as well?'

'Serbian, but his mother was the daughter of a Bosnian crime supremo. Later he married into Camorra's most powerful family – that's how he got to run the cash. But now he needs to do something about his fund, and fast. If he keeps losing money, his "investors" might decide to cut him off. Literally.'

'I see. Well, at least I get to visit Tuscany, I guess.' She looked at the empty plates on the table and smiled. 'Are you done?'

Walker sat back in his chair and lit a cigarette. 'I'm stuffed.'

Layla slid her fringe aside, staring at him. 'No room for the dessert?'

'No, none at all.'

'We'll see.' She stood, leaned forward to give him a quick kiss and walked off to the bedroom. 'Don't go anywhere. I'll be back in a minute,' she said before shutting the door.

Walker pushed back his chair and headed for the window, staring at the night sky as he finished his cigarette. His thoughts were in turmoil, and he wondered if he was about to make a massive mistake. He still knew very little about Layla, and there were so many other things...

He shrugged and returned to the fridge to pour himself another vodka, struggling to keep his hand steady. Images flashed by of her smile and her naked body, of her vulnerability during the boat trip and of the hard, unflinching toughness she could turn on like a shield. There was something magnetic, almost too hard to...

The bedroom door reopened and this time the music pounded louder, a South American beat drumming below flutes and eerie high-pitched voices. Layla approached him, wearing only a sheer silk vest and panties, her long legs encased in thigh-high fishnet stockings. Her hair hung loose again, back down below her shoulders. Walker felt his mouth go dry and waited for her to reach him, still feeling a little uncertain.

Layla stopped just a few inches away and his breath caught, just as a strand of her dark hair brushed his face – electricity seemed to pass between them, though they had not touched yet.

'Are you still hungry, then?'

'Yes,' he said, staring into her eyes, finally ready to ignore the tendril of nervousness that lingered in his stomach. 'Are you?'

'No. But I think I'm in love.'

Walker shivered, felt his hands go cold. 'Then that makes two of us.'

Her mouth came up to meet his and they kissed hungrily, falling to the floor.

...

Walker woke from a nightmare, his heart thumping. He glanced to his side but Layla was fast asleep, shifting a little as he slid his arm from under her and sat up to check the time. 2.37 a.m. – and he was wide awake. *Great.* Cursing under his breath he dragged back the blankets, bending lower to give Layla a soft kiss before shuffling to the living room.

He managed to find his cigarettes in the dark and fired up DeepShare, spending a few minutes scanning the processes the software was running. The Pienaar file wasn't ready yet, most of the results still in machine-code that DM had presumably been capable of reading, but that were far too difficult for Walker to decipher. He checked the logs: Omega thought the search should be completed in another four hours.

Which meant sleep would be hard. But after twenty minutes of fruitless clicking and studying an increasingly blurry screen Walker yawned and gave up, deciding to return to bed. He was about to open the heavy wooden door when he heard a soft noise from inside and stopped still, trying to identify it.

Was that... sniffling?

It took a second before he realised what it was. She must have been crying softly, trying not to be heard. Not knowing what to do, he went back to the sofa and lit another cigarette. *Why?*

CHAPTER THIRTEEN

Truth

The sky outside still shone with a few stars when Walker gave up trying to sleep and returned to the living room, his hands tingling with anticipation. Deep had to be done by now. He logged onto his computer and connected the tablet, waiting for the software somewhere in the Cloud to respond. Within a few seconds the icon of a new file named PIENAAR appeared and he grinned, clicking on it and whispering, 'Let's see what we've found, you son-of-a-bitch.'

The data started with biographical information and childhood stuff, progressively going deeper with an astonishing amount of information. Walker was shocked by how comprehensive Omega seemed to be, and once again he marvelled at how DM had managed to extract order out of data chaos. Then a section towards the end caught his eye and he froze, before clicking through links and nodes in a frenzy.

Please, no.

...

Walker heard the bedroom door open and raised his head from his hands, struggling to keep calm. He stood up and switched off the monitor, gazing at Layla. His throat caught at how beautiful she looked, with just a white sheet wrapped around her naked body. He steadied his voice and took a step towards the window, forcing himself to stare outside.

'Why now?' he said.

Layla must have noticed his tone, and she answered tentatively. 'What... what do you mean?'

'You knew Pienaar from before, didn't you?'

She didn't reply. Walker turned back, his anger building as he saw her biting at her lower lip.

'How...?' she whispered.

'Deep found the connection once I ran his name and face. It thinks you've known him since Mexico. And the guy is part of the Blackspring network. You've worked for them, too.' Walker paused, sucking some air in. 'I can't believe it – they're mercenaries, people too damaged even for the special forces.'

Layla nodded imperceptibly, looking down at her feet, silent.

Walker kept staring at her, his insides twisting. There were so many things he wanted to ask, explanations he wanted. But only the important stuff mattered now. He had wasted enough time, and the wolf could be just around the door. Still, there were things he needed to know.

'Were you there when they killed DM? Did you help them?' he spat.

She shook, tears forming at the corner of her eyes. 'Oh God, no. I only found out later, when I brought your computer to Pienaar. I had nothing to do with it, I swear.'

'But you returned to look for me. Why?'

She grabbed a chair and sat down, elbows on the table, her hands going up to her face. 'Pienaar realised immediately you didn't have DeepShare on your machine. They were going to come after you, but I asked them to let me try and get the access my way.'

'So you were trying to help me?' Walker groaned, a bitter taste in his mouth. 'Protecting me from the monster?'

'I... I didn't want to see anyone else hurt. Pienaar is dangerous, mad.'

That he could believe. But she was only telling him half-truths, he could feel it. There had to be more, and though it hurt, he needed to dig deeper. His very life might depend on it, not just his feelings.

'Very noble,' he said flatly. 'And you wanted your money, I guess. More, probably, if you got them whatever I knew.'

'They agreed to give me a few days... Pienaar planted the blood in your flat to give you a push. And yes, more money. But...'

'I don't care.' Walker turned back towards the window, his hands holding onto the sill as he shook. 'So Reims was a set-up as well, your wound...'

'No!'

'Come on.'

'No, *please*. I had no idea, I guess something changed and they decided to track us down. Maybe they were in a hurry, I don't know...'

'Then how did they find us?'

'Your phone, no?'

Walker snapped back, feeling colder now. She was not giving him the full story, and he was too shocked to think clearly. He'd had enough. 'A Dorfmann secure BlackBerry? I can't believe I fell for that. How the fuck would they trace it?'

Layla stood and took a step towards him but he held up his hands, freezing her into place. 'I... maybe they have someone on the inside,' she said.

'You're not that good when you have to make up lies on the spot.'

'I almost died after Reims. Please, Scott, don't do this. You can't think...'

'*No*. I couldn't think before. But maybe now I'm starting to.' He glanced outside, concentrating on the darkening clouds. It was time to find out the rest, if he could. If she'd tell him. 'Are they coming here?'

'I haven't spoken to them since London –'

Again Walker lifted his hand, still looking away. It could be true. 'Did you send them stuff from my tablet?'

'No.'

'Then why are you here?' he growled. 'Why did you tell me his name?'

Tears ran slowly down her cheeks. She didn't try to wipe them away. 'Everything since Reims has been real. You have to believe me. I... I want to help you.'

'Shut up.'

'Please. I know you can't trust me now, but I gave you Pienaar's name because... to help you bring these bastards down. I *was* afraid DeepShare might find out, I just hoped I had a little more time to make you understand.'

'Understand what?'

'It – it's not been easy. But I'm in love with you now, and...' She trailed off, uncertain.

Walker sighed, lit a cigarette and blew out the hot smoke. It had sounded plausible, in a way. But it was hard to tell – she had proven too good an actress till now. And he wasn't going to risk it, not any more. He stared into her red-rimmed eyes and nodded, exhaling.

'Fuck you. I never want to see you again.'

He picked up a small white envelope from the window sill and threw it at her feet. Layla glanced down, then up at him again.

'It's fifty thousand Euros,' he said. 'Take your fee, get dressed and disappear for a couple of hours. When you come back, I'll be gone.'

Layla nodded, wiped away her tears and turned back to the bedroom. Before shutting the door she looked at him and whispered, 'I understand. But I'll wait for you. If you change your mind, if you need anything – I'll be here.'

Walker flicked his cigarette out of the window and hurried to his computer, starting to pack the wires.

'That's going to be a long wait.'

...

Pienaar had thought several times about bailing and getting back to Africa in the past few days. He needed the money, but Europe was just too hard for him to stay long. His tastes couldn't really be satisfied, and what he liked to do was considered uncivilized around here. Goddamn wimps, they just didn't understand that man was either predator or prey. They had all their little laws and rules, but the beast could not be chained. Not for long, anyway.

At least the Englishman had called at last: they were in a hurry, now. Desperate for results.

That's what he was good at.

Pienaar smiled – organization, the right time and place, a bit of planning. All he needed, to get them results. And maybe have a little fun in the process.

Siena

The beauty and uniqueness of Siena's main square, Piazza del Campo, left Walker almost dazed as he sat at one of the outdoor bars and sipped a Campari soda without really tasting it. Throngs of people milled around the nine white-stone slashes in the travertine pavement near the ancient fountain and the central drain, weaving and talking, snatching pictures of the ancient palaces and homes, enjoying the early evening air.

Walker lit a cigarette and his mind bounced back to Layla again. He cursed himself in a low voice and finished his drink, signalling to the waiter for a second one. He needed to concentrate: Mosha would arrive soon and the Serb was going to need a lot of convincing. He opened his rucksack and took out DM's tablet, making sure the connection to the mainframe was active before diving into the software, finally becoming engrossed just as a hand came to rest on his shoulder.

'*Buonasera,*' a gruff voice said.

Walker half-turned and nodded at Mosha, attempting a nervous smile. The last three years had apparently not been kind to his old classmate, who had gained a large amount of weight and shed most of his hair in return. Walker stood and shook his hand, uncertain about how to proceed.

Mosha took off his jacket and sat down, just as the waiter arrived with a drink. The big Serb took it, ordered another one and sighed, his expression grim.

'So.'

'It's good to see you, man.'

'Yeah. Can you tell me what the fuck is going on now? There's all sort of stories, and the UK police seem pretty interested in talking to you.'

'I didn't kill DM Khaing.'

Mosha smiled crookedly, sipping his stolen drink. 'Of course not. Who did?'

Walker slid his chair nearer and lowered his voice, their heads almost touching. He rushed through the events, leaving Layla mostly out of it. When he mentioned Pienaar's name, and Blackspring, the Serb interrupted him, clearing his throat.

'You've heard of him?'

'Not the guy. But Blackspring – I've heard of them all right. Nasty muscle, many former black-ops. Active in Iraq, Afghanistan. They're guns for hire: the darker the business the better they like it.'

'I know. Could Frankel be using them?'

'Sure. A lot of banks have, in the past. Surveillance, industrial espionage and worse. I looked to them too, once, but then...' Mosha coughed, almost embarrassed. 'We... decided to keep it in the family.'

Walker shivered. 'Jesus. Do you think they can be linked?'

Mosha motioned for one of his cigarettes, lit it and took a long drag.

'That might be hard.' He paused for a second as Walker finished his drink. 'The only ones who might be able to dig out something like that are the madmen at...'

The big Serb stopped suddenly and jerked to his feet, flashing a smile at someone sitting a few yards away.

'Franco, good to see you!' he said loudly.

The man, a well-dressed Italian in his mid-fifties, smiled back and looked about to come and join them. Mosha dropped a couple of banknotes on the table, then gestured apologetically. 'I'm afraid I've gotta run, *Direttore* – but I'll call you later.'

He picked up his jacket and glanced over, whispering, 'Let's get out of here. Everyone in Siena seems to work for their damn Colle Bank.'

Walker shrugged and they hurried across the square, heading for one of the little side streets leading away from the piazza.

...

The Range Rover entered the garage and the wide aluminum shutter started to close. Pienaar waited for a couple of seconds, his gun ready. As soon as he heard the car-door click open he rushed from behind a pile of old crates and slammed the panel into the driver. His timing was perfect and Luigi Seu shouted in pain, falling back on the seat.

Pienaar pointed his Beretta at the man's face, grinning. 'Move slowly, you stupid fuck.'

A dazed Luigi nodded and got out gingerly, and the big Australian readjusted his backpack, waiting. His gun didn't waver, still trained on a spot just below the man's nose. Luigi glanced at him, his hands fumbling with the keys. 'What do you want?'

'Just to talk.'

'Are you...' The Italian's voice shook. 'Are you the one who killed DM?'

Pienaar didn't reply, shoving him through the side entrance and sending him sprawling to the floor. He slammed the door shut and glanced around, making sure they were alone in the house.

'Maybe. But no one needs to get hurt, if you tell me what I want to know. Where is Walker?'

Luigi struggled to a sitting position, staring wide-eyed at the Australian. 'I... I don't know, I haven't seen him...'

Pienaar's small gun went off, a muffled sound coming from the silencer. The Italian jumped back as the bullet dug a hole right between his legs.

'Wrong answer.' The Aussie circled quickly and reached out to the massive window overlooking the lake, drawing one of the curtains closed. He was about to pull the second one when Luigi shot up and sprang around the sofa, trying to reach his study.

Pienaar turned in a flash and cut across, diving after him. His hand locked around the broker's ankle and Luigi tumbled forward, banging his head on a side table and rolling to the floor, groaning.

The Aussie spat on him, his features twisted in a mask of fury. He lowered his gun into the Italian's face, pointing it at his forehead.

'You're a feisty one, yes?' His lips turned up in a rictus of savage glee. 'I like those.'

'Please...' Luigi panted, his pupils swivelling towards the barrel. 'I have no idea...'

'Turn around.'

'What?'

Pienaar pulled the Beretta back and lashed at the broker's face with the barrel, dropping him to the floor again. He picked up his rucksack and snarled, 'If you are not kneeling, palms on the floor, by the count of three, I swear I'll kill you right now.'

Luigi coughed, blood dripping from his broken nose. He pushed back on his hands and tried to sit up.

'One...'

...

Mosha hurried along a cobbled road, leaving behind a large group of French tourists. After a few steps he swore and tracked back into a side street: it was so narrow and twisty that there were no balconies above them, and Walker realised he could touch both walls without extending his arms fully. They walked on in silence for a couple of minutes, following the sharp angles as the alley became even smaller, only a sliver of dusky light falling through the buildings.

'Where are we going?'

'The Bottini.' Mosha stopped in front of a low wooden door that looked a thousand years old. He pulled out a key and turned the rusty lock, swinging it back into darkness and disappearing. Walker followed him inside and the big Serb closed the door behind them, fumbling in the pitch-black entrance. A click echoed, and a string of dim light bulbs lit up a narrow stone corridor, with ancient steps disappearing lower into the ground. The air was musky and humid – Walker coughed, shivering with mild claustrophobia.

'Bottini?'

'The medieval water-system for Siena. Twenty miles of tunnels, below the city. It's from the thirteenth century, abandoned now but still useful.'

'Great.'

'I have an office down here.'

'Are you kidding me?'

The Serb grunted and started descending the steep stone staircase, quickly disappearing from view. 'Afraid of the dark? There's only rats, I think. Tourists visit another area, below the Palazzo Ducale.'

'And you have an *office?*'

'You know Colle is our main bank. I come to Tuscany too often for my liking, and we sometimes need secure lines of communication. Follow me and be careful; it's slippery down below.'

Walker sighed. 'As you say, chief.'

Mosha continued into the ancient maze, choosing his way seemingly at random among the stone corridors, going up and down worn steps until they reached a rusted iron door, barely illuminated by the last flickering light bulb. The Serb pulled out a thin magnetic card and pressed it to the centre of the doorframe, waiting.

Something clicked and a stone near the side shifted. Mosha dislodged it, revealing a gleaming steel-and-glass sensor, then rested his thumb on it. The rusted panel sprang open and he pushed it back, turning to glance at Walker. 'Welcome to my den.'

...

Luigi struggled to a kneeling position and looked up at his tormentor, wondering what the man had in mind. His heart thumped and his head swam in pain; he tried to force his breathing slower and raised a hand to clear the blood from his nose.

The Australian pulled out what looked like a second, larger gun from his bag and walked around the sofa, slipping behind him. 'Put your hands on the floor in front of you, and keep staring ahead.'

'What...?'

The silenced handgun went off again, and a shower of plaster fell from the ceiling, near his feet. Luigi followed the order and closed his eyes, images of his wife and daughter flashing in the darkness. Thanking God that they were away, he felt a cloth slip around his head to tighten on his mouth. Then a loud noise, followed by a shock of unbelievable pain from the back of his leg.

Luigi screamed but the cloth muffled him, before another popping sound caused a second, monstrous explosion in his other knee. He fell forward and blackness overtook him as the floor crashed into his face.

...

'Hackernym.' Mosha leaned back in his plush chair, staring at the ceiling.

The hidden office was a high-tech space filled with monitors and computers, with a small side bathroom and even room for a secretary in a closed-up corner. Dozens of monitors covered the walls, the largest one silently tuned to Bloomberg TV and CNBC. 'Those cyber-pirates are the only ones who might be able to figure something like this out.'

'How do you know?'

'Because they did it to me!' The Serb groaned and stood up, pacing about the narrow room. 'They first called about eighteen months ago, threatening to expose a few of my... investors. They had all sort of insider documents, amazing.'

'Hackernym broke through your firewalls? Nothing ever came out, though.' Walker was nonplussed, and suspicious. Why was Mosha opening up so much? The DeepShare data he'd been shown was good, but he'd hardly offered anything until then. Maybe he was in more trouble than Walker thought.

'How did you stop it?'

'We cut a deal.' Mosha sat back down with a grimace and poured himself a whiskey from a squat crystal bottle, offering a second one to Walker. 'I give them stuff, and they keep quiet.'

'Stuff? You mean money?'

'No. Data, information. They have plenty of money, I think.'

'What type of information?'

'All sorts. From central banks' backdoor meetings to political pressures, anything. The murkier it is, the happier they are.'

Walker hesitated, surprised. Hackernym had pulled a few spectacular stunts in the last few years, like attacking the servers at Eurex or paralyzing Wall Street's settlements for a couple of hours, but they weren't known for any Wikileaks-type operation. They seemed more like a cyber-terror underground, trying to cause havoc in payments and financial market systems, attacking the infrastructure. 'Why?'

'No clue. But I got the feeling we were only small fish to them.' The Serb chuckled, his fat jowls wobbling.

'With over ten billion under management?'

Mosha nodded and finished his drink with a gulp. 'Yep. Those guys, they're very smart. And I think they are planning something... scary big. But they hold me by the balls.'

'Do you know if anybody else...?'

'Know? No.' Mosha shrugged. 'We all have our secrets, and weaknesses. But when their name comes up in casual conversation – I've seen a few worried faces. Famous faces, in our world.'

'I had no idea.' Walker paused, considering. *Maybe.* He needed all the help he could get.

'Few do. You should talk to them. They might find your story interesting.'

'How?'

'I'll make a call. Hackernym has a man in Rome, I think.'

Rome was only two hours away. An easy call. 'Great. I can go tomorrow.'

'Okay.' Mosha poured another drink and gestured at one of the monitors, switching it to a screenful of data. Walker recognised some of the analysis he had been sending over in the previous week. 'Now let's talk business, Yours.'

...

Luigi woke slowly, his blurred eyes struggling to focus. He tried to lift his cheek from the floor and his head exploded in pain, but his mouth refused to open in a scream, some sort of tape sealing it shut. He groaned instead, staring at the gleaming steel circle that stuck out from the back of his right hand.

His bruised brain failed to comprehend what was happening for a second, before recoiling in horror.

A nail.

His right hand had been NAILED to the floor.

Suppressing another scream, Luigi shifted his weight to his left palm and more pain shot up from his legs, almost breaking him. His head turned inch by inch, carefully, as he pushed off the floor on his good arm. He couldn't shift his knees...

The agony coursed through him like fire, as if sight had reawakened his shattered nerves. Two more large metal heads stuck out from the back of his legs, the steel going through his kneecaps. He was... almost crucified. His eyes started watering as fear and suffering flowed through his body, in waves, relentless like the tide.

Luigi blacked out again for an instant, but came back immediately as his face struck the floor, searing lightning into his mind. His chest shook in muffled heaves as his eyes refocused on a pair of scuffed brown shoes, just inches away.

He looked up into the Australian's placid eyes and tried to open his mouth. To plead, to beg. Anything, just to make the pain stop.

Pienaar grunted and cleared his throat, a slight smile on his thin lips. 'Now you'll behave better, won't you?'

Luigi nodded, the tiny movement spreading more fire through his limbs.

The Australian knelt lower, taking the Italian's good hand almost tenderly, and lifted the nail-gun from the floor. 'I'll pull the tape off your mouth in a second, mate. But there's something I need to finish off, first.'

Luigi watched the weapon move up in slow motion, drifting through the air. He let the big man push his left hand down without resistance, the rational part of him already broken, unable to fight.

The kiss of the steel barrel on the back of his hand was cool, quite pleasant.

Then a click, and hell opened up for him as iron went though flesh, his hand now entombed on the floor. Luigi thought it looked a bit like a dead crab on a brown beach, waiting for the tide. Then, thankfully, darkness overtook him again.

Underground Blood

'The market swings you forecast were impressive, and the logs match.' Mosha sat back and grabbed another one of Walker's cigarettes, putting it in his mouth unlit. 'And how Deep predicted the Italian mess... that's just astonishing.'

'There's more. It thinks the Euro could really break because of this. Rossini, Spain...'

'What probability?'

'Over sixty per cent. In less than five months.'

'Shit. And I can't get my hedge fund out of this fucking country.'

Walker smiled and lit his own Marlboro. 'There might be a way.'

'No. I've tried, but Banca Colle is basically state-run now, since the morons almost went bust a few years ago. The Minister and the Bank of Italy know where our capital comes from and they won't go after it – if I leave it here. But I'm not allowed to take it out.'

'Still, you can manage the fund as you want.'

'Yes.'

'And you have credit lines abroad. That you could lever up, in London and the US.'

'They won't let me hedge for Italian or Eurozone risk, here or abroad. It sends bad signals, apparently. That was made *very* clear.'

'What about betting against a big bank, like people did in '08? You might even get to do a good deed, for once.'

'Maybe.' Mosha looked at him askance, trying to guess where this was going.

Walker took a deep breath and sipped his drink, his mind rushing through the steps he'd been working on for the last few days. He pulled the tablet out of his backpack and logged onto DeepShare.

'If you set up the trade correctly,' he said, 'taking one side in Italy and splitting the opposite hedge abroad, you could lose here and make the money back in safe havens. A small risk if the bet doesn't come off, but if it works you effectively transfer a big chunk of your cash wherever you want, Switzerland, Cayman, anywhere.'

The Serb stood up again, his eyes losing focus as he started considering the process. He was silent for a couple of minutes, pacing, then came over to Walker's chair, his hand out for a lighter. 'I need to think about it.'

'It could be almost symmetrical. Or you could go all-in, and make a fortune abroad.'

'Only if there's an event that suits. Something that will make my big trades look unimportant.'

'Deep seems to think that something bad is brewing at a bank. A massive one.'

Mosha stepped aside, staring at one of the screens flashing through market information. A few graphs appeared and vanished as he gestured at the monitor, then he took a long drag of smoke and coughed. 'The market is awfully quiet for something like that to be lurking in the background.'

'It was the same when the London Whale almost sank JP Morgan. Or when Long-Term Capital went under.' Walker sniggered. 'You never know what investment banks are running, and when it'll blow up. Maybe someone liked Italian assets way too much. Or maybe something exotic we have yet no idea about will crack.'

'And your software has forecast this?'

'Possibly. Your capital might be the final trigger that Deep is looking for.'

Mosha shrugged and finished his own drink. 'So you say. But for something like this, logs are not enough. I'd need my tech people to look at your DeepShare. The entire code.'

Walker nodded, expecting this. 'I guessed as much. But I don't have Omega with me now.'

'When can you get it?'

'Soon, I think. But I'll have to collect it from several locations, *and* I can't send it over the net.'

'Of course. That's not a problem – we'll find a way.' Mosha grinned, his trading brain obviously already engaging with the issues. 'What about a little preview of what you know?'

Walker unlocked his tablet and waved him over. 'Well, as you know there's one bank that I don't like at all...'

...

'I can make the pain go away.' Pienaar looked down at the sobbing figure of the idiotic Italian. Blood spatterings covered the floor and the man's clothes, and he was careful as he shifted his feet to put away the surgical scalpel he had used so artistically until a few minutes before.

'Please... I've told you everything. The car, the phone...' Luigi's hoarse voice broke down again.

'I know, I know.'

'Please. My fingers...'

'The skin will grow back. So Walker is in the Nuorese, you reckon. But you're not sure.'

'No, we thought...'

'Yes, safer that way. But some of his family comes from there, no?'

'Please, the pain...'

Pienaar grimaced. This was becoming boring, and he was sure the wretch had already given him everything. Now he would start to make up stories, anything to please him. There was no more fight in the broker.

They all shattered quite easily in the end, you only had to take a few bits here and there...

'Okay. Look at me now.'

Luigi's head rose, twitching as he tried to straighten his neck. The nails in his left knee and right hand had come a little loose, Pienaar noticed. He walked around the bloodstains and lowered himself to stare straight into the red-rimmed, swollen eyes of the Italian.

'No more pain, I promised.'

He brought the nail-gun up from the floor and rested it against Luigi's forehead, then slowly squeezed the trigger, jumping aside as blood fountained forward.

CHAPTER FOURTEEN

Train

Walker rushed through the underground passage below the train tracks, swivelling to avoid an old man and almost tripping over some rucksacks. He dodged a bunch of teenagers with their heads buried in their smartphones and jumped into the carriage just as the doors started to close. The train shook and lurched forward as he stepped into the first-class wagon and looked around, checking the faces of the few passengers. No one he'd ever seen before. He exhaled and tried to slow his breathing, drying droplets of sweat from his temples.

A couple of businesswomen looked at him askance, before returning to their laptops. Further ahead a harried mother with two young children was desperately searching for toys to keep them entertained. The rest of the carriage was empty and he sat down by a window, still shaking with adrenaline. Florence had felt too small as he had tried to disappear among the tourists, wasting time to buy a few clothes and some pre-paid debit cards. And a cheap new phone after Mosha had called with the details to meet with Hackernym in Rome.

Around every corner there had seemed to be someone staring at him, and he was certain that a young man had tried to follow him through Ponte Vecchio. Or maybe he was just cracking up. Still, he was glad he had made the train just in time; an hour of waiting at the station would have been too long to contemplate.

The carriage rumbled away towards Rome and Walker sighed and lay back, his head aching. He had managed only a couple of hours of sleep, battered by visions of Layla as soon as he closed his eyes, uncertain whether the nausea was caused by the paranoia or her betrayal. As he grabbed and played with the new Nokia her eyes gleamed in his memory, mixing with the feel of her body and her scent. Which made him curse under his breath, before he took out DM's tablet, hoping to lose his mind in the spires of DeepShare.

Maybe it's not as bad as you think. It might have started for the wrong reasons, but in the end she told you what you needed to know.

He threw the tablet on the seat and angrily tried to shut off his inner voice. There had been too many lies, and he couldn't trust Layla ever again. She was just a leech after the next buck. A dangerous, beautiful leech. He stared outside as the autumn landscape flew past him, darker shades of yellow and brown descending on the fields of Tuscany and Lazio. And again he wondered why she had chosen to help him, in the end. Even if she must have guessed that DeepShare would eventually...

Walker stood up, placing his head against the cool window. This hurt too much, and he had a meeting that could seal his fate in a few hours. Hackernym was not going to care about Layla, and he desperately needed help in tying Frankel to Pienaar, if his plan was going to have even a small chance of success.

He had not told Mosha the entire truth. Frankel was vulnerable, but even DeepOmega did not know how or why it could be taken on yet. There were too many uncertainties – he still needed proof, information. He had to...

You should talk to her, give her another chance.

Which one was the real Layla? She could have brought Blackspring down on him, but hadn't. How could he be certain? That was something, he guessed: he was still alive – but maybe Deep had been compromised. Then again, DM's systems would have noticed, for sure.

He sat back down, his head spinning and twisting on itself. A waiter came by and he ordered a coffee and a bottle of water, his stomach scrunching up at the idea of anything more solid. Calling her was just too risky and she would be long gone, anyway. He had walked out of Sadali two days earlier, and now she had the money owed her. He sighed and pulled out his phone. He couldn't call her, but perhaps the old woman at the hotel had seen someone...

Walker's fingers must have dialled without him noticing and the ringtone buzzed painfully in his ear. It took a few seconds before the raspy voice of the Agriturismo's owner answered.

'Pronto?'

Walker hesitated, almost surprised. Then he started talking, his Italian sounding a little artificial to his own ears.

'Miss Sanna, it's Romeo. I just wanted to know if anyone has come along looking for me in the last couple of days?'

'Signor Romeo! No, no one has come...' She lowered her voice, sounding conspiratorial. 'But...'

'What?'

'I was wondering when you're coming back. The lady, Miss Juliette, she is a bit...'

Walker recoiled from the phone. Layla had said she would wait. 'She's still there?'

'Well, naturally. She looks a little... sad, though. Hardly ever leaves the room.' Her voice dropped even lower and Walker had to struggle to make sense of the words.

'A lovers' spat, maybe? Be good to her, she seems a nice lady. And so pretty, too. I remember when I was young...'

'Of course, of course.' Walker cut her off, trying to regain his composure. 'Sorry but I have to go now...'

'Should I tell her you rang?'

'Yes... No, I'll call her later. Thank you.'

He dropped the phone, hands shaking, and lay back in his seat. The waiter arrived with his drink and Walker downed the coffee, ordering another one. Then he picked up the tablet and headed for the second-class toilets, hoping the fire-alarm had been disabled.

Italian trains were notorious for people smoking in the restrooms, and he was desperate for a cigarette.

Bad News

The old man opened his eyes and sighed. Doctors and nurses had finally left the room, after more useless prodding and probing.

There was hardly any point.

He'd been trying to cheat death for too long, and knew he had run out of time. A month – maybe Christmas, they had said. It would be nice to see the New Year, but he doubted he would.

He rasped something and a pretty young woman brought him the speakerphone. It was time for final preparations. He might be around for Act One, if he was lucky. Act Two was still too far, but it should be able to run on without him.

Pity, he would have enjoyed the ugliness.

...

The train toilet was a mess, as usual. Dirty, unkempt, stinking of piss. Someone had ripped out the fire-alarm and wedged one of the windows open. A light taint of tobacco permeated the air, and a few butts floated in the broken bowl.

Italy, eternally unchanging.

Walker closed the WC and sat on the lid, pulling a cigarette out. *What now?*

His mind spun with possibilities, Layla's parting words tormenting him. She was still at the hotel. She hadn't called anyone, and was waiting. For him. Or maybe she was just bait. Maybe the trap had already been set, was ready to snap shut.

He lit the cigarette and swore at himself. Was he becoming paranoid? What was real and what were just shadows in his mind?

He needed to talk to someone.

His fingers flashed through Luigi's number, as if speed would make it less dangerous, but a part of him was beyond caring. He had to make sure he wasn't going insane. The call went straight to voicemail and he swore again, crushing his cigarette and lighting another one. He checked his watch – it was after five, and Luigi might already be home. He tried the house phone and a woman answered after the first ring.

'Hello?'

Walker hesitated. Luigi's wife wasn't due back for another week, and the voice sounded odd. 'Susan?'

'No, this is Officer Tarelli, of the Ticino Police. Who's this?'

Walker's heart sank and he dropped his cigarette.

'Uh, hello...' His instincts took over as he stumbled on the words. 'My name's Ginelli, I'm a friend of Luigi's. Is he around?' His brain looped images of DM's broken body but he refused to believe them. It couldn't be true.

'Mr Ginelli, I'm afraid Luigi Seu has been assaulted.'

'Assaulted? Is he all right?' Walker croaked, already knowing the answer.

'I'm sorry, but I can't tell you anything. If you leave your name and number, we will get back...'

Walker cut off the connection and almost slammed the phone against the wall. His lungs turned to ice and he forced himself to breathe, taking a step towards the mirror. He stared at his reflection for a second, noticing red-rimmed eyes and deep shadows under his lids. Then he threw a punch, shattering the glass and shredding his knuckles.

There was no pain. Not from the hand. Not from anything. Just a tsunami of rage that seemed to grow and rise impossibly as it swallowed him.

...

Layla's phone rang and she jumped off the bed, dropping her laptop as she rushed to the little side table. The digits on the tiny screen were an Italian number she didn't know but her heart accelerated and she bit on her lower lip. '*Sì?*'

'Get out of there.'

'Scott! Thank God, I was so...'

'They've killed Luigi. Get away *now* – it's too dangerous out there.' Walker's voice was steely, almost emotionless. Layla was speechless for a second, shocked.

'I'm... I'm sorry. What happened? Where are you?'

'It doesn't matter now. Fly to the States, I'll get in touch in a few days. But you have to leave Sardinia – Pienaar must know we went to the Nuorese, and they'll have the car plates.'

Layla's mind raced through scenarios, Pienaar's scarred face laughing at her. Walker was right, she had to run. 'Okay, of course. I'll...' She stopped, caught her breath. There was something else. 'Scott, wait.'

'What?'

'You know I had nothing to do with... with this?'

Walker missed a beat. 'Yeah. No point in going after Luigi if you were talking to them, right?'

'Right...' She struggled for words, hearing the pain that had suddenly surfaced in his voice. 'I'm so sorry, he was a good man.'

'He was. And I swear I'll find a way to make them pay, no matter what it costs me.'

'Do you want my help?'

'I need you.'

'Then you have me. No matter what it costs.'

CHAPTER FIFTEEN

Rome

Walker checked his watch as he completed his twelfth circle around the inside perimeter of the Pantheon mausoleum. Five minutes to go – about fucking time. He glanced at the tomb of an old Italian king and wondered what Luigi's grave would look like. Then he swore at himself quietly, glad of the silence, darkness and lack of cameras inside the ancient building. Killing an hour wandering the streets of Rome would have been too much to take, and his cramped hotel room felt too stifling. He had needed to move, to burn off the tension and anger. To think. To plan a way of getting even.

Taking a deep breath, he left the Roman temple by a side exit and hurried across the circular plaza, wading past one of the open-air cafes into the maze of cobbled alleys beyond. After a couple of minutes he reached 'Er Fagiolaro', a small restaurant that seemed carved into the corner of a run-down palace. It was too early for dinner in Rome and the few tables scattered around the black limestone floor were empty. Behind the bar a middle-aged man glanced up from the dishes he was scrubbing, asking, 'Micovich?'

Mosha's last name. Walker nodded, and the barman pointed to his right, to a little side door.

'Lady's waiting for you.'

Walker crossed the room, entering a private alcove almost entirely taken up by a rough table and chairs. A young woman looked up from her laptop, smiling at him. She must have been in her early twenties, pretty with long brown hair and hazel eyes behind narrow glasses.

'Hello, Scott. You can call me Mira.'

Walker hesitated, feeling out of place. Was this his Hackernym contact, the emissary of the feared cyber-pirates? It seemed wrong, somehow. Unreal.

A young woman, maybe still at university. It couldn't be right.

Mira stood and shook his hand, her smile never wavering. 'Don't worry, this place is secure. We use it every once in a while and sweep it regularly.'

'Secure?' *For you, maybe.*

'Yes – thick solid stone. No phone signals, no radar-mikes...' She giggled. 'I hate bugs.'

Walker sat down, dropping his rucksack under the table. The world was getting weirder by the second. 'Great. Listen, I don't know what Mosha told you, but I...'

'Micovich didn't need to say anything.'

'Really? Why are you meeting me then?'

Mira glanced at her laptop and typed something, her hands flashing over the keyboard. She turned it around, showing him a large picture of Pienaar.

'We know.'

'What?' Walker stared at the screen, shocked. His stomach twisted at seeing the murderer's face, and he had to restrain himself from grabbing the computer and smashing it on the floor.

'How?'

'You're just a little piece in a much bigger game, Yours.' She paused, letting her words sink in. 'We've been after Frankel for a long time, and we know about their links with this... monster.'

Walker's throat felt dry. This was exactly what he needed. 'Do you have proof?'

'Some. Not enough, yet. And we need to learn your story, that's one of the keys we've been missing. Do you have all of DeepShare?'

A knock on the door interrupted them, and the fat barman wobbled into the room with a tray heaped with slices of focaccia, some cold cuts and a bottle of vodka. He placed the tray next to Mira, who popped a piece of bread in her mouth and started chewing vigorously, then he handed Walker a tumbler filled with ice and a small ashtray and left with a grunt.

Mira smiled, a few crumbs still stuck to her lip. 'See, we even know what you like.'

Walker poured himself a large drink and rummaged in his pockets for cigarettes, trying to gain a few seconds. This was a world away from what he had expected. He wondered whether they could simply be using what he had told Mosha and wasn't sure how to go on. His brain felt addled, slow. But they must have known he'd check back with the Serb – there would be no point in pretending.

'I'll have all the pieces of the code soon,' he said in the end.

Mira nodded, studying his face. 'Good. We need them fast.'

'Why would I hand Deep to you?'

Her stare never wavered. 'To take Frankel Schwartz on, you'll need us.'

'Who the hell is *us?* All I know is Hackernym blew up a few servers, and you claim to know stuff about a bank.'

Mira typed something on her computer without glancing at the keyboard. 'I know it's been terrible for you, and I'm sorry for the loss of your friends. But we are not your enemies. These guys are.' She pressed a button and the speakers came to life, with a hint of static noise.

Voices, low music in the background. Tinkling of glass.

Walker tried to concentrate on the chatter but she signalled for him to wait. Some restaurant or pub, maybe.

An American man came on mid-sentence, louder, his words quite clear. *'Now they want proof though, something tangible. It's a big step for them.'*

Someone responded and Walker shuddered. It was a voice he had heard before, hundreds of times. A London accent, bass tones, certainty. Arrogance.

'Blackspring is on the ground, but it might take a while. A few weeks, months maybe.'

It was Beano Friedman, Dorfmann's London CEO. The Englishman had helped him in his career too many times to count, even on his last day on the trading floor. Walker swallowed, bile rising in his throat.

After a brief pause the American's voice came back on. *'That might not be a problem, as long as you can deliver the machine. You know I trust your vision, but... they'll need to see some data, soon.'*

Mira closed the laptop and waited, giving Walker time to process the information. She picked up a crumb of bread and played with it for a few seconds. In the end he just nodded, not trusting his voice, and she cleared her throat. 'I guess you recognise the English guy.'

'Yes,' he managed.

'The American is Wendall Welsh, one of the main powerbrokers on Frankel's board. He's working to get Friedman in the top spot at Frankel Schwartz. He couldn't do it at your bank, so he decided months ago to look for pastures new.'

'And DeepShare...'

'Was to be his engagement gift. Apparently they need it bad; there's something wrong in their back books.'

'I know.' Walker sank back down and took a sip of his drink, struggling to slow his breathing.

Friedman. That was how they had traced his phone to Reims – Frankel didn't need anyone on the inside at Dorfmann. One of the bank's highest-level managers was already working for them. The bastard's ambition had first killed DM, and now Luigi. Walker wanted to scream.

He stood up and lit another cigarette, trying to make sense of what he had heard. 'But... if you knew this, why didn't you stop them?' His voice rose, anger seeping in. 'Maybe you could have saved DM...'

Mira stared back at him, her friendly smile now gone. 'We didn't have any details, no real idea of what DeepShare might be or who was working on it. After DM's murder we put the pieces together, but by then you were gone and we couldn't find you. Until...'

'Until I met with Mosha.'

'Yes.'

Walker sighed, exhaustion catching up with him. The world had just twisted on itself again and he needed time to reflect on what he'd just been told. 'What happens now?'

Mira shrugged. 'This is all I know. I'm not so high up in Hackernym yet.'

She poured herself a glass of water and bit into another piece of focaccia. 'It's your call, I guess.' Her eyes glinted. 'Will you go to the US and meet up with the Old Man?'

'Who is he?'

'The Boss. God, maybe. I don't know, but he *is* Hackernym. Created it, financed it. He will have answers for you, I think.'

'I need more than answers.'

Mira shrugged and stood up, folding her laptop into a small handbag. The meeting was over. 'Go to Paradise Cove in Malibu and ask for him at the beach restaurant. He's very interested in you. That's all I can say.'

'What's his name?'

'Just ask for the Old Man. Someone will come.'

Running

Layla stuffed a couple of bags in the tiny trunk of the Fiat 500 and drove away from the Agriturismo, heading back into town. She rushed through the country roads, knowing that she only had a couple of hours to make the flight in Cagliari. Her mind was in turmoil, and she was worried about Walker. He had sounded weird, almost *changed* by Luigi's murder. She hoped he didn't do anything crazy out of rage or carelessness – things had become extremely dangerous again, and she knew how good Pienaar and his people were.

She accelerated onto the highway, checking her mirrors to make sure no one was tailing her. If they had the car plates, and access to some good data-miners, Blackspring could be catching up with her any time. She needed to get away from Sardinia as soon as possible and Walker had told her to fly to the US, where it would be a lot simpler to disappear.

Scott.

Layla wondered whether his meeting with Mosha had gone well, but she realised that his plan was starting to sound more and more like a broken dream. A lot of the details were unclear, and she could not hope to understand how DeepShare worked or even if Walker's ideas were feasible at all.

What's going to happen if... when I see him again?

After he had called, though it was sad and scary, a small part of her had rejoiced – maybe they could have a second chance.

But now she understood why it was impossible, and wrong.

Layla changed lanes and honked at a truck driver as she took the exit towards the airport, still glancing behind every few seconds to make sure no cars shadowed her turns. *You've been through this before, bitch. You have betrayed your loved ones for most of your life. There's something wrong in the setting of your brain and heart. Leave him alone, if you truly care for him.*

She sighed and wished for one of Walker's cigarettes, or maybe just the smell of him and the sound of his voice. Luigi's murder had sadly proven that she had not gone behind his back, that her link to Blackspring had been truly and definitely severed. But she still owed Walker a lot of explaining.

She skipped the airport exit and took the next one, deciding to leave the car in a semi-abandoned industrial estate – she could hitch a lift to the terminal and the vehicle might prove to be harder to find, maybe gaining them a day or two on Pienaar's men. *What are you going to tell him when you meet him? More half-lies, to make you look better than you really are?*

Layla swore at the voice in her head and gritted her teeth. He deserved the whole truth of who she was and what she had done in the past.

The entire ugly story, to make him realise he was better off without her.

Walker needed her help, and she swore she would do anything in her power to save him. But they couldn't be together, ever again. His plan was too fanciful, and she guessed in the end he would just have to disappear and rebuild a life somewhere else, if he survived.

A life without her, though it would break her heart again. If she couldn't trust herself, she couldn't allow him to put his faith in her.

It was that simple.

Colosseum

Walker turned into the wide boulevard of Via del Corso, leaving the tangle of ancient alleys behind. He had walked away from the Pantheon across the old heart of Rome in a daze, not knowing where he was going. His brain swam, looping around what Mira had shown him. Was it really possible? Friedman – how could the bastard have betrayed them, how could he be involved in murders...

All just for the sake of a bigger job, more power, fame? It was astonishing, but then the man's ambition had always burnt too brightly. The son-of-a-bitch didn't even need to work, had been worth hundreds of millions as a teenager, the scion of an insurance dynasty educated at the best schools in England. But as Mendes – who had known him well for years – had once told him, Friedman had always needed to be the best, the chief, the man. He craved recognition and power, headlines and business magazine covers, but Dorfmann, only a mid-tier player, could never be enough for him. Frankel Schwartz on Wall Street, though – that was the ultimate trophy, the bank that could truly put him on the map as one of the great financiers of the age. Again, Walker wondered if that was all the reason such a man could need. But Mira had been convincing, and the recording...

His head hurt, and he lit a cigarette to burn off the acrid taste at the back of his throat. Friedman and Frankel – a marriage made in hell. It just felt true, now that he knew. But his guts had failed him before. He needed more proof. And if the Old Man could help... he had to go and see him. No point hiding around Italy, not anymore.

He coughed, threw away the Marlboro and started thinking through the trip. He knew there was a direct flight to LA from Rome's main airport, but it might be better to take a longer route. Layla would probably be going through the same terminal, and at this point it was much better not to... A car honked and he stepped away from the road, focusing back and realising he was lost. He turned into a small side street and waded through the crowds of a busy outside bar, looking for a waiter to ask for directions.

The place was heaving. People chattering, busy ladies dodging and dancing through tables, glasses and plates in a precarious equilibrium. As he waited for a white-aproned girl to finish serving he glanced to his left, and noticed two men wearing dark suits slip into the side street. One stood taller than the other but both were thick with muscles, shoulders wide, biceps straining their sleeves. They were rushing, studying faces, checking the tables near the bar's entrance. *Shit.* Were they looking...

The taller one swivelled and his pale eyes fixed on him.

Walker swore and jumped back, overturning a chair. He shifted his backpack and spun off just as the man shouted something, then he accelerated into the side street, turning left again after a dozen yards. The smaller road beyond was overcrowded with tables from a tourist restaurant and he dodged through them, stumbling into one. Plates crashed to the ground and he checked back, managing to cross the last few steps as the two men in suits started weaving through the customers. He jumped a wide flowerpot and rushed forward, sliding through a group of old ladies and taking a couple of sharp turns into tiny alleys, before emerging into the circular plaza fronting the Army Mausoleum.

Crowds: he needed a place filled with tourists. Heart thumping, he sprinted across the roundabout, just missing a couple of cars that honked at him angrily. He risked a look over his shoulder – the taller, faster thug was only twenty yards behind him, and closing. Trying to remember Rome's geography, Walker pushed on harder. On his right the Roman Forum beckoned, but the last few visitors were leaving the ancient cobbles – it was too late in the day, and most monuments were closing.

Lights turned on in the distance and he grunted in relief – the Colosseum would stay open into the evening, and large queues always snaked around its entrance, even after darkness fell. The man behind him shouted something, sounding even closer.

Walker ignored the stitch in his side and tried to accelerate again, then he turned sharply and jumped into the traffic of the main road, swerving around a bus travelling in the opposite direction. A van blared and almost hit him before he was through to the other lane, dodging a motorbike and two more cars. A side-mirror glanced his shoulder and he rolled to the kerb, managing to stand up and start off again towards the bright lights, now only a couple of hundred yards away.

He checked behind him but the two thugs were still stuck on the other side of the road, wary of the vehicles whizzing by. Just a little further... He lengthened his stride and cut across the Colosseum Square, rushing past the long queue. He slid a hand in his pocket and sped to the entrance, ignoring the shouts of protests from the tourists and throwing a fifty Euro note at the gatekeeper, then rushed up the stairs towards the third Ring, the highest level of the massive arena.

How the hell have they managed to find...

He stumbled on one of the steep marble steps and almost fell, just managing to grab the handrail. Wheezing, he dived left at the second Ring, glancing at the signs that pointed upwards, then pushed harder into a couple of tunnels, flying by the ancient pillars and straining his eyes in the semi-darkness, careful not to trip on the uneven stone floor. A few moments later he emerged back on the plaza side, almost sixty feet above the tourist queue outside.

Breathing hard, he slid against one of the pillars, attempting to remain in its shadow. He scanned the square below and saw the shorter thug standing near a group of teenagers, under a tall streetlight. He was staring at a smartphone but immediately looked up at the second Ring, almost straight at Walker's hiding place. He shrank back into the tunnel, wondering how they seemed to be tracking him, and where the other man was.

His phone beeped and he swore. *Fuck.* They must have traced his number when he'd called Luigi's house. He grabbed the handset and flung it at the square below, aiming for the thug. Hurried footsteps echoed from the direction of the stairs and Walker looked around, trying to decide what to do. He needed to find another way out of the monument.

He crossed the tunnel and poked his head through to the inside of the Colosseum. The new wooden flooring – replicating part of the old surface where gladiators used to fight – covered about a third of the interior of the building, right below him. Further out, the labyrinth of the old Roman service passages still gleamed under the spotlights, a maze of ancient arches and tunnels that crisscrossed the underground of the arena.

The steps were getting closer.

Walker slid down the side of the second Ring, dangling from his hands as he tried to reach one of the old buttresses that used to hold up the spectators' bleachers. He let himself drop a few feet, almost slipping on the grass that covered the age-old bricks, then made his way down the slope onto the first Ring.

A few tourists ambling about the replica floor stared at him but he ignored them, jumping down with a thud. He looked back and saw the taller man had already followed, and was about to reach the same buttress. Glancing around, he noticed a crowd of people trying to leave by the main exit. Too slow.

He rushed to the edge of the wooden area and looked below to see what supported the platform – a network of metal scaffolding sparkled rustily in the half-light and he reached over the edge, grabbing the nearest pole and climbing down into the bowels of the Colosseum.

As soon as he touched the floor he spun, diving into one of the tunnels away from the platform. He took a couple of random turns, trying to remain in the shadows at all times and looking for the lower level. A few voices echoed eerily around the ancient pillars and he stuck to the darkest passages, not knowing where he was going. A little side door beckoned, half-open, and he entered it, sliding it shut behind him. Dim light bulbs illuminated a more modern corridor that descended lower, before turning into a grotto filled with stone cisterns.

On his left a few more rooms were blocked by wrought-iron bars and he ignored them, following the corridor's twists and turns for about a hundred yards. Something clattered ahead, and footsteps grew nearer. Walker glanced around and hid behind a pile of creaky metal chairs, waiting.

His heartbeat was so loud it felt as if it could give him away and he held his breath, preparing to jump from his hiding spot. A shadow turned the corner and shuffled closer, then stopped.

Walker sprang forward, ready to throw a punch, and a thin old man shrieked, stumbling back and falling awkwardly. His shouts of fear filled the narrow space and Walker cursed, rushing ahead to where the old man had come from. The corridor split and he hesitated, trying to figure out which way the centre of the Colosseum lay. Undecided, he shrugged and sprinted left, and after a dozen paces glimpsed the ghost of a green light. *Better lucky than good, I guess.*

Hoping the emergency exit wasn't alarmed, he stepped forward and pushed on the bars, emerging into the shadows near the Constantine Arch, on the other side from the Colosseum entrance. A few taxis waited under a streetlamp and he hurried to the nearest one, slamming the door shut just as the shorter thug appeared on the far edge of the small plaza.

'Let's go, fast,' he croaked in Italian to the driver.

The cabbie glanced at him and sighed, then he turned left into traffic, back towards the Roman Forum. 'Where to?'

'Anywhere. Just get me away from here, now.' Walker slid lower in the seat, studying the side-mirrors. The second thug had arrived, but both men were still checking the area near the Arch. He saw them studying the crowds, then approach a policeman.

'Lady trouble?' The driver shifted gears, accelerating past a wide roundabout.

'Yeah,' Walker took a deep breath, trying to calm down. 'Angry boyfriend – it was just a kiss...'

The driver chuckled. 'Must be the romantic ruins.'

'I guess.'

'Of course. I used to go after pretty tourists all the time...'

Walker let the cabbie ramble on about his amorous past and considered what to do. They drove past a few ministries, heading towards the Tiber and across one of the old bridges near the Vatican. The lights shone on the majestic dome of St. Peter's and Walker wondered whether Layla was okay. But she was not as dumb as him, and would probably be on a plane by now.

'So where are we going, then?' the driver asked.

'The airport.'

'Fiumicino or Ciampino?' Rome had two airports, the smaller one mainly for domestic flights.

'Naples.'

The cabbie turned sharply, staring at him. 'What? That's a three-hour drive.'

Walker rummaged in his backpack, pulled out a few large banknotes and pushed them into the man's hand. 'This should cover it. And I need to borrow your phone.'

'Sure.' The driver sniggered. 'That must have been one pissed-off boyfriend.'

'You have no idea.'

CHAPTER SIXTEEN

Back to Basics

All airports look the same. Walker tried to shrug off the feeling of foreboding that haunted him, and glanced around. The ticketing office was supposed to open at 6 a.m. but a fat woman had groped her way into her cubicle twenty-seven minutes late, and she hadn't pulled up the window grate yet. Some early travellers were sipping coffee at the counter down in the far corner, and a couple of bored Carabinieri shuffled through the empty spaces, submachine guns dangling from their necks. Nobody had glanced at him for hours, it seemed. He tried to look like part of the furniture, another bored guy waiting for his flight.

He had spent the night on a narrow bench, thin metal tubes digging into his back and thighs. Capodichino Airport was small, the departures lounge empty but for the janitors cleaning shiny surfaces and sharp angles. Empty had been perfect. He had needed time to think and sleep would have been impossible anyway. As a result he looked somewhat like a tramp: unshaven, stinky, hair plastered back as he had tried to wash up in the lounge's toilet. Not that he cared, as long as he could get away with it unnoticed. As long as he could get onto a plane.

The fastest way from Naples to LA was via London, of all places. He had known this since his taxi trip, but still hadn't decided what to do about it. It might have been the tiredness, but Mira's words were starting to ring a little more hollow as his mind spun through disaster scenarios and unlikely possibilities. Why did he have to go all the way to LA, and couldn't she have shown him more proof down in Rome? Who was this Old Man, and what was he really after?

DeepShare, of course. Like everyone else.

Like Friedman. Maybe.

Unless it was another lie that he couldn't see through. He had been a step behind the game since the beginning, and just as he felt he was catching up something else had been thrown his way. He needed certainty before he could decide how to move forward. He needed to know if Hackernym had been telling him the truth. And there was only one person who could answer the question for him.

A squeaky noise, metal on metal. The ticketing office lit up, the window yawning open. Walker stood up and approached the fat woman, a fake smile plastered on his face. She squared a telephone and glanced at him. 'Yes?'

'One way to London, grazie.'

She nodded and typed something on her computer. 'Flight is full. Waiting list or Business Class?'

'Business.' *What kind, though?*

...

One hour later Walker joined the queue for passport control. Two lines of people, approximately a dozen travellers in each. He chose the one to the left, behind a young family: mother father, little boy. Up ahead was the plastic cubicle, two windows, one opening to the left, one to the right. Two policemen, full uniforms, glancing at faces. Blank expressions. Scanning passports. Letting an old lady with a small trolley through.

The left-hand guard was older, mid-fifties. Out of shape, cheeks sagging. He looked bored, tired, like he had been working through the night. That was why Walker had chosen left. Younger could mean an extra fussiness, a deeper check. Old and counting minutes before it was time to go home meant better odds.

The queue slid forward and he followed, fingering his passport. The Sicilians had seemed scarily good, but he wondered what type of effort had been expended on him. The forgery felt perfect, but he had no idea if it really was up to scratch. Especially in Italy, the country that was supposed to have issued it. He sighed, trying not to fidget. Sweat trickled down his back as another couple was let through. The policeman was only yards away now, behind a plexiglass frame.

A quick scan, a better check on the good-looking girl's arse. Time for the small family. Walker shuffled forward again: just a few paces to go.

The border policeman sat up and craned his neck, trying to see below his white sill. The mother whispered something and the little boy stood on tiptoes, the top of his head barely reaching the plexiglass. A bored smile. Passports back, all through. Walker reached the window, trying not to blink.

The policeman offered his hand, palm up. The passport looked good and Walker handed it over, then glanced beyond, to the boarding gates. Four of them, about twenty yards away. He could sprint there in three seconds flat, he guessed. Not that it would help. He rested his hand on the sill, waiting. The policeman was staring at something, shuffling through the passport. Two pages forward, then five. One back. He looked up, a small sparkle in eyes as saggy as his cheeks. Walker sucked some air into his nose, fighting the urge to move his hand from the sill. His feet felt rooted to the ground and he glanced at the back of the monitor in the cubicle, trying to stare through black plastic.

The policeman grunted and slid the passport out of view, hands dragging side to side, slowly. A scanner of some kind, faint red light bouncing off the fiberglass counter into the man's face. His eyes tracked down, then up, then back to the screen. Walker felt a droplet of sweat trickle down his temple, waited.

Seconds ticked by. Too many. He reckoned he was busted. The policeman in front of him swivelled, glanced back at his younger colleague. Not a great pick, after all. Then back, quick taps on the keyboard, a shaking of the mouse. The eyes focused, fixed on Walker. Rechecking his face, back down to the passport, back to Walker's face again. Then fingers forward, up to the last page in the booklet. Walker wondered if the guards had a panic button hidden underneath the sill, or a pedal somewhere to call for reinforcements. A lady behind coughed, complained about wasting time.

The policeman grunted again, annoyed at something. Walker tried to breathe, finally blinked. The passport headed back towards him and he lifted his hand, took it.

The policeman nodded, gestured forward with his head. To the departure gates.

Walker stepped sideways, half-turned and slipped towards a row of chairs. His calves ached with tension and he exhaled. He had always hated airports, and he guessed it wasn't going to get better any time soon.

...

Walker readjusted the hood on the 'Love England' sweatshirt he had picked up at London City Airport and sipped his coffee, leaning against a wall on the small side-street opening onto Broadgate Circle. The day was cold and wet, the grey sky overcast with low clouds. Dozens of people were streaming out of the banks and law offices around the plaza, dispersing in cafes and food kiosks, hunting for lunch. He sighed and tried to shrink deeper into a small nook, worried about someone recognising him. *This has been a really bad idea.* Most people just hurried past, though, rushing to whatever takeaway place they fancied for the day before getting back to their screens.

Walker kept his eyes trained on the Dorfmann side exit that he knew Friedman used when he popped out for food, counting down the minutes. It was almost midday and the Englishman was due – like most traders, he liked to get his lunch early, before the US data started coming out around one o'clock. Fighting the urge to light a cigarette, Walker buried his hands in the heavy jumper and fingered the carving knife he had bought on the way. The blade was cold against his skin, the edge keen. He forced his breathing slower and focused, embracing the adrenaline thrumming in his veins. He had to stay sharp, but cool. It was time for some answers, and he wondered if they would be what he expected. His guts believed that the young woman in Rome had been telling the truth, but he needed to look into Friedman's eyes now. He needed to be sure. The side exit opened and a vaguely familiar face stepped through – some bigshot on the Fixed Income floor – followed by a couple of guys Walker had never seen before. Clients, maybe.

Taking a deep breath, Walker pushed off the wall and paced back and forth, trying to get his circulation going before leaning back into his original position. His watch beeped: midday. He needed to be back at the airport in a little over one hour to make the flight for Las Vegas. This was taking too long, and what the hell did he think he was going to...

The side exit yawned open again and Beano Friedman marched past the security guard, heading to his left towards a smaller alley that wound back to Liverpool Street Station. *Perfect.* Walker felt his mouth go dry, counted to five and followed the big man wrapped in a cashmere coat, eyes focused on the broad shoulders. When he saw the CEO turning into the narrow street he accelerated and shot past the corner, bumping him from behind and pushing the knife against his lower back. He leaned into him just as Friedman was starting to turn, and hissed, 'I'll kill you right now if you don't do as I say.'

Friedman twitched, his eyes widening as he recognised him. 'Walker? Yours, what the hell are you...?'

'Get your arse into the station.' Walker twisted the blade hidden in his hoodie, pushing it into the CEO's kidneys. The tip pricked the heavy wool coat, and he felt it rest against something more solid. 'I'll rip into your guts right here. Don't try anything dumb.'

'Okay, okay.' Friedman nodded and started walking again. 'Have you gone mad? Look, I know you didn't kill DM, but you shouldn't have run from the police...'

Walker almost broke his neck there and then. 'Just shut up. Once you've gone past the bookshop turn left into the small passage, away from the Tube.'

'Fine.'

They walked on in silence for a few hundred yards, inside Liverpool Street Station and then back out, along a little tunnel and onto a pedestrian way running parallel to the train tracks. The crowds thinned, until they were almost alone. Walker had scouted the place earlier and knew exactly where he wanted to go. He steered Friedman past an empty construction site, towards the bottom quarter of Finsbury Square. The walkway descended below street-level, bent in a couple of doglegs and finished in a cul-de-sac barred by the gate of the vacant building yard. Walker pushed Friedman away, making the big man stumble, and then he pointed to the husk of a half-finished disabled lift. 'Get in there.'

Friedman straightened. 'Or what? What the hell do you think you're doing?'

Walker stepped forward and hit him with a left jab, his fist crashing into the Englishman's jaw and sending him staggering against the concrete wall. Before Friedman could react he had grabbed his coat and shoved the CEO inside the narrow shaft, then followed him into the dark cluttered space. He stumbled over some discarded junk and the knife fell from his jumper's pocket, clattering to the floor and into some deep crack. He swore and regained his balance, slipping in a boxer's crouch.

Friedman glanced down in the semi-darkness, then back up with a narrow smile. A thin line of blood sneaked down the side of his mouth. 'A carving knife. You *have* lost your mind. What do you want, then?' He straightened up and brushed away some dust, almost composed again. 'If you need money...'

'You have no idea, do you?' Walker spat.

'About what? Calm down, Yours. Please,' he sighed. 'I know people at Scotland Yard. You shouldn't have run, but we'll prove you are innocent.'

'Really?'

Friedman opened his arms, tried to sound reasonable. 'You are, aren't you?'

Walker hesitated for a second. The Englishman still looked surprised but relatively calm, and sounded sincere. He had thought he could glimpse the truth just by staring into the CEO's eyes but now that he had... he was less certain than ever. His need for revenge, of any kind, might have clouded his senses. He could be making a monstruos mistake.

The evidence he'd been shown? Just a voice-recording from some pub, listened to in a restaurant in Rome. Hackernym could have faked it – God knew they had the capability. They probably could have faked an entire bloody movie, if it suited their purpose. Maybe *they* were the ones after DeepShare, and it was all part of some weird plan to force him to hand the software over.

'Scott, please. I know DM's death must have hit you hard.' Friedman shuffled forward, away from the back of the shaft. 'I think you're confused, and in shock. But...'

'What do you know of DM's murder?' Walker heard his voice shaking and cursed himself for it. But the world felt like it had once again tilted on its axis, and he didn't know how to go on. Too many things had been happening, too quickly. And now he was out of time, with a decision to make. He stared at Friedman, tried to see beyond the man's eyes, into his thoughts.

Friedman shrugged. 'Just what the police told me. They thought it was drugs, but then you disappeared and – still, I'm sure we can sort it out. Dorfmann's lawyers will help you, if you want...' He tailed off.

'What about DeepOmega?'

'It wasn't on –' Friedman froze for a split instant, realising he'd blundered. He shouldn't have known about Omega's existence.

Walker almost smiled as he tensed but the big man moved faster than he expected, jumping him in a bear hold and crashing him into the wall before they both rolled to the ground. Walker's head slammed against the concrete and his brain exploded in pain, his vision failing. By the time he'd recovered Friedman had straddled him, kneeling on his lower chest and pinning his arms to the floor. The CEO lowered his head and spat in Walker's face, blood dripping from his mouth. 'Almost had you there – but no matter now. What do you know?'

'Everything. Walsh, Pienaar...' Walker bent his neck forward and tried to flex his arms but the pressure from Friedman's weight and strength was too much. He rasped out a breath, struggling to think as his battered brain spun with nausea.

'How?'

'You –' Walker coughed – 'you have more enemies than you think.' He sagged back to the floor, relaxing his muscles. Waiting for a chance.

'I hope they're all as fucking dumb as you.' Friedman spat more blood in his face, then lowered his head, so close that his nose was almost touching Walker's. 'Where... the fuck... is... Omega?'

Walker slammed his head forward, head-butting Friedman for all he was worth. His forehead connected with the bridge of the Englishman's nose, shattering it, and as he howled and reared back Walker slid to the side, rolling away. He pushed off and pivoted on his right hand, then twisted and rammed his knee into Friedman's chest as he struggled up from his crouch.

The CEO fell back into a corner of the shaft, on all fours; Walker rushed him, aiming a kick at his midriff. He swung back with all his strength and almost lifted the big man off the floor before he crashed back to the concrete, chin first, beaten. Walker took a deep breath and stepped nearer, bending to grab his head by the hair, pulling it up a few inches. 'I'll come after you forever, you son-of-a-bitch.' He smashed Friedman's face against the wall, hearing teeth cracking, then swung back for another go. Blood dribbled onto his free hand from the CEO's broken features and he paused, inhaling deeply. It would be easy to kill him now.

The adrenaline still pumped and his muscles twitched, but Walker forced himself to unclench his fist and let go of Friedman. He stood up, still trembling, and stepped back. *No. I'm better than this.* He exhaled, turned around without a second glance and ditched his jumper, hurrying back towards the pedestrian walkway and Liverpool Street Station before he could change his mind.

Within twenty minutes he was back at City Airport, heading for the Transatlantic Lounge. He found a small sofa and sat down with a sigh, struggling with a wave of nausea. His head felt like some critter was trying to dig out of it, and he was exhausted. Going after Friedman had turned out to be a really dangerous idea.

But at least now he knew some of the truth.

And it was bloody time for someone else to feel hunted.

Santa Monica

LA's sun burnt through the open windows of the Georgian Hotel as Walker fiddled with one of the high-capacity storage drivers he had just rebooted, making sure it was working. After landing in Vegas he had jumped on a Greyhound to San Diego to buy the equipment, before making his way to Santa Monica. He was reasonably proud of himself: even if Pienaar had somehow managed to get his details from the Sicilians, Blackspring should have lost him again in the immensity of the States. Until he was ready to go after Frankel, at least. He glanced at the thick metal boxes – soon they would contain the DeepShare code, which he needed to collect from the servers where DM had hidden it, behind super-secure firewalls.

He had located half of the software at one of Stanford's Cloud facilities in La Jolla, while the other half sat at DM's alma mater, MIT. The access keys had been hard-coded in the tablet but he had copied them to a couple of new smartphones, just to have a backup. And one for Layla, perhaps.

Walker sighed and stood up, pacing around the living room in his suite; he studied the furniture again, trying not to think. A chaise longue, a fifties-style wooden table. An ancient cupboard. The hotel was trying hard to look Art-Deco. Almost succeeding. Like him, but thinking was difficult to avoid. He shrugged and dialled the reception, asking the guy to bring up a drink.

Luigi's smiling face broke through his mental walls and he dropped onto the small sofa, fighting to remain in control. Then DM's broken body grimaced at him and he lit a cigarette, strangling his emotions. There was no time to go to pieces. He had to keep his cool, to gauge whether Layla could really be trusted. Whether he could face working with her once more. Or even being in the same room as her.

Someone knocked and he went to open it, preparing a tip for the porter.

Layla burst through the door and hugged him fiercely, almost knocking him over.

'Thank God,' she whispered, kissing his eyes and face. 'I thought... I was sure I'd never see you...'

Walker pushed her away and stepped back, slamming the door shut. He forced some steel into his voice. It cost him a lot: more than he had thought he would need. 'Go and sit down. And start talking, or this is going to be short.' *And not painless.*

Layla nodded, then she shrugged out of a new black leather coat and curled up on the chaise longue, checking the room. She took a deep breath, unable to keep her eyes on his face. 'Of course. What do you need to know?'

Walker studied her, taking his time. Her face had fallen in a bit, and she looked thinner in a long-sleeved cotton dress. He didn't know where to start, anger and attraction warring inside him. 'Why the hell did it take you so long to help me?' His voice cracked, the distrust still burning.

'I... I didn't know what to do.' Layla paused, searching for words. 'I was about to run away so many times – I didn't want to get involved.'

'Why?'

'At the beginning I just thought you were... only another banker, a man with no morals, only money.'

'Whom you wanted to rob.' Even after she'd seen what had been done to DM. Walker shivered, uncertain. A part of him wanted to let her back in, but there were too many holes in her story.

'I was afraid of Pienaar. And yes, I still believed I could get Deep from you. Then Reims happened...'

Walker groaned, his guts twisting in knots. 'And after that, you still didn't say anything. You must have thought I had no chance.'

'I didn't see the point – it was not my fight, and I wasn't even sure I liked you. Besides I was wounded, in pain: I couldn't think clearly.'

True. But Luigi had ended up dead because he had tried his best to help them. Perhaps, had she come clean earlier... Walker shook his head. No, that was unfair. Pienaar would have been unstoppable anyway. Probably.

'Go on,' he sighed.

'Then you saved my life. But, beyond that... what really struck me then was your steel, your resilience.'

'In running about like a doomed, headless chicken?'

Layla glared at him. 'Don't be ridiculous. You're still around. You're still fighting.'

'I couldn't let DM's death be for nothing.' And he wouldn't. Even for her.

'That's when it hit me. You were not just a money guy. God – I'm not good with words...' She took a deep breath. 'There was more. A lot more.'

'So much that you still wanted to leave.' Walker's mouth tasted bitter, dry. 'Even in Sardinia, you just made up more stories, instead of telling me the truth.'

'I needed more time.'

'For what?'

'To...' Layla stopped, tears glinting in her eyes. 'I was falling for you, and it's always bad, in these... situations. You need focus, not –' She broke off and looked away, out of the window.

Walker waited for a few seconds. The way she had hesitated... Maybe there *was* a key to the hidden Layla. It was time to find out, once and for all. He went for the chair but decided to grab one of his cigarettes instead, and started pacing the small space. 'It's happened to you before, hasn't it?'

Layla nodded wordlessly, her face still turned away from him.

'Who is Rafael?'

She spun back to him then, shock flickering across her face. 'How do you know that name?'

'You called out to him, on the ferry. When you had a high fever.' When her defences had been at their weakest.

Layla squirmed, readjusting her short dress before answering. 'He was... When I worked for the Mexican police, I was sent undercover for almost two years – after a drug baron, in the Chiapas. Rafa was one of his younger sons. He was twenty-three and had dreams – he wanted a normal life, to get away from the family. We fell in love, but I never told him anything.'

'You just continued with your job. It sounds familiar.'

She nodded, wiping away a tear. 'I collected proof, told the army how to get around their security to catch them unprepared. The raid, when it came, was successful.' She sniffled, straightened her back. 'Only three people were killed, and the boss was caught alive.'

'What about Rafa?'

'He was one of the three. He died protecting his father, knowing I was just a government agent.'

'I'm sorry.'

She ignored him, the words tumbling out in a rush. 'I betrayed him. Apparently that's what I do. I should have opened up, told him to get away... I loved him, and his blood is on my hands. I can't trust myself, not after what I did to him.'

'And you thought the same thing might happen – with me.' And some of it had, he guessed.

Layla nodded, her hands worrying away at one of the buttons on her dress. 'I'm just damaged goods, Scott. You were right not to trust me.'

Walker crossed the room and sat on the other side of the chaise longue, concentrating on her face. She looked drawn, almost beaten. The last few minutes seemed to have taken a lot out of her. And it felt as if she hadn't lied this time. He wondered if he was going to regret the next few minutes.

'Maybe.' He shrugged.

'Do you... do you want me to leave now?'

Walker could see the fear in her eyes but he kept his voice cold. 'No. I still need your help, if you're ready. And I think you are now.'

'How do *you* know, when I can't even be sure of myself?'

She was shaking and he stopped himself from taking her hand. 'Everyone deserves a second chance. This is yours – don't fuck it up.'

Layla sucked in a breath, staring at him. 'Okay.' A long pause, as he waited. 'I'm sorry, Scott. I...'

His hand chopped the air. 'No more, for today.' It had been hard enough, for both of them. 'We have some planning to do now.'

'Okay,' she said again.

Walker let a few moments pass, staring at a dubious painting: a woman stepping out of the ocean, clad in an ancient bathing suit. Saint Tropez, early 1900s, he guessed. He finished his cigarette and put it out, letting some emotion seep back in his voice. There were things that couldn't wait, not after London. 'We can't waste any time. I want to destroy Frankel Schwartz for what they've done.'

She must have sensed the change in his mood and nodded again, still looking uncertain. 'How... how did Luigi...?'

Walker shivered, lit another cigarette. 'He was tortured, badly,' he answered, the strain in his words impossible to hide.

'Do you want...'

'No. Pienaar is a monster, and I don't want to think about what they did.'

Layla bit her lip and looked away, giving him a few seconds. 'Is Mosha going to help you then?'

'Maybe. But there's someone else who is going after those bastards.'

He told her of his meeting in Rome with Hackernym, and about their recordings. Layla listened, looking surprised, before asking, 'So you believe these guys?'

He thought of Friedman's broken face, of his lies. 'I *have* to believe them. It could be my lifeline.'

'When are you going to see this Old Man?'

'Tomorrow.'

'What if he just wants DeepShare? Maybe that's the only thing they're after, like Frankel.'

Walker fell silent for a second. That was exactly what he was worried about. But there were no other choices – he had to listen to them. 'I'm not sure. I'll have to see what he really knows, and what he's planning to do.'

'Do you want me to come?'

'No.' He ignored the hurt look on Layla's face. 'I have to do it alone, then maybe we can figure out the next steps together.'

The Old Man

Walker parked the rented convertible a few yards from the Pacific Ocean and climbed out, clutching his backpack. He hadn't noticed anything suspicious on the way and he still felt reasonably certain that Blackspring had lost his trail since Rome. And it should be hard to track him now. He'd been paying everything with cash and charge-up credit cards in a different name, and the bastards had no reason to think he might be in California. Still...

He took a deep breath and let himself enjoy a moment of peace. The drive from Wilshire Boulevard in LA to Malibu had taken him only thirty minutes, the sun was shining and some of the morning chill still stuck to the wind. He took off his shoes and wandered along Paradise Cove, under the small pier and across the sun-loungers scattered in front of the beach restaurant. A couple of families with young children played on the sand or ran after inflatable balls as he savoured the fresh ocean air, gathering his thoughts. There were too many questions he couldn't answer, too many doubts. Who was the Old Man, what was Hackernym really after, and what should he do if they wanted DeepOmega?

The software was his only bargaining chip, and DM's legacy. Was he prepared to risk it, on the back of some vague promises? He remembered the rage, the sense of betrayal when he'd heard Friedman's voice in the recording. Frankel Schwartz had schemed with Dorfmann's London CEO, hired Pienaar to steal DeepShare and murdered two of his closest friends. There was no real choice – Omega was promised to Mosha anyway, in exchange for his help.

Maybe not the full version, but enough of the algorithms to show how powerful it was.

Walker stopped and looked around, still uncertain. The restaurant beckoned, with its faux-fisherman's charm, and he didn't have another plan anyway. He bit on his tongue and hurried across the sand, into the bar area.

A pretty blonde girl was pouring beer for the only customer sitting near the entrance. Walker nodded to her and grabbed a menu, pretending to read it as he waited for his turn. Soon the bartender came over and threw him a fake smile. 'Will you be having anything, honey?'

'A pint of IPA, cheers.'

She took a second look at him, noticing his accent. 'Are you English?'

'Yes.'

'On holiday? You ever been to California before?'

'Sure.' He glanced down at the menu, thinking. Was she the one he should ask, or...

The other customer, a massive man with tattooed arms, left his stool and approached them. He wore a friendly grin underneath a baseball hat, and nodded in Walker's direction. 'Don't mind Pamela, she's a bit nosy but the fried shrimps are awesome.'

The girl stuck out her tongue and left, disappearing around the bar. Tattooed-man slid next to Walker and downed his small beer in one gulp, before winking at him. 'I think she likes you.'

'Good to know.'

'But I suspect you might not have the time.'

Walker sipped his own drink and shrugged. 'Do I know you?'

'No. But I was told you might be coming.' He put out his hand and Walker shook it. 'My name is Bill. Are you ready to see the Old Man?'

'Of course.'

'Follow me then.'

Bill led him out of the main entrance, to the carpark and behind the pier onto the long beach that curved back towards LA. They walked in silence for a while, across sheltered bays grazing the luxurious homes that littered the sand. Paradise Cove was the playground of movie stars and studio bosses, where billionaires from all over the world came to rest and hide near the ocean. Walker wondered how much a house would cost here, then was distracted as a former supermodel came bounding along the bank, running barefoot on the sand and surf.

Bill glanced back at him and turned away from the sea, opening a small gate that led to a spotless 1930s two-storey beach mansion. They crossed the small garden and waited under the porch, before a male nurse showed up to let them in.

'Is he awake?' Bill asked.

The nurse nodded. 'Not longer than fifteen minutes, though.'

'As if he'd listen.' He signalled to Walker, heading through a sparsely furnished living room to stop in front of a pair of oak double doors. A second nurse sat at a low table, staring at several monitors. She handed them two gauze masks, barely bothering to glance up.

Bill shrugged. 'Company policy. He's very ill, but don't worry – his mind is still sharp.'

He pushed open the heavy doors and Walker looked around the new room. Medical equipment and monitors hovered behind a high-tech hospital cot, still half-hidden from his view by the wide shoulders in front of him. A few stunning paintings hung from the walls – Walker recognised a Van Gogh and a Picasso – before a raspy voice from the bed caught his attention.

'Thank you, Bill. You can leave me with Scott now.'

Bill moved aside, letting Walker glimpse the shrunken figure of a sick old man trying to sit up. He was obviously dying, the face gaunt and discoloured, a few wisps of grey hair clinging to the gnarled scalp. An IV poked the man's skeletal arm; the rest of his ravaged body was hidden under a thin white sheet.

Even so, there was no mistaking him.

'Do you know who I am?' The old man's pale eyes still glinted with the famous, and feared, intelligence.

'Of course,' Walker croaked, surprised. Anyone who'd ever worked with money would know him. Gerard Soffet was more than a man, possibly the greatest living legend of the world of finance. An apex-predator, and one of the richest people on the planet. The genius who had built an empire gambling on markets for decades, with astonishing success.

Hedge-fund managers everywhere revered him, and politicians had feared his wrath ever since his raids on Currencies in the early nineties, crushing governments and central banks with the sheer force of his intuition, and money. For years now he had lived as a recluse, rumoured to be suffering from dementia.

'I guess I don't look much like myself any more.' Soffet's voice was creaky but his words still crisp. 'Then again, I'd rather lose my good looks than my brains.'

. . .

'I've found the place they were staying at. She's gone now, though.' Pienaar's tone bubbled with an undercurrent of anger, as usual.

Friedman ignored it, thinking quickly. 'When?'

'Three days ago. In a hurry, apparently. I could see if the old lady here knows more.'

'No.' Friedman shuddered. 'You're leaving too much of a trail, and your methods...'

'MY methods? I'm not the one who let Walker slip through in Rome. I get results.'

'Do you, really?' Friedman's hand went to his battered face. His guts churned but he forced himself to calm down. 'It doesn't matter, I don't want any more blood, for now.'

'They still think Walker's behind everything.'

'That's exactly why you should calm down.' He was surprised at how much those words had cost him. He wanted revenge, badly, but now was not the time for losing his cool.

There was a pause before Pienaar came back, his anger now apparent. 'I'm fucking tired of this. If you don't like the way I do things, just pay me off and I'll get out of your hair.'

Friedman sighed under his breath. He couldn't afford to lose the madman, not now. 'Look, Francois – she obviously ran after they found out about the broker. Where's the nearest airport to you?'

'Cagliari. It's a small one.'

'That's where she'll have gone. We'll hunt through the passenger manifestoes and figure out what name she is travelling under. And then we'll have them.'

'Fine. But I'm not going to hang around much longer.'

...

'Why am I here?' Walker sat on a metal chair near the head of the hospital bed. Soffet coughed a few times, then rasped a couple of shallow breaths and stared at him, his eyes watery.

'You're here to help me find a cure.'

Walker glanced around the room, uncertain. 'I'm not a doctor...'

'Not for me...' Soffet chuckled. 'It's far too late for that. But for the system. The world is sick, Scott Walker. And I'm trying to make it better.'

'With Hackernym?'

The old man nodded, his hand twitching. 'The disease has spread too much, we need a powerful shock. To cure, sometimes you must destroy, first.'

'And you're after Frankel.'

'Frankel Schwartz is nothing. They will suffer like the rest, when I bring the whole damn edifice down.'

'What?' Walker recoiled, his anger bubbling. 'They've killed people – my friends. Friedman, Welsh, Pienaar – God knows who else is involved. They must pay for what they've done.'

'And they will,' Soffet sighed. 'But they are not the cause, just a symptom of what's been happening.'

'Are you serious? Their entire fucking bank is a cancer. We all know Frankel has a finger on the pulse everywhere, like a corrupt giant spider. Bribing politicians, cheating clients, manipulating the markets... Now it's vulnerable for once, and we could take it apart for good.'

'I like your fire, young man.' Soffet smiled and coughed again. 'But let me tell you a story, first.'

Walker shrugged, struggling to keep his temper. 'Sure. Go ahead.'

'What am I famous, or infamous, for?'

'Your wealth...' Walker hesitated, uncertain. 'Philanthropy?'

'No, Yours. I am the man who...?'

'Broke the Bank of England.' Walker nodded. 'So?'

'And that of Italy, don't forget.' Soffet attempted a grin. 'But the way I did it – it's not quite as it was told in the books. I had lots of *hidden* help.'

'Hidden?'

'Powerful people in Washington and Berlin did not like the way the European integration was going, and thought a few countries needed to be taught a lesson. I came up with the idea and they stood aside, happy to... *facilitate* behind closed doors. I couldn't have caused a crisis and attacked the currencies of two large nations, not without having the US Federal Reserve and the German Bundesbank behind me. I knew everything before it happened.'

'Seriously?' Walker wondered if the old man had started to lose it, as people said.

'Yes. There's long been a cabal of central bankers, ministers, academics... You see them on TV, pretending to be working for the good of all, but there's always a special agenda. These people... they are the ultimate guardians of the status quo – they groom their successors amongst themselves, taking care only of the needs of the elites. You can't even become a famous economist unless you genuflect to their theories. They pick and choose, make governments fall... all in the interest of protecting the system.'

'That sounds like the IMF, or the United Nations.'

Soffet glared at him. 'Those idiots are only puppets, Scott. The real players, the Bilderbergs and their masters – they go deeper. I know them, I've worked *with* them for a long time. The last crisis, and the next one certainly – they were, and will be, partly planned. Years ago, they saw what was happening, and fed the cancer of subprime and excessive credit. They let the banks grow beyond any reasonable limit, because it was the ultimate opportunity to build their power and control social moods...' The old man trailed off, wheezing.

Walker leaned closer. 'Why?'

'Why? Lehman Brothers didn't have to go. They knew what would happen, and chose – *chose* – to break the world's markets. It was organised, decided to teach everyone a lesson: now you mess with us at your own peril. And they won – they are uber-rich, unelected, and do not answer to anyone.'

Walker sat back in his chair, dumbfounded. '"Give me control of a nation's money and I care not who makes her laws."'

'Rothschild. You *are* well read.'

'I've studied my Marx, as well. And you are sounding like him... or like a fringe blogger.'

'Many do not believe me, Yours.' There was no anger in the old man's voice, only a tinge of sadness, and pity. 'No matter, you will see the evidence we have been collecting for years...'

Walker nodded nervously, uncertain of what to say. Soffet was starting to ramble now, his voice gathering force, eyes blazing with passion. And though there was some truth in his words, it was becoming too much. No one could possibly have planned the financial crisis.

'First they piled on trillions of unpayable debts...' Soffet continued. 'And now they upend laws – so many, you have no idea. Bully, threaten, cover up crimes, all to keep the system ticking. Democracy has been broken, they alone decide what's best for everyone. But soon they will take a step too far, and then...'

The old man coughed again, a stronger attack bending his frail body in two. He looked as if he was dying and Walker froze.

'Sir, should I call a nurse...'

Soffet shook his head at Walker, twitched. His eyes closed and he shivered before calming down and breathing shallowly for a few seconds. 'I'm sorry,' he groaned. 'And I didn't want you here just to give you a speech.'

Walker sighed. At least the sick old man was still breathing. But for how long, and how could he get him to help? 'Listen, I'm not sure about this...'

'You will see, Scott. We hacked their most secret sanctums, and continue to record their messages and meetings. We are almost ready to unleash creative destruction – the true soul of capitalism...'

'I'm not sure I need to know.' Walker tried to sound soothing before the billionaire went off again. 'I just want to bring Frankel down, that's all *I* care about. Do you have enough to really hurt them?'

Soffet rolled his eyes at the interruption. 'Yes. Emails, intercepted phone calls, data and the rest. And we know of the mess in their Euro books.'

'Will you give it to me?'

'It's not quite finished yet. And we need to add your story to it. After you leave me, you can sit down with my people and go through everything that's happened since the beginning in London. It will become part of our case, and they'll show you all we have collected on them up to now.'

'All right.' Walker nodded. Soffet might have grown a little delusional, but if he really had what he said... 'What do you want from me in exchange?'

'You already know. DeepShareOmega. If it's as powerful as Frankel thinks...'

'It's probably better.' Walker paused, deciding it was time to gain some control over the conversation. He sat back, tried to look relaxed. 'Why?'

The old man's eyes sparkled, and his thin lips turned up in a hideous smile. 'I told you, Frankel is only a step. A bait, if you want. With your software we can probe the financial structure's weak spots, prepare our final attack. DeepShare could be our sniffer, telling us how and when we can really break them.'

Walker's blood ran cold. If all of this was true... 'Are you saying you want to destroy the entire financial system?'

'Of course not. What I want is to *shock* it. Look, for many years now Finance has grown like a monstrous parasite, sucking in resources, technologies, thousands upon thousands of stunning brains. For nothing. Just to make more money out of money, a kind of video-game arms race. But *real* wealth is production, resources, innovation... not paper. Don't tell me that DeepShare is not predicting another massive crisis in the near future. From what I hear, it's too good not to have seen it.'

'Yes, it is, but...' Walker struggled for words. 'Isn't there any other way?'

'When you have advanced gangrene...' Soffet pointed to his missing leg under the bedsheet. 'You cut a limb off – not just wait for the rest of the body to die.'

'But it's going to be bloody chaos. Bank runs, failures...'

Soffet smiled. 'Are you sure? I think they'll just freeze things for a while, and come up fast with better rules. With a stronger, more human system. It's only paper and numbers on a computer, anyway. As you have admitted, we are heading for implosion – at least I'll get rid of the madmen who are running things now before the damage becomes truly irreparable.'

Walker stood, uncertain. Could he allow the old man to have DeepOmega, or was there another way? He forced himself to think faster than he ever had in his life and the room faded as he worked through scenarios, possibilities. He needed Hackernym's help to destroy Frankel, and Soffet's plan just sounded impossible – there was no way he could break the world markets like that. Even with Omega. And if he got a few people to resign it wouldn't be such a bad thing; transparency was needed and Finance had to be reined in. *That* he could live with. He took the plunge, hoping he hadn't just signed a pact with the devil.

'Okay – but you'll only have Deep after I've seen Frankel Schwartz shattered.'

Soffet grinned. 'You could work for me. I like how you've survived, and I can pay well.'

'Thank you, but I'll pass.' A dying man's crusade was the last thing he needed to get involved in. 'I only wish to see Friedman and the rest of them pay. And I want my life back.'

The billionaire shook his head. 'You'll never have your old life back.'

'Of course not, and I'm not sure I'd want it, anyway. But I can build a new one.'

'With the Mexican woman?'

Walker hesitated, annoyed. *Do they know everything?* He shrugged. 'Maybe.'

'I hear she's a good one. Keep hold of her.'

Soffet's hand twitched and he pressed a button on the side of the bed. A second later the oak doors opened and Bill walked through, followed by a nurse. 'I'm tired now, my friend. Bill will take you to our analysts – they'll show you what we have, and add DM's story to the picture.'

'Thank you.'

'Don't thank me. I'm only doing God's work, repenting my sins,' he said. 'Ah, and please hurry up with Mosha Micovich. It might be a while until we are ready to act, but we'll need DeepShare very soon.'

'We'll move fast, if Hackernym's info is as good as you say.' Walker smiled, his stomach twisting in anticipation. 'I can't wait.'

'Neither can I, I'm afraid.'

CHAPTER SEVENTEEN

Risk and Opportunity

Layla met Walker for dinner at a Japanese restaurant a few blocks away from the Georgian Hotel. She was nervous and would have preferred to hide in his room, but Scott had been adamant. He seemed to be getting cabin fever as the countdown ticked faster. To what, she didn't know. He was already sitting at the back of the room, in a dark corner cut off by a few tropical plants. He jumped up when she approached, his expression intense.

'Did you find the guy?' he said.

Layla sighed and sat back, just as a waiter arrived. She ordered a red wine and turned back to Walker. 'Yeah, but it took forever. He's moved from Compton to Venice – guess the business is doing well...'

'Great. Are they going to be as good as my Italian IDs?'

'I've never had a problem with Karl. But he will need a week, especially for your British passport.'

Walker slapped the table, swearing in a low voice. 'A week?'

'Maybe just three or four days, he wasn't sure. Why?'

'We don't have a fucking week to waste,' he growled. 'I want to move on Frankel now – seven days is a long time in Finance, and Pienaar is still out there. I need to get to Boston and download the second half of the code.'

Layla rubbed her forehead, considering. 'Do you really have to go? It's digital stuff – can't you send it over the net, or something?'

'No. DM made sure it could not be done, and even if I managed to get around his protections – and I probably can't – it's too big. And the Internet is not reliable, or secure enough. The only way is a physical download, in one of those storage drivers in my room.'

'Are you sure?'

Walker exhaled, annoyed. 'Of course I am. Look, a lot of secret technologies works like that – a quant stole some high-frequency trading code from a bank some years ago, and he had to do it the same way.'

'It sounds dangerous.'

'It is,' he grimaced. 'They caught him after an FBI manhunt, and he got twenty years in jail.'

'Well, you can't fly, not with your Italian documents.' Layla looked around, lowering her voice. 'And after Naples... it's probably too dangerous.'

Walker finished his drink, struggling to keep his voice low as well. 'Tell me something I don't know.'

She glared at him. 'Don't crack up now, banker boy. If someone really has to – I can go.'

'You?' Walker forced himself to calm down, realising he was taking his frustration out on her. 'I'm sorry. But... you don't know anything about Deep.'

'You have all night to teach me. It's only a data dump anyway, isn't it?'

'Not quite...' He rested his head on his palm, thinking. 'There are going to be a lot of safeguards, and tricks. DM was very careful.'

'But you have the hard-coded keys, don't you?'

Walker fell silent. It could be done, he guessed. Layla would have to learn how to navigate the access portals, and the first-level subroutines, but... He glanced up at her, and tried to set aside his emotions. She was smart, and seemed truly committed. They had ten hours till the morning flights and no other real options. He nodded at her. 'Are you sure?'

She nodded back, looking a little nervous. 'Try me. I won't let you down, I promise.'

'I know.' Walker took her hand, felt her shaking. She'd need to be relaxed, and confident. *Take it easy on her.* He smiled, trying to make it look real. 'Fine, of course you can do it. It's gonna be easy. The Sicilians were faster than your friend, though.'

Layla attempted a small smile and he felt better. 'Not only that, he's become ridiculously expensive as well.'

'Hopefully I won't need many more.'

'No. And I've already paid anyway, consider it my treat.'

'I will,' Walker deadpanned. 'Especially since you still have my fifty grand.'

'God, you *are* a banker, aren't you?' She rolled her eyes and grabbed her menu. 'I'm starved, what's good here – to take away, I guess?'

Walker stood and grinned at her. 'Nothing you can have. We've got to go back to the hotel and start working. You can order a bite from room service.'

'Great,' Layla groaned.

...

They left the restaurant and hurried back towards the Georgian Hotel on foot. It was too close and taxis would have been hard to find in Santa Monica, anyway. In minutes they'd half-sprinted back to the tourist hotspot of Third Street Promenade before Layla grabbed at Walker's arm, pulling him to a stop. 'Please, not so fast,' she panted. 'I'm not at my best, yet.'

'Really?' Walker stepped back, smiled at her flushed cheeks. She gave him the finger and bent, winded, arms on knees.

'Okay, take your time. We're almost there anyway.' He checked the side streets as she caught her breath, seeing nothing. Then he just waited, considering a cigarette. Heartbeats later she straightened up, pushed her hair back behind one ear and grimaced at him.

'I'm ready.'

'You sure?'

'Shut up.' Layla grabbed on his arms and took off, pulling him along. Walker smiled and let her lead, knowing she would die before stopping again. Within twenty paces the crowds on the Promenade quivered, then dispersed as a light drizzle started to fall. They walked through the remaining tourists and shop-gawkers, past a bar where music thumped, screaming exotic beats. Some stores were shuttered, white-and-red rental signs looking conspicuous. A lonely busker played on, dancing intricate moves to some internal rhythm, oblivious to her sparse watchers. Layla stared at her for a second, then she bit her lip and leaned closer. 'So, what was the Old Man like?'

'Intense. And maybe slightly mad, but with reason.' Walker shivered, remembering the skeletal hands. And the words. And the Frankel file.

'How?'

'I'm not quite sure. He thinks that some banker cabal is... hurting the world. And he wants to break it up.'

Layla paused, considering. 'Is he right?'

'In my most paranoid conspiracy theories, yes. But in reality – I don't know. A lot of underhand stuff happens in Finance.'

'Like what?'

'We don't have enough time to go into it... But he talked about a global conspiracy to cause a crisis, cover-ups, governments being ordered about...' Walker shrugged. 'The man was a genius, but he's dying now. He might be delusional. Though a lot of it sounded plausible. '

He paused as they turned the corner. A blue car honked, someone shouted and a homeless man rushed through the street. Walker froze and glanced behind and around them, making sure no one was looking at them. Layla squeezed his arm, then let him go. 'Shit. We're too jumpy,' she said.

'Probably.'

'We are. Now go on, and try to look normal.'

'Okay.' Walker stepped past a traffic light, couldn't resist another check down the road. 'The stuff they have on Frankel Schwartz is lethal, though. And with what I told them happened to us, they'll be able to put even more pieces of the puzzle together. What they've managed to hack is incredible.'

'Couldn't they have done the same with other organizations?'

'I'm sure they have. But I don't really care, not after all that's happened. This is for Luigi and DM.' Walker stopped, his eyes losing focus. 'I just want those bastards to get caught. And the old man needs DeepShare.'

'Will you give it to him?'

Everything has a price. 'Only after they go public on Frankel.'

Layla nodded, considering. 'Is what they found enough?'

Walker started walking again, running through the possible chain of events in his mind for the hundredth time. 'I think so. We've cobbled together the bad trades they're hiding in their books. When Hackernym's stuff comes out, most of the bank's top management will be in serious trouble, a lot of people arrested. Frankel is going to be headless.'

They had reached the turquoise-blue facade of the Georgian and he stopped in front of the marble steps. 'By then, it will only take a further push – the event that Deep has predicted should erupt in a crisis, wiping their positions away. The bastards will be in a panic, having to sell in a crashing market. Frankel's trades are so big and levered that most of its capital will be gone in hours. I expect it to happen so fast they won't know what hit them.'

Layla recoiled and stepped back, looking horrified. 'Is this what you've been planning with Mosha? You're going to cause a world crisis just to destroy Frankel Schwartz?'

'No.' Walker raised his hands, palms out. 'No... I swear, DeepShare had already seen this shakedown coming – it's going to happen anyway. It's only another small step in our descent to hell, according to Omega. But this episode should blow over again, just like it did before I met you. It won't be a real systemic event, I hope.'

'You *hope?* Have you forgotten what happened after Lehman Brothers?'

'Never,' he said. 'But that's why I'm not too worried. Look, Lehman going bust changed the world. You can split Finance in Before '08 and After Lehman.'

'Like B.C. and A.D.? That's ridiculous.' Layla looked at him askance.

'It's not, ask any senior banker. And the lesson was learnt, Frankel won't be allowed to go bust. What they'll do – they'll simply break it apart, cut off the pieces and sell them on the cheap, to other banks.' Walker smiled, savouring the words. 'The top guys will get the blame, but no one else will lose a penny. And it's an investment bank anyway, no deposits or mortgages...'

One of the hotel porters spotted them standing just outside and opened the door. Walker pulled gently on Layla's arm, started up the steps.

'You make it sound too easy.' Layla shook her head, unconvinced.

'Maybe.' Walker tipped the smartly dressed man and entered the foyer, turning right towards the bar. 'But I've ran it on Deep so many times... it's going to work. Trust me – what we are doing will simply stop Frankel from having the time and resources to react, because we'll get those bastards to jail.'

Or he might go down as one of the men who had broken the world's economy, he guessed. Walker needed to believe his plan would succeed, but there was a part of him that felt stuck, trapped between massive grinding mills. Frankel Schwartz on one side, the Old Man and Hackernym on the other. There had to be a chance that either could grab hold of him, break him and use whatever was left as some sort of scapegoat while they went their own merry way. He was only one man, with a risky plan. But he had Deep – and a fury to make things right, or die trying. He grinned and checked around, found a room-service menu and handed it to Layla. 'So, what are you going to order?'

She looked queasy. 'I'm not that hungry, right now.'

...

The nightmare was always a reflection of itself, full of anguish and pain. Pienaar knew it was a dream because he was his grown-up, powerful self, still dressed in a kid's pyjamas, sleeping in his little old bed. And, like the six-year-old he had been, there was nothing he could do aside from watching, horrified.

As so many times before the men had broken the door down and he ran to his parents, scared by the noise and shouting.

Just in time to see them shoot his kneeling father in the back of the head.

Mother tried to grab and protect him but they attacked her, beat and kicked her, ripping her nightdress off before...

...before a phone rang, insistently. Again and again, unwilling to stop.

Pienaar opened his eyes and was instantly awake, his hand shooting for the clumsy sat-phone. 'Yes.'

'Good news, Francois.' Friedman's voice was chippier than usual, and the Australian wanted to vomit.

'We have narrowed it down to three, but by tomorrow we should be certain of where she is,' the Englishman said.

'Good.'

'You're going to the US. Get on the first flight for the West Coast.'

'And Walker?'

'He will be near her, we're sure. I'll let you know what the next step is – once we've located them.'

'I'm ready, but I'll need some good men. Michel and his team should do.'

'Of course. We'll fly them over later, but this time you have to make sure Walker really has DeepShare, when we go in. No more mistakes – we're already out of time.'

Pienaar sighed, restraining himself. 'Tell the others. I'm not the one who screwed up.'

'I think...'

'Make sure of it, mate, or after this I'll come after you and reopen your face up.' Pienaar grinned and closed the connection.

Code

Layla swore quietly at the computer, digging deep into her reservoir of Mexican insults for the vilest descriptions she could think of. The small cubicle in one of MIT's Cloud facilities near a new industrial compound outside Boston felt stifling, the grey plastic walls threatening to close in on her. DeepOmega had frozen again, and now she'd need to wait for five minutes before she could try with the second random-generated code. It was a fucking nightmare.

The first part of the download had been quite smooth, as Walker had predicted. The access portals were easy to navigate, down into the unlock screens buried beneath a couple of fake searches. And the software had flowed into the storage driver without a hitch, faster than she expected. But she had been stuck on the second part for over an hour, bouncing off a couple of number-algorithms that should have been straightforward to bypass. Should have, according to Scott.

Layla sank back in her chair, trying to keep the frustration at bay. She forced her mind back to their tests through the night, struggling to relive the scene as accurately as she could. *Concentrate, bitch.* They were sitting on the bed, two laptops next to each other. Walker clicked on the second window to the right, and input a string of numbers. She glanced back to her notes, making sure she had it. Then he quickly shifted to a black-and-white code screen, typing a question. The answer materialized somewhere else, on a tiny corner-icon, a sort of inverted arrow that she needed to drag...

Layla swore again. She couldn't remember. *Fuck. What am I going to do now?* In his paranoia, DM had picked the most secure Cloud facility in the US. The building was screened, with no connectivity to the outside world beside its own massive cables. Mobile phones were disabled, and if you left the room you couldn't come back for forty-eight hours. Walker would kill her – he needed the code, fast.

The computer beeped, ready to let her try again. A message flashed on the screen in capital yellow letters: THIS IS YOUR LAST ATTEMPT. IF YOU FAIL TO FOLLOW THE CORRECT PROCEDURE THIS WINDOW WILL LOCK FOR TWENTY-FOUR HOURS. Layla's head dropped, and she desperately wished for a cigarette. Or Scott. Or a miracle. Forcing herself to focus, she tried to go back in time again, with more clarity. The little corner icon... where the hell...?

YES!

The bloody arrow needed to be trashed, of all things. And then her second hard-coded formula should work. Holding her breath, Layla went through the procedure carefully, rechecking her notes, making sure there were no mistakes. After minutes that seemed to last forever the black background inverted and shuddered, folding onto itself. Random lights flickered on and off, before the download screen appeared in all its stark beauty. *I did it.* She thought Walker would be proud of her. She certainly was, for once.

...

Sprague watched the whore leave the MIT building, still carrying the heavy bag she had gone in with. He turned the ignition and his Toyota grunted into life as he waited for her to get in a cab. The Corolla – possibly the most common car in the US – was the perfect surveillance vehicle. He was certain she wouldn't notice it in Boston's traffic, or anywhere else. He reversed out of the parking bay as the whore climbed into a yellow taxi, following a couple of vehicles behind, all the way onto the I-90 that would take them to Logan Airport.

The heavy traffic would slow her down and Sprague smiled, pressing a speed-dial key on his phone. It rang twice before the team-leader answered.

'Talk to me.'

'She's done.' Sprague hated using extra words, if he could avoid it. His voice was too high, almost girlish, he thought.

'Okay. Where is the bitch going?'

'Back to the airport, I guess.'

'Makes sense. Follow her into Departures and check that she gets on the direct flight she's booked for. Someone will pick her up in LA.'

'Uh uh.' Sprague grunted and turned his attention back to the road, concentrating on the taxi ahead.

...

Walker sipped his coffee, glancing at the storage driver he had secured to the passenger seat. He was driving back towards John Wayne Airport to pick Layla up, before they could leave Los Angeles and go to ground somewhere small and safe. He suppressed a yawn, the fading light playing tricks with his tired eyes. He'd been working almost non-stop for the past twenty hours, first preparing Layla and then simulating scenarios and events and watching DeepShare crunch numbers for the ambush on Frankel Schwartz. Prepping and downloading a copy of the Omega code out of Stanford's mainframes had proved a simple but tedious process, but at least he had been able to use the time to perfect his scheme. Deep finally showed high probabilities of success, especially if they moved fast. Now he needed Mosha to prepare the terrain, and start shorting Frankel's stock and bonds in size. Smoke signals for all the hedge funds and computers out there.

Walker's phone beeped and he checked the message: 'All done, L.'

He sighed, relieved, and lit a cigarette. His thoughts wandered for a while until a car honked and he swerved just in time, realising he was crossing into the opposite lane. He cursed himself and slowed down even further, finding a rest-stop to pull over and take a short break. He exhaled and sat back, still shaking with adrenaline. With the plan about to kick into high gear, he forced himself to relax a little and let his thoughts linger on the future for a second. If it worked, maybe there would be...

The rumble of a large truck shook him out of his reverie and Walker finished his coffee, lighting another cigarette. He breathed in the crispy sea air and considered his phone – with the entire software in their hands, he was at last ready to call Mosha.

Let's light the fuse.

The Serb must have been wondering what the hell had happened to him, and why there had been no further progress. Walker dialled from memory, a slow grin spreading on his lips as he waited.

'About time, you son-of-a-bitch.' Mosha's voice was coarse from sleep. 'Do you even know what time it is here?'

'I'm guessing around four in the morning.'

'Yeah.'

'I thought you might be in a hurry.'

'I've been shitting my pants, that's what.' Mosha mumbled something in Italian, probably to his wife. 'Give me a minute...'

'Sure.'

After a few seconds the voice came back on the line, all traces of sleep vanished. 'So?'

'Has Hackernym been in touch with the info?'

'Yes.' Mosha exhaled. 'Amazing stuff.'

'Frankel's books are filled with Southern European stocks and bonds. Italy, Spain – they've gone all-in, a massive bet.'

'Madness. But the market is very calm at the moment.'

'Not for long. Deep is certain that our brand new Italian PM, Rossini, will manage to push through a public vote on the Euro membership.'

'Seriously?' Mosha sounded uncertain. 'My analysts think it's less than a one-in-four probability, for now.'

'Fire them. It will happen, and fast – in the next few weeks, maybe. Then Frankel's trades will crap out on the possibility of Italy breaking the Euro.'

'They'll never get enough yay votes in the ballot, Yours.'

'Of course not, but it doesn't really matter. Once Rossini makes the announcement, Hackernym will go public with the Frankel files. Welsh will get arrested, and Friedman. At least three more big shots on the board, the CEO and more senior managers will have to resign. And a few hours later their secret portfolios are going get published as well. What do you think will follow?'

Mosha grunted. 'When they sense the blood, a lot of hedge funds will start shorting whatever Frankel Schwartz needs to sell. Run the market against them.'

Walker's voice dropped lower, an edge of nastiness in it. 'Indeed. And their stock will crack. Frankel's capital is going to get slaughtered, and they won't be able to raise more. Certainly not quickly enough.'

'Like Lehman Brothers.'

'Exactly. With their shares dropping to zero, they'll be finished. You can close your short, clean up and load your books with cheap Southern European stuff in the frenzy. You buy a lot of Italian bonds, in a very public way, showing great faith in your adopted land. Deep is certain that the country won't leave the Euro after all – markets will bounce back, you'll make a fortune on the return to normality and look like a hero to the Italian powers-that-be.'

'A good scenario. What if it doesn't work?'

'It will.'

Mosha sighed, his voice suddenly tired. 'Maybe. But as I told you in Siena, I must see the DeepShare code before I start shorting in size and alerting the market that something might be amiss with Frankel. I need to have my quants run it. Your word is one thing, but numbers are better. The trade is too big.'

Walker had expected this, and didn't flinch. 'That's fine. I have the whole code with me now, on storage drives. But they have to be physically delivered.'

'When can you get it to me?'

'I can't fly for a few days, and I shouldn't take it out of the States myself, anyway. It's too dangerous.'

'Are you in the US? I'm about to zip to New Mexico on business. We could meet there, at the old place.' He paused for a few seconds as keyboard clicks echoed. 'Tomorrow night, five in the morning.'

Walker thought hard, his tired brain rushing back through time. 'Seriously?'

'Why not? It will be empty.'

'Not completely.' He wasn't sure if this was a good idea, but when he checked the date on his watch he realised the Serb was right.

'Well, you know your way around the ruins, don't you?'

Walker sighed. 'I guess.'

The Road Trip

Walker stared at the monitors, willing Layla to materialize out of the arrivals lounge at Orange County's JW Airport. The trip to Stanford and the backpack with the storage driver he carried were making him nervous, like an athlete on the final straight worrying about someone catching up to him. He wanted to slip out of LA, get on the road and drop the code to Mosha before anything else could go wrong. And airports made him nervous. Especially at the moment.

A crowd of people streamed past the glass doors, coming from a hidden entrance to his left. Businessmen, women with children, a few older ladies on some trip. He glanced at their luggage, trying to read the tags attached to suitcases, struggling to make out the codes. A good-looking woman slid past him and he concentrated on her trolley. MIA on the white sticker, from Florida. Wrong flight. He swore quietly and shuffled forward. Layla's plane had landed forty minutes earlier from Boston – she should already be out.

The crowds thinned, dispersing as the passengers slowed to a trickle. Walker readjusted the straps on his rucksack, attempting to get comfortable. The damn driver was heavy. He considered popping out for a cigarette but just forced himself to breathe more slowly instead, and to wait. It couldn't take much longer, unless... *Unless* someone had managed to intercept Layla – maybe they had tracked her from Italy, and caught up with her in Boston.

Maybe she'd taken Deep.

He swore at himself – Layla only carried half of the program anyway, and she knew it. Besides, there was no way she would, not after all...

Another crowd of people bulged from the side entrance, oozing towards him. Suited businessmen, trolleys, laptop bags. A couple of surfers hurried past, carrying a board. Its decorations were gaudy, bright colours on a blue background. Behind it he caught a glimpse of dark hair on top of a black coat and stood on tiptoes, trying to see past a massive, obese man.

Layla.

The stink of sweat assaulted his nostrils as the fat man wobbled by and there she was, head turning as she looked for him. Walker lifted his hand, waving, just as a tall guy rushed past a couple of children and ran right into her shoulder, almost knocking her over.

Walker jumped forward, trying to make his way through the crowd. He dodged a huge suitcase and approached Layla as she regained her balance, just in time to see her glaring at the tall guy. She was rubbing her wounded arm and readjusting a big rucksack – Walker hoped she hadn't dropped the storage driver. He called out her name and she turned quickly, flashing him a smile.

'Excuse me,' said the tall guy. 'I was in hurry…' He had a strong French accent and looked embarrassed. He placed a hand on Layla's shoulder, near her neck, and she shrugged him off.

'Asshole.' She turned away and stepped towards Walker, grinning. 'I did it!'

'Great.' He glanced around the airport, the nervousness returning. 'Now let's get out of here.'

…

Walker woke groggily, the pain in his neck and shoulders washing away his exhaustion. He glanced out of the window and saw darkness, the rental Chevy's headlights struggling to illuminate a desert landscape. Joshua trees rose from the sand and cast long shadows that disappeared towards distant mountain peaks.

'Where are we?' he croaked.

'Just past Santa Fe, we should be arriving soon.'

Layla sounded as tired as he felt and he checked his watch. They had been on the road for over thirteen hours straight after he'd picked her up from Orange County's airport, and he had been asleep for the last four. He groaned. 'Why the hell didn't you wake me earlier?'

'There was no reason to. I haven't seen another car for hours.'

'Are you sure?'

Layla half-turned to him, her eyes looking bright in the dim light. 'I thought I was the trained one here.'

'You might be tired.' They were too close to get caught, and it made him nervous.

'I *am* tired, but not stupid,' she glared at him.

'All right. Let's just stop at the first hotel we can find outside of Taos.'

'Fine by me.' Layla stretched her neck and stared ahead, angry.

Walker lit a cigarette and exhaled, trying to slow his heartbeat. 'I'm sorry. And... just terrified, that's all. I don't wanna fuck up now.'

'I know. Neither do I.' She grabbed his Marlboro and took a long drag. 'So this is it?'

'What do you mean?'

'You give DeepShare to Mosha. By the way, where exactly are we meeting him?'

'A place called Montezuma. It's a crumbling hotel in the middle of nowhere.'

Layla turned to him, surprised. 'Why?'

Walker shrugged. 'No idea. But at least we're both familiar with the place. He might have something else to do there, I guess.'

'And you know the drop spot? How?'

'Long story. I'll tell you on the way back.'

Layla sighed, sounding annoyed. '*Fine.*' She concentrated back on the road, let the seconds tick by. 'So what happens afterwards?'

'We rush back to LA to get our new passports, and disappear.'

'Seriously?'

Walker nodded, taking his Marlboro back. 'Yep. There's nothing else to do, anyway. Mosha will set up his positions, and after that we only need to wait for the fireworks. I'll have to stay hidden, at least until Frankel is taken down and Pienaar and the rest exposed.' He paused, eyes lost in the darkness outside. 'Deep thinks the events in Italy will happen fast, then Hackernym goes public. Let history unfold – we just have to avoid being found in the meantime.'

'Or there might not be an after.'

Walker could feel ice cubes sliding along his spine. 'Don't even think of that.'

'I'll try not to. Where are we...?' She hesitated for a second. 'Are we going together?'

That's a great question. Walker finished his cigarette, flicking the butt out of the window. He wasn't ready for the answer. 'No.'

Layla went quiet for about a minute, then she slowed and stopped the car on the right side of the road, her hands turning white as she held onto the wheel. 'Will you ever forgive me?'

'I don't know.'

'You said you loved me. Was it true?' Her voice shook a little.

Walker opened the car door and stepped into the desert night, marching a dozen yards away. The air felt thin and freezing and he remembered the altitude of the plains. Was it true? Of course it was fucking true – he had fallen for the damn woman from the first moment. But he still didn't know if he could trust her again, now or ever. He heard her climb out of the car but kept his eyes fixed on the horizon, trying to find something in the moonlight, anything.

Her steps crunched on the sand as she drifted closer. He held his breath, felt her hands circling his lower chest. Before Layla could let her head rest on his shoulder he slipped away and turned, facing her.

'Yes,' he answered simply.

She took it in, paused for a second. 'And now?'

'Now I need to think. A lot.'

Layla nodded, her eyes pools of darkness in the car-light haze. 'I see.' She sighed and pointed back to their Ford, her voice lower. 'I guess we should go.'

Walker watched her hurry back, not trusting his legs. He could feel himself trembling and fought to remain in control for a few seconds, his blood loud in his ears and thumping his temples. When he had calmed down enough he retraced his steps to the car and sat down without another word. She started the engine and eased away from the shoulder, back to the empty, dark tarmac.

...

It took over one hour for the atmosphere to thaw and become breathable again. Layla eventually glanced at him, then back to the road. She was biting on her lip again, uncertain.

'What?' Walker asked.

She cleared her throat. 'Where are you going to go?'

'I haven't decided yet.' Walker sat back in his seat, raising the backrest a little as he tried to get more comfortable. He lit another cigarette and cracked the window, considering the Old Man's plan and concentrating on the days ahead. After a few minutes of uncomfortable silence Layla glanced at him again, whispering, 'It's okay if you don't want to tell me. I understand.'

'It's not that. I just haven't thought that far ahead.' He relaxed a bit, feeling wrung out. There was other stuff to worry about – no point in raising the tension further. 'I've never been to the gulf coast of Mexico.'

Layla gave him a little smile, stretching her neck. 'The capital of Yucatan, Merida – it's a lovely town. Big enough to get lost in.'

'Does it have beaches?'

'No, it's inland.'

Walker shook his head. He'd already checked it out. 'Nah, after all this... I want a sea view.'

'Italians,' Layla groaned. 'What about Tulum, on the Gulf?'

'Never heard of it.'

'You'll love it. Tiny bays, little shacks on the beach, a quiet town. Good bars.'

'Sounds great. What about you?'

Layla shrugged. 'I don't know – I'll just be glad when this is over.'

'What, you don't enjoy being chased by a homicidal maniac?'

She glanced at the rearview mirrors, shivering. 'I want...' she sighed. 'I just want to be happy, for a while. Not running, not worrying, just...'

'Just being.'

'Yes. And... after all – if your plan works? What will you do?'

'I'm not sure.' Walker exhaled, considering. He'd been wondering the same thing for days. Or years. 'Something useful I hope. With Deep, maybe. The way DM wanted it to be used.'

'What about money? You might need a fortune for something like that.'

Walker nodded. That hadn't really crossed his mind, but he guessed it made sense. Using money for something good – what a weird thought for an investment banker. 'True. But you forget...'

'What?'

'I'm a derivatives trader. Don't you think I can make a buck or two in bringing a bank down?'

...

'They've stopped at a road motel in Taos, in New Mexico.'

Pienaar's voice was muffled by a static hiss, and Friedman had a little trouble in making out the words. His face still hurt, badly. 'New Mexico? Why?'

'No idea. You have the line to the smart guys – I just follow the bug on the bitch. Should we go in?'

'No. We don't know yet if they're carrying all of the software.' Friedman thought for a second. 'Maybe it's in the servers at Los Alamos?'

'They wouldn't drive so far east. And Los Alamos is mainly military.'

'Good point.' Friedman glanced through a couple of files. 'There must be something in the area. I'll get the team to run background checks on both – perhaps there's a connection in their past, someone they know.'

'Do it fast. The shadowing game is tricky and we could lose them again.' Pienaar's anger was surfacing again, always close to exploding. Friedman shivered – the Australian was a time-bomb that would need to be defused when they had Omega.

'I will. Just be ready to act, Francois.'

'I'm always ready.'

CHAPTER EIGHTEEN

<u>UWC</u>

No more suffering.

The old man closed his eyes, knowing it was for the last time. He bid farewell to his paintings and his consciousness spun, numbed by drugs. Images flashed by him fleetingly: his children, his friends. His enemies. He had many regrets, but the work of the last few years – Hackernym – that would be his legacy. Bringing the scum into the light, remaking some of the world. There was hope, a chance of redemption.

His mind drifted off into the past, circling onto itself. Faces, words...

Oddly, Walker's steely gaze came back to him and he wondered whether the young man would understand. It was a little betrayal, one of too many, but done for the greater good. Maybe things would be clear to him, in the end. He hoped so.

But now it was time to go, and the silence engulfed him.

...

After sleeping for a sweaty few hours in a motel that looked like it had been crumbling for most of the previous century, they hit the road again. Walker drove through darkness for seventy miles straight south of Taos before turning into a small town named Las Vegas, NM. He sped past a couple of empty intersections, scoured his memory and took a side street that wound further into the hills, through ancient conifer woodland. Minutes later he swung a sharp left onto a rutted dirt track and followed it for a while, headlights bouncing up and down, before parking their Chevy in a small clearing hidden among cypress trees.

The road must have been half-abandoned for years, and the little pathway he remembered was now overgrown with plants. He got out of the car and led Layla into a couple of dead-ends, deeper into the forest. He knew the hotsprings he was looking for were just a few hundred yards away and he kept pushing through the woods, using his flashlight as little as possible. After a few minutes of scrambling in the dense vegetation they chanced on a newer track, emerging behind the old hut that served as changing rooms by the steaming rock-pool.

The abandoned hotel – The Castle – was a vague grey outline on top of a low hill a few hundred yards away. Walker once again decided that it did look a little like a medieval castle, three stories tall, a large round tower spurting off by the right side. He tightened his backpack, heavy with the storage driver, and turned to check on Layla. She had unzipped her black leather coat and was fiddling with the knife holster on her left leg. 'You okay?' he asked.

'I'm fine,' she said. 'How the hell do you know this place so well?'

'I went to school here. For two years – Mosha, too.'

Layla swore. 'School? What about the students?'

'It's half-term. And the security guards are old retired policemen, happy to stick to their booth at night.' He shrugged and moved off through a scrub-infested backyard, with Layla just behind. They climbed a low wall and pushed on in the half-moon light, circling the bubbling waters, then sprinted onto a small bridge that led behind a classroom building, and ran on. Two hundred yards later they paused, crouching against the rear wall of the college auditorium. Walker glanced at Layla: her breathing was ragged, but she looked all right. 'We'll have to go around the corner over there, pass through a hedge and follow the bike track up the hill.'

He pointed towards the top of Montezuma Hotel, a few spotlights illuminating its conical turrets. 'The bush continues almost all the way up – no one should be able to see us from below.'

Layla nodded and shadowed him as he made his way, sticking to pools of darkness before rushing beyond the thick bramble. It took them less than five minutes, walking fast and bending low to remain out of sight as they curved around some halls of residence, with only a couple of lights shining from the student rooms. Half a dozen turns later they reached the top of the hill, past a badly illuminated parking lot close to the entrance of the hotel.

Walker stopped and moved into the vegetation by the bike-track, whispering, 'This is a side access, and the service area is very close. Mosha should be waiting for us in a nook of the grand ballroom but be careful – the planks could be rotten, and it was dangerous even twenty years ago. There are lots of tunnels and storage spaces underground, so mind your feet.'

He looked around, waiting for a few seconds to see if anyone had spotted them, but the night was quiet and still. Taking a deep breath he hurried through the pitted concrete and climbed some steps to the old doors. Swatting aside broken strips of yellow 'Danger' tape, he studied the handles. The latch was broken and he pushed open a panel, holding his breath and shining his flashlight into a bare room.

The walls were fissured and peeling, with the remains of a table and chair still waiting in a corner. Layla followed him inside and they slipped around a soggy area in the middle of the floor towards the exit on the farthest side. A wide corridor led off into darkness, tall windows flanking it on the right, doorways opening on the other side. The glass panes were dirty and broken and Walker switched off his flashlight, whispering, 'If I remember right, it's just another few rooms ahe...'

A floorboard behind them creaked and Layla turned, quick as a cat, hand shifting to her left hip. Walker pivoted and clamped his fingers on her mouth, pulling her back and into one of the doorways. He slid against the wall, reaching a shallow corner and following it blindly, around another dogleg. The darkness was heavy, complete. He held on to her arm and stood still, straining his ears.

Nothing. Then more creaks from above, and a low squeaking sound somewhere ahead. Maybe the joints of an old building letting out some stress. Layla's breath near his neck felt impossibly loud and Walker stepped a little further, hand creeping along the wall. Crumbling plaster, then a thin wooden post. Another door.

He leaned across, willing his eyes to adjust faster to the blackness. A couple of faint shapes, some mild bio-luminescence from mossy walls. A sliver of light shot through the room a few yards away, less than two inches wide. Then gone.

Walker swore inwardly, swung back behind the wall. Was someone walking around with a torch? Why? He checked his watch: they were late, and Mosha should already be waiting for them.

Unless the Serb had sold them away.

It would explain why he'd wanted to meet in such a remote place, perfect for Pienaar or Hackernym or...

Layla's mouth came up to his ear. 'What did you see?' she whispered.

He held up his hand, breathed out and counted to five. Silence, again. Then more creaking noises that could have been anything, or nothing. He crouched, the rucksack digging into his back, and poked his head through the doorway, inches above the floor. Dust got into his nose, nearly made him sneeze. The beam of light was still there, not moving.

Something clanged nearby, wood against concrete. A shutter slamming in the wind.

The light vanished, then came back again. Maybe a broken window. And a paranoid brain. Walker bit on his tongue and stood up, going through the door. 'Nothing. Just nerves, I guess,' he whispered back.

Layla followed him and he ducked under a timber that had crashed through the ceiling, into the L-shaped room, stepping over the sliver of faint light. A window on the other side opened onto the night, the moon shining through the broken glass. A splintered blind swung back and forth in the wind.

Walker grimaced and passed underneath it to enter a larger hall, the ceiling sloping away into darkness. A floorboard creaked and gave way underneath his foot. He stumbled, almost losing his balance as the weight of the backpack dragged him down. Layla grabbed on his arm, helping him upright. 'Fuck,' he swore quietly.

'Use your torch. I don't want to get impaled by something.'

He nodded and risked a quick pass of the torch, trying to memorize the layout of the wide space ahead. He didn't really know where they were: the hotel was huge and almost twenty years had passed since he'd last walked the place. But the moon was on their right, meaning they had to go around the other side, back towards the heart of the building. The grand ballroom started squarely at the centre of the ground floor, flowing to the farthest end where massive windows opened onto the mountains beyond. He was trying to decide which of the two doors in front of him to take when a distant coughing sound echoed from the rightmost corridor, before cutting off sharply.

Walker flicked the torch off, freezing, waiting for another sound.

'Mosha?' Layla asked.

'I hope so,' he whispered back. Though the world had tilted many times in the last few days, there was no way Pienaar could have tracked the Serb, or bought him. It had to be Mosha, probably starting to get bored and spooked as he waited. Walker took the door from which the sound had come, followed a couple of turns and a longer passage, more windows bouncing moonshine into the hotel, this time from the left. They were getting closer to the ballroom, travelling in the right direction now. His foot tilted forward and he felt another floorboard oscillate, then drop a few inches.

He swore and slid back before switching the torch on again. Several planks were broken and rotted, the entire aisle ahead sagging like an old hammock. He exhaled and tried to see further along, wondering if the floor got better a couple of yards on. It looked like it, and he considered jumping across instead of doubling back.

Layla must have guessed what he was thinking. She took his arm and leaned closer. 'It's too dangerous, I think.'

He nodded, started to say something.

The window behind him exploded in thousands of shards. The noise was deafening and Walker felt little glass bullets smash into his jacket and the back of his neck and head, like painful wasp bites. Stunned, he pivoted and saw Pienaar climb through the shattered frame as his beam of light fragmented on the broken glass. He was swiveling a large pistol in his hands, the barrel impossibly elongated. A second man emerged behind him from the far corner, pointing another torch mounted on some submachine gun.

Walker glanced at Layla as he stepped back. She nodded and he lunged forward, pushing off his left foot, trying to get as much lift as he could. Light bounced off the ceiling and he saw the rotten floorboards slide backwards below him. The heavy rucksack dragged against him, slowing his momentum. He flexed his legs in the air, trying to gain extra inches like an Olympic long-jumper. Then his right foot touched down, the wood giving away. He could feel something fly through the air behind him and a gunshot exploded, whistling above his head.

The floorboard crumbled. Walker let go of his torch and bent, almost diving, emptiness below his feet. He landed on his hands and slid further, something heavy thumping to his right. Layla bounced up and twisted just as he struggled to his feet. A heartbeat later they had pushed on through the last few yards, off the corridor and behind a dogleg. Another gunshot echoed, spraying Walker with plaster. Then heavy running footsteps, as the hunters prepared to jump after them.

Walker pulled on Layla's arm and steered her into a doorway on the left, past a couple of empty rooms. They hurried along a narrow passage and through a cloakroom, slipping past massive doors into some kind of foyer. Behind them steps echoed on the old wooden boards, quick but not running. Pienaar must have realised how dangerous the floor could be, and was following with care.

Walker slid to a stop in the centre of the enormous room, Layla just a pace behind. He swung the beam around, searching and praying the planks were sturdier here, then found the staircase he was looking for and ran to the broken steps, climbing sideways and keeping his back against the wall. They were about to disappear from view when the huge doors smashed open and Pienaar walked into the foyer, his torch sweeping around. Walker pulled Layla up and stopped still, trying not to make any noise. A bright light circle slid up the staircase, stopping just a few inches short of her shoulder. Then it flowed back down.

Someone hissed angrily, footsteps retreated and the doors swung shut. Walker counted to ten in the deep darkness, still holding onto Layla. Her breathing was as ragged as his, and they were both shaking. He took a deep gulp of air and let go of her, rummaging in his pocket and finding his lighter. He risked a quick flick of the flame to get his bearings and pushed on along another service corridor, past a larger landing into one of the wings of the old hotel. Dozens of bedroom doors waited on their left, some shut, others splintered or hanging off rusted hinges. On their right a few widely spaced small windows opened onto the hills beyond, faint moonlight barely lighting the way ahead.

'Where are we going?' Layla whispered.

'I think we can circle around from the third floor, to the main exit on the other side.'

'Now?'

Walker shrugged, thinking. 'Maybe not. Pienaar will be expecting that, and we don't know how many men he has. I think we can stay hidden for a while – till daylight if we move about.'

He pushed on, turning a couple of corners, back towards the centre of the building and away from the windows. Eventually he found a door in perfect condition and tried the handle. The panel swung back into an empty windowless room and they hurried in, using Walker's backpack to wedge the door closed. *What now?* He walked around with care, making sure the floor was safe. Layla sat down in a corner, exhaling. 'Shit.'

'How the fuck did he find us?' Walker swore. 'Do you think it could have been Mosha?'

'No idea. I told you Pienaar's good, though.'

He grimaced and flicked on his lighter again. The deep darkness split, revealing a second door on the far wall. 'What do you think we should do?'

'Isn't there another way out somewhere?'

Walker thought for a second. 'There is an old service tunnel that goes back past the hotsprings, but I've only walked it once. I don't think I could find it again, it's like a maze down there.' He exhaled and went to check the handle on the second door, found it locked. When he turned he noticed a ghost of light from a mobile phone in Layla's hand. 'What...'

The doorframe exploded inwards, stinging him in a shower of splinters.

Smoke billowed from the opening and he coughed, unable to breathe. As it dispersed, bright light flooded the room from a couple of torches and Walker was blinded for an instant. When his eyes readjusted he found himself staring into Pienaar's grinning face, the Australian's large pistol aimed at his chest. He almost considered jumping him, rage and fear boiling his blood, but a second man walked into the room and pointed a short rifle at Layla. It was the tall French guy who had bumped into her at JW airport and Walker's heart sank – they had been running behind since then, at least. A part of him wondered what had happened to Mosha, and how badly it was going to turn out for them. He shivered. Very badly.

'Look what we found here, two scared little sparrows...' Pienaar's voice resonated in the narrow space. 'Hands on your head, fuckers. Let's go.' He gestured with the torch, still keeping his gun trained on them.

Layla glanced at Walker, then she shrugged and stood up calmly, heading out of the room. He followed her into the corridor where the Frenchman took up the tail position, sticking his rifle in Walker's kidneys.

Pienaar barged past and grabbed Layla's arm, chuckling. 'Come on – there's a friend waiting for you.' He led them down a service staircase, back to a ground-floor room decorated with an arched ceiling. He paused for a second before taking them along a couple of corridors, skirting some debris and turning again through a wide passageway that Walker remembered well, into a cavernous hall. *The Grand Ballroom*. Shining his torch to the floor Pienaar shoved Layla forward, dangerously near a gaping hole in the rotten boards.

'Careful, pretty one. You're on thin ground here and we wouldn't want...'

'Stay on the right, Layla,' Walker interrupted him. 'I think it's the first room past that window.' He realised his voice was shaking and swallowed, just as Pienaar turned to him with a snarl. A torch swung at Walker's head and he swayed back, but the rough plastic glanced his temple. He felt skin rip and blood dripped into his eye.

'Shut up. You'll speak only when I tell you to.' Pienaar faked another swing, then he chuckled and glanced at the Frenchman. 'Good job, Michel,' he said. 'Now go back out and keep an eye on the entrance. We don't want any accidental company, not when the fun is about to start.'

Michel left and they skirted the damaged floor, entering a windowless suite illuminated by a weak light bulb. Walker saw another armed man, wearing a balaclava. He was pointing his gun at Mosha, who sat on a stained mattress next to a pile of old blankets. The Serb's hands were tied but he held his back straight when he looked up with a grimace. 'Not quite what we planned, Yours.'

'I'm sorry, man...'

Pienaar's fist hit him just below the ear and Walker crumpled to the ground with a metallic noise as his backpack half-cushioned the fall. He groaned and tried to slip his arms through the straps but Pienaar kicked him hard in the stomach, driving the wind out of him. 'I told you to be quiet.'

The Australian was about to hit him again when Layla raised her voice. 'Enough! The stuff you want is in Scott's rucksack. Take it and leave us alone. You win.'

Pienaar stepped back from Walker's prone body and pointed his gun at her. 'Shut up, bitch. If you had done your job instead of disappearing with this idiot –' he waved the light at the trader's face, just as he struggled to get back up – 'we wouldn't have to go through all this *unpleasantness*.'

'You tried to kill me.'

'Not my call. The client felt a bit rushed.'

'Because you murdered a man.' Layla's tone was angry, defiant. Walker managed to get back to his knees, scared but proud of her courage. 'You're a monster, Francois. And a stupid one at that,' she spat.

Pienaar slid forward and slapped her hard, sending her tumbling onto a mattress, just a step away from Mosha and his guard. She rolled sideways, then pushed off one of her elbows and crouched, knees bent. Walker saw that her lip was split as she struggled up.

The Aussie grinned. 'Do you like her, Temur?'

The man in the ski-mask grunted and Pienaar nodded. 'Maybe I'll let you have a go, after I'm done with her.' He stepped forward, pointing his torch at Layla's face.

'The lady is right, big man.' Mosha's voice stopped him. 'Take what you came for, and run. If you hurt any of us... my friends will come after you, forever. They will squash you like a bug.'

Pienaar spun, angry. 'I know about you, you fucking Serb. And I'm not worried about the Neapolitans. Dead men don't talk.'

'How did you find us?' Walker croaked, trying to gain some time. He didn't know what for, but things were crashing too quickly. He climbed back to his feet, the rucksack discarded.

Pienaar swivelled and punched him again, hard. He holstered his gun as Walker doubled over, then clubbed him on the back of the neck, dropping him. Walker's face hit the floor and he struggled to breathe. Pain shot through his limbs, his insides on fire. He tried to inhale deep and push the suffering aside, as he would in the ring. *It's only pain.* He prepared himself for another blow, but the Australian just stood over him.

'Is it all in there? Your stupid program?'

'Yes...' Walker coughed, dragging himself to one knee. 'Everything's in the storage driver.'

Pienaar grabbed his hair, forcing his head up. 'No fancy tricks, like the last time?'

'No...'

A shout echoed from outside the hotel and they all froze. Pienaar pressed his hand to the receiver in his ear, then turned to Mosha. 'What the fuck is this?'

The Serb stood, a tentative smile on his lips. 'No idea, but it sounds good...'

Pienaar swore, looking around the room. He nodded to Temur and growled, 'Kill him.'

Balaclava-man raised his gun and Mosha dove away. The assailant managed to fire off a shot just as Layla sprang from the floor, tackling his legs. They both went down and Walker saw a flash of metal as she tried to free her knife. Then he reacted, bending lower to grab his rucksack.

Pienaar was about to pull out his pistol when Walker hit him with the heavy bag, swinging with all his strength. He caught the Australian across the shoulder and the gun flew away through the open door, into the large hall beyond.

Feinting to the right, Walker dodged left and squeezed past Pienaar as he recovered from the blow. He glimpsed Mosha lying on a mattress and heard a shout from Temur as he struggled with Layla, before another gunshot echoed. Then he rushed through the door, eyes scanning the floor for the Aussie's weapon. He heard footsteps behind him and saw the barrel glinting in a shaft of moonlight. He dived for it but just as his fingers closed around the grip Pienaar's heavy body landed on his back. The old wooden boards screamed and they crashed through the floor, tumbling into darkness.

Tunnels

Layla rolled on top of Temur, struggling to keep his gun away from her chest. The man shifted below her, shoving back, and she realised he was too strong to hold down. She let her grip slacken for a second, allowing him to turn his shoulder, then pivoted and kneed him in the crotch. Temur's body convulsed, breath exploding out of his mouth when she hit him again, savagely.

As his body contorted she pushed off, drawing her knife and bringing it up in a smooth movement. The blade slashed his throat as she swung it back, before thrusting it down into his chest, again and again. The steel sank deep with a soft, squelching sound of freed blood. Steady rhythm, grunts, a letting of fear and anger and frustration.

Seconds passed, until a loud noise brought Layla back from her frenzy. She breathed in and stood up, glancing at Mosha's prone body and Temur's bloodied torso.

Neither was moving.

Knife in hand, she sprinted into the main hall and saw a cloud of dust floating up from a large hole in the floor. She grabbed someone's discarded torch, approached the edge and looked down, into the void. Rubbish and broken timbers shone back at her, a cloud of dust still floating upwards.

Pienaar's voice drifted out of the chasm, angry, followed by the noises of a fight. The hole was maybe five yards deep, the bottom a mess of debris. She was about to look for a way down when Walker's shout echoed from below, followed by the mad Australian's laughter. Without a second thought

Layla closed her eyes and jumped into the gap, preparing for the impact.

...

Walker fell for what seemed a very long time, in the end landing awkwardly on his shoulder, the wind driven out of him. He rolled to the side, left arm spasming as he bumped against a broken board, splinters penetrating his skin. He shook his head and tried to clear his vision as he got up, then dropped again to one knee to avoid Pienaar's fist. *Jesus, he's fast.* The big Australian was on him, unleashing a flurry of punches that he struggled to block in the dim light, stepping sideways, away from the hole in the ceiling.

Pienaar stopped chasing and glanced around, bending to grab a long beam of wood to swing it in a wide circle. Walker scanned the floor as well, found nothing. He backed out of range, swiveled and ducked at the last second, the staff grazing the top of his head. He knew he needed some weapon but Pienaar was harrying him, and he was too busy trying to dodge the staff's sweeps. He feinted and jumped to his left, going for a kick to the Aussie's legs but the big man just danced back, twirling the beam in his hands and stubbing him in the stomach.

Walker doubled over and slid back; his left foot tangled in some old cable and he stumbled to the floor. The shaft cracked against his left wrist and he shouted in pain, driven down by the force of the impact. Pienaar cackled and closed up to him, lifting his arms for a final blow.

Something heavy dropped to the ground a few yards away and they both froze for an instant. Walker glanced sideways and saw Layla, crouched, pointing a torch at them. She stood and brought her right hand back, then snapped it forward again. A bright shadow flashed through the air, just intersecting the light beam. It hit with a solid noise and Pienaar growled in pain, turning away. Layla's combat knife was stuck in his shoulder blade, more than halfway to the hilt.

Someone shouted 'Francois!' from the room above and a gunshot echoed.

Walker saw Layla stumble, heard her cry out. He struggled back to his feet just as she half-fell, half-jumped to hide behind a mountain of rubbish. Fear and rage exploded more adrenaline through his muscles and he slashed into Pienaar's legs, almost knocking him over. Arm pulsing with pain, he spun and pushed off his left foot, connecting with a right cross that sent the Aussie reeling backwards.

Pienaar recovered, tried to swing the beam and his shoulder caught, Layla's knife still buried in his back. He grimaced and dropped his staff. Another gunshot crackled but they were hidden away from the hole, deeper into the tunnel. Walker ignored it and attacked in a flash, feinting to the head and landing a couple of uppercuts to the midriff, just missing the solar plexus. The Aussie grunted and swayed, still holding his stance. Walker feinted again, dipped his right shoulder and whipped his torso around, letting his abdominal and dorsal muscles generate torque as he went for a massive left hook to the face. His arm rang with pain as the fist connected but Pienaar's nose burst and he stumbled and fell back onto a large pile of debris.

The Australian landed with a thud, his eyes widening in shock. He convulsed and screamed, an animal wail of suffering so intense the thick air shook with it. Walker bent and glanced down, hands finding the discarded wooden beam. A thin rod was coming out of Pienaar's right calf, like a skeletal finger dripping with blood. The Australian had impaled himself on a steel pipe, its sharp tip entering the back of his upper leg to burst out just above the knee. *Finish him. Now.* Walker inhaled and stepped forward, swinging his makeshift staff. Somehow Pienaar parried it with his forearm and the wood broke, splintering.

Letting the momentum carry him Walker pivoted on his left foot, slicing back just as the Aussie struggled to free his leg. The tip of the beam lashed his face and Pienaar's head bounced against the low mountain of rubbish. Walker maneuvered the broken timber, pressing it against the big man's throat, pinning him back.

Pienaar's good arm shot up to try and shove it away but Walker leaned forward with his entire weight, choking him. Rivulets of blood appeared as the splintered end dug into the Australian's skin and his pupils widened in panic. Walker hesitated for a second, uncertain, before Luigi's face and DM's tortured remains ghosted through his mind. Howling in rage and grief he braced himself and pushed harder, his entire body shaking with the effort. The world went blank for a few seconds, then he felt something break and he blinked, finding himself staring into the whites of Pienaar's eyes. The Australian's arms shook for a couple of heartbeats, up and down, before his fingers unclasped and his body went slack.

Walker stepped back, sucking in the stale air. His hands trembled as he glanced down at the dead killer, blood dripping from the battered mouth and nose. Pienaar looked like a giant broken toy, the scar on the right side of his face spotted red. Walker half-expected blackness to be oozing out of him instead of blood. He thought of DM and Luigi, wondered if they could see him now. Wondered if they felt better, somehow.

He didn't.

The coldness in his stomach had just gotten worse, if anything. There was an emptiness that dead bodies could never fill, he guessed.

Another gunshot echoed in the underground corridor and he glimpsed someone's feet, still hovering on the far side of the hole he had fallen through. The fucking Frenchman, probably. He checked around and found the pile of stones and junk behind which Layla was hiding. The gunman was stepping around the edges of the fissure, looking for a safe way down.

'Layla, can you move?' he hissed.

'I... I don't know.' Her voice was full of pain and Walker's heart skipped a beat. Had she been hit, and where?

'Pienaar's dead, I'm coming for you.'

'No, wait. The guy'll shoot you...'

Walker ignored her and rushed forward, dodging as he heard another gunshot crackle close. He dived behind Layla's refuge and came up, his left arm a mass of twisted nerves. She was half-crouched, leaning on a thick broken plank. He reached for her and slid his hand on her hip – her legging was drenched in blood. 'Fuck. We need to go, before he finds a way down.'

Layla ground her teeth and croaked, 'Go where?'

'Into the tunnel, over there.' Walker pointed towards Pienaar's body. 'It follows on under the ground floor, and will connect to other service passageways.'

'But...' Layla struggled up, then collapsed again. 'You said you weren't sure you could find the way.'

'Do you have a better idea?'

'No.' She leaned on him and groaned, her face twisted.

'Can you walk?'

'I'll try.'

Walker helped her up and placed his right arm under her armpit. He grabbed a stone with his other hand, ignoring the screaming in his shoulder, and threw it across the tunnel under the gaping hole above. A couple of gunshots echoed and they staggered the other way, stumbling under the protection of the whole part of the roof, past Pienaar's body and into the darkness beyond.

He half-carried Layla through twists and turns into the maze-like corridors, pausing often to check his surroundings with the tiny flame of his lighter. Minutes passed, maybe a dozen. The tunnels were still in decent shape, though cracks often appeared along walls and in the limestone ceiling. The floor was covered in dust and the odd pile of rubble, broken cables sneaking along to some forgotten machine. He cursed himself, trying to remember the general layout as they struggled along. Layla didn't complain but was slowing too often – he could hear her gritting her teeth and her breathing had become more ragged. A small noise made him turn his head and he realised that footsteps were bouncing their way from some passage behind. God only knew how close or far away they were.

He forced himself not to think of the tall Frenchman hunting them and just pushed through narrowing passageways, deeper into the ground and, he hoped, away from the abandoned hotel. Eventually they reached a larger cave-like room, the roof disappearing into darkness. Walker found and lit a small stick before looking around: three smaller tunnels opened away on the far and side walls, yawning blackness back at him. A few broken crates sat abandoned in the middle of the floor. He could feel a faint breeze and his mind flashed back to twenty years earlier. He knew where they were. The hotel had used the cave to stash coal and gasoline.

Layla groaned, her voice strained. 'Scott, I can't do it anymore.'

He bent down and checked her calf again – the gunshot wound still bled, but it looked like the femoral artery was not spurting. The problem was that if the bullet had only nicked it she might still tear it open. And then she'd be dead in a couple of minutes. He took a deep breath, struggling to calm down and think. 'We've almost made it, I swear. You can do it.'

'I just...' She coughed, then her legs gave way and Walker stumbled trying to hold her weight. He lowered her to the floor gently. 'Okay, but we can only stop for one minute. Pienaar's guys might be catching up to us.'

Layla didn't answer, her hand squeezing his fingers, almost hurting him. She drew a few shallow breaths before whispering, 'I'm sorry. You should...'

'Shut up. I'm not leaving you here.'

He knelt and slid his hands under her legs and shoulders, ignoring the agony in his left arm. With a grunt he lifted her to his chest and took a few halting steps towards a narrow tunnel on the other side of the cave. Layla held the burning stick and he carried her for a few long minutes, straining every sinew in his body to go as fast as he could. *Not fast enough.*

The flame flickered out and a heavier darkness fell around them. He struggled onwards, straining his eyes in the mild bio-luminescence of lichens and fungi, the rhythm of his footsteps almost hypnotic. Every few seconds distant noises rebounded around the tunnels, a mild screeching, thumps, a cracking of wood.

The world had become a grey mist, darker and lighter shadows mixing and coalescing, forming into solid corners and walls before floating away. Time had stopped, perhaps. But he knew the Frenchman must be behind them, slithering in the darkness, weapons ready to finish the job. And every sound felt closer, every step seemed to echo.

He was making too much noise.

Layla was hardly moving any more, her breathing low and shallow. A couple of times she groaned in pain, but when he asked she whispered she was okay. Walker tried to believe it, digging deep within himself. He pushed on, beyond the edge of exhaustion, spurred along by a faint brightness he could see growing in the distance.

Suddenly the tunnel shrank, with shadows and light now clearly visible. He prayed it wasn't his battered brain playing more tricks but soon the tunnel widened again and a waft of fresh chilly air hit him. He struggled through a few tangled plants and emerged into a clearing in the forest where moonlight shone on damp grass. His muscles were screeching with the effort and he lowered Layla to the ground, winded. Her eyes fluttered open and she gave him a little smile. Then she coughed and tried to sit up before giving up and lying back. 'Where are we?' she croaked.

Walker sucked in a few breaths, wondering if they had really made it. He picked her up again for a few paces, then propped her against a wide tree-trunk. Both her leggings were dripping blood, a dark stain on the pristine grass. 'The woods. Our car is only a couple of minutes away, I think.'

Layla nodded, struggled to speak and coughed. Her legs twitched and Walker bent lower, trying to ignore the stab of fear in his chest. 'I'll carry you again, let's go. We need to get you...'

'Wait... please.' She raised her hand, then lowered it by her side, reaching into her coat pocket. When it came out again she was holding onto her phone, the low-green light turning her face into a mask of shadows. She studied it for less than a second, he guessed. Though it felt a lot longer.

'It's okay...' she rasped, letting the phone drop to the ground. 'We can wait here.'

Walker froze, his heart skipping a beat. *Oh God, no.* It couldn't be right. 'What?'

'I'm sorry. I...' She choked, tried again. Her voice was low, almost a whisper. 'The hotel has been secured, and Pienaar's men are dead or have run off.'

'How... how do you know?'

Layla shrugged and lay back against the tree, almost spent. 'We can stay here – they'll be coming to pick us up in a few minutes.' She took a deep breath and closed her eyes.

It should have been good news, Walker guessed. He groaned and stood up, turning away from her. 'Of course. Who are they? The US Government or...'

'Hackernym.' Layla's voice cracked. 'I'm sorry, Scott. But they saved us.'

'Because you work for them. It's your *job*, again.' Walker was surprised at the ice in his voice but he felt strangely flat, emotionless. Hollow.

'Just for the Old Man... directly.'

'From the beginning?' He knew she was wounded, fading. But he didn't care any more, and kept pressing. She owed him this much.

Layla nodded, her voice dropping even lower. The night was so quiet he could hear faint noises coming in their direction from the Castle, far away. 'I've known Soffet for a long time. He hired me to infiltrate Pienaar's team...' She paused and breathed shallowly, then looked at him again. 'He didn't really trust anybody, even his own people... not with this.'

'I see.'

The first step away was almost impossible. The second threatened to break his soul, and he hesitated. Then DM's dead voice spoke with Luigi's accent and he took a third, longer step, reaching the treeline.

'Scott,' she whispered.

'What?' Walker didn't turn around. Looking at her would have been too hard.

'Aren't you... won't you come back with us? You could really help with DeepShare and...'

He spun back then, letting some anger creep into his tone. 'That's not the real Deep. The storage driver only contains DM's baby version, with what I wanted Mosha to see.' He felt a sad smile crease his lips. 'You didn't think I was just gonna hand the full Omega to a bunch of crooks, did you?'

He turned around again and stepped into the undergrowth, disappearing among the shadows of the forest.

CHAPTER NINETEEN

Sharing

Walker resisted the urge to throw the newspaper into the water and he poured himself another juice. He stared at the article again, ignoring the twitch in his left shoulder, before sitting back and lighting a cigarette. The ocean lapped calmly a few yards away from his porch and he tried to relax and enjoy the beauty of the little bay hidden among the mangroves. But Tulum's emerald coast was not working. Nothing would work. His friends had died, Layla had betrayed him even while saving his life, and now this.

Once more he went through the words, not really wanting to absorb them. It was only a background article, written days after the events, in The Wall Street Journal. The quiet raid on Frankel Schwartz, Friedman's disappearance, some new faces on the executive board. At least Wendall Welsh had had the decency to commit suicide. Your run-of-the-mill corporate scandal.

Nothing more.

The bank still stood, continued with its business, its share price already stable. All sorted, somehow. He crumpled the newspaper and opened his laptop, bringing his email up.

The work on the baby version of DeepShare had taken him several days, but now everything was ready. At the touch of a button the software could be made public, access given to large banks and government agencies around the world. Since what Hackernym had taken might still become too powerful in their hands, balance needed to be restored. And as far as anyone else was concerned, this was the real Omega. A little trap that might also give him an alternative, the zero one. Because if you ever needed to capsize a boat, you wanted everyone to move to the same side first. And it was what DM would have wanted anyway, and the only chance Walker had to be free.

Not from his nightmares and memories, but at least free to try and rebuild a life of some kind.

Alone again, as ever. Could he do it once more?

Walker shrugged and took a few steps down the beach, enjoying the feel of warm sand on his feet. He turned and studied the small shack where he'd been living for the last few weeks, since the cursed night in New Mexico. Layla would probably have liked the small wooden house, shaded by an ancient tree. But she had chosen Hackernym.

Familiar faces appeared in front of his eyes – Luigi, DM. Mosha had survived, barely, and was still in hospital. All gone now, because of greed, and fear. Because of the hubris of wanting more, knowing the future, gaming the system.

Even the Old Man is dead. Walker wondered once again whether Hackernym's betrayal would have happened with

Soffet still alive, or if it had only been caused by the panic of a headless organization.

It didn't really matter any more. Revenge, what little of it he had tasted, had left him only with a bitter, empty aftertaste.

Walker exhaled some smoke, returned to the porch and put out his cigarette. His hand hovered for a second above the keyboard before finally hitting the send button.

A Visit

He was almost drunk, as usual.

Walker tried to focus on the words in the Reuters article but his eyes weren't quite working and he gave up, closing the lid on his computer. It didn't matter. DeepShare had been right once more – the Italian government had called for a popular consultation on its Euro membership in the run-up to Christmas. The markets had initially swooned but now, a few weeks before the actual vote, things seemed to be stabilising.

The referendum was expected to fail, and Italy would continue to honour its trillions of dollars of debt and stick to the Union without making a mess of the world economy. Which sort of made sense. *Unless...* Walker tried, but he couldn't summon the energy to rethink the scenarios through. Financial markets just didn't matter to him any more – not now he knew how the system was rotten to the core. They could all go to hell, for what he cared.

He poured himself another beer, knowing there were still many to go before he could sleep for a few hours. He was about to down it when a voice interrupted him from the darkened beach.

'Are you going to offer me a drink?'

Time stopped. Walker felt his throat go dry as the question bounced around his brain, echoing in the empty spaces of his skull. A part of him had been expecting something like this, waiting for it. Hoping for it.

Dreading it.

It wasn't a hard question, really. Just a yes or a no would suffice. The past month had given him a long time to think, to remember, to wish for a different past. He'd seen Layla's eyes shining in his mind so many times that he could count the tiny freckles in her pupils. He had felt her hot mouth and body in his dreams, over and over. He had remembered her voice, cracking. *I've known Soffet for a long time. He hired me to infiltrate Pienaar's team...*

Words that didn't really give him a whole lot of room to wiggle. Words that brought DM's death back, in sharp relief. Words that might get Luigi to thrash in his grave. It was impossible to tell if things might have turned out different, though. *You can't change your own history.* But he guessed the future was still up for grabs.

And the question was whether his future could somehow forget a part of his past.

The betrayed part.

The part that knew he had only been a job, for a long time. An involving one, certainly. One that had shaken Layla to her roots, he guessed. That she was prepared to die for, as she had shown. To love for, maybe.

The problem was, Walker knew himself. And he had too good a memory. He knew how he would always wonder if there was something else lurking behind a corner, another slice of uncertainty. Another dark shadow above his head, ready to break him again. Not a way to live, though his life felt scratchy and flat like a worn-out jumper, hardly wearable any more. But what choice was there: did he have anything left, beside his pride?

He shrugged and narrowed his eyes, his tone cold. 'I thought you'd never ask. How long have you been out there?'

Layla stepped with a slight limp into the circle of light thrown by the large candle he kept on the table. His heart struggled to beat. She looked as gorgeous as ever, in a short strapless summer dress. 'Not long. Half an hour, maybe.'

'What were you waiting for? The more I drink, the less pleasant I am.'

She picked her way over the sand and sat on the porch steps, her expression uncertain. 'We need to talk.'

'Why did they send you?' His voice was steadier than he felt. At least the trading floor had taught him something.

'I didn't give them a choice. I wouldn't tell anyone where you were.'

Walker nodded, almost relieved. It was a good start, he guessed. 'Why not?'

'You're asking silly questions again.'

'Maybe.'

She paused a beat and shook her head, pushing her hair behind one ear, as she had so many times before. 'I run the Hackernym action team now.'

Walker sat back then, his mind made up. 'Congratulations. So what do you want?'

She hesitated. 'You already know. Now that you've released the baby version, we need the full Omega to...'

'No.'

Silence.

Walker stared at her. 'And if you're not going to drag me away in chains, you can piss off now.' He sipped his drink and half-turned, looking into the night.

Layla remained silent for a few seconds, waiting. Then she inhaled, cleared her throat. 'I'm sorry it had to end like this,' she said.

Walker snapped, getting up so fast his chair fell to the ground. He stood over her, his voice crackling with ice.

'Did you really think that I'd never find out, even without Pienaar showing up at the Castle?'

'I... I don't know. I tried to... I really cared for you.'

'Right. Forget it – you just *finished your job,* as ever, and I should have seen it. But what's really pissed me off is the bullshit with Frankel. How could you be so fucking stupid?'

'We went to the SEC and the Federal Reserve with our files,' she replied, her eyes widening.

'Exactly.' Walker exhaled, trying to calm down. 'And what did you expect? They buried most of it, of course. Friedman vanished. The bank will get a new CEO, some fresh faces on the board. A slap on the wrist. They are still around, and DM and Luigi died for nothing.'

'We had to do it like that.' Layla's voice was still calm and Walker's anger grew again, like a storm breaking.

'Did you?' he shouted. 'Why couldn't you just go public, and let everyone know how corrupt and criminal the entire fucking bank is?'

'Listen...'

'For God's sake, their stock is already bouncing back. You let them get away with it.' Walker returned to the table to finish his drink. 'Did the Old Man plan it like that, or was it just sheer fucking stupidity on your part?'

Layla stood and approached him, taking a sip from his water-bottle. 'It went the way it should have.'

'Why?'

'Because it was always part of the plan. Didn't the Old Man tell you that Frankel would only be the first step?'

'Yes.' Walker remembered Soffet's eyes, shining with the rightful zeal of a prophet. *I was right.* Maybe it wasn't over yet.

'You just believed what you chose to,' Layla said. 'Hackernym has always been about bringing down the entire system, not just one bank. We knew the central bankers and Treasury bureaucrats would cover up anything to save an investment bank of that size: Frankel Schwartz is too-big-to-fail.'

'And?'

'And now we can prove it. We are ready to show the world how they will stop at nothing, will protect killers, break every law – just to keep the status quo. As you know, Hackernym has been spying on those criminals for years, and with Frankel they've gone over the edge once too many. The Fed, the European Central Bank, the market regulators – we'll bring them all down.'

She fiddled with her shoe and pulled out a tiny USB key, handing it to him. 'Have a look at this, it's only a small sample of what we'll hit them with.'

Walker took the driver and plugged it into his laptop. The screen came alive, flashing a quick summary of the contents; there were dozens of hyperlinks to actual recordings, audio and video, documents, memos, mails. It was structured like the Frankel files he had seen, but on a much larger scale.

Banks and hedge funds, central banks and ministries... all the way to the top, to the names and faces that had decided the fates of the financial world for the last decade. He scanned some of the information, shocked at the depth of illegality and corruption in the data. It was dynamite. If they published it, so many heads would roll everywhere...

Layla interrupted his train of thought. 'I've been learning, Scott. The entire Western world runs on credit, you said it yourself. Money, banks, *everything* is credit. I guess you know the root of the word?'

'Of course. It's from the Latin *credere.* To believe, to trust.'

'And when trust is broken...'

Walker sat back in his chair, his head spinning with possibilities. Then he smiled sadly, understanding everything at last. 'All the King's horses and all the King's men...'

'Couldn't put Humpty together again.'

'Maybe.' Walker stared at her, his voice cutting. 'But maybe Hackernym is just a bunch of dangerous cranks.'

'How... why?'

'It's going to be a mess, no doubt – but the markets are way too resilient. You'll cause a disaster for nothing. Governments are going to intervene, great promises will be made and as the scandals subside...'

Layla sat down, resting her head on her palms and nodding slowly. 'Things will go back to what they were. One crisis after another, getting bigger all the time.'

'Yes. This stuff is big but...' He pointed at the screen. 'It's not quite enough.'

'That's what we're afraid of.'

'And that's why the Old Man wanted DeepShare,' Walker said. It all made sense, in its own insane way. 'He needed to simulate the events, figure out the right conditions and exact timing for releasing the files. Every structure has pressure points, but if you really want to shatter it, you need to find the perfect spot. Deep is ideal for that.'

'Yes. But you've made a lot of it public,' Layla bit her lip and poured herself another drink. 'Everyone that's important now has some of its foresight. I've seen what DeepOmega can do, and we all know they'll use it to their own ends, even the baby one. No more jokers in the pack, if you keep the full one secret.'

Walker smiled sadly, his eyes still fixed on her gorgeous face. 'You should trust Old Man Soffet more.'

'What do you mean?'

'He understood Deep's role, and its limits. He *wanted* it to be public, in whatever version.'

'Why?' She paused and looked at him askance. 'It's still another massive weapon, once more in the wrong hands.'

Walker closed the laptop and the night crept closer, kept at bay only by his candlelight. A small animal croaked from the mangroves and the shadow of a bat flickered across the sand. He looked at her, sighing. 'What the Old Man understood is that DeepShare is great, but it's not God.'

'What do you mean?'

'I mean it's very good at predicting the future, based on the facts it can gather. But the Deep version everyone is running now doesn't know about Hackernym, and the stuff you'll make public. It's drawing a mistaken conclusion. Ever heard of GIGO?'

'Garbage In, Garbage Out?'

'Indeed.' Walker half-smiled.

Layla went silent, considering his words. 'So... the big banks and the hedgies have been building the wrong positions over the last few weeks?'

He hesitated for a heartbeat, still uncertain. But it was far too late anyway. Nothing could stop the avalanche, not anymore. He could only hope to give it a push in the right direction. 'If you hit them with the Hackernym files at the perfect time, yes.'

'And that's why you made the baby Omega public.'

'Not only that,' he grunted. 'It will be needed to rebuild, after you guys are finished. The more people know and understand of it, the better it will be.'

'So you agree we're doing the right thing?'

Walker lit a cigarette, his eyes drifting to the liquid darkness of the sea. What did he really think? Was he just letting anger overcome his senses?

No. Deep is right.

As a part of him had suspected all along. There was only an abyss ahead – the system needed a reboot.

'I don't know, it's an impossible question,' he said. 'But I can't stop you, anyway, not alone. This... it's the best I can do, I guess. And it's what DM would have wanted – use Omega to shape unavoidable events, to steer them towards a better outcome.'

Layla nodded and finished his water, then poured herself a large rum. Her voice was subdued when she finally asked him, 'How long have you been planning this?'

'Ever since I met the Old Man. Maybe even earlier than that. It's sort of always been there, at the back of my mind. But planning is too strong a word. Hoping, I guess.'

'And you've run it on the full DeepOmega.'

Walker stood again and took a couple of steps towards the surf. The waves crashed noisily yards away, but the blackness was almost impenetrable, no matter how hard he stared. Heavy clouds covered the moon, and crickets chirped away to his right. Loud, annoying, almost drowning the thumping of his heart. He forced himself to breathe, deeply.

Exhale.

Inhale. 'I think you should go, now.'

Silence.

He heard her chair scrape the porch, the creaking of old boards as she shifted her weight and stepped aside. Or forward. Or backwards, it didn't really matter.

'I understand.' Layla's voice was so low he almost couldn't hear her as waves broke in the distance. *Better that way*.

He waited, guessed she had turned around. He cleared his throat and heard her stop. 'You can tell them I've run it a billion times, of course. It's like watching a computer play chess against weaker copies of itself. The strongest one always wins.'

CHAPTER TWENTY

Into the Light

December had dragged along, crawling on its belly as events matured, but now it was almost time. Walker readjusted his chair and waited for the fireworks to start, the old tingling of anticipation alive in his body and mind. It was 5.12 p.m. in New York, just over one hour after the market closed. On a Friday evening, obviously. Having a weekend for the powers-that-be to panic could only work in Hackernym's favour. The newspapers and TV channels would have plenty of time to dig, and speculate, and sharpen their knives.

The media had been forewarned an hour earlier of a huge, anonymous data dump – confidential documents, phone intercepts, the full works would be published online on dozens of websites around the world, in countries where controls were weak. Walker ignored the links in the email; he had already seen the files, and was only interested in the immediate reactions.

DM's tablet was switched on, with the expected events of the following few days charted by DeepOmega in tiny scribbles and graphs, probability trees breaking in terrifying directions. It looked too much – Deep couldn't be right. But Walker's trading instincts had gone to sleep. He had no real idea of what might happen.

He stood up and was tempted to walk away along the beach, abandoning everything. The price he had paid for this was too high, and he didn't really know if he had anything more to give. Unplugging the laptop was a temptation he had fought many times in the past few weeks, and he wondered how DM's tablet, strong as it was, would fare in a close-up meeting with the salty seawater.

Suddenly his computer beeped an alert – the data was out. Walker sat back, knowing he had to stay. The world would need Omega after this, and he was the one who knew it best, now that DM was gone. He went back into his kitchen and poured a large rum. Good vodka was hard to come by in this remote part of Mexico, and he'd had to change his habits. Marlboros were everywhere though, and he lit one before returning to his table under the tilted porch.

It took exactly thirteen minutes before the enormity of the revelations in the files hit the global consciousness. Another seventeen, and the world went into crisis mode.

...

Walker rubbed at his tired eyes, rereading the Reuters headline a couple of times before it disappeared along the fast-scrolling ticker. Several hours had passed since the Hackernym download, and reactions were starting to hit.

'(ECB) – THE PRESIDENT OF THE EUROPEAN CENTRAL BANK,' the screen read, all in bold capitals, 'HAS RESIGNED ALONG WITH THE ENTIRE EXECUTIVE COUNCIL. PRESS CONFERENCE TO FOLLOW – FRANKFURT, 05:34:17.'

It was a good start: strike one for Deep. Waiting for the rest, he went to the ancient percolator and filled his cup to the brim. He missed Italian coffee, its sharp flavour and pungent smell, the little layer of creamy foam that you could only see on top of a proper espresso. Maybe one day – but even if he had been cleared by UK police he was in no hurry to return to the Old Continent. Too many memories, too much pain.

Still... Out of curiosity, he switched to a BBC channel to check what was going on in London. And he chuckled.

No riots, perhaps not yet. But a massive crowd had gathered in Exchange Square in the City, and cameras on Threadneedle Street showed a bunch of black-hooded youths trying to storm the Bank of England, only getting beaten back by water cannons. The Prime Minister, the Leader of the Opposition and a couple of Royals were due to speak soon. He guessed the only thing missing was Oliver Cromwell.

A lot of Europe was almost quiet. Stunned, waiting. Trying to understand what was going on. Africa, South-East Asia and most of South America had hardly budged, while Australia and Hong Kong crumbled. He guessed Finance was mainly a worry for rich countries. Or the world's poor knew better than to get upset over something that wasn't a sustenance issue. *Good on them.* He picked up a tired novel and settled down to pass the time; the headlines would continue to hit as the Western world woke up.

The book was almost finished when CNBC, the live-feed sitting in the top-corner of his laptop screen, broke more news. The overweight announcer was breathless, tension and excitement sharpening her German accent in an almost painful way: *Following an emergency conference call of Eurozone Heads of State, several Finance Ministers have resigned, in Germany, Italy, Spain, Austria, and the Netherlands. No news from Paris, but apparently the Chief of the Bank of England and the Chancellor are about to go as well. This is the biggest day...'*

Walker killed the volume, and returned to the last few pages of his book. Europe was already old news; he expected Asia to come in soon. He bet with himself that Omega would get something wrong – the Chinese were not going to wait for Sunday, he was almost certain.

...

This time it was Bloomberg that got there first. On the classic black background the new top headline suddenly flashed in bright orange: 'CHINA IMPOSES CAPITAL CONTROLS. NO TRANSACTIONS ABOVE 5,000 USD ALLOWED WITH FOREIGN INSTITUTIONS.' Walker grinned, picked up DM's tablet and whispered, 'One-all. Humans strike back.'

DeepOmega did not reply, continuing to crunch its calculations somewhere in cyberspace. When Japan announced its Premier was gone, together with the emergency closure of all its financial markets within seven minutes of the machine's predicted timeline, Walker shrugged and turned the screen off. As expected, he had lost his bet. It was time for another bad coffee. He slipped into his tiny kitchen and froze. Layla was standing next to the sink, preparing a tea.

'What are you doing here?' he said.

'I've quit my job.'

Walker paused for a beat. 'Why?'

She studied him, biting at her lower lip. 'It was getting in the way of my life.'

'I guess that's never good.'

'Where's the sugar?'

Walker sighed, gave up. 'It's in the lower cabinet. I'll be on the beach.' He walked outside in a slight daze. A small smile broke through on his lips, though he had tried to kill it. She didn't quit easily.

Maybe it was time to forget his pride and give life another chance.

Last Rites

It was 6.17 on Sunday morning when Ted Harris, the Chairman of the Federal Reserve of the United States of America, walked into his office. His hair was slightly dishevelled and his eyes sunken from lack of sleep.

The Treasury Secretary nodded to him and poured a coffee before sitting down across the breakfast table. Harris sighed and ignored the food, handing over a white envelope. 'Mr Ginter, here's my resignation letter.'

The Secretary took it and placed it in his jacket without raising his eyes. 'I'll give it to the President this afternoon, together with mine.'

'Has he decided what to do?'

'Yes. The markets will open as usual on Monday.'

Harris slumped lower in his chair, groaning. 'But that's madness. Europe has already announced they are staying closed, and Asia too. We'll be swamped with selling; the entire world is going to use New York to get out of their positions.'

'I'm aware of that. We've all advised him against it, but Congress is already calling for the President's impeachment. He thinks what we need now is transparency, a cleansing. The pieces can be picked up later.'

'The markets will crash. It will be like nothing we have ever seen before, much worse than Black Friday.'

Ginter shivered, his hands playing with a silver spoon. 'What about the big banks and the hedge funds, can't they step in and hold it?'

'I've been speaking to them through the night.' Harris's voice was tinged with resignation. 'Most of them have the wrong positions. They all thought the Euro crisis was about to

blow over, and have gone massively long. They'll need to sell as well, to protect their capital base and depositors. Many will go bust.'

'So there's nothing we can do?'

'No.' Harris buried his face in his hands. 'Too many people have been compromised by this, anyway. We can only let it play out, and hope something else doesn't crack. The entire financial system will be teetering on the edge as it is.'

The Secretary stood up, his expression a mask of worry. 'Then let's just pray nothing pushes us into the abyss.'

...

Late Sunday night, something did.

Results of the Italian consultation were tallied and made public. Horrified by the Hackernym files and the exposed betrayal of the country's interests, Italians had reacted and voted to leave the Eurozone and return to their old currency. The country would default on the largest debts in history, and over three thousand billion dollars of debt held around the world suddenly became worthless.

The Euro was no more.

EPILOGUE

It lasted less than a heartbeat.

Red.

A picosecond in the virtual world of markets, a shadow fleeting by a server that was closer than most, just as the speed of light snitched the atomic clocks before the next micro-tick.

Maybe it was a mistake.

It had to be, really. This was not even supposed to be possible.

Then the headlines crashed the screen. Big, bold, screaming headlines that would echo across the media for days to come. All markets had been closed, suspended. Frozen in time at the previous Friday's close. The President had just announced an emergency G-10 meeting, all the major players involved. New rules would be set, a new design for the great game. Most countries would co-operate in reworking the financial system before anything could reopen.

Like after 9/11. Like during World War II.

There were flaws in Wall Street and around the world, the President had said. But it was only paper, numbers on computers. The real economy could and would go on until they were fixed.

Scott Walker agreed.

He looked away from the beauty of the blood-red screen and allowed himself a sad smile. The ocean beckoned to him, the surf breaking on the beach to his right. He had been staring at the market for hours, wondering if he should trade anything. Sweating, his palms wet. A part of him wanting to get in on the action, sell a thousand Futures and trade the crash. Like the old days – make some cash, enjoy the adrenaline screaming through his veins. But he hadn't.

And now it was too much, even for someone nicknamed 'Yours'.

The Dow Jones Industrial Average had just flashed out in the greatest collapse of all time. You couldn't go lower than 0.01, and that was a good thing.

Walker smiled and pressed the button that would release the full DeepOmega onto the net, available to the entire world.

It was time for everyone to try again.

– The End –

ACKNOWLEDGEMENTS

There are many people to thank, and all of them have contributed to make Zero Alternative a lot better than it was, while the mistakes left are obviously mine.

Three Hares Publishing, by Yasmin Standen and Helen Bryant (nee Corner): I'm awed by your skills and tenacity, thanks for believing! Jennie Rawlings for the jacket and Sarah Quigley for proofreading: your excellence and great professionalism have made it a pleasure to work with you.

Lorenzo, who's almost forced me to write it, and whose support, suggestions and friendship have been so important that I have no words left, for once. My early conspirators Luigi (as always above and beyond the call of duty), Eve, Cliff, Daria, Klaus, Luca R., and naturally the long-suffering Franchi – you've all slogged through the sludge, giving me the belief that there was something there.

Asia and Joshua, because you still loved a Dad who'd been using his computer far too much.

And finally all the good, weird and interesting people I've met through all my years in Finance – bankers are not all bad, believe me.

13431980R00226

Printed in Great Britain
by Amazon.co.uk, Ltd.,
Marston Gate.